STORM
WARNED

STORM WARNED

DANI HARPER

Montlake
Romance

Published by Montlake Romance, Seattle

www.apub.com

Amazon, the Amazon logo, and Montlake Romance are trademarks of Amazon.com, Inc., or its affiliates.

ISBN-13: 9781477827925
ISBN-10: 1477827927

Cover design by Jason Blackburn

Library of Congress Control Number: 2014955022

Printed in the United States of America

To Dad, who encouraged my first submitted work when I was barely fourteen. It was a letter to the local newspaper, and when it was published, I remember the incredible thrill of seeing my name in print. The biggest thrill, however, was when you told me I had a way with words. If I do, I'm certain that it came from you.

*Every heart sings a
song, incomplete,
until another heart
whispers back.*

—Plato

*Music gives a soul to
the universe, wings
to the mind,
flight to the imagination,
and life to everything.*

—Plato

ONE

⁊⟊

Beddgelert, Snowdonia Mountains, Wales
1820

A strange horn sounded, deep and long, the notes bouncing off the mountain slopes and echoing down the valley. Something about the odd tone, the bell-like timbre, sent a shiver down Caris Dillwyn's back and made her redouble her efforts.

She had one last sin to accomplish.

The ash tree's exposed roots made kneeling awkward, especially in long woolen skirts, but after a dozen years of practice, she was used to it. She was grateful that the forest floor wasn't muddy today as she carefully placed the battered fiddle case inside the half-rotted trunk. She gave the wooden box an extra push to make certain it would stay in its familiar hiding place, then scrambled to her feet and brushed the dirt from her clothes. The guilt, however, could not be so easily swept from her mind, and she sighed. *A whole afternoon wasted when I should have been working.* Surely that was an extra sin even though her day's chores had been done early, and she would work several more hours when she got back to the farm. Usually she came to the woods only at dusk, but the rare sunny afternoon had beckoned her. For the first time in a very long time, she'd said *yes.*

And oh, how she'd enjoyed it, even though the pleasure likely made her list of misdeeds even longer.

As an extra precaution, Caris gathered handfuls of last year's leaves and piled them at the base of the tree to cover the hollow spot. She would take no chances on losing her one and only treasure, her great-grandfather's forbidden fiddle.

The plaintive horn sounded again. *A strange time of year for a hunting party*, she thought. *But the wealthy do as they please.* And sometimes they pleased to holiday in the little stone village of Beddgelert, where Prince Llywelyn the Great had once kept his sporting lodge. Such guests were more devoted to drinking and didn't usually venture far in search of game, certainly not this high up the mountainside. How strange that the sound seemed to come from somewhere above her . . . *A trick of the echo,* she chided herself. But she couldn't deny that the call of the horn was unusual in its tone, if not its origin. A hunting horn signaled that a quarry had been sighted. It beckoned both riders and hounds. Its call put a thrill in the blood and caused the heart to leap with excitement in both man and beast.

But this horn invited no joyful response. There was something ominous in its voice, a warning rather than an exultation. She thought of the preacher's sermons about the book of Revelations, the great trumpets that heralded sorrows and judgments, and the reaping down of sinners . . .

Sinners like her.

Her stocky cob, named Eira for his snow-white coat, seized her jacket sleeve with strong teeth and tugged hard. His rubbery lips left flecks of chewed grass behind. "That was quite unnecessary." She scolded him without heat, however, and was already putting a sure foot in the stirrup. She mounted easily, sitting comfortably astride even though her stockinged legs were nearly exposed to the knee. (And was that a sin, as well, if there was no one to see?) Thank goodness she'd grown up on a farm, and not on some upper-class estate. Try as she might, she simply could *not* imagine trying to curl herself around a sidesaddle.

Eira was normally steady as a rock. Now, however, the pony stamped his feet impatiently, then abruptly lurched down the winding mountain path at an awkward trot without her urging. It wasn't like him at all. He'd been content enough to graze the afternoon away while Caris practiced old bardic ballads, wistful songs of farewell and lost love, and lively Celtic reels. She even dared a bawdy song she'd overheard outside the Royal Goat last week. As usual her da had stopped at the pub for *just a pint*—which always turned into several—leaving Caris outside to keep an eye on their wagon. Could she help it if she overheard a shanty through the open windows? The randy lyrics had reddened her cheeks: "I wish I was in bed with the captain's daughter . . ." Yet her fingers had twitched all the same, anxious to apply the bow to the old fiddle and try the tune's rollicking rhythm for herself. Without its scandalous words, of course—she had faults enough already. The local preacher sermonized often about the devilish nature of music played purely for enjoyment, and hadn't she spent countless hours over the years doing exactly that? There was no help for it, though. The music seemed to bubble up inside her like a lively spring of achingly cool water, ever-flowing and impossible to contain.

But contain it she must, at least when she was at home. There Caris tried to remember to sing only hymns within her father's hearing. But all too often, she'd be moving the sheep or gathering eggs or forking out hay, and a merry folk song would simply spring from her lips. That's when the lecturing began. *Music be given to man that he might praise his Creator*, said Da, echoing the stern sentiment of their preacher. *And naught else.* But drunk or sober, Dafydd Dillwyn would never raise a hand to her. Instead, she'd end up in her room or, much more likely, with more work to squeeze into an already long day.

Once in a while, however, when her gruff father was well into his cups, he seemed a different person entirely—perhaps the one he'd been before his beloved wife had died and left him with a tiny girl child to care for. Sometimes he'd even use his fine baritone voice to share some of the old songs he remembered, ones that had once been handed down through generations, music all but lost to time and the church's strict influence. *The Welsh language survived both the English and the church*, he'd say, thumping the tabletop with his thick-fingered fist and making the ale slosh from his tankard, *but its true song did not, and so Wales is naught but a bird without wings.*

The following day, when he was sober (and no doubt contrite), it was strictly hymns for him—and therefore for her as well. She had nothing against them. Some were pretty enough, and a few even utilized simple folk tunes. But to her musical heart, they seemed both limited and limiting. Of course, it could only be another sin to think like that . . . As for her stern father, she knew he loved her in his way. His lectures about music were driven by concern that she wouldn't attract a good husband with her seeming lack of piety—and sure enough, here she was, long past twenty and not a suitor in sight. A spinster, a *ddibriod*, as some wags in the congregation whispered.

Caris told herself she didn't mind a bit, that she was much too busy to be lonely, and most of the time it was even true. She had her father to care for, as well as the farm—and the more Da drank, the more both needed her. Besides, she reasoned, wasn't it better to be alone than be wed to someone who couldn't understand her soul-deep need to create music? It had pulsed through her as long as she could remember, and even singing didn't assuage it fully.

The discovery of the precious *ffidil* at the bottom of an old trunk when Caris was ten had changed everything. She knew better than to show the instrument to her father—at best, he'd make her put it back. At worst, he might take it away or even destroy it. Musicians and bards, according to the preacher, were heathens, *the devil's servants* for certain. And so hiding the fiddle had been her greatest sin to that point.

Caris's next transgression, however, had been her most daring—to visit the Romani, the Kale, and ask them not only to teach her to play the instrument, but also to share their songs with her. The Gypsies camped in the high forest above the Dillwyn's isolated farm every year, and although the preacher had nothing good to say about the travelers, most of the Beddgelert farmers were glad enough to see them. The men mended roofs on barns and houses and sheared sheep. Their women sold bright dyes of every color, made from plants they'd gathered on their travels. What Caris liked best was that the Kale played a great deal of Celtic music—including *Welsh* music—around their campfires at night.

Perhaps it was fitting that the free Romani should be the keepers of Wales's heritage, preserving the old songs and daring to play them in the open air. Caris didn't know if her country would ever want its music again, but *she* surely did, and any other tunes she could learn as well. Irish, Scottish, English, and more— the Gypsies knew them all, plus haunting tunes from Europe that thrilled her blood. And so she'd begun a secret life. She still worked long, hard hours on their hillside farm, but at night, when Da was well and truly *feddw* (strange that the preacher had few complaints about ale and spirits!), she headed for the forest with the fiddle under one arm. In the other hand, she carried buttermilk or oatcakes to trade for music lessons, tunes, and songs.

Persisting in a bad habit was undoubtedly an evil all its own, but she sometimes wondered whether it was a new sin each time, or just a large one overall. Whichever it was, long after the Gypsies left each season, she continued to visit the forest for as long as the mountain weather would allow. There she would play to her heart's content without fear of anyone overhearing her. The first few years, she'd been afraid that Da would wake and find her gone, and what could she say that would make a lick of sense to him? He'd be certain that she had a lover—or was just plain daft.

Would he prefer to think that, rather than know what I'm really doing?

As time passed, however, Da began to drink earlier in the day. The farm did well enough under Caris's management, and her father conceded more of the business of it to her until she ran it all by herself. It was harder to find the time for her fiddle, but still, she seldom chose her bed at the end of a fourteen-hour day. What did she care if she spent her days bone-tired? Better that than doing without her music, which had grown by leaps and bounds until she improved upon the old songs and began to create new ones, tunes that were less and less tame by the day.

Ballads and lays and reels seemed to burst forth from the old instrument with a life of their own until she danced as she played . . . She not only led two lives, but she had become two people. One was the hardworking, businesslike Caris, who pulled lambs from birthing ewes, raked out pony stalls, took sheep to market, sold wool, and bargained keenly.

And the other Caris? She could only shake her head. *Who is this wild woman who leaps about in the woods, making music for only the trees to hear?*

The dire hunting horn was definitely closer now, and her sensible cob extended his stocky body into a fast canter. Caris frowned as she adjusted her seat to his rapid pace, yet she didn't dare rein him in. Though her da had often said, "'tis dangerous to run a horse to his barn," something was terribly wrong if Eira was so bothered. *But what?*

Although the Dillwyn farm was isolated, she'd explored this thick forest on the hills high above the valley since she was a small child. There were no wild boars left anywhere in the country, never mind here, no fierce animals bigger than a badger or a fox, and Eira never spooked. Now the forest seemed far darker than it should. It wouldn't be the first time she'd stayed too long, lost in her music, but a break in the trees revealed dark clouds overhead that doused the bright daylight as surely as water doused a fire. It was a long way back to the farm, and she could find her way there blindfolded if need be—yet a mountain storm was nothing to trifle with.

A flash of lightning half blinded her. Thunder crashed like the world was ending, and her steady, dependable Eira did something unheard of: he threw his rider and bolted for home.

By the time Caris got her breath back, her white pony was long gone. She got to her feet slowly and with care. Nothing broken or sprained, thankfully, but she'd have some bumps and bruises on the morrow. The wind had picked up, thrashing the limbs of the trees, and above the din, the mournful horn wailed like a lost soul. She'd never heard the like of it, and the hairs on the back of her neck prickled.

It's coming this way.

Caris saw nothing unusual in the dim forest. The storm above, bearing down on her with incredible speed, was something else entirely. The blackened clouds roiled like an angry sea, lit within by flares of unnatural lightning—green and blue and vivid mauve.

I'll never make it to the farm. But staying among the trees in such weather was a poor plan. There was little other shelter to be had—unless she went to the dolmen. On their way to their camp-site each year, the Romani waved bits of red cloth at the ancient stone structure and spat in its direction, giving it as wide a berth as the rutted forest paths would allow. Evil or not, Caris hoped the great white capstone, supported by three half-buried boulders, would shield her, and she ran as fast as she could in its direction. Her heart was in her throat as the wind whipped her long black hair free and yanked at her clothing with invisible fingers. Lightning struck behind her, close enough that she could feel the ground shake, and she nearly lost her footing.

As the clap of thunder died away, instinct made her cast a glance over her shoulder, and what she saw *did* make her stumble and fall: great coal-black hounds of monstrous size were bounding in her direction, their red and glowing eyes revealing their identity: grims!

Panicked, she scrambled to her feet. The dark fae dogs, called *barghest* or *gwyllgi* by some, were said to foretell one's death, but they weren't the most frightening thing she saw. Following the hounds were forty or fifty riders—*and their horses' hooves didn't touch the earth!*

She was completely surrounded by the otherworldly company before she could scream.

Caris choked down her fear and forced herself to stand still, her hands in front of her gripping each other so hard that they hurt. She needed the pain to help keep her wits together. All these years she'd thought the Wild Hunt was just a story to frighten children into being good, and that the Tylwyth Teg, the Fair Ones, were nothing but make-believe. She knew, however, that many of her neighbors believed them to be real—real enough that they set offerings of bread and milk on their porches at night to avert fae pranks and beg their favor. Even the preacher must have thought them real, as he occasionally spoke out against the evils of consorting with demons and faeries. Perhaps he thought them to be one and the same. Whatever they were, no one wanted to actually meet them.

But here she was.

The storm boiled overhead, and chains of lightning shot through the inky clouds. Several of the massive hounds paced in front of her, all of them at least as high as her waist, growling low in their great shaggy throats and occasionally showing their long white teeth. Yet Caris instinctively knew that the dogs were unlikely to attack unless commanded. It was the Fair Ones themselves she had to be wary of, as they towered over her on their gleaming mounts—though it was difficult to remain on her guard. Tall and slender, the Tylwyth Teg were so beautiful that it actually hurt to look at them. Their ethereal faces were exquisitely sculpted and seemingly lit from within. Their iridescent eyes, never a single hue for more than a moment, glittered with countless secrets, and their long white hair fell free in wild, wind-stirred waves. As in the old stories, the fae wore brilliant colors, reds and blues and greens more vivid than anything found in nature. Their leader wore riding leathers the deep, rich hue of communion wine, trimmed with finely wrought silver.

Caris felt a strange longing well up as she studied her captors, a desire to look upon the Fair Ones always despite the ache it caused within her human heart. Perhaps they were accustomed to being admired, for the fae returned her gaze without expression. Even their horses were like nothing Caris had ever seen. Long-limbed and glossy-coated, they danced in place on polished hooves. Their great eyes showed more than a little interest in Caris, but the natural curiosity of a mortal horse was lacking—and so was the friendliness. Instead, there was an icy anticipation, as if the fae horses were keen for the signal to chase her down. It was then that she noticed that several of the creatures had tusks or fangs, and a few even boasted horns!

Acting quickly to hide her fear, Caris turned her attention to the rest of the hunting party—then immediately wished she had not.

Behind the bright allure of the Tylwyth Teg, the accompanying riders were all human, or had been once. Their faces were haunted and drawn, their clothing tattered and dirty but still distinguishable. Here, a businessman slumped over his horse's neck, his fine white shirt and waistcoat mere rags, with his watch chain swinging free. There, a woman in a muddy gown sat sideways on her thin steed, her hands tangled in its mane, her bonnet fallen away and her long hair hanging in ropes. *There are so many . . .* A miner, his face smeared with coal dust, and a shattered lamp still strapped to his hat, sat astride a white-eyed pit pony. A carthorse, still wearing his traces, bore a butcher with his bloody apron. A red-coated soldier with a broken musket listed in his saddle. Not one of the mortals looked at Caris, or even seemed aware of their surroundings at all. All their lathered mounts were thin, wild-eyed, and frothing at their bits.

That's when Caris saw the knight with the broken sword, his ancient armor rusted, his stallion bony and unkempt. As a child, she'd heard exciting tales of brave knights, but she knew full well that wars were no longer fought in such a manner—two of her own uncles had served in the Royal Welsh Fusiliers against Napoleon. *Enchanted*, she thought suddenly, and swallowed hard as she realized the hapless people who followed the Hunt were not only from different walks of life but from different times as well! *They're enchanted, every one of them!*

In her childhood stories, the Wild Hunt meted out a rough justice of sorts. Liars, thieves, traitors, and murderers, caught out of doors when the Hunt was passing, were often ridden down and compelled to follow in their wake forever. The greedy and the unfaithful were likewise punished. Had her small sins attracted their attention? Had the Hunt come for *her*? Caris strained to be calm, to tamp down her terror. Even if she were not their intended quarry, she knew she was far from safe. The fae were said to be capricious in nature, and they could take offense where none was intended. She must be very, very careful.

"Girl." The leader of the Hunt addressed her, his voice a cadence of deep, resonant bells. "Who are you, and what are you doing here in the forest alone?"

"Caris Ellen Dillwyn, and I'm not a girl; I'm twenty and eight," she said at once, and very nearly put her hand over her own mouth. *Where did that come from?* Had they spelled her to tell too much of the truth? Every child in Beddgelert knew it was unwise to give your name to the Fair Ones—it gave them power over you.

He made a dismissive gesture. "I am Maelgwn, prince of the House of Ash. And we are a thousand *thousand* times as old as you, *girl*. You have not answered us as to your purpose here."

"My life is not as long as yours, good prince, but I have lived here for all of it," she said, smothering the dangerous impulse to retort that she had far more right to this spot than the creature that questioned her. Perhaps she should demand what *his* purpose was. Instead, she quietly added, "My father's farm lies below, past the trees and over the dry stone wall."

A fearful splintering sounded from elsewhere in the forest, like a tree being clawed asunder, and Caris turned in time to see one of the hounds emerge from the brush. To her horror, the beast had her fiddle case in his great drooling teeth. "That's mine!" she burst out. Heedless of the danger, she took several steps toward the monstrous dog with an upraised hand, as if to smack an errant cow that had broken into the garden. "Drop that *this minute!*"

The fae leader raised a fine eyebrow and signaled the hound, which released the battered wooden case at Caris's feet. She knelt at once to retrieve it, brushing the slivers and spittle from the container as carefully as if it were a live thing. Withdrawing the fiddle, she cradled it in her arms, feeling gently along its neck and strings for damage. Her whole body sagged with relief as she found none.

"Play for us, girl," said Maelgwn.

Play? Caris rose slowly, her fiddle and bow clutched to her with uncertain hands. Dear heavens, what could a mortal play for the fae? "My lord, surely your own musicians far surpass my simple skills."

"Play for us." It wasn't a request, and for a moment she bristled. She was not their servant to order about. Yet perhaps if she amused them, they'd let her go. At first Caris was certain her fingers would shake too much to play a note, but as she tucked the fiddle under her chin, she felt a small measure of comfort from the familiar instrument. And thanks to the repertoire she'd gained from the Romani, she knew exactly which song to begin with . . .

How many mortals, she wondered, *have performed "The King of the Faeries" for the Tylwyth Teg themselves?*

She drew the notes with her bow, slowly, quietly at first. Her body rocked and swayed as she built upon the old Celtic tune, as she added the flourishes that begged to be included. By the time she slid smoothly into "*Saith Nos Olau*," she'd all but forgotten she had an audience, and a dangerous one at that. Her feet launched her upward and she landed on her toes. The music seemed to flow through her as if from the earth itself, her steps were light and sure, and there was power in her rendition of "*Nydd y Gwcw*." Darkness broke apart with flashes of light, and the storm released a pelting shower. Yet the rain seemed only to add to the music, bouncing like silver notes from the shining surface of the fiddle as Caris's unbound hair flew about almost as rapidly as the fraying strands of the bow cord. Here was a tune she had never known, a dizzying reel with depth and strength, blossoming from so deep within her that Caris was no longer aware of anything . . .

That is, until the last fiber of the cord snapped, and she suddenly held a useless bow in her ice-cold hands. Shocked, she remembered where she was and lowered the fiddle to her side as water ran down her face and dripped from her clothing. Her breath was ragged and her heart pounded loudly in her ears. The entire Hunt stood silent as a graveyard, as still and motionless as marble statues, completely untouched by the driving rain. Untouched by the music too, it seemed, as their beguiling faces were yet devoid of expression. Caris sighed inwardly. *No matter if they didn't like it,* she told herself. *No matter, I have given it my all. I have played with everything I had, and I can do no more.* She stood quietly, awaiting her dismissal.

Maelgwn, however, smiled. It lent a saintlike radiance to his perfect features, but like the winter sun reflecting off mountain snows, there was no true warmth in his countenance. "It is apparent that you do not belong in this place," he announced. "You will come with us."

Her heart lurched in her chest. "I would but slow you down, my lord," she said with care. "My pony is gone, and in truth, I must make my way home to care for my father."

A female in a riding habit the color of spring leaves laughed aloud, reminding Caris of the tiny strings of bells on Romani wagons. "Wouldn't you rather play for us at Court, dear child? The queen's palace is a splendid place. Think of the wonderful dances we might invent together! And what songs you might learn from us as well."

If the old stories were true—and with the Fair Ones standing before her very eyes, she had to believe they were—Caris knew what would surely happen next. Those foolish enough to enter the vast faery lands beneath the mountains were seldom seen again.

She steeled herself as she regarded Maelgwn. She must be firm, yet not offend.

"The Tylwyth Teg are said to be generous hosts, and your offer is truly kind, good sir. Yet I would be a faithless daughter if I left my father to run the farm alone. Come for me in twenty years, which is naught but a moment to you," she offered. Her heart hurt as she realized for the first time that at the rate her dear da was drinking, he'd be unlikely to last so long. "I will practice my music every day, in preparation to go with thee willingly at that time."

Maelgwn's smile disappeared as if it had never been. "Think you to bargain with us, girl? Your loyalty to your father is admirable, but in your absence, he will simply drink more and care nothing that you are gone."

"That's not true!" declared Caris. "He misses my mother, and it would be cruel for Da to lose me as well. He'll have no one to run the farm, he'll—"

"Enough." The leader of the Hunt dismounted. Holding a silver stirrup in one hand and extending his other to her, he obviously intended her to ride with him.

Caris had sins in abundance, but abandoning her father would never be one of them. If the Fair Ones were intent on having her music, *then there must be none for them to have!* Quickly, she took the old fiddle in hands made strong by years of hard work . . .

And broke the beloved instrument over her knee.

The shattering of the varnished wood affected the Tylwyth Teg far more than her music had. There was anger on some faces, disbelief on others. As for herself, Caris might as well have torn her own heart in two. Tears streamed unchecked, but still she stood straight. "I cannot play for thee, my lord," she said simply. "I am a faithful daughter."

"Faithful, are you?" he mocked. The prince's handsome face was twisted with fury, as he seized a coiled silver whip from his elegant saddle. "*Then you should have a faithful form!*"

The heavy whip glowed with a strange light of its own—dear heaven, was he going to beat her? She pressed her lips together tightly, refusing to plead for mercy, and simply waited for judgment to fall.

"Maelgwn, please! Surely you don't need this child?" It was the faery in green who protested.

He rounded on her at once. "Do you think me foolish, Rhedyn? A ruler gathers *every* weapon against future battles," he snapped. "I would not leave a sword upon the ground, and neither will I leave this one behind."

What weapon? Caris frowned. *What sword?*

Rhedyn bravely tried again. "But the girl does not deserve such—"

A blinding flash of light, hot and bright as a dozen suns, split the air with a deafening crack of thunder. Caris could no longer see or hear, and the air she dragged into her lungs was thick with the smell of sparks. Agony overtook her until it seemed her body would break apart as surely as the precious fiddle had. She had never fainted in her life, but she was grateful when blackness swallowed her.

When next she was aware, Caris found herself stooped and racing along the ground, neck in neck with the great hounds that followed the Hunt.

And realized she had become one of them.

TWO

༄

Eastern Washington State, USA
Modern Day

Not interested," Liam Cole said into his smartphone. That was true. "I'm happy doing what I'm doing." That, however, was a total lie. He hadn't been happy for a minute since he'd turned his back on his old life, what little of it had been left after his world imploded.

"Yeah, well, no one's asking you to give up the farm, you know," said Mel, who had been his agent once and would still like to be. "Just come out of isolation long enough to do a few gigs. I've got a couple open-air festivals at the end of the summer—nothing too big, just a little something to keep yourself in practice. It'll be enough to let people know you're still *here*, and then you can go right back to being a hermit. Buy some extra fancy cows with the money. Just tell me you'll think about it, okay?"

"I'll think about it," said Liam. Another lie. He wouldn't, although guilt pricked him. Mel was a good guy, but he didn't understand. Nobody did, least of all, Liam himself. Tossing the phone onto a side table, he rose from the wicker armchair on the wraparound porch, slapped on a faded Mariners ball cap—a long-ago gift from his Aunt Ruby, who followed baseball like a religion—and headed down the steps. As soon as he left the shade, the day's accumulated heat hit him like a wall; it wouldn't even begin to cool down for another few hours. But if he didn't get busy and do something, anything, he'd start *thinking*, and it sure as hell wouldn't be about doing a concert.

Of course, the damn thinking happened anyway. *A little something to keep yourself in practice.* What would Mel say if he knew that Liam's guitar and mandolin hadn't been out of their cases in three years? Not even his beloved fiddle had seen the light of day since his last gig, the one in Minneapolis, the one that changed everything. *Maybe I should have paid attention to the damn number.* Not that he was superstitious, but it was the thirteenth stop in Liam's first tour as an honest-to-God headliner. The reviews had been nothing short of stellar, representing a ginormous step forward in the career he'd been struggling to build since high school. And Liam was on fire that night, improvising on the bluegrass ballads and newgrass numbers he'd written himself. The audience had demanded three encores, and he was on top of the world . . .

Unaware that some voyeuristic pervert had just uploaded a video to YouTube.

After wishing for years that the media would spare him a little more attention, Liam Cole was pleased to see the after-concert scrum of reporters, the biggest gathering yet. But they didn't want to interview him about what was plainly his best performance ever. No, they were all asking for his *reaction.* He didn't know what the hell they were talking about. *Thank God for Mel.* Not only had his agent run interference for him with the press; the man somehow conjured four plainclothes security guards the size of linebackers to act as human shields. They bundled Liam into a plain gray SUV, and the driver (Mel's brother-in-law, as it turned out) took him to a hotel room—and *not* the one that was booked and waiting for him.

When the door closed and he was finally alone, Liam had sat on the edge of the bed, peering at the screen of his phone, unsure exactly how to go about searching for something he didn't want to find.

In the end, it found him. Any email from an address he didn't recognize normally went straight to the trash bin as spam—but there was one that stood out. It wasn't advertising hot women or blue pills or credit cards; instead, the subject line simply read, "Sorry." Opening it revealed a link to the video that complete strangers were now talking about: Jade Marshall Cole, Liam's love since middle school and bride of less than a year, in bed with Vic Raymond, the guy who'd been his best friend and best man. Certain parts had been blurred, but it made no difference. Like his Uncle Conall had said, "If you're naked, it's a sure bet you're not fishing."

Liam had known loss. He'd felt his mother's death keenly, and still missed her. And yet he hadn't known heartbreak could produce such raw physical pain. He even ran his hand over his chest, certain that there must be a hole there, that his ribs had been sawn asunder and his heart torn out by the roots.

She loved me. She said she loved me. She showed *she loved me. How could she do this to me? To us?* If everything he'd had with Jade was a lie, then what the hell was left in his world to believe in? What was real?

And as for Vic, anger flooded Liam's gut, mixing like acid with the agony. Leaving Mel to cancel the rest of the tour, Liam rented a car from the first place he found that opened their doors at 6 a.m. Originally he'd intended to drive straight through to his home in Portland, but even ignoring speed limits could trim only so much off a twenty-six-hour trip, and he hadn't slept a wink to start with. The inner pain and fury that wrestled each other for dominance exhausted him, and he finally conceded to catch some z's in a couple of truck stops along the way. Afterward he chugged bad coffee and filled up on doughnuts and burritos that he couldn't taste and that sat in his stomach like rocks. He *willed* his body to digest them, to take in the "quick and dirty" fuel. It would do no good to collapse on the goddamn doorstep before he even confronted Jade. Besides, he wanted his head clear—or *clearer*, since it was already buzzing with volatile thoughts like a frickin' hive of angry bees.

It was just past noon the next day when Liam finally turned onto his own street. His brain had finally settled, somewhat. Although he hurt like he'd been gutshot, he'd carefully rehearsed what he wanted to say, what he planned to ask, what he needed to know—and every last reasonable word of it went right out the window as he spotted an all-too-familiar vehicle parked in front of his house, a yellow Jeep Wrangler that was strangely clean for once.

Apparently Vic's been too damn busy sleeping with my wife to go off-roading!

Rage bubbled up from the depths of Liam's soul, like magma making its way toward the earth's surface, as he parked halfway down the block and stalked to the house. The drapes were drawn, but it was the middle of the day and that just ratcheted up his fury. There was no disguising his approach from his own dog of course—Homer was barking wildly from the backyard. Maybe Vic and Jade would suspect Liam's presence, but more likely they'd attribute the dog's excitement to the neighbor lady's half-dozen cats. After all, Liam wasn't expected home for another three weeks.

He had his keys. It was his own damn house. He had no idea why he didn't simply burst in, except that some small corner of his mind that was still sane told him he didn't want Jade in the middle. Instead, ringing the bell like a frickin' stranger brought him exactly what he hoped for . . .

Vic Raymond, former best friend and current betrayer, opened the door.

In a heartbeat, Liam had seized him by the shirtfront and yanked him outside hard enough to throw him off the porch. With a growl that was very far from human, the volcano within Liam finally erupted with world-shattering force. He was blind to everything but the need to let his fists express all the anguish and anger that words could not. If the traitor got in a punch or six of his own, Liam didn't know or care. Some distant part of him was vaguely aware of Jade screaming in the background, of people gathering, of Vic's face going from white and shocked to bloody and unrecognizable, of sirens coming down the street. And still he could not stop.

Liam woke up in a cell, not certain how he'd gotten there and with no idea what time or even what the hell day it was. Waiting for him was pain with a capital *P*, more than he ever imagined possible. Not from the bruises on his face, or the split knuckles, or even from the spots on his back where a taser had connected— though they all hurt like a sonofabitch—but from the throbbing ache in his chest.

Also waiting for him was an arraignment on an assortment of assault charges (he sure as hell didn't *remember* hitting a cop). Uppermost in his mind, however, was that he still hadn't gotten the chance to talk to Jade. Maybe he shouldn't have made that his first and only permitted call, but he'd already thumbed the number pad before he thought it through.

It went straight to the machine. What the hell had he expected? He left a nondescript message and hung up. Christ, he should have had the sense to call Mel to find him a lawyer, or better yet, he should have called his uncle, if he could reach him. His agent would have taken care of it. Uncle Conall would have, too—right after the big man threw a haymaker at Vic himself. That mental image cheered Liam briefly, but it was the only bright note in a long and dismal morning.

Dead last in a lengthy line of defendants waiting to be formally charged, he had far too much time to reflect on what he'd done—or might have done. No one had mentioned what condition Vic was in. Liam's hands were damaged, so he'd obviously beaten the living shit out of the guy he thought he knew. Hell, he could have killed him, but damned if he could dredge up much regret . . . Well, not on the surface, anyway. *How could Vic have done this to me?* They'd been inseparable since they were twelve, when Liam had first moved in with his uncle and aunt. He and Vic had been in the same classes (and skipped more than a few to go fishing), competed as team ropers in junior rodeo, partnered in 4-H projects, played football, gotten stupid-ass drunk for the first time, set the chemistry lab on fire by accident, double-dated, and finally graduated. All of it as best friends. Vic had been his best man, and Liam was due to be Vic's in only a few months. *What the hell is up with* that?

As for Jade, Liam would rather not think about her—*not here, not now*—but it was like trying to stop a river with a teacup. He was one big, throbbing ball of hurt from the top of his head to the soles of his feet, and he wasn't certain if he was going to explode again or just sit down and bawl like the brokenhearted kid he felt like. Because while he was infuriated by Vic's betrayal, Liam was utterly devastated by the thought that his sweetheart, *his Jade*, had cheated on him.

He never saw it coming. If there were signs, he hadn't clued in to a single damn one.

It has to be my fault. Has to be. She'd *never* do such a thing to him otherwise. The stress must have gotten to her, with him being gone so much. He'd been so wrapped up with preparing for this tour that he hadn't paid enough attention to her. And money had been so damn tight lately, thanks to the overwhelming costs of promotion. He could make changes, make it better. They could work this out, put this behind them. *People overcome shit like this all the time, right?*

Liam pled not guilty, and bail was set and so was a return court date. More fun and games for later, but he didn't give a damn at the moment. He was worn out right to his very soul. First on the list was to get a room, to get some real food and real sleep, and *then* figure out what the hell to do next . . .

Or that would have been his plan if Jade hadn't been waiting outside the courtroom for him, grim-faced and red-eyed, clutching her purse in front of her with both hands. It killed him that he didn't even know what to do, how to feel. Shouldn't he be running to hold her? Shouldn't she be holding him? Instead, they approached each other warily, like strangers, almost like *enemies*. Even acquaintances would have given each other a warmer greeting.

"We have to talk," she said, and he could already tell it wasn't going to be good.

"Now you want to talk? Seems to me we needed to talk a helluva long time ago."

"You weren't here."

Through some shred of willpower he didn't know he had left, Liam clamped his mouth shut. It would do no good to air their dirty laundry in the middle of the goddamn courthouse. Instead, he followed her outside, where dark, heavy clouds matched his mood perfectly. They got into her car and drove home—or rather, drove to their *house*—without saying a word.

They avoided each other for a while, saying nothing. He stripped off his clothes to shower and was astonished at how much blood was on them, Vic's blood. The clothes went straight to the trash, and Liam stood under the hot water for a long time until he felt somewhat human again, as human as a person *could* feel when his damn heart was missing. He lingered some more, until he couldn't hold off talking to Jade any longer.

Things did not improve when the silence was finally broken. All the things he'd guessed were wrong truly *were* wrong—but those things were only the tip of the iceberg. He opened the curtains in the living room and let in the gloomy gray light. It barely illuminated the damn room, never mind their relationship.

"I didn't want to get married," she said quietly. "I don't want to be married now."

He stared at her as if he'd never seen her before. "How can you even say something like that? We love each other. We've always loved each other. It's always been me and you. Hell, we couldn't imagine anything else."

"That's the problem. It wasn't possible to imagine anything else. I didn't get a chance to imagine anything else. For God's sake, Liam, I was barely fourteen when we started hanging out together. Fourteen, and you were just sixteen. That's way too young to plan out the rest of your life."

"But you planned it anyway. We both did. Jesus, every year we had a different song picked out for our wedding dance. We planned houses and argued over kids' names. Hell, I even used to sing that old Beatles song to you, 'When I'm Sixty-Four,' and one day you dumped a bowl of flour in my hair to make it white. We had an epic flour fight in your mother's kitchen, remember?" Liam reached for her hand, but she pulled it away and went to stand on the other side of the living room. The carpeted space between them might as well be the Grand Canyon.

"I don't want to remember. Everything I remember has *you* in it."

He stood stock still, as the hurtful words crashed into him. "Exactly when did that become a bad thing?" he managed.

"That's not what I meant, not really. It's more like—I've never had a relationship with anyone else. I've never done anything else ..."

"Until you did Vic?"

23

"You don't understand!"

How he managed not to leap across the abyss, to grab her and shake her, he'd never know. Instead, he turned his back on her, shoved his hands into his pockets, and stared out the window. "No, I don't understand. You haven't told me a damn thing. You've never said one word to me that might have given me a clue that you were unhappy or that you didn't want me. In fact, if someone hadn't sent me a fucking YouTube link, *I'd still be in the goddamn dark.*"

He wasn't seeing much now, either. Not the manicured yard and newly planted trees, not the pretty residential street, and not the kids playing next door. Only his entire life exploding in front of his eyes. "Nice video work by the way. What the hell did you do, leave the blinds open? Invite the neighbors?"

"Vic did it. He told me at the hospital. I swear I didn't know he was filming us—it was a crass thing to do, but he wanted to tell you and I didn't."

"Yeah, I can see how that would be difficult for you."

She ignored the sarcasm. "I didn't *know* how to tell you. I wasn't ready to. I didn't even know what to call what we were doing."

"Funny, I can think of lots of words for it."

"God knows, I didn't love him or anything. I swear I didn't. It just happened and then it kept happening." She stopped then, as if she'd said far more than she'd intended to say.

Liam turned around very slowly. "How long?"

Her lips trembled in a face gone pale. "Off and on. A couple of years, maybe more."

She might as well have shot him between the eyes. Incredulous, Liam blinked once, twice. It was a few moments before he found his voice. "Even before the goddamn wedding?" He swallowed hard, again and again. The lump in his throat felt like a golf ball. Finally he worked it out of the way long enough to shout, "*Jesus frickin' Christ*! If you didn't want to marry me, *why the hell did you say yes*?"

"I thought it was what I wanted! I thought I loved you, that Vic was just some kind of stupid-ass fling, something to get out of my system. And I felt like I *had* to marry you, don't you see? Everybody expected it." She threw up her hands. "Everybody. Name someone in the county who didn't know us and expect us to get married. It wasn't just us, playing and pretending, it was jeezly *everybody*. Even my own family, my folks, were in on it. My mom talked about it all the time, started a hope chest, not for me but for us. *Us*! Everywhere I went, I wasn't just me, I wasn't Jade, I was just half of you. *We were like Siamese twins for God's sake!*" Tears burst out as forcefully as her words. "I was Mrs. Liam Cole before you ever put a ring on my finger. Because everyone could see only you. As soon as I said my name, it was 'Oh, you're so lucky' and 'He's so talented' and 'You must be so proud.' It was always about you. I was invisible."

"You should have told me. We could have done something— hell, we *did* do something: we left." It was crystal clear now why she'd been so insistent that they move to Portland. "It must be getting better now that we're here. You just haven't given it enough time."

"Time isn't going to fix this, Liam. It can't. You're the one with the music, with something to build, something to dream about and create."

"I've been building it for *us*! And it's yours, too. We've been building it together."

She shook her head. "I get to promote *you*, remember? That's my part in it. And when I'm not doing that, I'm just another member of the audience. Don't you get it? I don't have anything that's just *mine*."

"Is Vic yours?"

She glowered at him. "That's over. It wasn't anything to begin with."

Wasn't anything, my ass. Only a ten-point earthquake that had torn away all the ground from under Liam's feet and destroyed everything he held dear. "So you're saying you cheated on me because I had music and you didn't?"

"For God's sake, it's not that simple. But if that's all you can understand, then yes. And when you were gone, when your music took you away more and more—*I couldn't find myself!* I didn't even know who I was anymore. I don't now."

"Most people take a few college courses, get a hobby, you know? Even take skydiving lessons or something! If you were trying to find yourself, why the hell would you go looking in Vic's bed?"

"I don't know. I don't know." She put her hands to her head, and her misery was evident as she sank into a chair. A part of Liam—maybe his little finger—whatever part *wasn't* emotionally destroyed, felt a tinge of sympathy for her. Maybe it was habit, but for a fleeting second he wanted to hold her and tell her it was all right, tell her they'd work it out and everything would be all right. And then the moment passed. *It's never going to be all right . . .*

As if she'd heard him, she said, "I can't live like this, Liam. I'm done. We're done."

"Tell me you love me or tell me you don't," Liam dared, already knowing the answer but not able to live another minute without hearing it. "Say it out loud. Tell me to my face."

The tears flew as she shook her head. "I've been trying to tell you, *I don't.* I just don't love you the way you want me to, and I'm never going to."

∽

And I'm never going to . . .

The cloying clouds of remembrance finally cleared from Liam's head just as he finished moving the last of the square bales of straw from one side of the barn to the other. The bales hadn't needed to be moved of course. It was just something he did when the past reared its ugly head and he had a crapload of unwanted emotions to work off. Some men drove fast, some drank, some drugged, some picked a fight, and some hit the gym. Liam Cole moved bales.

He peeled off his sweat-soaked T-shirt and used it to dry his face and wipe flecks of straw from his perspiring arms. Liam was tall, and he'd always been on the lean side, but his muscles were rock-hard and defined. Hard work was good therapy for him. He'd learned that when he was ten, when his mother first took sick. Emotionally, he had his music. It gave his heart an outlet, his fear and hurt a voice. But some days, there was just no substitute for physically working his body until it could barely move. Achieving exhaustion was the only way he'd been able to sleep at all during the two years Mom had stubbornly fought her losing battle with ovarian cancer.

When she died, Liam had gone to live with his Aunt Ruby and Uncle Conall. They doted on him and he loved them dearly, but in truth, it was probably their farm that had saved his young sanity. They had an organic operation—Steptoe Acres—south of Spokane Valley, Washington, along Hangman Creek. Lots of land to wander, with places to explore, hills to climb, rivers to swim in and fish, horses to ride, and solitude when he wanted it. *Real* solitude, out in the middle of the quiet wilderness, away from all human voices. And, as with all farms, there was a ton of chores that always needed doing. It was an ideal location for a grieving boy to work through his pain. He'd become whole in this place.

Now here he was, a grown man, and damned if history hadn't repeated itself: his life had blown up in his face, and it seemed like everything he'd ever touched lay in jagged pieces. Where else would instinct take him but the farm where he'd been healed once before? Liam had needed something to do and a place to do it that was out of the way. And when Uncle Conall and Aunt Ruby moved to Arizona soon afterward, he'd taken over the operation. Liam strongly suspected the couple had moved up their retirement plans just a little for his benefit, and if so, he was doubly grateful. Because Steptoe Acres was exactly what he needed.

For one thing, if you had dairy goats, you damn well had a *schedule*. There was no lying in bed wondering about the meaning of life when forty Saanen and LaMancha does were waiting to be milked at 6 a.m. No wondering what you were going to do with yourself at night either. Second milking started at 6 p.m. The raw liquid had to be cooled down quickly after each milking, then put through the pasteurizer before going into the storage vat. Sanitizing all the equipment after each milking was a production in and of itself, not to mention all the care that went into the animals themselves.

And then there was kidding season over February and March. Regular barn checks had to be made throughout the night in case a doe needed help or newborn kids had to be warmed up or hand-fed. Meticulous records had to be kept, and—hardest of all, in his opinion—Liam had to come up with a hell of a lot of new names.

After the spring kidding came spring planting. To help retain its organic certification, Steptoe Acres had always grown its own feeds and hay, which produced multiple harvests throughout the long growing season. Fields of market vegetables and fruits had to be planted, watered, weeded, picked, and delivered to the cooperative.

Nope, Liam Cole was in no danger of running out of things to do. With the dairy alone, he was usually too busy to think or feel, and that's exactly what he wanted. In fact, he quickly found himself a little *too* busy and had to make adjustments. He soon leased out the orchards to a neighboring organic farmer who would take good care of them, then he hired seasonal help for the fields. He'd thought about carrying on the cheese business, but in the end conceded defeat. Aunt Ruby had made fresh goat cheese, called chèvre, plus slow-aged cheeses dipped in wax, for the area wine-tasting and restaurant markets. Liam had helped every summer since he was twelve years old, so he knew the process well, but in the end, he contracted to provide pasteurized milk to a gourmet cheese maker in Spokane Valley.

His uncle and aunt had been understanding of the change. After all, they'd worked the farm as a team. As a one-man show, however, Liam had only two hands—and he wasn't interested in acquiring any more than necessary.

Despite all the work, the farm gave Liam as much or more than he put into it. Everywhere he looked was a vista of open land and open sky, with rolling hills to the south and mountains rising along the Idaho border. A man could breathe here. There was something deeply satisfying about working the land, being close to the earth. And the livestock? He'd always liked animals, and while there were classic frustrations—like the escape-artist goats finding yet another way out of the pasture—there were also moments of profound connection.

It was a damn good thing he could still connect to *something*, because he sure as hell didn't care to be around people. All his efforts over the years to be recognized, to be noticed, to stand out from the crowd, had come back to haunt him. People noticed him, all right. He wasn't sure which was worse, the whispers behind his back, the furtive looks, or the well-intentioned remarks that would have been better left unsaid. *You looked so happy together. That girl must have been crazy to leave you. What a damn shame—why, you two were made for each other!* And Liam's all-time favorite: *Well, better to have loved and lost, they say.* Personally, he'd like to get his hands on the writer of that particular little saying . . .

Not to mention all the damn reporters who *still* called him up and asked if he was working on a new album or when he was going to give another performance.

They didn't know that he couldn't, of course. Nobody did. Inside him, there was still a lot of anger wrapped around pain. And within that? A whole lot of *nothing.* His natural feelings for music appeared to have been amputated. Playing, writing, singing—gone, just gone. Where once he couldn't live without a tune in his head, now there was a terrible silence. It should have scared him, and maybe it did if he looked deep enough. But when it came right down to it, he wanted nothing more to do with music anyway.

Of course, it didn't take a shrink to figure out a whole shitload of *whys.* He wasn't stupid. Jade and his music were intertwined, had been since before his first public performance at age fourteen at the state fair. Gangly and tall, he hadn't been a popular kid then, hadn't filled out the promise of his height, or gotten what Aunt Ruby called his "heartbreaker looks" yet. And still, pretty blonde Jade Marshall had cheered him on and encouraged him to follow his dream. She attended countless little performances as he filled in last-minute slots in playbills and did backup work for some concert bands. By the time high school was over, Liam was opening for some of the larger acts that came through the area. Over the following five years, both the shows and the audiences got bigger—and Jade was still there. How many times had she sat behind that rickety folding table, selling CDs of his songs and handing out business cards? *No wonder she'd felt so invisible.* He could see that much now.

Nevertheless, it had been Jade who had first encountered Mel and talked him into listening to Liam's work.

Mel had offered to represent him at once. And within minutes of leaving the office of his brand-new agent, Liam asked Jade to marry him. It seemed natural and right. No matter how often he tried to think back to that night, he still couldn't see any hint that she might not want the same things he wanted. Theirs was a shared dream, or so he thought. But then, he'd been young and riding high on enthusiasm—how could he see anything but a bright future ahead?

He'd understood, of course, when Jade started staying home more. She had a wedding to plan and a house to furnish and a college program to enroll in, if she ever figured out which one. And besides, she was his sounding board for every new song before he debuted it, so she knew his music inside out. It wouldn't be the same without her input, their shared analysis of each performance, but he understood that she might be getting bored. Liam took a week off so they could get married, and then he went back on the road. He missed her of course, but they were both busy, just like every other modern young couple, right? He was creating a future for them both. She'd gotten him started, and he didn't blame her a bit for being tired of the road life. She had better things to do, and it was time she did them.

He'd just never imagined she had *someone* better to do. Maybe what goaded him most was feeling like such a damn idiot. How stupid he'd been to assume Jade was happy, how dumb to take for granted that they were on the same page. Especially when hindsight now rudely pointed out all the flashing neon signs he'd missed. The future he'd imagined was now a pile of ashes. Either he blamed his music for the loss of Jade, or he blamed himself and gave up the music he loved as a kind of penance.

Whatever the cause, the songs that had once flowed so freely were now blocked. Three whole years had passed since the ending of his world as he knew it, yet his talent couldn't be more inaccessible to him if the vast concrete walls of Hoover Dam were holding it prisoner. He could beat his fists bloody against it, yet the music—*his* music—simply could not be reached.

And he didn't give a beggar's damn if it stayed that way.

In the human world, the horizon was just blushing with dawn, yet evening was new as Caris returned to the Nine Realms, and the moon had not reached its height. The cool air was thick with the scents of exotic night-blooming flowers, and strange constellations glittered high above. She would never understand how the faery kingdom could lie far beneath the Black Mountains of Wales and yet have a sun and moon and stars! It should be black as Hades here, dark and suffocating, but all was brighter and more vivid than the world above, even at night.

The beauty did not cheer her, however. Her appointed task had taken her to a sullen young man who routinely stabbed his body with needles. Thinking the great black dog in his room was a hallucination, he'd thrown an ale bottle at her, then laughed out loud when it passed right through her as if she were a ghost. Like most of the human world, he had forgotten the old faery legends—if he had ever heard of them at all. But whether or not he understood her purpose, he would still be dead the next day of his habit.

The thought made her soul sick, and as always, Caris loathed her morbid role. She *cared* about the people she appeared to—and surely that was the worst quality in the world for a death dog to possess. She couldn't seem to help herself, though she suspected the heartache would eventually kill her soul.

So far, she hadn't forgotten what it was to be mortal herself, hadn't forgotten what it was like to be part of the human world above. *Not yet.* Other grims, she knew, eventually lost sight of their origins, especially the ones who had been among the Fair Ones for a very long time. Some began to worship their fae captors, who surpassed all human dreams of beauty. Other grims became despondent, wishing that the death they foretold was their own, or they stopped feeling emotion at all, as if their hearts had died within them. Far too many turned cruel, deriving great pleasure in frightening or tormenting those whom they were sent to warn.

Caris still attempted to lessen people's fears. She behaved calmly, tried not to surprise people, and she certainly didn't chase them. In fact, she tried to model her behavior from the loyal and friendly collies her da had kept with the sheep. Sadly, it didn't work very often. Not surprising when all grims were black as sin itself, and monstrous in size. Most were like mastiffs or like wolves. Some had glowing eyes, and their very appearance was designed to inspire raw terror, even if the person had no idea what the dog's morbid mission was.

Though tall as a man's waist, Caris was more slightly built than the other grims. More like a deerhound, she thought—as far as she could discern without being able to see her reflection—or perhaps it was because she was female.

And the only female grim at that.

When Caris first arrived in the fae kingdom on the heels of the Hunt, Rhedyn, the green-clad faery, tried once more to influence the prince. "At least permit the girl to be as she was. There are other ways of hiding her, other ways that she can serve you. The work of a death dog is simply too morose to be borne by a mortal woman's heart." Maelgwn's heart—if he had one at all—remained completely untouched. As the pair argued, Caris learned that the prince had cobbled together a hunt of his own for sport. His entourage, which had so terrified her, was but a pale imitation of the real thing!

Finally, Rhedyn declared she would take the matter before Lurien, *true* Lord of the Wild Hunt—but Maelgwn's vile temper erupted. He struck his lovely companion hard enough to knock her down and ordered her to silence. "A prince," he declared, "enjoys a status far superior to any mere lord. And do not forget that one day soon, I will elevate my royal standing above all."

She rose slowly but with dignity, her exquisite mouth bleeding blue, and bowed her acquiescence. Caris felt almost as heartsick for the green-clad faery as she did for herself.

She soon learned that most of the Tylwyth Teg were as Maelgwn: selfish, uncaring, quicker to anger than any other emotion, and altogether contemptuous of mortals. A few, like the faery who had spoken up for her, possessed some semblance of fairness, even kindness, but they were rare—although it was said that Gwenhidw herself, queen of the Nine Realms, had once held dear a human friend.

There was no one left for Caris to hold dear. She'd been a captive of the Fair Ones for close to two centuries, a fact she knew only because her task took her to the mortal world above. There she had witnessed for herself the deliberate march of years in her country, the struggles and the progress, the changes and the growth. But in the strange kingdom of the fae, the old stories proved true: time not only didn't move the same; it might not even exist.

Had she not been human only days ago?

Certainly the grief in her heart was still fresh. Dafydd Dillwyn drank himself to death, just as the cruel fae prince had predicted. That it would have happened anyway was no comfort to her at all. Had she been there, her father would still have liked his ale too much. But he might not have slid into perpetual drunkenness so quickly, and she would have cared for him to the very last. Because of Maelgwn, her father had died alone, his farm in ruins around him.

She blamed herself just as much as the ice-hearted prince. If she had repented of her music, if she had not been so determined to play, she would never have spent hours hiding herself in the woods, would likely never have encountered a faery hunt in her lifetime. The preacher would undoubtedly declare that Caris was being punished for her long list of sins—but if that were so, it seemed horribly unfair that her father had been made to suffer as well.

As for her soul, its most raw and agonizing wounds were not caused by guilt for the music she had made but by *frustration for her inability to create more*! How often did she hear songs and tunes, both human and fae, that enlivened the deeply buried remnants of her spirit. As a grim, her clever fingers had been replaced with useless toes, yet she could still sense a tingle in them, the yearning to express the spark of music that was still part of her. It was like starving in the face of a sumptuous feast, her hands and mouth bound so she could not partake.

Perhaps this is hell after all.

THREE

⌒⁊⩙⌒

T he fae smith lay in a pool of his own blue blood. Maelgwn paid the body no heed, nor did he spare a glance at his own blade as he spelled it clean and sheathed it. His attention was wholly on the exquisite breastplate. It was painstakingly fitted and elaborately tooled, a thing of great beauty, but he cared little for that. Nor did he particularly care about the quality of the faery-forged silver that it was made from, although it was far stronger than any steel that mortals could make.

No, the prince had eyes only for the twenty-two small stones and eleven large stones that adorned the breastplate. They gleamed in their double-sided settings like darkly iridescent pearls, facing inward toward the wearer as well as outward, and he stroked a finger over each one as if caressing a lover. *At last.* Maelgwn had spent centuries accumulating the rare nuggets that possessed the priceless capacity to amplify magic. As a member of the royal family, he'd been given a *bwgan* stone—a very tiny one, commensurate with his distance from the throne—when he reached adulthood. Its expansion of his magical abilities was likewise unremarkable, but he'd realized the potential immediately: *more bwgan stones equals more power.*

Now, finally, he had thirty-three—only the queen herself possessed more. Many he had won by gaming, a few he had purchased with his winnings, most he had stolen outright. None were from any bwgan he'd ever slain on a hunt. Very few of the aggressive, sharp-toothed creatures, perhaps only one in ten thousand, ever developed a precious stone within its skull. But the prince made certain he was seen hunting the massive salamander-like creatures often, lest anyone should ever catch sight of the handful of stones he always carried with him and question how he came by them. So far, the only one who had ever witnessed the complete collection was the smith who had crafted the breastplate. *And he won't be telling anyone.*

Slowly Maelgwn stripped off his fine clothing until he was naked to the waist, then hunched into the breastplate like a knight donning a cuirass. The process was far easier than he thought it would be, a testament to the smith's fine eye for fit and design. Breathing deep, the prince reveled in the sensation of silver and stone against his skin. And in a sudden rush, his magic reared up within him like a rampant stallion, powerful and potent—and with it, the dizzying desire to dominate. For a long moment, Maelgwn stood with his head back, eyes closed, and arms outstretched as the intense energies from the stones burned through his body like thirty-three flames. A whirlwind of power raged within and without, gathering strength, looming larger and larger, filling the very room and threatening to consume him . . .

Until the magic abruptly merged with him, becoming his to command.

Maelgwn opened his eyes. Like an impatient hound brought to heel, the power sat uneasily as if eager to be sent out. Accordingly, the prince's first act was to flick a finger toward the fallen smith and reduce the body to ash. At a word, a spectral breeze gathered the particles and bore them up the chimney of the forge, to be scattered over the swampland beyond like so much dross.

It pleased him immensely.

Usually the prince would have a servant dress him, but now that would have to change. *A small sacrifice*, he thought, as he fastened his new secret securely beneath his fine clothing. *And a good trade.* No more stones sewn into the hems of his garments, no more stones tucked into hidden pockets. Now, all of his bwgan stones would be with him, with all of their enhancing qualities available to him, *at all times.*

Maelgwn's followers had been attracted to him partly by his station but mostly by his magical prowess and his power; they had no idea of its source. They admired him and obeyed him—and they did both without question. That would not change. If anything, now that he had even *more* power at his disposal, he would also gain more followers to carry out his plans.

The thought of those plans brought a fresh rush of energy, almost sexual in nature, and the stones heated to the point of pain. Mentally, he beat down the flames. *Not yet, not yet. It is not time!* If he was to achieve his ultimate goal, he must take every precaution, make every preparation—including the careful accumulation of every possible tool and weapon.

Fortunately, he had a very important weapon already at hand, hidden in the form of a voiceless female grim.

On the way to the stone kennels beneath the palace, Caris usually gave the Court as wide a berth as possible, mindful of those grims who ended up completely bewitched by the Fair Ones, following them like supplicating shadows. She *would not* adore her coldhearted captors. *Not now and not ever.*

Today, however, raised voices spilled from the throne room, and Caris paused in spite of herself. The voices of the Tylwyth Teg were hauntingly alluring but generally devoid of emotion. Even their bell-like laughter was mirthless, reminding Caris of ice crystals in a glacial stream. But this was different—never had she heard such agitation and excitement among the fae.

Instinctively placing her black paws with care so that no toenail clicked on the polished agate floor, Caris entered the massive ancient room. The crowd was far larger than she'd first thought. Still, even with so many gathered within its mighty walls, the size and splendor of the throne room overwhelmed the senses. The impossibly high ceiling had been created from a single great translucent gemstone, varying from the deepest purple where the dome met the exquisitely carved agate columns that bore it, through shades of mauve and sea green until, in the exact center, the stone became as transparent as a great glass bubble. Through it, the mysterious sky of the faery kingdom could be seen clearly.

At the moment, she half wished the bubble would break and release some of the noise from the building. Usually, the barest murmur bounced about the polished walls of agate, jasper, and crystal until a whisper was as loud as a shout—and no one was whispering now. *If grims could get headaches, I'd have one now for certain.* Caris slipped in and out along the edges of the throng, finally shrinking shadowlike against a wall to watch and listen from behind a pillar of striped stone.

While the Tylwyth Teg were the ruling class, they were not the only fae present. The Nine Realms hidden beneath Wales were populated by countless creatures—and some were as horrifying as the Tylwyth Teg were comely. A grim was scary enough in its own right, yet Caris couldn't suppress a shiver as her gaze traveled over the endless shapes and sizes of faery beings. Some looked like trees, some like rocks, and some resembled animals that should exist in only the worst of nightmares. Even creatures that didn't usually venture onto dry land were present. *Kelpies*, the great water horses that drowned unwary humans, stamped and sent flecks of seaweed flying into the crowd. Tree nymphs—no less dangerous for their exotic beauty—quarreled and pulled at each other's hair. Dark and light, massive and tiny—the variety of faeries seemed endless.

And so did their animosity toward each other. There was no harmony here. Almost all the tribes or factions kept to themselves, crowded into defensive clusters, with each group keeping a wary eye on the ones around it. The only thing any of them had in common was the making of loud demands.

Caris ceased studying the assembly and focused instead on a faraway dais of mottled green jasper. From its layered heights rose the Glass Throne. During her time in the realms, she'd overheard countless conversations. Most of the fae spoke freely to one another if a grim was present—after all, though they understood a thousand languages, grims couldn't utter a word—and because of that, Caris knew the enormous throne was not glass at all but a fanned array of natural crystals the size of timbers. A fae song had caused them to burst forth from the surrounding rock when the earth was yet young, and the music encouraged them to take on their unique shape. *Such a song that must have been!*

As always, however, the spectacular throne stood empty. Since the murder of King Arthfael at the hands of traitors long ago, the queen seldom graced the chattering Court with her presence. Some said her heart had shattered with her beloved's death. Some said she feared for her own life. A few said she simply had no interest in the posturing and gossip that seemed to be part and parcel of Court life. Whatever the reason for the monarch's absence, Caris had never seen her.

She recognized Lurien, however, standing to the right of the great seat. Unlike most of the Fair Ones, his hair was as black as the riding leathers he wore, and swung to his waist in hundreds of whip-thin braids. He was the true Lord of the Wild Hunt. Of late, however, Lurien was more often seen acting in the office of the queen's *Llaw Dde*, her Right Hand, than leading the Hunt. And it was as the *llaw dde* that he raised his hands for silence and addressed the assembly.

"With her generous permission, I speak in the name of Her Benevolent Grace, Queen Gwenhidw of the Nine Realms, *Brenhines* of the Faery Kingdom *dan Cymru*." The noise of the crowd diminished, though it did not cease entirely. "This is our ancestral home, and we have lived here since before the Black Mountains rose. The time has come when our—"

Lurien stopped as genuine surprise, then pleasure, passed over his strong features. Without warning, he knelt where he was, and the entire vast assembly fell to their knees in utter and complete silence. Even Caris dropped to her belly in her hiding place. Although the hall was crowded with fae from every corner of the realms, a wide path opened immediately all the way from the steps of the dais to the massive arched doorway farthest from it.

Where stood the queen.

The Tylwyth Teg were rightly known as the Fair Ones, but they were coarse and common compared to the unearthly beauty of Queen Gwenhidw. Her porcelain features seemed to glow from within, accentuated by the impossible hues of the night sky captured in her gown. It needed no cape or train; instead, her own shimmering hair tumbled to the floor in a pearl-colored cascade, unbound and unadorned, save for tiny flickers of living light. Her crown was a delicate circlet of woven silver that graced her forehead, and her only jewelry a long silver chain that disappeared into the bodice of her gown. Nothing more ornate was required to prove her office, as her power radiated from her as from the heart of a star.

No attendants, no guards, no entourage followed her. Barefoot, she walked the long path with unhurried grace, and with each delicate step a vibration sang through the polished agate floor. The pulse of Gwenhidw's power built until Caris could feel it like a heartbeat in the stone column she hid behind. Still the sovereign took her time, pausing right and left to greet her subjects with genuine warmth. As she finally neared the dais, Lurien made a move as if to offer his hand, but she simply smiled and shook her head. She mounted the steps of the high platform without escort and sat upon the enormous throne unaided. As tall as she was, she looked almost childlike in the throne's great translucent arms—and Caris was reminded that the throne was designed to seat two monarchs at once—yet Gwenhidw seemed perfectly at ease, even comfortable.

"Peoples of the Nine Realms, we are gathered on a matter of great importance." Strength was woven through the clear, crystalline tones of the queen's voice, and Caris found herself leaning forward in spite of herself.

"As the Lord of the Wild Hunt indicated, this is our home. It will always be our first home. However, our numbers are many, and the mountains here are old. The power that flows through this earth, that forms the very touchstone of our magic, is not infinite. It is no longer great enough to support us all. At best, we risk stagnation. At worst, we risk war among ourselves.

"As you know, we have proposed to follow the example of many other fae kingdoms. Our brothers and sisters to the north and to the west have established new holdings in the younger lands, and so must we.

"When the king lived . . ." Here Gwenhidw paused, but Caris didn't think it was for effect. "When *my husband* lived," the monarch continued, "he negotiated with other fae tribes for many years until he succeeded in claiming a choice territory for our people. Arthfael rightly named it Tir Hardd, the Beautiful Land. There the earth magic pulses like a thousand hearts, and on its surface alone, it is nearly seven times the size of the human country of Wales above us. Below, however, where earth magic holds sway, Tir Hardd is vast, many times as large as all the Nine Realms taken together."

The crowd had obviously heard this before. There were many heads nodding, and a few soft murmurs, but some in the assembly seemed to struggle to be silent. Finally, a gnomelike creature near the front, one of the *coblynau*, could not hold his tongue any longer, and stood up. "Begging yer pardon, good Majesty. There's been talk of the new territory fer a long time, and I'm sure it's every bit as grand as ya say, but that won't matter to my clan," he said loudly. "Won't change a thing fer us. The Tylwyth Teg control everything here, and they'll do the same there. They'll own everything and they'll run everything. There's not a thing in Tir Hardd fer the rest of us to look toward."

Though those immediately around him drew away as if he were about to be struck by lightning, many more in the hall jumped to their feet and clamored their agreement. Unfazed, Gwenhidw smiled. "Your point is well taken, Druce Aldergrove. Some have too much power and others do not have enough, so there is no longer a balance in the Nine Realms. This is exactly why we must not build on old foundations if Tir Hardd is to be a sanctuary and a new beginning for all. In short, we must change."

"And exactly how would you have us *change*, my Queen? The Tylwyth Teg have always ruled because we are fit to rule." Caris recognized Maelgwn by his voice before she spotted him on the far side of the vast chamber. He continued without waiting for an answer: "It has been so since the beginning of our worlds. Surely you would not have us discard our traditions because of a few malcontents?"

Not surprisingly, the place erupted into shouts and roars, the tumult amplified by the rock surfaces. It seemed that everyone was arguing at once . . .

Until an explosion of light shook the immense room to its foundations. Grateful she was already lying down, Caris struggled to put her clumsy paws over her ears as thunder reverberated off the walls and vibrated through her body. The heart-stopping display startled the vast assembly into absolute silence, but Caris was one of the few who knew what had happened: Lurien, as *llaw dde* of the queen, had used the full power of his light whip upon the steps of the dais. A magical weapon, whoever held a light whip could summon and control a hunt. The guilty were chased down with it, and captives were driven like cattle before it. Hounds were compelled with it. And she, Caris Ellen Dillwyn, had been changed by it when Maelgwn led a hunt of his own.

She doubted that a light whip had ever been used to bring order to the throne room before.

All were once again kneeling, even Maelgwn, as Lurien's words replaced the silence. Quiet and deliberate, they carried to every ear, and his tone was far more frightening than even the weapon he still held uncoiled in his hand. "You will remember that you are in the presence of your monarch, and you will receive her words," he said, then bowed to his queen and moved to stand at the foot of the dais—next to a smoldering pile of stone rubble, where his supernatural whip had struck.

Caris could swear that Gwenhidw looked amused, but the queen continued as if there had been no interruption at all, and her voice was solemn. "Our new territory lies across the Wide Waters. It is beneath rolling plains framed by two mountain ranges that mortals have named the Cascades and the Rockies. I myself have made the journey there several times, to determine that this land is suitable for all of my people—not just the

Tylwyth Teg, or just the Bendith, or just the Gwyllion, but *all*. The earth beneath is rich with magic and raw materials, fed by the energy of living volcanoes and mighty rivers. Tir Hardd merely waits for our people to shape it to their will."

The throne room remained quiet as the monarch described a detailed plan for the transplanting of the faery kingdom. It would require a staggering amount of magic that could be achieved only if the many tribes put aside their differences and worked together. But it was when Gwenhidw explained how the new territory would be *governed* that the monumental room erupted with commotion once again. This time, however, it was with cheers and blessings upon the queen's bold proposal.

Only a few were displeased, and as Caris expected, the naysayers were all Tylwyth Teg, with Prince Maelgwn at their center.

"You have said that we cannot build on old foundations," he declared boldly. "If so, then I say that a new land requires a new ruler."

"And no doubt you wish to be that ruler," said Gwenhidw. Her face was composed, her voice calm as a summer breeze, yet there was power behind her words like waves gathering before the wind. "You are quite free to bring your claim before a meeting of the envoys, Maelgwn. They will decide whether it has merit."

"What envoys?" he asked, clearly surprised.

Her answer was directed not to him but to the assembly. "I call now for a delegation of envoys not only from each of the Nine Realms but also from every tribe and every clan in the kingdom. *Mark me now, that all must be fairly represented.* Send them to my courtyard when six suns have risen. But be certain," she cautioned, "that the leader you select is the wisest and most trustworthy among you. And he should have at his right hand and his left those who are your most magically gifted. Because it is your chosen envoys who will work together not only to expand the

Nine Realms but to ensure that each and every group receives a fair and generous share of the new territory. *And it is your chosen envoys who will assist in governing it.*"

The queen rose from the Glass Throne then and motioned with her hands that all should rise with her. "My beloved subjects, we are embarking on a great adventure to a greater destiny. I foresee the day that Tir Hardd will be the envy of all fae nations. Those of you who wish to remain in our ancestral home may do so, for we relinquish not that which is ours. Those of us who imagine greater things for our peoples, however, will be traveling across the Wide Waters. I myself will go with you, and together, we will build anew."

To the shock and delight of her subjects, Queen Gwenhidw bowed to them, her palms outstretched as if in supplication.

Magic must have revealed her hiding place, because Caris couldn't imagine how else Maelgwn had managed to find her in the chattering chaos of excited faery beings. His face was a mask of fury as he shoved a sinuous *beannigh* and a monstrous *fire drake* aside as if they were nothing and seized Caris's silver collar in his hand, lifting her clear off the ground as if she were merely a rabbit, not a massive dog that nearly weighed as much as he did. "I need grims for a hunt," he declared, shaking her roughly. "Many of them, do you hear me? Search the kennels quickly and bring every grim you can find to the stables. We leave at once." She dangled from his fist—and knew to make herself as limp and lifeless as possible, lest she attract his attention—as he snapped a command to the Fair Ones who followed in his wake: "Leave nothing that you value behind. Bring every weapon, every artifact, every relic that possesses a modicum of power in it. We will need it all."

"We're not coming back?" whispered Rhedyn. Caris was sorry to see her still among the prince's retinue—especially when a faint shimmer along the faery woman's ear revealed that she wore a *glamor,* an enchantment often used by the Tylwyth Teg to heighten their beauty and mask real or imagined imperfections. *Hiding the evidence of Maelgwn's bullying, no doubt.*

"Did you not hear Gwenhidw's words? She has forced our hand," said the prince. "We have no choice but to carry out our project a little earlier—but we will reap the rewards that much sooner."

The prince threw Caris against the stone pillar and stalked out as she slid to the floor. Of the entourage that followed him, none spared the black dog a glance, save Rhedyn. She said nothing, but her gaze was filled with apology. And something that looked like shame.

As soon as they were gone, Caris glanced about wildly. *A hunt?* The shadows had left the human world above by now. While grims could come and go at any time, there were ancient laws governing both the true Wild Hunt and those, like Maelgwn's, that were organized privately: all hunts were restricted to the hours of mortal night.

Whatever is Maelgwn thinking?

Suddenly she guessed the prince's destination . . . A grim's heart did not beat, but that didn't seem to prevent it from rising up in her throat. For a long moment, Caris considered disobeying. Would he notice if she didn't show up? *Of course he would.* While there might be hundreds of black grims, she was the only female, and that had been the cruel prince's own doing. Maelgwn would not forget her any more than he would ever forget—or forgive—her act of defiance in breaking her fiddle. *Too bad I didn't break it over his head.*

Of course, then she'd be dead—or, much more likely, *worse.* Death or a continued existence as a grim were nothing compared to what Maelgwyn could inflict if angered. He'd surely punish her if she disobeyed him. He'd also find a way to punish her if she ran to Lurien, or even the queen, and told them . . . *what* exactly? That she suspected the prince was going to Tir Hardd? Not only did she have no proof to offer; she didn't even know if Maelgwn was forbidden from going there. After all, he was highborn, a great-grandson of the late king's sister. And she?

She was just a voiceless dog. She couldn't tell anyone anything, even if she had evidence and witnesses aplenty. All she could do was fulfill the command she'd been given.

Slowly, Caris rose from the floor. With her head down, she made her way unnoticed through the happy, chattering crowd to the door that would take her to the stone kennels far below.

FOUR

~~~

The sound of shattering glass woke him, and for a moment Liam didn't know where he was. Another crash from somewhere above cleared some of the sleep from his brain, but the roaring in his ears continued. *Wind*, he realized. A hellacious storm was shaking the entire house to its century-old foundations. He'd fallen asleep in front of the damn TV again, but it was off, and so were the lights. *Power must be . . .*

Twin bolts of lightning struck close by, and instinct had him diving for the floor behind the couch just as something exploded in the yard. Before he could take another breath, thunder battered his senses until he had to clamp his hands over his ears. The floor beneath him vibrated, and shards of glass and wood rained down around him. And something huge, dark, and heavy came crashing down beside him, narrowly missing him.

When the tumult finally died away, lightning continued to flare and flicker, enabling him to see part of a tree impaling the living room wall, stripped of all branches like a giant's spear—and right where Brewster the Mooster had always hung. Uncle Conall's ancient trophy had been named by a three-year-old Liam and was practically part of the family. Now the searing flashes of light revealed the enormous stuffed head upside down, mere inches from Liam's hiding place. Its monstrous antlers had been driven into the floorboards, and one glass eye hung free like something out of a horror movie.

Every window in the room had shattered, and the force of the wind drove the rain sideways through the opening, the furious drops soaking everything.

Cautiously, Liam rose and felt his way to the kitchen, where a collection of candles, flashlights, and battery-filled lanterns collected dust on top of the fridge. He grabbed a lantern and tucked a small penlight in his pocket, but with the near-continuous flashes from the storm, he quickly realized there was little point in turning either light on. No point going upstairs either—the sound alone was enough to tell him that the windows were gone up there as well, and he couldn't do anything more about that than about the broken glass blanketing the living room. Without warning, the house shook hard enough that pictures fell from walls in every room—this was no ordinary thunderstorm. Tornadoes were rare here but not unheard of, and Liam decided to err on the side of caution, taking shelter in the bottom of a solidly built hallway closet. *Whose bright idea was it to put the door to the damn cellar on the outside?*

The door of the closet was heavy, made of thick hardwood, and he left it open a couple of inches so he could still keep track of his surroundings—but Liam also kept one hand firmly on the knob, ready to slam the door shut. Heaven only knew what was happening to his poor goats. Panicked, no doubt. He'd put them all in the barn for the night as always—the forty dairy does and the twenty-odd yearlings that were slated to be the next generation of pedigreed milkers. But the barn might not be enough. Hell, at this rate, even the damn *house* wasn't going to be enough. Worse, he had thirty-five head of Red Angus cattle out on summer pasture, and his two Appaloosa horses, Dodge and Chevy, were with them. There was an open-sided shelter at the base of the ridge for them, but it would be worse than useless in this maelstrom—and the mare was heavily pregnant.

He kicked the closet wall in frustration. There wasn't one single damn thing he could do to help any of his animals right now. *At least you're not here, Homer.* Liam's German Shepherd had been his best bud for just over sixteen years, but during that long canine life, the big goof had always been reduced to wedging himself under a bed during a storm. This time, Liam might have been tempted to do the same. Multiple lightning strikes continued to hammer the area as if the storm system had parked itself directly over Steptoe Acres. The strobing light that pierced the darkness surprised him with its colors—green, blue, even red, as if the aurora borealis had turned violent and was attacking the earth. Thunder slammed again and again until Liam's head pounded painfully, but he was thankful for what he *didn't* hear: the unbroken roar that might have signaled a twister.

It was a relief when he could finally count more than a couple of seconds between a flash of lightning and its partnering peal of thunder. He waited a few minutes more until he was certain that the storm was truly moving away to the west. Liam left the closet then, keeping low as he headed into the main floor's guest room. He needed to get a look outside. Tornadoes usually formed off the trailing edge of a storm, and he wasn't taking any chances. He hugged the wall beneath the window as the house shook again, then eased himself up until his eyes were just above the sill.

It was a full-fledged electrical event out there. Lightning split the sky in all directions and stabbed the hills, but not all of it was coming from the clouds. Liam blinked hard, straining to see in the pulsing *light-dark-light-dark.* There were ropes of bright lightning flicking upward here and there along the base of Finger Ridge, slashing around wildly like whips. *What the hell?*

He'd read something about upward streamers in connection with lightning, but whatever he was seeing disquieted him on some primal level, bothering him even more than the battering of the house and farm. There was a wrongness to it that he could feel, an *otherness*—and the moment that impression formed in his brain, the clouds lit up like lanterns, enough that the area around the bizarre ground lightning was illuminated for the barest fraction of a second.

Riders. Jesus, Mary, and Joseph, there was a dark band of riders out there in the midst of hell itself.

Without warning, agony detonated in Liam's head and bright stars burst behind his eyelids. He seemed to hover in that state, suspended for a long, sickening moment before blackness obliterated everything.

It was far from dark when Liam finally woke. He cursed as bright sunlight stabbed his eyeballs, setting off a headache from hell even as his body protested the unyielding mattress. Wait—there *was* no mattress. He squinted at his surroundings from beneath the shade of his hand. What was he doing on the floor? And in the guest room, no less? He made a move to get up, and his stomach lurched as the room spun. *Christ.* Slowly, he put a hand to his head and felt carefully along the hairline, hissing as his fingers came in contact with a palm-sized goose egg. There was a wet smear of fresh blood on his hand when he pulled it away.

It seemed to take forever before he could manage to sit up, bracing his back against the bed for support. The effort drenched him in cold sweat, and he had to take a break until the nausea settled and his vision cleared. It was then that he spotted the culprit that had coldcocked him: a heavy crystal vase belonging to Aunt

Ruby. How many times had he seen the oversize heirloom piece on the kitchen table, filled with big, showy cut flowers from her garden? How much did the damn thing weigh? Three pounds? Five? It was empty right now . . . and completely unharmed. That seemed more than a little unfair when his skull felt cracked in two. Instinctively his gaze tracked upward, and Liam realized that the vase had been sitting on a bookshelf built along the top of the window, an accident just waiting to happen. Perhaps he should be grateful. The way the storm had shaken the old house, it was a wonder the entire wall hadn't fallen on him instead of just the vase.

Gotta get up. Liam rose shakily and sat on the bed, waiting for the pattern on the wallpaper to stop moving before he dared stand. A few deep breaths later, he felt steady enough to shuffle his way carefully into the unholy mess that had once been the living room. Inspecting it, however, would have to wait—his top priority was his livestock. The poor animals could be trapped or scattered, terrified or injured, or perhaps even dead. He *had* to get to them. Sliding his feet into his boots by the door, he gripped the jamb for support as he rode out another wave of dizziness and nausea. Finally he made it outside, shambling onto the porch at a ridiculously slothlike pace. *Come to think of it, even a damn sloth would laugh.*

Liam didn't feel much like laughing himself as he looked over the storm's aftermath.

The morning was calm and bright, as if nothing had happened. Blue sky, faint breeze, heat already beginning to build. Chickens were busily feasting on the worms driven to the surface by last night's rain—but they were doing it amid downed branches, shapeless lumps of wet hay, and sodden piles of debris. He eased down to sit on the only furniture left on the porch—a heavy bench that Uncle Conall had bolted to the wall so it wouldn't move under his ample frame when he took his boots off at night. The many chairs and tables, the bright profusion of plant pots and window boxes, and even the porch swing, were nowhere in sight, replaced by unrecognizable garbage and a sad scattering of dead starlings. In the house yard, every one of Aunt Ruby's elaborate flower beds was shredded. Even sadder were the many broken trees—and worst among them were the matching pair of century-old chestnuts. When Liam was six, those magnificent trees had supported a pirate fort and a rope bridge. Now they lay split from crown to root, and he guessed it must be part of one that had speared the house.

Beyond the yard, the farm looked even worse. There was no doubt in his mind now that a tornado had touched down. A trio of forty-foot metal grain bins lay crumpled on their sides like giant beer cans. It was the nature of tornadoes to be destructive. It was also their nature to be bizarrely capricious as to *what* they destroyed. Last night's twister had played hopscotch throughout the farm, razing this building and that building to the ground, flattening some things beyond recognition, sweeping away many heavy farm implements altogether—and yet a few structures had been left standing. The house stood, the milking parlor stood, and so did a scattering of equipment sheds. Even the four walls of the main barn stood, although its entire roof was missing.

One good thing was that the goats appeared to have escaped the barn somehow—a large group of them had crammed themselves into the farthest corner of their corral. He'd have to get out there and inspect them one by one, but at first glance it looked like almost all of his milkers were there. They seemed pretty damn calm considering what they'd been through—but perhaps the poor things were in shock. Liam had shut them in the ill-fated building last night, something he always did to keep them safe from predators like coyotes. He hadn't expected danger from the sky. Thankfully the monster storm had carried the roof clean away, rafters, ceiling joists, and all, and not brought it crashing down on the heads of his herd. In fact, the entire roof structure was mostly in one piece—about a quarter of a mile away in the midst of his alfalfa field. The alfalfa itself was unrecognizable, and the scent of wet, crushed plants hung heavy in the still-humid air. Even from where he stood it looked like an army had trampled the young crop into the ground, leaving a swath of destruction that was nearly half the width of the field.

An army. Had he really seen riders last night? Or had he dreamed it *after* he'd been clobbered by Aunt Ruby's five-pound vase?

He shook himself free of those thoughts and focused on the disaster in front of him. A storm was a normal, natural occurrence, and a tornado, while rare here, wasn't unheard of. The truly strange thing, however, was that there had been no warning, and that made Liam angry. There hadn't been the faintest indication of bad weather on the local news, no emergency warning message scrolling across the bottom of the TV screen, no annoying sound signal. What the hell happened to the Doppler radar and all that other high-tech shit that meteorologists had at their disposal?

He made his way down the steps—and was compelled to stop and rest on every damn one—then picked his way slowly along the sidewalk stones. Every couple of feet, he had to step over or around something: splintered boards, shapeless blobs of wet insulation, twisted shingles, a pair of Uncle Conall's ample hip waders, an upside-down lawn mower, a broken shovel, countless lawn ornaments. Liam was sorry now for sometimes wishing Aunt Ruby wasn't so crazy about gnomes. As far as he could tell, her entire collection, numbering more than a hundred—maybe even *two* hundred—and lovingly collected over the course of decades, now lay smashed all over the lawn. The many little pointed hats, disembodied faces, and broken limbs made the yard look like a bizarre battlefield.

Liam finally made it all the way to his truck, but his sense of accomplishment was short-lived. A full-length two-by-six had speared the windshield and buried itself in the driver's seat. Three flat tires underscored that he wasn't going to town for a while, or even—as he had hoped—around the farmyard and the pastures. Dizzy and still nauseous, Liam leaned against the vehicle for several minutes before he turned and looked back at the house. The two-story Victorian had survived the storm well—if you didn't count that damn tree stuck in the living room wall. A few bundles of shingles, and some new glass, and the old house would probably be as good as ever. The house was a hell of a lot older than Liam, even older than his aunt and uncle. Perhaps it had weathered similar storms in its long lifetime and had learned how to deal with them.

Mentally Liam shrugged off that odd line of thinking. He'd grown up loving the house and the farm, but they weren't alive, weren't sentient, didn't feel or know anything. The animals needed him. He had to stay focused, dammit, had to get to his livestock and help them.

Glancing past the house, it was plain that the power lines along the road were down for at least a mile. Liam sighed heavily. That meant he had to get the generator hooked up and running, or he'd be milking forty goats by hand. If he still *had* forty dairy does. And where were all the yearlings? He'd only seen a couple in the tightly packed herd. As for his cattle, they were nowhere in sight, and they would have to be rounded up from wherever they'd fled to. A sensible horse could pick its way through this mess, but he didn't have one available to him—Dodge and Chevy had been pastured with the cows. The shed containing his four-wheeler lay in a splintered heap.

Shit. Not only did he have a hell of a lot to do, but he had no choice but to do it on foot. And somehow he had to manage it all without passing out or . . .

Liam leaned over and threw up some bile, narrowly missing his boots. A round of dry heaves followed, nearly taking him to his knees as the top of his skull threatened to tear off. He knew he should probably get the lump on his head checked out, although how he would fit that on the to-do list that was growing by the minute, he didn't know. *Gonna be a long damn day.*

He'd made it most of the way to the heavy steel corral that attached to the west side of the barn when he spotted something large and dark crossing the field toward the other side of the big building, the shaded side. An animal, definitely, and limping badly. One of the does? Saanens were pure white, but LaManchas came in every color—and his herd's best bloodlines resided in four does that were mostly black. *Christ, I'd better check her first.* Although the ground seemed to move beneath his unsteady feet, he finally made it to the wire fence that provided a token separation between plowed land and dirt farmyard, and he gripped it with both hands like a lifeline.

But the approaching creature wasn't a goat at all. It was a dog.

Not *his* dog of course—he'd buried his best friend, Homer, only a few months ago. The big gold shepherd had passed on in his sleep, in his favored spot on the thick sheepskin-hide pillow beside his master's bed—and Liam hadn't been too manly to let honest tears fall.

This animal was one he'd never seen before, and it wasn't a creature that could be easily forgotten. Its dark fur was muddy and bedraggled yet couldn't hide the handsome lines of its body. Liam immediately thought of an ancient sight hound that might have run alongside a pharaoh's chariot. Despite its size, the dog's body was lean like a greyhound's. The downcast head was elegantly shaped, ending in a delicate pointed muzzle. Long, graceful legs promised cheetahlike speed—or they would have if the poor thing hadn't been using only three of them. The fourth was held off the ground, and even from a distance, Liam's practiced eye noted the odd angle of the limb.

The black dog stopped when it saw Liam but didn't raise its head. Instead, the animal seemed to expect rejection and slowly turned as if to leave.

Liam whistled and the dog hesitated. He whistled again and its ears pricked. The lowered head swung back to look at him. "Come on, that's the way," he called gently. "Come over here! Good boy, come here!" Clinging to the fence to steady himself, he made his own way to the open gate as quickly as his battered head would permit. He whistled again as he slipped through, then grabbed the post for support. He'd only meant to get down on one knee, to make himself smaller and less threatening.

He hadn't expected to slide down the gatepost like a rag doll. The jolt of landing on his ass sent spikes of purest agony through his brain, and he moaned aloud. *Goddamn it . . .* Liam felt like he was holding his skull together with his hands, and for a long moment he half expected his brain to start leaking out of his ears. Through the haze of pain, however, he saw that the dog was now facing him, head up and alert. And slowly, painfully, it limped over to him.

It was huge. Even seated as he was, Liam was a tall man. Yet the strange dog was looking *down* at him. "I sure hope you're not looking for easy prey there, fella," he joked. As if in answer, the animal pressed its nose to Liam's knee and lay down—albeit gingerly. Big, intelligent eyes focused their gaze on Liam with unmistakable concern, and the dog's tail wagged weakly.

"Well, shit." He had to rub a bit of moisture from his eyes then. The dog was doing exactly what Homer had done when a fourteen-year-old Liam had been thrown from a horse. He was far from the house with a badly busted leg, cold and scared and in pain. Good old Homer—still a pup himself—had stayed right there with him for hours until Uncle Conall had come looking for him.

Liam reached out a hand and rubbed the soft ears, the intelligent forehead. The dog's tail wagged once more, but it shivered then, and he remembered it was injured too. He struggled to his knees. "Let's have a look, fella, see what's wrong here. Maybe I can help." For a moment he didn't think the animal would comply. Then slowly it relaxed onto its side and closed its eyes, and Liam felt along its body with gentle hands. The leg was definitely broken—he didn't need to touch it to know that—but he thought some ribs might be busted up as well. And there was a wide strip of black fur missing from the back of its neck and across its shoulders, the exposed skin blistered as if burned. Was it possible it had been struck by lightning? Liam thought he'd seen a silvery collar when he'd first spotted the big dark creature, but there was nothing around its neck now. Whatever had happened, the dog was probably in a world of hurt, yet it was calm and stoic. "There's a good fella," Liam said, stroking its flank. "There's a good boy." Suddenly he realized he'd missed something important. "Good *girl*," he corrected himself.

Despite the sun's warmth, the shade of the barn felt downright cold to him. Had the storm brought in a cool front? The dog was shivering again too, and Liam immediately unbuttoned his shirt and covered the creature, wishing he had something warmer to blanket her with. *She's probably thirsty.* He struggled to his feet—standing very still for a long moment to make sure he was going to remain on his feet—then shuffled his way to a nearby trough, holding on to the fence wire for support.

A few minutes later, he sank down beside the big dog, holding a cracked and dented bucket at an angle so she could reach the few inches of water in it. She drank every drop. Satisfied, Liam leaned back against the gatepost with a heavy sigh.

"We're one helluva pair," he said to her. "You can't walk far and I can't carry you. In fact, I don't think I can go anyplace." It was true—not only was his brain clearly trying to escape his skull, but that little jaunt to the water trough had exhausted him beyond all reason. "We're gonna have to call in some help, girl."

He patted the pocket of his jeans and was relieved to find his phone still there. The screen lit up at his touch, and he was amazed to see he had three whole bars plus half a battery to work with—apparently Murphy's law hadn't located him yet! Quickly he flipped through the numbers stored on the device, but he realized there weren't very damn many to choose from. Aunt Ruby and Uncle Conall had been the only family who lived in this area. He was close to his cousin Tina, but she was in Seattle—she'd drop everything to come and help him, of course, but it was more than a six-hour drive. As for friends, the ones he'd had growing up had moved away, and he hadn't made any new ones. In fact, hardly anyone could be called an acquaintance either. It was his own stupid fault of course: he hadn't wanted company, so he hadn't even tried to be friendly. *Way to go, Einstein.* How many times had he heard his uncle say, "A farmer can't get along without his neighbors"? Liam recalled the families who used to own the farms on either side of his, but not the names of the people who lived there now. They were miles away in both directions too, so walking for help sure as hell wasn't an option.

Although the sensible voice in his head insisted he needed to get checked out by a doctor, Liam was far more concerned about the injured dog. Plus, although he hadn't had a chance to check on his poor goats yet, they were certain to need medical attention as well. Heaven only knew what condition his cattle and horses were in—if they were still in the county. *What I need most is a vet*, he decided. The only one he'd ever trusted to treat old Homer was up in Spokane Valley—his cousin's high school friend, Morgan Edwards. It was definitely out of her way, yet she had cared enough to drive all the way out here twice in those last few months of Homer's life. *It couldn't hurt to ask, could it?* At the very least, Morgan might know of some other vet who could come on short notice.

Liam tapped the screen where her number was displayed. And hoped.

FIVE

⌒⫯⌒

C aris lay on the ground near the man's feet, grateful for his kind words—how long had it been since she had heard the slightest expression of concern? And he had covered her with his own shirt. The fabric was too thin to provide much heat to her battered body, but her heart was profoundly touched. She hadn't known many men who would do such a thing for a mere dog, especially one that wasn't their own. He'd struggled to bring her water as well, even though it was plain that he was injured too— and here she was with no hands to help, and no strength if she had them. He slipped into unconsciousness soon after he'd talked into the palm-sized phone, and blood still oozed freely down the side of his face.

It's a fine face. When she'd been human, she would surely have sighed over that intelligent brow and determined chin. She'd sigh over his handsome frame, too. The man's shirtless body was lean and well-built, his arms strong, and well-acquainted with hard work. Light brown hair dusted his chest and she had a shockingly wicked wish to trace his muscles with her fingertips. Unbidden, Caris's gaze followed the pattern of hair as it lightly encircled his nipples. Below his navel, darker hair formed a vee that disappeared into the waistband of his jeans.

The rush of unfamiliar feelings flustered her. As a grim, she'd seen men's bodies countless times over many decades as she bore dire witness to their impending doom. Although she'd felt compassion for the men, no other emotion stirred within her. Certainly no appreciation for their form. Now, deep inside, something long buried and long forgotten was suddenly wide, wide awake.

If the man was awake, of course, Caris would never have indulged in studying his appealing form. Not only would she be shy about it, but she'd be far too busy puzzling over his striking blue eyes. Their vivid color was so like the high skies of autumn, yet there were shadows in them too, dark depths of heartache and raw anger buried deep.

And still he gave me the very shirt from his back . . .

She'd needed it, and she'd needed the water. Needed more, too, and she licked her dry lips with a tongue turned sticky. Caris hadn't known thirst since she'd been changed all those years ago, but she was parched now. *What does it mean?* Other sensations, equally unfamiliar, rippled through her body. A grim's heart did not beat and Death's herald had no need to breathe. A grim felt neither heat nor cold, could be as solid as stone or as insubstantial as a ghost. A grim certainly did not suffer *pain.*

Yet her ribs now hurt as if she'd been stabbed in many places, as the heart beneath them pounded far too fast. Her lungs labored to suck in air as if they couldn't get enough. One leg would no longer bear weight, and it throbbed like a bad tooth. Worst of all was her back, where Maelgwn had struck her with the light whip. It stung sharply as if on fire, and she could smell singed fur—and burnt skin.

The collar. The collar must have borne the brunt of the blow, or surely she'd already be dead. It must have been damaged, perhaps even broken, by the impact of the magical weapon. The heavy silver links had slid off her neck and dropped to the ground when she'd struggled to heed this man's call . . . How many long decades had she borne the choking weight of faery-forged silver around her throat? The absence of it might have made her feel giddy if she hadn't been in so much pain.

Caris's vision blurred and darkened at the edges. Had the impossible happened? Was she a mortal creature again? She was injured for certain, possibly dying . . . but free at last. *Anything is better than being controlled by that spiteful prince for one more minute!*

From nowhere came the thought that her gruff father would have had far stronger and more inventive words for the pitiless faeries who had stolen away and enslaved his only daughter, and that thought suddenly made her miss Da so terribly that her heart ached as much as her whole body. Apparently her emotions had found their way back to her as well. How typical of the fae to restore those things that were the most painful to bear. She closed her eyes, so tempted to just let herself go, *and yet . . .*

And yet she found that there was the tiniest spark within her, kindled by the lingering warmth of this stranger's concern. Caris thought she sensed a flicker, then a solid glow, as that internal spark developed into a sparse flame. Gradually it grew and warmed, flaring from candle fire to cheering hearth, until the shuddering cold was dispelled from every inch of her body. Pain released its grip, and even the agonizing sting of the wound across her back was soothed. She breathed easier then, a long, deep sigh, as though she were relaxing into sleep.

Sleep, however, was not what her body had in mind at all.

~

"So the guy we're going to see is a cousin of your friend Tina? We're talking about the same Tina who owns the man-eating dachshund, right? Please tell me this relative of hers doesn't have one too!"

Morgan glanced over at her younger partner, Jay Browning, in the passenger seat of the clinic's truck. He was wearing his long hair in a single braid today, and his T-shirt read "Veterinarian by Day, Ninja by Night." She could well believe it—the man had more energy than anyone she'd ever met. He was a huge asset to her clinic as well as a good friend. Plus, he and his wife, Starr, had a very eclectic range of interests—for instance, they'd just returned from a UFO convention the week before last. Their open-mindedness to the unknown had proved a huge bonus over the past couple of years, as Morgan had discovered for herself that there was much more to the world than she'd ever suspected.

"Jake's not a man-eater," she said. "He's just defensive about having his toenails trimmed."

"*Dragons* are defensive about their toenails. I had a perfect career record of zero dog bites until I met that little wiener. Then *bam*—nine stitches!"

"I've a charm fer that." A gnarled brown face with bright blue eyes popped up from the club cab seat behind Morgan. The brim of his much-prized baseball hat—a souvenir of the Toronto Blue Jays—bumped her shoulder but somehow managed to stay on his small head. She didn't know if it was because of his thick braided hair and the odd leaves that sprouted from it, or if he'd spelled the precious cap to stay in place.

"Ranyon, you know you're supposed to wear your seatbelt," she chided.

"I've a charm fer that too," he said brightly.

She didn't doubt it. The little *ellyll*'s magical abilities were all out of proportion to his diminutive height. Out of the corner of her eye she could see him straighten his other treasure, a T-shirt that matched his hat (and hung to his knees). It was the only clothing he wore. Beneath the royal-blue material were more brown leaves that covered his body like a coat made from the forest floor, while his arms and legs resembled narrow tree branches.

He rested the sharp elbows of his spindly arms on the console between the seats. "Are there chickens where we're goin'?" There was a hopeful note in his voice. He was absolutely fascinated by birds of all kinds.

"Maybe a few. But mostly goats. Liam has a herd of about forty does."

The ellyll was only disappointed for a moment. "D'ya think Leo would like a goat when he comes back? They make fine gifts."

She tried to keep a straight face as she imagined her friend's reaction to finding a goat in his backyard when he returned from his Marine Corps reunion. The old veteran had a big heart. He'd practically adopted her now-husband Rhys, even accepting his strange story of having been imprisoned by the fae. When Ranyon came along, Leo had taken his existence in stride—and adopted him as well. Rhys had moved in with Morgan of course, but Ranyon remained Leo's roommate and dearest friend. The ellyll used his magic to make the old man's life as comfortable as possible, while Ranyon's habits kept Leo's life interesting. Lately they'd begun keeping a small flock of hens. *But a goat?* "The goat will eat Leo's prize dahlias," she said at last. "And your fence isn't tall enough to keep it from eating the neighbor's flowers as well."

"Oh, aye, Mrs. Kettleson wouldn't take kindly to that. She nearly had three kinds of hysterics when poor old Spike wandered onto her front lawn and pissed on her garden statues. I had to put a charm on the woman to make her forget she'd seen him."

"It's a wonder Spike didn't bite her," said Jay. Leo's old terrier had reigned supreme for years as the clinic terror until Jake the dachshund came along.

Spike probably has a charm on him *as well.* Morgan slowed the truck to leave Highway 195.

Jay looked around. "I know you said this guy lived outside our usual area, but I didn't think you meant *this* far out. What is he, an old boyfriend or something? Is that why you didn't bring Rhys along?"

She punched his shoulder as hard as she could while still driving.

"Guess not," he moaned, rubbing the spot where she'd hit him. Morgan doubted she'd hurt him a bit. Despite his lean wiry build, he regularly competed in sword competitions at Renaissance fairs, and she knew from her husband's training that such skills required a high degree of athleticism. Jay was slightly built but fast and strong—pretty useful attributes for a veterinarian too.

"You big *turkey,* you know darn well that Rhys isn't home from California yet, or he'd be calling you up right away to tell you how things went with our horses," she scolded, though without heat of course. "As for Liam, yes we're friends, but we're not very close. He was a few years ahead of Tina and me in high school, so I never got to hang out with him much unless he was visiting at her parents' farm. That's where I met him, you know. Tina was having one of her famous summer campouts, and he happened to be there with a guitar." She sighed inwardly. The difference in age hadn't kept Morgan and her girlfriends—Brooke, Sharon, Katie, and Lissy—from having a crush on the guy with the sky-blue eyes. Tina often complained that it wasn't fair having such a hunk for a first cousin, but even she had been completely captivated by the music that poured out of him like water from a mountain-fed spring. "It was amazing, Jay. I've never heard anything like it, before or since." Morgan sighed aloud then. "He had so much talent, I was sure he'd make it big someday. He nearly did, too."

"Wait a minute, this isn't Liam *Cole* we're talking about, is it?"

"Yeah, that's him."

Jay whistled and sat back. "Starr and I saw him perform once at a bluegrass festival. I know what you mean about his talent. Didn't seem to matter what instrument he was using, whether he sang or just played—the music seemed to surge out of him like he was channeling something bigger than himself. It was a damn shame when he dropped out of sight. We've got all his recordings, but I don't think he's put out anything new in a long time. Hey, he didn't fall into drugs or something, did he?"

"No, thank goodness," she said. "Tina says it's a pretty bad case of broken heart. His wife cheated on him, they broke up, and he took it all pretty hard."

"Hard enough to give up on his music? Might as well have cut off an arm or a leg. It'd be like you giving up working with animals—it's part of what makes you *you*."

Morgan nodded. "Yeah, well, he's amputated even more than that. He's pretty much buried himself alive on his uncle's farm for the past three years. Lives alone there, runs the whole operation by himself. Doesn't interact with people at all if he doesn't have to, especially if he doesn't know them."

"Guess that explains why he called you instead of a vet in his own area."

"Exactly. I always thought you had to be old to become a hermit. Don't get me wrong, though, Liam doesn't really act weird or anything. He works hard, he takes great care of his livestock, and Tina says the farm is flourishing. He's a really good guy, Jay. But he's locked inside himself and determined to keep it that way."

"Must have been one mean-ass breakup."

"Yeah. Yeah, it was," said Morgan, keeping an eye out for the highway sign that pointed to the turnoff. "Liam and Jade had already been a couple for something like three years when I was still in ninth grade—they were the proverbial high school sweethearts and all that, you know? I don't think either one of them ever dated anyone else, so that's over a decade of togetherness. But it's been three years now since the divorce, and Tina's getting worried."

"Could be depression."

"Tina and I talked about that, but she doesn't think so. It's more like grief." Even if nobody had died, there was still the death of the relationship to be mourned, the death of dreams. And Morgan knew from her own experience that grief was a process that varied from person to person. *No one can say how long is long enough.* "I told Tina that Liam will rejoin life when he's good and ready—but I confess, I was crossing my fingers when I said it. He has to make that decision for himself, and while most people do, some don't."

"He'll be fine," said Ranyon. The ellyll sounded sure of it. "All a man needs is a good enough reason to live, and he'll pull himself out of the jaws of Death herself, if need be."

"He's not dying," Morgan said, then wondered if that were strictly true. Music had definitely been Liam's life, and now it was gone. "But you're right about one thing—he's going to have to find something new to live for." That she understood. Morgan's best friend, Brooke, had recently proved to be just such a motivation for Aidan ap Llanfor. The big Welsh blacksmith had been on a quest for vengeance before he met—*more like crashed into*—the attractive young witch. Morgan couldn't help but smile at the thought. Brooke and Aidan were currently on an extended honeymoon in Catemaco, Mexico—a charming city renowned as a center of magic and witchcraft. *Bet he never saw that coming.*

"Say, Ranyon, you don't happen to have a charm that'll help Liam, do you?" asked Jay.

The little ellyll shook his head. "Nay, there's not a spell in this world or any other 'twill give a man purpose. Each must find his own."

"Seems like some purposes come and find you," Morgan murmured. *Or hunt you down.* She certainly hadn't been looking for all that had come to her—especially her husband Rhys. His love would always be a source of wonder to her. Her life had been full and satisfying before he literally jumped into it. Now she couldn't imagine a day without him. *What if I lost him? What if he walked away, like Jade walked away from Liam?*

It wasn't so hard to see why Tina's cousin had built a wall around himself.

The crunch of the gravel road beneath the truck tires was the only sound for several minutes until Jay tried to lighten the mood. "Hey, I hope that deal goes well with the horses today."

"Me too," she said, grateful for the change of topic. "Selling a pair of fully trained Friesians to the current world champion jouster? It would be incredible advertising for our center, and a pretty big feather in Rhys's cap."

"I'd like a feather in *my* cap," piped up Ranyon. "Maybe a bunch of 'em."

Jay looked doubtful. "Not sure they'd go well with the baseball theme you have going there, bud."

"Well a'course they would," the little man retorted. "Blue jays are *birds*, dontcha know? And where d'ya think *yer* name came from?"

"It's short for Jacob. My parents didn't name me for the bird. Or the team, for that matter."

Ranyon snorted as if he didn't believe a word of it, but he let it go. "If I could get close enough, I could charm the tail feathers off a live one," he continued. "All I'd need is a few peanuts—blue jays like their peanuts like a *warth* likes his live meat."

Knowing that the ellyll was sensitive, Morgan fought hard not to laugh at the mental picture he'd just painted. "What Jay means is that professional ball players don't put anything on their hats. It's a—a *distraction* to the game."

Ranyon seemed to ponder that carefully. "Certain are ya?"

She nodded solemnly. "Have you ever seen Brett Lawrie or Chad Jenkins decorate their hats?"

"Ah, well, then, that's a point," conceded Ranyon. He'd been introduced to baseball by her dear old friend Leo, and it had been a life-changing experience for the ellyll. The game was practically sacred to him. "But it woulda been a *brammer* of a hat."

Morgan was about to agree with him when an all-too-familiar sensation, gentle yet repellent, strummed her nerves like a silken cobweb brushing her hand. "Ranyon?"

"Aye, I feel it too."

"Feel what? I don't feel anything," said Jay, frowning. "Please tell me it's not—"

"Fae," she breathed, her hands suddenly cold on the steering wheel. The *knowing* that she'd inherited from her grandmother was dead certain. "There's fae close by, or they've been here very recently."

"They're not here now," assured Ranyon, standing up on the seat and looking out each window in turn. He pressed a button to lower the window behind Morgan and leaned far out, as if to scent the air like a dog. "And a good thing too. 'Twas not just any fae," he called back, the wind whipping away his words. "There's too much power lingering here yet."

Jay lived up to the slogan on his own shirt by diving halfway into the rear seat and seizing the little ellyll's T-shirt in a death grip. He needn't have worried. Despite the wind that whipped past the window, not so much as the hat on Ranyon's head fluttered—evidence of the ellyll's easy command of magic.

But there were other forces at work.

"I don't like this. We're almost at Liam's farm, and I can feel it getting stronger," said Morgan. "What on earth were the fae doing in this area?"

"Whatever pleases them, to be sure," declared Ranyon. Morgan didn't like the sound of that. She didn't like the look of it either when they rounded a bend and got their first view of Steptoe Acres . . . And the devastation that surrounded it.

"Holy crap," breathed Jay. "What kind of a storm did this?"

Ranyon leaned on the console between them and shook his head, making the many copper bells and charms around his neck jangle together. "'Twere no storm that brought this mess about. The Tylwyth Teg were here."

SIX

hit, shit, shit!

He'd fallen asleep—how long had he been out? People with head injuries were supposed to stay awake. Liam didn't know who had made up that rule or why, but he did remember it was important. Did it still count, he wondered, when he'd already been out cold all night?

All he knew for certain was that he was exhausted. His eyelids felt like they had lead fishing weights hanging from them, but when he finally talked his eyes into opening, a brilliant blue-and-gold light seared itself into his already-tender brain. He threw his hands up in front of his face and cursed at the rapid movement as well as the glare, certain that the agony in his head would drive him back into unconsciousness—or perhaps angry that it didn't.

The light vanished abruptly, leaving him half-blinded. Gradually he pulled his hands from his eyes, blinking away the spots in his vision.

And then he blinked in disbelief. There was a woman kneeling beside him. A naked woman. A *curvy* naked woman with dark chocolate eyes and smooth olive skin. Her long black hair fell like a soft curtain over full breasts but failed to hide their luscious nipples. *I'm hallucinating here. Gotta be.* But as delusions went, it was a damn good one. Liam's gaze traveled inch by delicious inch all the way down to her soft thatch and slowly back up to her compelling eyes.

Strangely, she didn't disappear. Maybe he'd blacked out again? He could be dreaming, perhaps even in a coma. Or hell, he could be dead for all he knew—and wouldn't that suck, to be taken down by a damn flower vase? Liam was not a religious man, but he might reconsider if all angels were naked and built like the goddess in front of him.

"Am I delirious?" he wondered aloud.

"I don't think so, but 'tis a bad bump you've taken. You were gone away for a time." The woman's voice was sexy as hell, its low tones caressing his ears. Even if she were fully clothed, she could make his body sit up and pay attention just by reading a phone book. Her words lilted with an unknown accent, and he found himself wanting this shapely vision to say more, to say anything.

That is, until she stretched her hand toward his head.

Liam's instincts had him pulling back until the fence post was pressing into his spine. Until he knew for certain if the stranger was real or imaginary, she could damn well keep her distance. "Where did you come from? Who the hell are you?" he demanded.

Her hand dropped. "Caris. I'm Caris Ellen Dillwyn." She paused, frowning, as if remembering something. Bright color flushed her cheeks, and she threw an arm over her beautiful breasts. "*Mae'n ddrwg gen i*—I'm sorry. I'm so very sorry. I guess I'm not used to this." She glanced around and seized a crumpled shirt from the ground, pulling it on like a robe and clutching it closed. The wrinkled material was dirty and bloody, yet it didn't detract from her looks in the slightest.

"Not used to what?" he asked crossly.

"Why, being mortal of course. Being human again." Caris sighed. "It's been a dreadful long time, you see, and a very confusing day."

Right. That's what I get for asking. "I'm with you on the *confusing day* part," he muttered.

"I thank you for the shirt. 'Twas no small thing to care for a lesser creature in need."

Several facts connected in his unreliable brain at once: It was his own damn shirt she was wearing. And the last place he'd seen it was on the great black dog. He looked around but the animal was now nowhere in sight. "Where's the dog? She's injured." He tried to sit up, but a riptide of dizziness nearly pulled him under the sea of unconsciousness again. "Did you chase her away?" he gasped out as his head swam.

"Now, don't be trying to get up," she said, seizing his wrists with surprisingly strong hands and leaning over him. The fact that her shirt gaped wide again was far more effective at holding him in place, however. "You'll be doing more harm to yourself. And you need not worry about the black dog you showed such kindness to."

"Why the hell not?" Wait, since when had he told her what color it was?

Caris released him and sat back, once again holding the shirt closed. "Because 'twas not a dog you found, sir, but a grim."

Maybe he wasn't conscious after all. "A *what*?"

"A grim is a messenger of death. A *barghest*." The woman studied his face, obviously frustrated that she wasn't getting through. "A *gwyllgi*?" She threw up her hands. "I'm sorry, I don't know what names you give to fae creatures here. I'm trying to tell you that what you found was not a mortal dog. *It was me!*"

Uh-huh. Liam considered the possibilities: Either he was out cold or down a damn rabbit hole. *Or the beautiful Caris is off her meds.* "Do you really expect me to believe a bullshit story like that?" he asked. "I saw the dog with my own eyes. For something that's not supposed to be *mortal*, it was pretty badly hurt. And I need to find it so I can help it."

"You're too busy thinking I'm daft to listen to me," she declared. "I'm telling you that I was the dog you tended. The faeries changed me when I refused to go with them, and I've been a grim ever since."

"Faeries?" *Jesus, this just gets better and better.*

"I wasn't sent here to warn you though—you're not about to die."

Liam goggled at that little revelation, then recovered himself. Hadn't he watched plenty of werewolf movies as a kid? He knew exactly what to ask: "If the dog was really you, then where are your injuries?"

She looked down at her left leg and slowly rubbed it. Her hand gliding back and forth over that smooth thigh sparked all kinds of ideas in Liam's mind—and other parts—that he didn't have patience for at the moment.

"*Fel y boi*," she declared. "Right as rain. Perhaps it was the changing that healed me."

Christ. "Guess if I change into a unicorn, I'll feel fine too."

"I know you're mocking me. But you're not yourself, not with a lump like that. Let me get you something to drink. I'll bet you're fair thirsty."

Liam could certainly get behind the *thirsty* part. And hey, maybe that was the way to deal with this bizarre situation: just pick and choose whatever made sense. In fact, he'd once read a psychology article about directing and controlling one's dreams—what if *this* was a dream and he could change it? Maybe he could even give it instructions . . .

"Fine, I'll have an ice-cold beer. And a kiss." His hand snaked behind her head and yanked her face to his. Her full lips tasted even better than he imagined, and her breasts brushed his bare chest.

A split second later her fists thumped on his solar plexus hard enough to knock the breath from him, and he lost his grip. As he gasped for air like a fish out of water, Caris stood a few feet away, her arms folded tight around her and her expression telling him plainly that he'd crossed a major line.

But hallucinations weren't supposed to have lines to cross . . .

"What the hell? You're *real*? You can't be real!" he half shouted, depleting his air again and aggravating the ringing in his head.

"You'll find out how real I am when I'm boxing your ears."

As gorgeous as this woman was, Liam sure as hell didn't want her to be flesh and blood. Dreams were fun. Fantasy was a release. But *real* was a whole different animal. *Real* meant he had to deal with her—not to mention deal with his body, which was craving her the way a starving lion yearned after a gazelle. His jeans were still excruciatingly tight despite the fact that the shirt she'd commandeered was now painstakingly buttoned all the way to the neck. Since it also hung halfway down her thighs, all the glory he'd witnessed earlier was hidden—though the thin material couldn't do a thing to disguise her shape.

"Nothing makes a damn bit of sense today," he muttered.

"Not to you, I'm sure. I'm thinking that lump on your head has not only addled your wits but made you forget your manners," she said. "And it's clear that my lack of proper garments has given you notions. So in case you're not really a *dihiryn*, I'll explain it to you. I'm not a barmaid, so you'll be keeping your hands to your own self. Are we clear on that?"

"Crystal." Liam had no idea what a dihiryn was, but the tone clearly said *asshole*. "So no cold beer either, huh?"

"As I'm not seeing any pub nearby, you won't be getting any ale."

She picked up the cracked bucket he'd offered to the dog. "You'll be having to make do with some water from the trough," she said. "What you brought me was clean enough and tasted fresh."

"But, but . . . I brought water to the *dog*, not you," he insisted.

"Have it your way." She shrugged and disappeared from his line of sight, and Liam wished that Morgan would hurry the hell up. It was weird enough when he thought that his subconscious had conjured the naked goddess. The fact that she was a living, breathing human being was far more bizarre. Especially since Carol—*no, Cara? Caris!*—was insistent that she'd been a *d-o-g*. How cruel was it that a woman so pretty should also be certifiable?

He jolted, rattling his bruised brain and making him curse, as the woman reappeared at his elbow.

"Sorry that I startled you." She offered him a strange little pottery bowl with uneven edges and waited patiently until he had both hands wrapped around it before she let go. "I thought this might be easier to drink from than the bucket, but take care you don't cut yourself on it," she warned.

The dish was plain white bisque on the inside, clean and porous. The outside felt smooth as glass, however, with strange bumps and protrusions, and he glimpsed several bright colors through his fingers . . . Still, the water called out to him, drawing his attention away from the container. It was cold and sweet, and he drank every bit of it. "Thanks," he breathed.

"Grateful I am that I could return the favor of a drink to you."

Ri-i-i-ght. Because you used to be a dog. And I'm Alice in Wonderland. His thirst sated for the moment, Liam lifted the odd bowl and risked a glance beneath. The wizened face of one of Aunt Ruby's countless garden gnomes grinned back at him.

More than a little creeped out by the makeshift bowl, Liam's beleaguered brain desperately kicked out a new thought. A good thought. A *damn* good thought. He pointed at the woman. "Tell me, did you get caught in the storm?"

"I was in the very midst of it, for sure."

Bingo. Just like that, he had a whole lot of answers. *Nice, comfortable, sane answers.* One, the woman must live in the area—hell, she could be a relative or friend of his closest neighbor, for all he knew. Two, she'd been affected by the storm just as he had been. Liam's barn roof stood in the alfalfa field as testament to the violence of the weather. If a twister had touched down here, the damage to the surrounding farms might be even worse. It was no big stretch of the imagination that someone could be wandering around in the aftermath, confused and in shock, just like disaster victims on the news.

Liam went from angry and confused to protective and concerned in the space of a heartbeat. The storm had struck in the middle of the night and probably yanked her right out of her bed. No wonder the poor woman was naked.

And here I've been acting like a complete moron.

Resurrecting his manners, Liam began by keeping his gaze strictly on Caris's face (although he'd be seeing that curvy body every time he closed his eyes for a long, *long* time to come). "I . . . I owe you an apology, a big one. I'm really sorry for being a jerk. I don't usually grab pretty women, at least not without asking. I think you're right about my head playing tricks on me." He pointed at the lump, and she nodded.

"Aye, probably why you're cranky as a wet cat too. In our town, Kynan Jones took a bad blow to the head when he was shoeing a horse. He had trouble with his temper ever after, and with his remembering as well. Couldn't think of his own name half the time and had to be reminded where his house was, though he was just as good a farrier as ever."

"That's not very comforting."

"Well, do you remember *your* name?"

For a split second he hesitated. He'd never been rock-star famous, but since he'd turned his back on the music world, he seldom introduced himself to anyone. He didn't want to remember that time in his life, what he used to do, and maybe not even the person he used to be. Introducing himself meant risking that someone else might remember—and then he'd have to talk about it. The more sensible side of him knew that was *totally messed up*, but his other side, the emotional side, didn't give a shit.

Which was why he couldn't account for the words that came out of his mouth before he'd even finished his thought.

"Liam. I'm Liam Cole."

It was good name, *a strong name for a strong man,* thought Caris. An apt name in another way, too—*Liam* meant "protector," and surely it fit someone who would give their own shirt to a dying dog. She was about to offer him more water when he began shouting.

"Here! Over here!" He tried to sit up higher but quickly paled and broke into a sweat, putting a hand to his head as if trying to hold it in place. The other hand he waved in the direction of the house, where a man and woman were climbing the steps.

"Easy now. I'll hail them for you." Caris stood up at once, shouting and waving. The couple saw her, thank goodness. They hurried as much as possible too, each carrying a case of some sort, but it was difficult to negotiate the piles of debris that littered the ground. Both broke into a jog as soon as they could get close enough.

"Liam! Omigod, are you all right?" The woman dropped down next to him and began checking him over.

"Man, am I glad to see you guys," he sighed.

"Glad to see you too, bud, but holy crap, why didn't you call the EMTs? They would have been here a lot sooner than us. You're hurt." The woman frowned at the huge, bleeding lump on Liam's head and felt carefully around it. She pulled a penlight from her pocket and shone it directly into each of Liam's blue eyes. "Your pupils match—that's something to be thankful for," she said.

Meanwhile, her partner remained standing and extended his hand politely to Caris. "I'm Jay, and *this*"—he inclined his head toward the woman examining Liam—"is my partner and friend, Morgan. Are you all right? Are you hurt?"

Caris could feel her cheeks heat as she remembered her half-naked condition. Liam's shirt was large, but it was as thin as a summer nightshift—and a whole lot shorter. Small wonder Jay was asking if she was all right: she probably looked daft as a brush, undressed as she was. "I'd be very much better if I had something proper to wear," she said.

At her words, Morgan's head whipped around. She scrutinized Caris for a long, piercing moment before turning her attention back to Liam. "Jay," she said. "I've got spare scrubs in the bottom of one of these bags she can have. Maybe even some coveralls in the truck. But call 911 for me first, will you?"

"I'm fine," protested Liam, although Jay whipped out a phone and pressed the numbers anyway. "Morgan, I need you to look at the dog."

"I'll be glad to check him too, right after we get you sorted out," she said.

"What dog?" asked Jay, glancing around with the phone still pressed to his ear. "Where is it?"

Caris was about to explain but stopped herself just in time. Liam hadn't believed her, so why would these people? In fact, why would *anyone*? For some reason, Morgan had already eyed her with raw suspicion—how would the woman react to the truth?

Caris opted for a half-truth instead. "There was a lost dog here that Liam was trying to help. I . . . I don't know where it's gone off to. I was more worried about him, and trying to keep him still."

"I'll just bet he was really cooperative too," said Morgan. She was holding a finger in front of her friend's face. "Pay attention, Liam. I need you to look this way . . . now that way."

Liam winced and pressed the heel of his hand into one eye. "Dammit," he said. "That hurts worse than my head does."

"Ambulance is on its way," announced Jay. "You know, I got crowned by the flat of a wooden broadsword during a Ren fair a couple years ago. The concussion gave me a monster headache, but my eyes were the worst. Felt like they were being stabbed in their sockets every time I moved them."

Liam snorted. "Wish I could say it was something noble like a sword that hit me. Unfortunately, it was a goddamn flower vase."

"A formidable enough weapon if an angry woman is wielding it." Jay looked over at Caris and grinned.

She was appalled at the notion. "I did no such thing!" she protested. "I only just met him!" But then, she *had* shoved him hard, and she'd used her fists to do it. It had been purely instinctive when he grabbed her. Could she have injured him further?

Liam glanced up and met her gaze for a moment, giving her a lopsided wink that let her know she didn't need to worry. "It wasn't Caris," he said. "But even that would've had a little more dignity to it. Aunt Ruby's big crystal vase fell off a shelf during the storm. Knocked me colder than a pickled herring."

"You were *unconscious*?" Morgan put the penlight away. "If we hadn't already called 911, we'd be doing it now. You're *so* going to the hospital, mister."

"But I've got to find the dog! And my goats—I don't know if they're hurt, and they haven't even been milked yet! I don't know where the cattle are, and my horses are with them, and . . ."

Morgan shushed him. "We'll find all your animals, and we'll look after them. You know you can trust us to do that, or you wouldn't have called us."

"And I can help as well," declared Caris. "I've worked my father's farm and cared for plenty of ewes in my time, and a few cows and goats as well. If they're waiting to be milked, they're sure to come to us." Again she noticed Morgan studying her. *Why?*

"The goats can be fussy about being milked by strangers," began Liam.

"I've a charm fer that!" A brand new voice—and an odd one—entered the conversation. "And you can count on my helping hand as well." A knee-high being hove into sight through the tall grass and walked boldly up to the gathering, with a spotted hen as big as he was tucked under one skinny arm.

An ellyll! Caris knew the ellyllon were powerful elementals, wielding the most ancient of magics. Yet, among all the creatures of the Nine Realms, they were one of the rarest. Most said that bwganod, giant salamander-like creatures with wicked teeth, had eaten them. Caris, however, had overheard a different story: that a dark faction of the Tylwyth Teg resented the power of the ellyllon, which far exceeded their own. The power-hungry group had conspired to use blood magic, forbidden by the most ancient of laws, and enacted a curse that temporarily weakened their rivals. With their ability to defend themselves diminished, every ellyll found by the conspirators had been slain in a single night.

"Hey, Ranyon." Jay mouthed the words quietly. "Where've you been?" He wasn't a tall man, but the little creature had to reach high to slap him on the arm with his twiglike fingers.

"Looking about, seeing what's what. Ya could have waited a mite," he declared, not softening his own voice one bit. "Not everyone has great long legs like *you*, ya know."

"Nice to think I've got long legs compared to somebody,"

whispered Jay. "I always feel like a skinny kid compared to Rhys."
He glanced around, apparently to make sure that Morgan hadn't
heard that remark—or perhaps to be certain she was blocking
Liam's view. Caris quickly pretended to be facing another direction entirely. From the corner of her eye, however, she saw Jay and
Ranyon exchange a complicated system of clasps and knuckle
bumps. Both grinned like fools afterward, and Morgan looked
over her shoulder and winked at them.

Caris didn't know which was more surprising, that this rare
fae creature was *here* of all places or that the humans could see
him. A grim was intended to be seen by the person it was sent to
warn, but not many mortals had the ability to perceive the fae on
their own. Nor did any fae show themselves readily. Yet Jay had
demonstrated he could both see and converse with Ranyon. Morgan saw the little ellyll, but she didn't speak to him as she tended
Liam. Jay fell silent as well. Ranyon didn't seem to mind a bit, as
he simply kept up a running conversation all by himself. After a
moment, Caris understood why his human friends were so quiet.

Liam cannot see or hear the fae.

Considering what the prince's outlaw hunt had done to
Liam's once-lovely farm, she wasn't sure if that was a good thing
or not. As it was, he probably blamed the destruction on a storm.
What would he do if he knew the storm was not a natural one?
She couldn't guess the answer to that either, but she did know one
thing: the trio of newcomers expected *her* to be as blind and deaf
to the faery realm as Liam was. And for now, it seemed safer to
let them think that.

SEVEN

It was her fault. She had forced him to do it.

Maelgwn was in a foul mood as he paced the crystalline cavern he'd chosen for his temporary chambers. *Temporary* until his palace could be built, a structure that would outshine the queen's own residence in the Nine Realms. But thinking about the splendor he would surround himself with as he ruled Tir Hardd failed to cool his rage. Caris Ellen Dillwyn had spoiled his plans. Oh, not beyond recovery, of course, never that—no one was *that* important, and Maelgwn prided himself on his resourcefulness. But her value as a weapon would have made his plans far simpler to implement.

As a grim, it had been easy to hide her, but it should also have been easy to control her. For a time, it seemed to work. The same foolish mortal girl who had defied Maelgwn's orders, and broken her pathetic little *ffidil* in front of him, had been his obedient dog for nearly two human centuries. Yet no sooner had he brought his hunt to Tir Hardd than he'd been forced to make an example of her. One of the other grims had spotted her attempting to escape and raised the alarm.

Where did she think she could hide that I could not find her? Most of his followers felt that mortals weren't very smart, and

Maelgwn was inclined to agree. *But they could be trained.* And he was determined that this particular human should learn once and for all. In his rage, however, he had wielded the light whip too fiercely. Lightning had struck repeatedly, and she hadn't gotten up again.

Even now, he swore he could still smell the stench of burning dog hair.

How dare she die!

Maelgwn's fury had known no bounds as he led his hunt on a rampage throughout the human countryside. The mortal plane would soon know they had a new master, and even now his fists clenched to think of it. He would be as the old gods, feared by all and worshipped with offerings. The stones in the silver breastplate beneath his tunic hummed, as if they liked the idea as much as he did. It made him think of the rich collection of relics and artifacts that he and his followers had brought with them, all possessing power in one form or another.

The prince had left the dead grim exactly where she had died, of course—after he had kicked her repeatedly, of course—but perhaps he should have someone retrieve the silver collar. The intricately designed torcs worn by the big black dogs were forged in such a way that they retained magic. At the very least, Maelgwn could bind a new grim with it. *Perhaps I'll bind Rhedyn with it . . .*

Normally, the prince would simply send out grims to get the job done. But this could be an opportunity in disguise. After all, hadn't he just forged a brand new partnership? Surely this was a perfect little task with which to test that alliance.

～

As Morgan sat with her friend to wait for the ambulance, Jay grabbed a bag and headed around the other side of the barn to check on the goats. The mysterious Caris went with him to help. The simple dark-green scrubs Jay had found for her looked absolutely rich next to her olive-toned skin and glossy black hair "Your girlfriend's quite beautiful," Morgan ventured. "Lovely accent too—sounds like she could be Welsh, though not from the same area as Rhys."

"She's not my girlfriend," Liam said firmly. "And I have no idea where she's from. I've only known her a few minutes more than you have."

"Really? How did she get here?"

"Not a damn clue."

"Well, it must be your lucky day if pretty women are dropping out of the sky."

He snorted. "Not if I'm not looking for one."

Defensive much? "Well, I just meant . . ."

"Besides," he added. "She's had a tough time of it. I don't know what happened to her in the storm, but she's really confused right now. You'll look after her too, right?"

She blinked at his odd remark, but her answer was sure. "Of course we will."

The ambulance pulled into the laneway of the farm just as she was about to ask Liam what he meant. *Caris didn't looked confused—in fact, she was taking care of Liam before we got here.* As the EMTs made their way across the obstacle course that had once been a yard, Morgan squeezed Liam's hand. "Look, I know you don't want to be fussed over, but I really think you've got a concussion, possibly a bad one, and they're nothing to mess around with."

"Yeah, yeah, I know. I watch football," he said. "Believe me, I have a brand-new respect for guys that take a hit on a play."

Morgan moved back out of the way to stand with Ranyon, who still had the chicken tucked under one scrawny arm. No one could see the ellyll unless he allowed them to—but she couldn't help but wonder how he managed to hide the hen as well! Ranyon undoubtedly was hoping to take it home to Leo's house, to join his growing flock of "found" fowl. *Do I need to talk to him about leaving it here? It's got to be Liam's chicken.* She knew Ranyon would never steal it, but would he try to "borrow" it? The fae had many strange ideas about ownership.

Together they watched as the EMTs carefully put a cervical collar on Liam to immobilize his head and neck. It was a sure sign of how lousy he must feel that he didn't protest, even when they strapped him to the stretcher. When it was obvious they were done, she put her hand on his shoulder. "Don't worry a bit about your animals, Liam. We'll take care of all of them as long as you need us to. Just get some rest, okay?"

"I'll probably be back in a couple of hours or so," he said, but the gruff certainty was gone from his voice. Instead, he sounded tired, and his face was nearly as white as the sheet on the stretcher.

No way would any self-respecting hospital release a head-injury patient without at least an overnight observation, she thought. Meanwhile, she'd do her best for his livestock and make arrangements for their care. If Liam wasn't worried about them, maybe he wouldn't be so damn anxious to come home. "I'll call and give you a full report on your animals," she said, then added, "And about Caris too."

"Thanks, Morgan. I'm glad you came. You're a good friend. No wonder Tina thinks the world of you."

"You just get better—and I'll call Tina to let her know where you are."

He frowned, then winced, no doubt sorry he'd moved the muscles in his battered forehead. "Shit, if you do that, she's just gonna worry."

"Sorry, but relatives have that prerogative. But I'll let *her* make the decision as to what to tell your aunt and uncle."

"At least Tina won't be able to find them right away. They're on some kind of archeological tour of Peru right now. Aunt Ruby's really into Aztec ruins and all that."

"I think those are Inca ruins."

"Same difference."

She patted his hand, then stepped back out of the way as the EMTs moved in. "See you later, bud."

"Make sure you help, Caris," Liam called out. "And find that dog!"

Morgan watched after them for a moment, not envying their trip through the debris-strewn yard and wondering whether she should go with them and try to help. That's when Ranyon reached up and tugged at her sleeve.

"Is he dying?" he asked solemnly.

"He's got a concussion for certain, but it'll heal in time."

"So yer certain he won't be dying?"

Morgan looked down at the little man in surprise. "Now you're scaring me. What's all this about dying?"

In answer, he held up his twiggy hand. It didn't look strong enough to hold the heavy silver collar draped over his palm. The wide band of intricately woven links hung to the ground on either side of his upstretched arm. Morgan recognized the otherworldly workmanship of the piece at once, but its perfection was marred: dozens of scarred and broken links glinted in the sun. Many even looked melted, as if the collar had suffered some great violence.

"Omigod," she whispered, as she took the collar from Ranyon. Her skin crawled at the touch of the faery-forged metal. She'd felt a strong fae presence here, but *this* she hadn't expected. All the clues had presented themselves almost as soon as she'd arrived, however. *A dog goes missing and a mystery woman from Wales shows up. What the hell else could it be?* "Liam said he didn't know Caris, but he was certainly worried about her. He said she was confused and wanted me to look out for her." Her voice trailed away as she looked around, quickly scanning the farm in every direction.

Ranyon shook his head. "I've never heard of a *female* grim afore, but there's a death dog here for certain," he declared. "There's naught else that wears a collar like this in all of the Nine Realms, and ya know that better than most. So if yer friend's not fated for death, what's a grim doing here? And worse came along with it, dontcha know."

The ellyll's words penetrated Morgan's frantic thoughts. "Worse? What the hell's worse than a messenger of death?"

"A fae hunt rode through here: it's them that brought the storm down on yer friend's farm."

Morgan finally shifted her gaze away from the collar to stare at her friend. "Ranyon, are you sure? The place is a helluva mess, but I didn't see any hoofprints at all."

"Nor will ya, not from fae horses. But the air is disturbed, dontcha know—the energies are stricken as sparks from a flint. I feel their path and their passing. 'Tis their power we've been feeling ever since we came close to this place."

Although she believed him, the situation made no sense to her. "But Lurien leads the Wild Hunt." Not that she trusted the tall, dark lord one hundred percent, mind you. Nothing personal, but it was usually a mistake to trust a fae. Although the queen herself had become as dear a friend to her as had Ranyon, others of the faery realm were coldhearted and amoral at best, malicious and deadly at worst. Lurien appeared to have a code of honor, but whether it matched human ideals was another matter entirely. Still . . . "I've never heard of him leaving a swath of destruction like this. Never. He's, well, too classy to do something so juvenile. And our friend, Aidan, certainly wouldn't do it if he was filling in for Lurien—and besides, he and Brooke have been gone for a month now."

"True on all counts, good lady. But I can feel the magic of this hunt everywhere, and it tells me another strange thing: the dogs were all grims, with not a single *Cŵn Annwn* to be found."

Morgan frowned. "My grandmother used to say the Cŵn Annwn were faery hounds—they're pure white, aren't they?"

"Aye, and marked with red ears and red eyes. Lurien has a great mob of 'em. There's nothing can follow a trail like a Cŵn Annwn. Grims might run along with the Wild Hunt for the sport of it, or because they've finally gone mad, but never in such numbers. There must have been half a hundred great black dogs here last night, and just as many riders." He placed his twiggy hands on his hips. "And so 'twas not Lurien's band at all that did this mischief."

Fifty grims? The enormous dogs would make a terrifying picture. And although the true Wild Hunt was not immune from being hijacked by those with ill intent—and Morgan would never forget the encounter that had nearly killed her and her husband at their own farm—the implications of Ranyon's words were much, much worse. "You're talking about something altogether new then, like a rogue hunt?"

He nodded solemnly. "There are many vile creatures and scoundrels, fae beings that defy the queen's authority and seek holdings in Tir Hardd unlawfully. Worse, they could bring harm to the human world above. We have the proof before us, good lady: someone has brought over an outlaw hunt, and look at what it's wrought in a single night." The ellyll waved a hand at the destruction all around them.

Great. Just great. The royally sanctioned Wild Hunt was terrifying enough, but they were bound by ancient laws. There were parameters, boundaries, *rules* for heaven's sake. But a rogue hunt? All bets were off. They would likely do whatever they pleased—unless it was possible for the true Wild Hunt to find them and catch them. "No wonder Lurien's been trying to patrol the new territory as well as the old kingdom. Now I understand why he needs Aidan's help so often."

Because of Morgan's unique relationship with Gwenhidw, she was well aware that the sovereign had been compelled to lean on Lurien more and more as her right hand. As powerful as he was, the Lord of the Hunt had been forced in turn to rely on someone else to fill in for him at times—and that person was often Brooke's husband, Aidan. The information was a well-kept secret, of course. Ranyon, Rhys, and Morgan hadn't revealed it to anyone, not even to Jay and Starr. The fewer beings who knew that a mortal had a covert hand in fae business, the better Aidan's chances of surviving the highly dangerous job . . . Personally, she was glad that his honeymoon with Brooke had made him unavailable for a while.

"We'll need to be watchful," continued the ellyll. "And you'll be having to get word to Queen Gwenhidw."

Easier said than done. Gwenhidw was her friend, true, but up until now, the monarch had always approached Morgan, slipping away from her heavy responsibilities whenever she could manage it unseen—which wasn't often. Morgan had never attempted to contact the queen, nor had she been invited to do so. Fae social mores were not the same as human ones.

"I'll try to figure something out," she said. "That or try to contact Aidan—he might know how to get hold of Lurien." She wasn't sure of that, though. It was far more likely that Aidan had the same kind of relationship with the Lord of the Wild Hunt that she did with the queen. *Don't call us, we'll call you . . .* Besides, she wasn't too confident she could even find Aidan right now. He and Brooke had chosen to honeymoon in Catemaco—but they had no itinerary. Brooke had wanted to play it by ear and travel around that area as her intuition moved her. Cell phone service seemed iffy. Morgan had gotten through to Brooke only once, and that was weeks ago . . .

As for herself, Morgan wished Rhys was with her right now. Although he was a skilled warrior, he couldn't fight off an entire faery hunt—but she'd still feel a whole lot better just being wrapped in his powerful arms, even for a few moments. She sighed inwardly and turned back to the ellyll. "But the hunt has left, right? There are no fae here?"

"Aye, my magic tells me they've gone—save one." Ranyon pointed at the collar in her hand. "Without the collar, a grim cannot be compelled to leave the mortal world, dontcha know. And I'm thinkin' we need to be asking her some questions."

Morgan nodded. "I'm thinking you're right." She set off at a jog in the direction of the goat corral where Jay had gone with Caris.

~

Like a parched desert flower absorbing dew, Caris drank in the myriad of sensations that surrounded her. It was a strange and contradictory mixture. The living warmth of morning sunlight on her arms and face, the peaceful breeze that stirred her hair, and the vivid colors that filled her gaze—all were a delight to her soul, even as the damage and destruction to the farm were an affront to her sensibilities.

Sounds and smells were different now of course, not as sharp or as keen as a dog experienced them. But she didn't miss that a bit. Not when she had hands to command, not when she could reach for something *and feel her fingers close around it*! Her heart ached with the sheer joy of being able to grasp and to touch. It was a miracle to her to stroke the texture of a goat's soft hair, to feel the frame and muscle of its body braced against her, as she held each animal securely but gently for Jay's inspection.

She didn't rejoice in the animals' distress—many had been injured in the storm, with long gashes and finger-length splinters of wood embedded in their thin hides. All were subdued, and many leaned their heads against Caris as if seeking comfort from their frightening experience. She murmured to them in her native tongue, just some soothing, lilting nonsense that she'd often used to quiet anxious sheep.

"Some of those words sound like they could be Welsh," said Jay, as he finished suturing a doe's leg. "Isn't *cariad* sort of a pet name for someone you love?"

"Just as you might say 'darling' or 'dearest,'" she affirmed. "Wales is where I was born, though most people there speak English." Suddenly she wondered if it was a good idea to be telling him where she was from. How careful did she need to be? Telling Liam she'd been a grim had been a mistake, that was certain. But what about her human origins? She realized that she had no reasonable-sounding explanation to offer anyone as to how she'd come to be here.

There were other concerns, too. While she'd observed the march of progress during her many years as a death dog, she had little idea of how to actually function in this time or what was expected of her. Here she was clad in a green tunic of some sort and a pair of matching *trousers*—not only had she never worn such things in her life, but the fabric wasn't much heavier than Liam's shirt had been. Practical for freedom of movement, she could admit, and very comfortable. Undoubtedly such garments would be a grievous sin in her former life, yet women now commonly wore far, far less. Times had changed . . . *Perhaps I can, too.*

Of course, modern fashion was the least of her problems, Caris knew. She might be human again, but she felt like a fish out of water. The wisest course of action would be to keep quiet, look for cues, and learn all she could. To that end, she decided to encourage Jay to do the talking. "How did you come to learn the Welsh language? There are many in Cymru itself that never master the tongue."

"Morgan's husband, Rhys, and our friend, Aidan, are both from Wales too."

Welshmen, here! She hid her surprise with difficulty. Would her fellow countrymen be quicker to discern that she didn't even belong in this century, never mind this decade? *What then?* Questions tumbled over each other as her thoughts raced.

Unaware of Caris's worries, Jay continued. "The interesting thing is that their dialects are not just different from yours; they're really different from each other's. I'm no expert on linguistics, though. I just picked up on a couple of words you said that sounded kind of familiar. Rhys calls Morgan *cariad* all the time."

"That's very sweet." No one had ever called her that. Her da had affectionately called her *bach* when she was a child. It meant both "little one" and "dear," and he used it occasionally even when she was grown. But *cariad*? That was for lovers to use. Without warning, she caught herself imagining Liam's masculine lips forming the word, just as he was bending to kiss her.

Her cheeks flamed and she cleared her throat, as she refocused on the conversation. "It's true, our language has a different lilt in each area, even different words for things," she managed to get out. "'Tis a little country, yet some in the South say they cannot understand those in the North."

Jay nodded. "It's the same here. You put people from Brooklyn, California, and Texas in the same room, and you wouldn't believe they're from the same nation, even though the language is the same." He laughed then. "Listen to their political views, and you'd be *certain* they're not from the same country!"

She smiled at that, and a single conclusion emerged from her whirling thoughts: if she was going to get along in this new place, she was going to have to trust someone. Her instincts—if they still worked—seemed to be at ease with Liam's friends. *And I'd take my chances with any human over a fae,* she thought.

But what about the ellyll? Strangely, she felt no danger from Ranyon either—he appeared to be a firm friend to Jay and Morgan. And if what she had learned as a grim was true, no ellyll had any reason to side with the Tylwyth Teg. So she would trust him, too, and hope she was right.

"What part of Wales are you from?" Jay asked.

"The Northwest. We had a sheep farm up in the mountains," she said, without hesitation now. "Above the village of Beddgelert. It's a bit isolated, so our way of speaking might sound different from your friends."

Jay stood up and brushed himself off as he studied the herd. "Looks like we've got the worst of the wounds looked after. I can finish the rest if you want to get started with milking—that is, if you feel up to it. I wish we could use the machines, but there's no power. And while I hate to waste it, we'll have to dump the milk for now. There's no way to keep it cold."

Regrettably, he was probably right. Caris could see no goat kids, only yearlings that probably wouldn't be interested. There were no calves, no pigs, nor any other creature—not even a farm cat in sight!—that could make use of the milk. And one look at the swollen udders of the does told her there would be a *lot* of it. She got down to business, choosing a site with a slight incline that would allow the milk to drain away from her work area. There was no rope at hand to restrain them with, but in their present condition, the animals might be happy to cooperate. Caris knelt on the ground and simply called the does to her. Some hesitated, but a big white one practically climbed into her lap, anxious to be relieved. Caris talked soothingly to her, massaging the tight udders so the milk would let down, then falling into an easy rhythm of right, left, right, left. The milk spurted onto the ground, where it ran in bright foaming streams among the grasses until it found a spot to pool that was several feet away. She'd barely finished before a smaller black-and-red doe was trying to bump the big white one out of the way and take her place.

"Here now, there's room and time for all," laughed Caris, and she milked the second goat, then the third. By the fourth, she'd happily lost herself in the familiar chore, taking joy in her ability to work with her hands again, and in the uniquely human satisfaction of simple work on a sunny day. It wasn't long before she was singing, a distillation of contented pleasure and exquisite happiness beyond anything she'd dared dream of experiencing again. All that was missing was her . . .

Suddenly Morgan rounded the corner of the barn at a run, with Ranyon (still holding his chicken) following as quickly as his short, twiggy legs would allow. Her heart in her throat, Caris jumped to her feet at once, startling away the goat she'd been milking. "*Duw annwyl*! Is Liam all right?"

"You ought to know!" declared Morgan, pointing directly at her. "You tell me what you did to him, right now!"

EIGHT

⌒⋒⋔⋒⌒

As a rule, Liam wasn't fond of hospitals. He'd spent far too much time sitting by his mother's metal-railed bedside to ever be comfortable in a medical environment again. Yet he couldn't help but appreciate that the staff was both kind and competent as they evaluated his condition. The CT scan had revealed no evidence of fracture, despite the howling pain in his skull. The neurologist had ascertained that there was no bleeding or clot in Liam's brain.

Word of the day, he thought. *Can you say* hematoma? He doubted he could spell it, but if he ever felt better, he'd probably be cheerful about not having one.

The vertebrae of his neck were deemed sound, and he was freed from the cervical collar. Now he knew how old Homer had felt wearing a big plastic cone from the vet's . . . That image led his train of thought back to the veterinarians at Steptoe Acres— he wondered what they'd found. Liam wouldn't feel at ease, of course, until he could check on his livestock for himself, but at least he knew the animals were in good hands.

Caris is helping Morgan and Jay.

That thought seemed to come out of left field, and it certainly had no business bringing such a surge of pleasure with it. An overused Internet meme came to mind, something like "what has been seen, cannot be unseen." And it was true. There was no way he'd ever be able to *unsee* such an attractive woman. Or stop his body from reacting to her curvy image in his head. Even now, his cock was starting to pay attention, headache or not. *Guess that proves there's no connection between a guy's brain and his dick . . .*

But even after Caris had covered herself up, something about the directness of her dark gaze and her fierce assertion of boundaries had made Liam's interest sit up and take notice for the first time in years. *She's a spirited one*, his Uncle Conall would say, and Aunt Ruby would probably take him to task for making the woman sound like a wild mustang.

But she's not wild at all, thought Liam. Maybe it was the concussion talking, but in their first meeting, he had sensed both strength and steadiness in Caris. A pretty weird conclusion, considering that she had claimed to be a dog at the time . . . Yet something in her beckoned him, a generous earthiness that appealed to him on many levels.

I must be cracked, no matter what the damn scan said. I don't even know her, and I don't want to. I don't want to be concerned about her, I don't want to care about what happens to her, I don't want to see her again, I . . .

I am such a frickin' liar.

~

"I did nothing to Liam!" protested Caris. "I only pushed him away from me when he became too familiar."

"Define *familiar*." Morgan's eyes narrowed suspiciously, even as Jay stared from Caris to her, and back again.

"He grabbed me and kissed me," Caris admitted, and she actually looked embarrassed. "But it wasn't his fault, not really. He was thinking I was a dream, you see. He'd already had that fearful lump on his head when he found me. All I did was remind him that I was as real as he is, and he need not be taking liberties. 'Twas not my intention to do him harm!"

Morgan was baffled. *He kissed you? Why would he be putting moves on a complete stranger? And whatever would make him think you were just a dream?* "Let's just cut to the chase. Why would Liam be hanging around with a grim? Or, more to the point, why would a grim be visiting Liam at all? Is he in danger?"

"I wasn't sent to him, if that's what you're asking. It's not his time to pass over. The man found me in his field after the storm, and that's the whole of it."

"You think she's a grim?" Jay slowly sidled a couple of steps away from the woman, and whispered to Morgan: "Nobody told me there were *girl* grims! Are you sure she's a death dog?"

"Think about it. She was dressed in nothing but Liam's shirt when we got here. Remind you of anybody we know? Like the naked warrior I found on my lawn? Or how about the naked blacksmith that showed up in Brooke's spell room?"

He shrugged. "Okay, so Rhys and Aidan didn't exactly have a wardrobe after their spells were broken. But that doesn't mean everybody in the buff is a former grim. I just figured Caris and Liam were, you know, a *couple.*"

"Me too—until he told me that he'd never met this woman before in his life."

"Maybe he got hit harder than we thought. Because if he could forget someone like *her,* he's got way more issues than you told me about."

"'Tis true that he doesn't know me," declared Caris. "But I know this about Liam Cole: he's a good man. He was kind without reason to a strange dog that was wounded and dying, and he gave me the very shirt off his own back, though he was injured himself."

Her words brought Morgan up short. *Kindness.* Rhys had spoken of it as an antidote to some faery magics, and most particularly to his own condition: he had been a grim when Morgan found him. Unaware of his otherworldly origins, she had loved and cared for the great black dog as her own dear pet—and Rhys had been restored to his human form because of her actions. *Has history repeated itself? Or is someone trying to fool us?* "You still haven't said it outright, but the dog was really you, right? Liam didn't know you were a grim, but we do—we found your silver collar. So I want to know right now why you're here. Are you spying for the fae?"

Caris was quite a bit shorter than Morgan, yet there was a solemn dignity in her bearing—and a flash of indignation in her eyes. "I have not denied that I was a grim. As for spying for the fae, why ever would I help them? Think you that I chose to be Death's herald? That anyone does? I won't be condemned for what was done to me, for all that was taken from me. And I will not go back to the Nine Realms."

"Hey, hold on a sec," said Jay gently. "We're the good guys here, right Morgan?"

Good guys still have to be careful. "Nobody is sending anyone to the faery world unless they belong there," assured Morgan. "I'm sorry to be such a hard ass about it, Caris, but we have to know the truth. The fae are dangerous, and they've caused a lot of trouble here. We can't trust just anyone, especially someone who's been in contact with them."

"Perhaps I shouldn't be trusting *you* then, since you have an ellyll for a friend," said the woman, folding her arms as if daring them to deny it.

Jay goggled, but Morgan wasn't surprised. There were only three ways that a mortal could see Ranyon. He could allow it, as in the case of Jay and his wife, Starr. Or a human might have a rare psychic gift, like old Leo Waterson. *Or the person had been to the fae kingdom.* As former grims, Rhys and Aidan could see the little ellyll—and any other fae beings.

And so could Caris Dillwyn.

"I protect my friends too, dontcha know." Ranyon's declaration sounded a bit breathless as he finally joined the group, no doubt because he was still carrying the big spotted hen. "And I'll just be testing this tale of yours. Here"—he passed the bird to Jay—"hold this lovely great biddy for me, will ya?"

Ranyon reached under his blue T-shirt with both hands and appeared to be searching for something. Morgan wasn't sure what lay beneath the leaves that grew thickly all over his body—Pockets? A kangaroo pouch? A chest of drawers? He always seemed to carry an unbelievable assortment of copper wire, old clock gears, buttons, feathers, pebbles—and once, a half dozen eggs! Any time he was overexcited, items were sure to tumble to the ground, and Morgan would bet that there was presently a trail of odd things leading like bread crumbs all the way back to the other side of the barn.

However, Ranyon's treasures were far more than a fanciful collection. The ellyll could whip up a charm or a spell at a moment's notice—and he did so now. Wrapping a stem of foxtail grass around a nugget of rich blue stone, he turned to Caris. "Now, then, there's nothing ya need worry about if you're speakin' true. Give me yer hand, and we'll be settling this beyond doubt."

To her credit, the young woman didn't hesitate. She thrust out her arm, and Ranyon placed the stone into her upturned palm. As he did so, something invisible crackled in the air around it like sparks from a fire. The ellyll leaned his head toward the stone, listening intently. After a long moment, he straightened up, carefully adjusting his Blue Jays cap as if adjusting his thoughts as well.

"There's not a bit o' guile in her," he declared at last. "And it's plain she holds no ill toward yer friend, Liam."

Morgan had to ask. "So does that mean . . . ?"

"Aye, she was a grim, and now she's not," said Ranyon, as casually as if he'd been talking about someone having gotten over a cold.

"Holy cow," said Jay, sitting down on the ground, forgetting all about the chicken he was supposed to be holding. Instead of running away, however, the newly freed hen sat down beside him, as if it were astonished too. "Lightning really *does* strike twice— er, I guess that's *thrice*."

The ellyll held up a twiggy hand at that and shook his head, making the charms around his neck jingle. "Not quite the way yer thinkin'." He glanced up at Caris. "I'll wager that while Liam was kindhearted toward this good lady, 'twas not enough by itself to shatter the spell. Kindness is powerful magic, but it's slow. It takes far more than a single mortal day to do its work."

"Then how could the collar be broken?" asked Jay. "I've seen firsthand just how tough faery-forged silver is. Nothing human can even scratch it."

"True enough, unless something of great power weakened it first."

All of them looked at Caris then.

"A light whip," she said, quietly. "I tried to leave the Hunt, tried to get away. That's when the prince lost his vile temper and struck me with the light whip."

Ranyon clapped both his twiggy hands over his heart as he fell flat on his back without a sound. The chicken came over and eyed him curiously. "And yer not dead as a doornail?" he gasped out.

"I thought I was. He thought so too, or he wouldn't have left me behind. The Tylwyth Teg do not let go of their toys. Ever."

The certainty in Caris's expression sent a chill down Morgan's spine. "But Rhys and Aidan . . ." she began.

The ellyll shook his head. "The queen herself intervened fer yer good husband, dear lady. And the fae that trapped Aidan was slain. Otherwise both men would yet be prisoners of the Fair Ones," he said solemnly. He turned a thoughtful eye to Caris. "'Twas surely the collar that saved your life. And the breaking of the collar freed you from your fate as a grim."

"Aye, I think that must be right."

"What's a light whip? Anything like a light saber?" asked Jay.

Morgan thought her friend sounded just a bit on the hopeful side. *He wouldn't be so thrilled if he saw one in action.* As for herself, she hoped she never saw one again. Each light whip held a ton of magical energy, all squeezed into a narrow, ropelike form. The weapon—for it was one—was powerful enough not only to summon but also to control the entire Wild Hunt, and to make every fae creature in it obey without question. She looked at Caris with new eyes. How had the young woman managed to fight such a terrifying compulsion?

"It's like a bolt o' lightning in yer hand!" Ranyon was telling Jay. "And few there be that can wield it aright. The light whip can slay the careless bearer as well as those he bends to his will."

Before the boys could start comparing the pros and cons of magical weaponry—and ever since Ranyon had been introduced to *Star Wars*, such discussions had become a regular occurrence—Morgan wanted to get the truly important information. "Exactly which prince are we talking about, Caris?"

"The prince who stole me away from my life, who turned me into a voiceless animal, is Maelgwn of the House of Ash." She spat out the name as if describing a snake. "And it's a pity that it pleased him to lead a hunt on that day. Lord Lurien might have been more lenient had I refused to follow *him*."

Ranyon's voice was uncharacteristically hushed. "You *defied* a prince of the Fair Ones?"

"For all the good it did me. I was taken away just the same. The farm went to ruin, and my poor father died alone, never knowing what had happened to me."

Morgan exchanged glances with Jay. "I'm so very sorry," she said to Caris. "You've lost a great deal. The fae don't think as we do."

"Nay, make no excuses for them!" The ellyll was rarely angry, but he was standing on his twiggy toes, all but shaking with ire. Morgan wished she'd remembered in time that Caris wasn't the only one who had suffered at their hands. Ranyon's entire clan had been killed, leaving him utterly alone.

"The Tylwyth Teg are without an ounce of pity," he continued. "They serve only themselves, and they leave naught but heartbreak and ruin behind them."

"You're right," said Morgan, putting a hand on her small friend's shoulder. "You're absolutely right. Most of the Fair Ones are self-centered and insensitive, and many are deliberately cruel. All of them are damn dangerous. But it's also true that *some* try to be different. Some have honor, like Lurien, and some have compassion, like Gwenhidw."

Ranyon simply crossed his skinny arms across his blue shirt and refused to respond.

Caris, however, sighed and nodded. "There are yet a few with a small grain of kindness. A faery woman, Rhedyn, tried to talk Maelgwn out of changing me, and she spoke up for me more than once, although it angered him enough to strike her. And I've seen for myself how much the queen truly loves her subjects. But that's little or no comfort to me when I think of my poor da, and what he must have gone through when his only daughter came up missing."

A moment later, Morgan saw the little ellyll slip his twiggy hand into Caris's. It was a childlike gesture but a kind one. The old stories often spoke about mortals being kidnapped and taken to the faery realm. How many lives had been stolen over the centuries? How many loved ones had mourned? She almost regretted standing up for Lurien and the queen; perhaps they didn't enslave humans themselves, but it appeared that they tolerated the practice. If so, then how different were they, really, from the other fae? She didn't know the answer to that.

Jay had questions of his own. "What was this Maelgwn guy doing with the Hunt? What happened to Lurien?"

"Prince Maelgwn has followers among the Fair Ones, every one of them ambitious or foolish or both," said Caris. "He cares not for the true Wild Hunt, nor for Lurien's lawful rule o'er it and the justice it metes out. Instead, Maelgwn calls together his own hunts, and they terrorize the mortal world for sport."

"Like Liam's poor farm," Morgan said. "But why here?"

"'Tis true that they have never before ventured to this place. But the queen announced that the new territory would be fairly divided between all the faery races and governed by leaders of their own choosing. Her words angered many of the Tylwyth Teg, and especially Maelgwn." Caris shook her head. "I've never seen him in such a rage."

"'Tis the same as always," muttered Ranyon. "They believe that only *they* should lead."

"Maelgwn called a hunt straightaway," she continued. "And I'm thinking he must have planned it long beforehand. The party was gathered much too quickly, otherwise, and well supplied as if for a long journey."

"He's using grims," said Morgan. "Why not the white hunting hounds?"

"The Cŵn Annwn belong to Lord Lurien. But Maelgwn favors the grims because they strike fear into human hearts—and many of them are mad enough to kill if he commands it."

"And you?"

She shook her head. "I don't know why he made me come along. It pleases him to trouble me, I think. When I realized where he was going, I wanted to tell the queen. But a dog has no voice."

"And no choice," finished Ranyon. He yanked his Blue Jays cap from his leaf-laden hair. "My hat's off to ya, good lady, for daring to try to escape once more. Glad I am that ya succeeded, and that the murderous lout didn't kill ya."

To everyone's surprise—and the ellyll's delight—she leaned over and kissed the top of his leafy head.

"Great, so not only do we have a rogue hunt, but now we have a dangerous faery prince running around," said Jay. "Didn't we *just* get rid of an evil princess? Are royal pains coming out of the woodwork now?"

Ranyon carefully replaced his Blue Jays cap, as if trying to preserve Caris's bestowal. "The queen is never out of danger, dontcha know. She may speak little of it, but the Royal Court is brimful o' plots to relieve her of her throne. It has always been so. A good many of her own relations would be quick to plunge the knife if it meant they could have her power."

"So how closely is Maelgwn related to her?" asked Morgan. "Please tell me he's not the new heir apparent."

The ellyll sniffed in disdain. "True it is that Maelgwn is a prince of the Tylwyth Teg, and the most toffee-nosed, arrogant fool of the lot. But he's a prince in name only. He's one of countless great-grandchildren of the late king's sister and has no hope of ever ruling anything."

"I only wish that were true," said Caris, slowly. "I fear he has hope aplenty now, though not for ruling the Nine Realms beneath the Black Mountains of Wales. Maelgwn wishes to be king of all of Tir Hardd."

Jay goggled. "Wait a minute. That's—"

"Right here under our feet," finished Morgan.

NINE

～⁊⎹₷～

L iam slept. He didn't ask anyone's permission, and no one cautioned him against it. He was exhausted, his injured head throbbed in time to his heartbeat, and he was certain that the insistent hospital noises would irritate him to death long before he was released. He gratefully left all of that behind as he plunged headlong into slumber, as a swimmer into cool, deep waters.

And dreamed . . .

The ancient mountain forest was lush with new summer, so thick and full that the sun could penetrate the leaves only enough to scatter droplets of light like golden coins. But it was the wild, cascading tune that burgeoned with life. *Drawn from a long-seasoned fiddle*, that much Liam could tell, but the song itself was unlike anything he'd ever heard, or even imagined. The eager notes flitted through the trees one moment and lingered in the air the next, like a vast assembly of hummingbirds.

His first instinct was to follow the tune to its source. His second, stronger impulse was to head in the other direction, to block out the melody that stroked his senses as intimately as a lover. The dream gave him no choice in the matter, however. Liam found himself following the impossible music through narrow, green-shaded paths, up steep overgrown inclines, and across glittering streams.

At last, the trees parted before him to reveal a sunlit clearing, made all the more vivid by a sea of yellow cinquefoil and marigolds—and in the midst of that bright glory danced the source of the song. The woman was clothed only in the music she created, save for her long dark hair that swung back over her shoulders with each sweep of her bow and each spring of her small feet. The arc of her hips echoed the curvature of her fiddle, and he envied the instrument as it nestled between her pert chin and the round of her breast. Liam knew her sumptuous shape by heart, though he'd seen it only once . . .

But the tune that Caris Ellen Dillwyn coaxed so effortlessly from the dark golden wood was something he'd never known. Nor had he known such yearning. *Primal*, he thought. The music was as primal as the desire that pulsed through him to touch her, as basic and raw as the need to breathe—and to feel the woman's resplendent form welcome his hard, muscled body.

Liam struggled at first, resisting the pull, shoring up the walls of his resolve to fend off all the things he had banished from his life. But he was powerless to keep the music from touching those dormant passions. For one brief moment, Caris looked up and appeared to meet his gaze . . . and the deep, dark songs of his soul called out to her, as if they knew they would find expression if they could just reach her.

Yet she didn't hear, didn't see. Immersed in her music and rapt in her dance, she spun away, and his heart spun crazily with her—until the bright sun dimmed abruptly. Enormous black clouds swooped and swirled like live things, so low that they brushed the tops of the ancient trees and blotted out the light. As ominous as the darkness was, some instinct told Liam the real danger wasn't from above.

"Caris!" he yelled, desperate to reach her, to get her to shelter—because *something was coming*. He could feel a strange shuddering vibration in the earth beneath his feet, growing stronger by the second, creeping closer and closer . . . Something was coming, something huge and evil and cruel. But the dream itself turned cruel then, rooting him to the spot. He struggled and fought to move, his muscles bulging and straining, to no avail. Worse, Caris seemed unable to hear him, unaware of his plight or her own danger. She simply danced upon the golden flowers, her bow coaxing the wild song into a new key that seemed to pluck hidden strings within Liam. But at the farthest edges of the forest beyond, he caught a glimpse of movement in the deep shadows.

Something squeezed Liam's arm, and he was abruptly freed from the paralysis of the dream. He was also very much awake and staring into the wide eyes of a startled nurse.

"You can let go of me now, Mr. Cole," she said, with a strained smile.

"What . . . Oh, hell." Liam released his death grip on her wrist. "I'm sorry."

"Bad dream?"

"Not exactly." No one could call any dream bad which featured Caris's exquisite form. As for the rest of that vision, however: "More like weird." And unwelcome—the strange, wild music from the dream was caught in his head now, like a shining fish struggling in a net.

"People often get bizarre dreams with a concussion." She removed the blood-pressure cuff from his arm. "I'm just sorry to have to keep waking you. Gotta check your vitals, you know. Can I get you anything? Some water maybe?"

Liam didn't have to think. "I need my phone."

∾

One by one, the goats were milked, the animals tended. In the early afternoon, one of Liam's horses found its way back to the farmyard, and thankfully the big speckled stallion was unhurt. Caris wondered what it had thought upon finding its home in disarray, its owner missing, and three total strangers doing the chores. Fortunately, the horse appeared relieved and happy simply to be near people after the terrifying events of the night. A good feed of grain, along with a soothing brush-down by Caris, seemed to put its world to rights.

If only the human world was as easily soothed.

At least I'm not the enemy anymore, thought Caris. Thanks to the little ellyll's truth spell, Morgan was no longer viewing her with suspicion, and Jay had relaxed considerably in her presence. They hadn't asked any additional questions, and she hadn't offered any further information—with all the livestock to look after, there'd been no time. It was a temporary but welcome relief, since Caris wasn't quite ready to tell all. She was every bit as mortal as they were, but she was painfully conscious that she didn't fit in. The world she'd known had vanished long ago, and there was no place she could claim as her own. *I'll just have to* make *it my world*, she thought, pressing her lips together in determination. *I'll work hard until I belong here as much as anyone else.*

It would be nice to call Morgan and Jay her friends one day; she couldn't help but like them both, even though they'd been on their guard at first. She certainly admired their skill with animals, their loyalty to their friend, and their determined compassion. *They're good people.* It would surely be good to talk with Rhys too—and hadn't there been another man mentioned as well? If they had once been grims like her, maybe they could help her figure out how to build a life as a human once more. *Just to speak with someone from my own dear country would surely be a treat.*

Still, it was Liam who had impressed Caris most deeply, even with that brusque and reluctant way about him. Several times she caught herself not only wondering if the man was all right but also missing him. And how silly was that, when she didn't even know him?

"Maybe ya know what's important."

Caris jumped as Ranyon abruptly appeared next to her. He'd been all over the farm, using his charms to coax badly frightened creatures out of hiding—over a dozen yearling goats, several more chickens, five gray geese, and even an entire family of barn cats. Every time he passed Caris, he had waved or grinned, as if they were the best of friends already. Now he looked up at her with a knowing expression.

"I didn't read yer mind, ya know. You said it all out loud as you was a-workin'. Seemed only right to answer ya." He winked and dashed away after another chicken.

Jay had wired together a few damaged places in the corral fencing so the goats wouldn't escape, but Caris was still relieved when Ranyon charmed the boundaries as well. Goats were as bad as sheep: if one got out, the entire lot of them would follow. Next up was to clear the debris from the barn. It might not have a roof anymore, but everything inside—equipment, hay bales, buckets, and feeders—looked like they'd been stirred into a prickly batter by a giant's hand. There was no choice but to set to work to put things right. Even open to the sky, the building would keep the goats and other creatures safe during the night. And it wouldn't hurt to plan ahead and close them in early. That way, the does would be already gathered for their evening milking.

Thank goodness for Ranyon, thought Caris. As his mortal friends did the heavier work at ground level, the nimble little fae climbed the timbers like a sailor climbing the mast and spelled the few remaining bits of the roof and rafters to fuse together. By midafternoon, the barn was fit for tenants—yet the poor goats continued to huddle at the farthest end of the corral. They wanted nothing to do with the barn, and Caris could hardly blame them after what they'd been through. But it was a problem she could deal with, one that required no magic to solve. She simply poured a big bucket of feed onto the cleaned and raked dirt floor. In seconds, every goat, big and small, couldn't wait to get inside.

From the barn door, Morgan gave her a thumbs-up—then reached in her pocket to answer the tinny musical summons of her phone. *What a clever little machine*, Caris thought. As a grim, she'd witnessed the inception of telephones in the human world, of course, but had never used one herself. Now these tiny glowing devices were everywhere, no longer restricted to the wealthy or the privileged. *Maybe I'll have one too, some day.*

Morgan didn't seem to be enjoying hers at the moment. "I just don't think it's a good idea. No, not that, I mean—yes, everything's under control. We're making real progress. Just give us a little time . . . *Look, do I have to call Tina to make you see sense?* She'll come down here, you know she will." Finally she put the heel of her hand to her forehead. "Of course you can, just a minute," she said, and held out the brightly lit rectangle to Caris. "It's for you."

Caris just stared. "I . . . I don't understand."

"It's an expression. It just means the *call* is for you, that someone is waiting to speak to you," Morgan whispered, cupping her hand over the phone's face as if to keep it from hearing her. "I had a hard time explaining that to Rhys at first—he thought I was giving him the phone as a gift. Pick it up like *this* so you can hear, and then just say hello." *It's Liam*, she mouthed, and made herself scarce as Caris gingerly put the strange device to her ear.

"Hello?" she said, trying not to sound as timid as she felt.

"Caris?"

Oh yes, it very much *was* him. His voice in her ear seemed incredibly intimate, and she could feel her cheeks burning bright. "Are you well then, Liam?" Caris managed to get out. "How is your poor head?"

"I'm going to have a headache for a while, a couple weeks at the very least, but it seems my thick skull protected my brain. The doc's insisting I stay overnight, of course. I just wanted to talk to you, make sure you're all right before I decide if I should listen to him."

He was that concerned about her? Caris put a hand to her feverishly hot face. "Well, *of course* you ought to listen to the physician. You needn't be worried about me—I do thank you for asking, but I'm well enough. I milked out the goats, and Jay's just finished looking after the ones that were hurt, and then Ranyon"—she caught herself just in time—"er, I mean we *ran about*, and we found thirty-eight does and eighteen yearlings." Caris heard his sigh of relief.

"That's all of them but four," he said. "Much better than I dared to hope. Any sign of Dodge and Chevy?"

"Dear heaven, are there people missing too? You might have told us that first!" she admonished.

Liam started to laugh, then groaned. "Damn, that hurts the head. No, no, I meant my horses. They were pastured with the cattle when the storm hit, and they're probably in the next state by now."

"There's a stallion that came to us, with a spotted coat."

"That's Dodge!" he exclaimed. "Is he . . . ?"

"There wasn't a thing wrong with the big beauty that some feed and affection couldn't fix. He likes his curry brush, that's for certain."

"He'll take as much of that as you feel like dishing out," Liam agreed. "I'm glad he's okay. I hope Chevy is too—that's the mare.

She'll be foaling soon, and I'm really worried about her." He paused, as if to measure his words. "I'm actually more concerned about you. Are you all right? Are Morgan and Jay looking after *you*?"

"Your friends have been good to me, though they'd be hard pressed to be as kind as you were when you first found me." It was nothing but the truth, but Caris wished she hadn't said it the instant it left her lips. He wouldn't welcome any reference to her time as a dog. *Not when he doesn't believe me.*

Sure enough, his tone grew serious. "Look, we kind of got off on the wrong foot. Neither of us was at our best when we met. You've said some really strange things—or at least that's how I remember it. So I need you to tell me straight: do you remember where your home is? Where you were, *who* you were, before the storm came?"

"I know right enough where I'm from, thank you, and exactly who I am. I'm not soft in the head, Liam Cole. And I didn't tell you a single thing that wasn't the honest truth."

That prompted an awkward silence, but she didn't care. He might not believe she'd been a grim, but she wouldn't stand for him thinking there was a thing wrong with her mind.

Finally Liam said, "Okay, well, lemme talk to Morgan again. I need a rundown on the goats' injuries and stuff."

I could have told you all of that, Caris thought, knowing full well that what he really wanted was to escape the conversation. Hiding her disappointment, she dutifully delivered the phone to its owner and went to help Jay with the speckled horse. He'd found a saddle and tack in the ruins of a blown-down shed and was soon riding out to look for the cattle. The flashy-colored Dodge looked grand in action as he cantered along the fence line. *What would it be like to sit astride a horse so tall?* Caris liked riding, and she felt a pang in her heart as she remembered her white pony, Eira. The dear old cob had been a good-natured beast, and a friend. She hoped he'd made it back to the farm . . .

A pang of sudden grief speared her heart. For Eira, for her da, for the farm, for all of it . . . *and she remembered her fiddle*!

Her heart stilled as she stood in the middle of the ruined yard, instantly back in the past. She heard again that hideous crack as the beloved instrument shattered in her own hands. Something caught in her throat and knotted in her chest until it pained her to breathe.

No! She was not going to allow herself to revisit this. She couldn't bear it. Her heart had been as broken as her dear fiddle, but dwelling on it would be like picking at the scab on a wound. *I'm human again*, she reminded herself as sternly as she could manage. *I have hands and fingers again, don't I? So I'll just be finding myself another fiddle!*

The instruments still existed, that much she knew. She'd seen them when she walked the mortal plane as a grim. What the cost might be to purchase a fiddle, she had no idea—but it didn't matter. If she had to work day and night for years to earn one, then that's exactly what she would do. Whatever it took, however long it took, she would play her music, her songs, again. *And this time, I won't be having to hide in the woods to do it.*

Still, there were tears on her face. The heel of her hand would have been enough to wipe away one, perhaps two, but there were more, and she had to turn to the hem of her borrowed shirt to blot them all. *I can't be thinking about these things from the past*, she thought fiercely. *If I do, I'll start crying like a perfect ninny and never stop. I have a second chance, a second life, and it's* now, *not two centuries gone.* How or where she was going to live that life, she didn't yet know, but surely she shouldn't waste a minute of it pining for what used to be.

Or yearning for what might be with a certain blue-eyed man . . .

~

Liam switched off his smartphone and stared at its dark screen for a long time. Sharp twinges in his forehead and in his eyes reminded him *strongly* not to frown—yet he kept doing it anyway. Frowning came naturally to him, and it seldom had much to do with his mood (even though his mood had been generally shitty for the past three years). Mostly, his brow furrowed when he was thinking.

And he was thinking hard about Caris Dillwyn.

His friend Morgan had given him every detail he could wish for about the condition of his livestock, but most of what she'd said was already forgotten. It was Caris's words that kept running through his mind—and all in that low sultry voice of hers, with that naturally sexy lilt of which she seemed utterly unaware. Why hadn't he kept her on the phone, kept her talking? Why did he have to get all pissy and ask for an update on the animals from Morgan instead?

Because Caris won't back down on her damn dog story, that's why.

He rolled that thought over in his mind a few times. *I didn't tell you a single thing that wasn't the honest truth*, she had said. A lawyer would point out that the woman hadn't mentioned anything specifically about the dog again—yet Liam's gut told him that was exactly what she was referring to.

His gut was telling him a few other things too, things he hadn't expected to hear. Living at Steptoe Acres, it was impossible to count the number of times Uncle Conall had given what Liam and his cousin Tina had nicknamed "The Famous Gut Speech." They'd giggled over it when they were kids, but as they'd grown older, their uncle's wisdom had become evident.

Liam knew the words by heart. *Everybody says you have to decide between the head and the heart, but that's just so much bullshit. Your heart and your head don't know a damn thing between them when it comes to other people. Your head can know facts about them, sure—like a criminal record or a Purple Heart—but that's about it. And your heart only knows how it feels and what it wants, not what the other person is feeling . . .*

And wasn't *that* a painful truth? Hadn't Liam once assumed that Jade felt just like he did, wanted what he did, cared about what he did? And maybe she had, once, but he'd never noticed a change. His heart was happy, so he'd cheerfully taken for granted that hers was on the exact same page. And if any nagging inner voice suggested there might be a problem, he had flatly ignored it. Christ, he'd been stupid.

. . . It's the gut you have to listen to, boy. That's your instinct, that's what tells you the things you can't see or feel. Aunt Ruby, now, she goes in for all that psychic woo-woo stuff, but it all boils down to the very same thing: your gut. *A million billion years of evolution telling you what* is *and what* isn't.

Liam's gut had plenty to say about Caris Dillwyn. For one thing, she wasn't crazy *and he knew it.* That part was a damn relief, really, because he didn't want her to be crazy. She wasn't lying, either, but that wasn't so reassuring, not when he was far from ready to believe what she was saying. Even less comforting was the dead-certain knowledge that *he wanted her,* period. His gut was telling him that as loud and clear as if someone had announced it over a cranked-to-the-max stadium sound system.

He wanted her, and it didn't make a single lick of sense. He knew nothing about Caris in the conventional sense, all that "head" stuff that his uncle talked about. His heart knew little more, only that somehow her presence had stirred up its ashes and uncovered an ember still faintly glowing. As for his dick, well, it had already registered its opinion. Sex was definitely on Liam's agenda—hell, he'd have to be dead and buried not to have reacted to Caris's gloriously naked body—but it wasn't the final destination, not at all.

He wanted her. All of her. In his arms, in his bed, in his heart. In his life. Period. It wasn't that fluffy love-at-first-sight stuff you saw in the movies—it was something far deeper, as tangible and solid as bedrock, and as real as rain. It was a revelation and a validation at the same time.

Now what the hell was he supposed to do with a thing like that?

In the past, Liam had known what he wanted and gone after it. He'd wanted a music career, and he'd started self-producing CDs of his own songs before he was even out of high school. Jesus, he'd played his tunes everywhere—hot and dusty street corners, weekend farmers' markets, school dances, rained-out parks, coffee shops, small-town rodeos, and the state fair. No venue had been too small, no effort too great, if it gave him a chance to share his music. He'd had a dream, and he'd pursued it with everything he had in him.

He'd set aside that dream (hell, he'd driven it over a cliff and set it on fire), but maybe it was time to find out whether the doggedly determined man who would fight for something he wanted was still inside him.

TEN

⌒⌒⌒

The cacophony of strident voices, loud shrieks, and bone-shaking growls echoed off the shadowed stone wall that Lurien leaned against with crossed arms. His stance was deliberately casual, and he even appeared to doze at times, though he was alert to every nuance in his surroundings. His long black hair usually hung in hundreds of loose braids that whipped wildly in the wind when he rode, but today he'd pulled it all back into a simple sleek tail that attracted no attention. Likewise, his dark riding leathers bore no silver, nothing to catch the sun or draw anyone's gaze from among the glittering costumes and elegant clothing adopted by the newly elected envoys.

Of course, most of them would recognize the Lord of the Wild Hunt if they really looked, but all were completely preoccupied in being seen themselves. And as they postured, they argued their causes and rehashed old wrongs. In fact, as far as Lurien could discern, no progress had been made at all since the envoys had first gathered in the palace courtyard. Seventy-eight representatives from the Nine Realms formed a ragged ring around the enormous mosaic map of their world in the garden's very heart. Most of the exquisite flower beds had been trampled early on, either by misstep or on purpose, as if the various delegates jockeyed for physical position as well as political.

No coalitions and no alliances had formed. No plans had yet been proposed, never mind decided upon. In fact, there was really only one thing anyone agreed on so far, from the largest *afanc* to the tiniest *bwbach*—they blamed the Tylwyth Teg for many of the kingdom's problems. The overwhelming majority felt that the Fair Ones had squandered much of the powerful magic beneath the Black Mountains, depleting it so badly that it might take millennia, perhaps even eons, to recover. Just as the allegations reached a fever pitch, and a fight was about to break out between a pair of giant sinewy *basilisks* and a troop of small but determined coblynau, the queen quietly appeared in their midst.

The arguing factions lapsed immediately into silence—and many individuals knelt—as she walked slowly around the broad mosaic map, where crystalline tiles and precious stones glinted in the sunlight yet failed to compete with the queen's radiance. Everyone knew that Gwenhidw was of the Tylwyth Teg by birth. But if she was insulted by the angry accusations (and there could be no doubt she'd heard them), she gave no sign. Instead, she once more stated her commitment to stand by and for *every* fae clan in planning for the future.

"Does that include dragon men?" A *pwca*, bolder or stupider than the rest of the assembled envoys, dared the one question that Lurien had dreaded. The proud Draigddynion—called *dragon men* for their reptilian features—were one of the Dark Fae races, and a band of them had been behind the assassination of King Arthfael. Gwenhidw herself had barely survived the attack that took her beloved husband's life. Lurien had devoted himself in the centuries since to ferreting out the venomous plot, but each time he uncovered one intrigue, another rose up to take its place. There seemed to be no lack of conspiracies, and almost all of them involved the Draigddynion in one way or another. He knew what he wanted the queen to say . . .

And he knew already what the queen *would* say, though they had never once discussed it. Lurien's blood ran hot then cold as she uttered the damning words.

"*All* the clans."

There was no audible gasp, but the Lord of the Wild Hunt could swear he heard one anyway as the shocked enclave shrank back. His queen stood calm as ever in the very center of the map of the realms. *How fitting,* he thought, *that the question had been asked just as she reached that spot.* She was as unyielding in her ideals as she was beautiful, as fierce in her love for her people as a warrior ferocious in battle. Such a sovereign there had never been.

But Gwenhidw was far from finished, and she turned her attention to Lurien. "If my *llaw dde* would kindly see to their reception, I do believe the Draigddynion delegation has arrived."

It was all Lurien could do not to gape at her. He was indeed the *Llaw Dde*, the Right Hand of the Queen and as such, he would gladly obey any order she gave, would kill for her or lay down his life for her, as she pleased. *But this . . .* She knew how he felt. Had he not brought the very king of the dragon men to justice for treachery against her? How could she ask him to not only allow an enemy into this sanctuary but also deliberately bring that enemy within striking distance of her?

Still, the royal gaze did not yield, and his lips formed the only words they could. "At once, Your Grace."

Lurien strode to the forecourt of the palace, his booted foot-steps echoing off the polished agate floor. His thoughts had turned as black as his clothing, his temper as dangerous as the light whip he wore coiled at his side. Perhaps it was the turbulent aura he carried that kept all other living beings well out of his path until he arrived at the great crystalline room where guests were received. It appeared completely empty, every carved jade bench around the perimeter unoccupied. He wasn't fooled, however. Even if he hadn't known of the dragon men's chameleon-like abilities, his well-honed senses told him someone *was* here.

Lurien simply waited.

A moment later, his sight seemed to refocus—and a single hooded figure, swathed in plain woven fabric the color of cold ashes, became visible by the tall columnar fountain at the center of the vast room. Strangely, the dragon man was facing away from him, though Lurien's entrance had been anything but stealthy. Was it a dare—or a taunt?

I could kill him right now. But Lurien could not bring himself to betray the queen's purpose, not even to save her from herself. "Our monarch will see you now," he made himself say, his voice devoid of all emotion despite the twisting in his gut.

The mysterious figure leapt to its feet and crossed the immense chamber faster than even Lurien's eyes could track— but an experienced hunter didn't need to see to fight. Instinct put his right hand on his light whip and gathered all of his magic into the palm of his left. There was no attack to meet, however. The creature simply stopped still—just outside the reach of the light whip, as if it knew its range—and threw back the gray hood.

Her hood. "And will you slay me as you did my uncle, oh mighty Lord of the Wild Hunt?"

The palace grounds were brilliant with flowers that bloomed nowhere else in the worlds above or below, yet it seemed that their colors dimmed before this woman's features, and Lurien sucked in his breath in spite of himself. The most ancient of fae legends claimed that the exotic beauty of Draigddynion females had been at the root of the bitterness and hostilities between the dragon race and the ever-jealous Tylwyth Teg. For the first time in his long, long life, he thought he might believe it.

Her skin was delicately gloved with smooth miniature scales of palest gold that shone warmly and invited the touch. Pearl-like prominences gleamed along her fine brows and blended into a jewel-like triad that laddered up her high forehead and vanished into the featherlike strands of her lustrous tawny hair. Her golden lips appeared full and soft, and might even have been inviting if not for the determined set to her jaw and the fierce look in her luminous amber eyes. As Lurien watched, her pupils flicked from wide and round to narrow and catlike, as if she had abruptly drawn curtains to keep him from seeing inside her.

And still, it was not her preternatural beauty but her *identity* that sent his thoughts spinning. He knew exactly who she was—it was his business as *llaw dde* to know such things. But nothing in the realms above or below had prepared him to meet her face-to-face, and especially *not here*. Mistrust harshened his voice. "Where are your fellow diplomats? Your retinue? Your guards?" he demanded.

She shrugged. "I came alone. I thought it better this way. My people are as suspicious of you as you are of them, and with good reason on both sides, wouldn't you say?"

Alone? This woman was incredibly brave or naively foolish to set foot in this part of the fae kingdom, never mind enter these halls by herself. It was far more likely that she was planning to sacrifice herself for the slim chance of disrupting the meeting of the envoys, or harming . . .

His thoughts were interrupted as she unclasped her heavy cloak and let it fall to the floor in a great ashen heap around her. "You may kill me now, or you may take me to your queen," she said simply, and she invited his inspection by turning in a small tight circle with her hands outstretched. A sheath of violet fabric, fine as thistledown, was gathered at one shoulder, and draped across her lithe form, hiding it and revealing it at the same time. "As you can see, I am without weapon or artifice."

But not without fear, he realized. Though she appeared relaxed on the surface, the Lord of the Wild Hunt had been stalking and studying prey for untold centuries. Every one of her muscles was tense and energized for fight or flight, and there was the faintest quiver in her breath as she awaited his decision. To feel fear was not cowardice, he knew. And acting in spite of fear was the only true courage.

Slowly, he lowered the light whip. Though he kept his magic close to the surface, like arrows in a quiver, Lurien's palm held no threat when he extended his hand to the dragon woman. Accepting his escort, she placed her long elegant fingers lightly upon his broad palm—and something like lightning raced through his blood and was gone almost before he could register the sensation. He studied her face, silently demanding to know what she had done, but the woman seemed completely unaware that anything was amiss. In fact, she wasn't paying attention to him at all. Her pearled brow was determined, her enticing golden mouth set, as she kept silent pace with him through the high-arched corridors all the way to the very heart of the palace. Again, he admired her courage. A stray snippet of poetry—not fae but human, Goethe perhaps—passed through his mind in deference to the woman at his side: *something mighty and sublime . . .*

As they emerged into the sunlit courtyard, Lurien fulfilled his role as *llaw dde* to the absolute letter by announcing the newest delegate to the gathering. "In the name of Her Grace, Queen Gwenhidw of the Nine Realms, I present Aurddolen o'r Draigddynion." And just in case any of the delegates were uninformed as to the significance of that name, he couldn't resist adding, "Recently crowned ruler of all the dragon territories."

The gasps from most of those assembled were loud and

unmistakable this time, but Lurien didn't hear them. His mind was automatically screaming a warning as the envoy stepped forward to take the welcoming hand of Gwenhidw and . . .

Nothing happened. Yet *everything* happened. The two rulers embraced for a heart-stopping moment as if they were simply dear friends meeting, then Aurddolen gracefully and graciously assumed the place hastily vacated for her in the circle of astonished diplomats.

"Now that we are all here," said his queen, "there is no time to lose. We have much to do, and"—she looked directly at Lurien then, and had the audacity to wink at him—"bold moves require bold plans."

As Caris watched Jay and Dodge disappear over the ridge, Morgan came striding into the barn, plainly exasperated. "Why does every man on the planet think he's a superhero?" she demanded.

"A what?"

"You know—oh wait, maybe you don't," said Morgan, blowing out a breath. "Well, it's just the way that men think they can do anything, no matter what."

Caris laughed. "Ah, like a man will say he's right as rain, even if he has an arm hanging off."

"That's it, that's exactly what I'm talking about. Liam just called back to say he's coming home right now, instead of waiting until tomorrow. I know that the doctors can't force him to stay—they're not allowed to tie the guy to a bed. But if Liam leaves the hospital, there's no way he'll take it easy, not with all of *this*." She waved a hand at the debris-strewn yard.

"Aye, he doesn't strike me as the kind of man to sit idle while others are working," said Caris. "You're worried he'll not be resting overmuch."

"Exactly. I told Liam I just plain didn't want him here, that it would make my job harder to have to babysit him as well as the animals. I gave him every reason why he should do himself a favor and stay in the hospital. Or in a motel *next* to the hospital, just for a night, just in case, but *no-o-o-o*. Nothing worked. And so now I owe you an apology."

"Me? My heavens, whatever for?"

"After I hung up, I called his doctor's office. They won't tell you anything if you're not family, so I lied my face off and pretended to be Tina so he'd tell me what the tests showed. Liam *does* have a concussion, but it doesn't appear to be serious. Still nothing to fool around with of course, and the doc said he'll have to take it easy, rest a lot, not overdo things."

"Right-o, everything a man is naturally bent to do," snorted Caris. "My da was the same once."

"So Liam needs some help around here, at least for a couple of weeks."

"Well, of course he does!"

"And I said you'd do it."

It was a long, speechless moment before Caris recovered herself. "You want me to work here on Liam's farm? With Liam?" Her voice wobbled a little. Something deep inside was fluttering like a bird—both appalled and excited—at the thought of spending so much time with the blue-eyed man.

"I know it's a lot to ask, especially when Liam's such a . . . such a . . . Well, *hell*, I don't know what else to call him but a grumpy old hermit. He won't be easy to be around, I know, but Jay and I have to get back to the clinic tomorrow at the latest."

"I don't know what to say."

"Look, I've watched you today, Caris, and you really know what you're doing." Morgan softened her voice. "I know you just got back to being human and all, but maybe this would be good for you while you get your bearings. Familiar surroundings, right? You said you grew up on a farm."

"It was a long time ago. Jay showed me the *machine* here that does the milking—I've seen them before of course. I know what all the equipment is, and what it's for, just like I know what all the machines are in the house. As a grim, I walked the human world, and I've witnessed all the new ways over the years—but I don't know how to use a single one of them myself."

"Anyone can learn to use technology, but you already know the animals, and that's the most important part. I know animals too, and I can see when someone is gifted with them. Please give Liam a hand for a little while, a few days maybe. Just until I can find someone else? You'd be paid fairly for it, of course. And then I'd love it if you'd consider taking on a position at my clinic. I'd like you to work for me."

Caris was grateful she wasn't the crying sort—she'd be in tears for certain at Morgan's kind offer. "And here I was wondering where on earth to begin, how to find a place for myself in this new life."

"You'll have more support than you know, I promise you that. Like I mentioned before, my husband, Rhys, was a grim once. And my friend Aidan, too. So you won't be alone."

"Fer certain ya won't be alone!" The familiar voice made Caris look down. Ranyon had his spindly hands planted on his hips—or where his hips probably were. "I'm not fer leaving ya here on yer own, even with Liam. I'm thinking you need a little backbone on yer side."

"A little *what*?" asked Morgan.

"You know, like in the TV shows that my friend Leo likes to watch. The police always call fer backbone when they fall into a tight spot."

Caris didn't know what on earth he meant, but she could see Morgan trying her best not to laugh.

"*Backup*," the woman explained. "They call for backup. It means—"

He waved a hand at her. "I know well enough what it means. It's when someone has yer back, right? Well, I'm not fer going anywhere until I know fer certain that *llygru* prince is gone fer good—and if he's not gone, I'm wantin' to know what he's up to! Seems to me, as well, that this good lady might need a bit of a friend while she's getting used to being human again."

"I'm sure Liam won't be *that* miserable to be around," began Morgan, but she trailed off when Caris shook her head.

"Liam won't be mistreating me, I'm sure, but he doesn't believe me one bit. I made the mistake of telling him what I was, so he already thinks I'm touched in the head," she explained. "As much as he needs help around the farm, he won't be trusting me, and he might not even want me here at all."

"Ha!" the ellyll snorted. "I'm thinking that Liam would like fer ya to be here far more than Liam himself knows."

Caris wasn't sure that was true, but she solemnly clasped one of the ellyll's twiggy hands and shook it gently. "I'm very glad of your offer, dear Ranyon. You're right about things being a mite strange right now, and a bit of understanding company would be welcome."

"Aye, well that's settled then," he declared, then charged off in the direction of the house.

"Wait—where are you going?" asked Morgan.

Ranyon didn't slow down a bit but called back over his shoulder: "We've got some planning to do afore Liam comes home, but surely we don't need to be doing it on empty stomachs, do we? I'm fair to fade away here!"

"He always is," Morgan whispered to Caris. "But for once, I can feel myself fading too. Breakfast was an awfully long time ago. Let's go see if we can scrounge up some kind of meal for the three of us, and then we'll put our heads together."

"He's *hungry*?" Caris was perplexed. "But he's fae—he could conjure a banquet for himself right here and now if he wished."

"Of course he could, but he won't. In fact, Ranyon could have done *all* the work for us today with just a few charms, but he didn't. He uses magic only where it's needed—at least, most of the time. He reminds me a lot of my friend Brooke that way. She's a very powerful witch, but she follows a strict code. She respects her gift by using it sparingly, and only to help others. You won't find her snapping her fingers to fold the laundry or wash the dishes for herself." Morgan hurried to catch up to the ellyll.

Caris followed, but slower, as she turned over the woman's words in her mind. It seemed respectful, felt *right*, that magic should be reserved for need. How different from the faery realm, from everything she'd experienced there. And how unlike the Tylwyth Teg, who used magic for everything and anything. *Can any of them so much as comb their hair with their own hands?* Small wonder that their hearts were cold, their emotions faded, and their desires forever unsatisfied. *They never touch anything that's real.*

Right now, Caris had never felt more thankful for her ability to work. She was dirty, hot, tired, and hungry—and it was sheer glory.

A little of the shine rubbed off that glory about halfway to the house. It was further than it looked to be, and as she trailed her companions, dodging wreckage and rubbish, Caris found herself wishing for a steaming pot of tea. How strange to want anything, to feel *need* after decades of nothingness. *It was like being numb,* she decided. Her body had continued to exist, certainly. But in its canine form, it was as if her human senses had been suspended, hibernating like dormice under an endless snow.

Now her body was making demands. It was bad enough that she'd had to adopt an enormous old pair of barn boots that surely were too big even for Liam, but at least Morgan and Ranyon had managed not to laugh. They couldn't help but chuckle, though, when her stomach growled like an angry bear.

They were most of the way across the ruined yard, stepping over and around a myriad of things so shredded and shattered that Caris couldn't even identify what they had once been, when she thought she saw movement from the corner of her eye. She paused and looked hard at a long, low-roofed building filled with old machines and tools. It was shaded and dark, but she discerned an immense shadow pooled beneath it all, blacker than the rest...

"Don't be looking at it!" hissed Ranyon, seizing her hand and tugging her along with surprising strength. "Pretend nothing's amiss."

She obeyed at once, clasping his twiggy fingers and swinging his arm lightly as if they were simply dear friends out for a stroll. It made sense to defer to the little ellyll. Goodness only knew just how old he was, but for certain he was far more experienced than she was in most matters, magical or otherwise. Just ahead of them, Morgan was completely unaware, explaining to them how the house had once belonged to Liam's aunt and uncle, and he hadn't changed a single thing since he moved in, and *wasn't that just like a man...*

Caris leaned down and whispered to her small protector. "You saw it too. What was it?" The ellyll just shook his head emphatically, saying nothing.

The roofed porch of the big old house was welcoming, partly because of its cool shade, but mostly for its sense of shelter, however slight. Still talking, Morgan opened the door and walked in—and she was startled as Ranyon abruptly shoved her out of the way and yanked Caris in after her. In a flash he'd turned the lock (an odd move, considering every window was already shattered), then planted his long thin hands against the thick wooden panels, as he chanted a brief but emphatic spell.

"What the..." began Morgan, but she got no further.

ELEVEN

A dull thud, like the fall of a giant's mallet, reverberated through the floorboards, and Caris could feel the vibrations in her bones and teeth. She peered through a broken pane as the charm's power spread out from the house in all directions like ripples on a pond. The magic itself wasn't visible, but its effects were. Every blade of grass flattened before it, and each fallen branch and scrap of debris arranged itself outward until the expanding circle reached the building.

The shed collapsed in an immense cloud of dust, both roof and walls, burying the machinery inside in a tangle of broken boards and twisted beams.

"Ha! 'Twas just as I thought," declared Ranyon, folding his thin, branchlike arms across his bright blue shirt.

"What the hell happened?" demanded Morgan. "Did I just see you wreck Liam's machine shed?"

"We had a bit o' company," he said. "And it was hiding in there."

"The fae are *still here*?" She fisted her hands in apparent frustration. "Dammit, I have the *knowing*, but I can't feel anything except that a whole parade of Tylwyth Teg trampled through here. Why didn't I sense that one of them was still within spitting distance?" Morgan pointed at Caris then. "For that matter, why didn't I know right off that you were a grim? If Ranyon hadn't found the collar, I might not have guessed."

The ellyll fanned his spindly hand in a calming gesture, encouraging Morgan to sit down. "Yer not losing yer touch, good lady. She wasn't a fae creature when ya met her, but as mortal as you are. I thought she was a human meself, dontcha know.

"But as for that great creeping *anghenfil* out there"—he pointed out the window in the direction of the ruined building—"'Tis neither mortal nor fae, and a danger to both."

Anghenfil. *Monster.* Caris found a kitchen chair and sat quickly before her legs refused to hold her. There were many kinds of faery beings, as she had witnessed for herself at the queen's gathering. But there were other things that lived in the worlds above and below, things dwelling in the Inbetween, *predatory* things that even the Fair Ones feared. She'd never seen an anghenfil herself, even when she'd traveled with Maelgwn's hunt to this land, but several of the riders had been very much afraid . . . "Jay's out there by himself," she breathed. "He won't know to beware."

"He won't be having to." Ranyon shook his narrow knotted fist at the closest window. "I might not be able to best a creature like that toe-to-toe, but I've given it a headache it won't soon be rid of."

"Are you certain it's gone?" asked Caris.

"Fer now. It's fled to whatever hole it crawled through to get here. And I'm hoping it's tellin' all its friends to steer clear o' this place."

"Great, it has *friends* too!" Morgan was punching numbers into her phone. "I'm warning Jay." Frustrated, she tried twice more. "*Crap!* The stupid thing says he's out of range. I should have thought about the hill behind the farm—Finger Ridge is practically solid basalt under the soil."

"*Pfft*, basalt!" The ellyll acted as if they were talking about mere paper instead of stone and abruptly plucked the phone from her hand with his long, twiggy fingers. He didn't press a single button but simply put the bright little rectangle to his ear. "Are ya there, Jay? Aye, it's Ranyon." They chatted as if nothing in the world was wrong, as if something huge and menacing had never been lurking nearby.

No doubt to channel her anxiety over Jay, Morgan started clearing broken glass from the countertops with a will. Caris followed suit, seizing a broom and attacking the shards that littered the floor. She was working on her second glittering pile when the ellyll finally revealed the existence of the otherworldly creature to their friend.

"A *what*?" Jay's voice through the phone could be clearly heard.

"Now, then, there's no cause fer alarm," soothed Ranyon, and after a short but vigorous conversation, Jay must have believed him. A moment later, the ellyll handed the cell back to Morgan. "I had a good look through the phone while Jay was talking," he said as he began piling books and magazines onto a kitchen chair. "Our boy's found most of yer friend's cows, and t'other horse as well. He's bringing them back to us. And you'll be pleased to know there's no anghenfilod anywhere near him."

Caris was relieved but also fascinated. "You can *see* through the little machines, too?"

"No, not the way he means," explained Morgan. "He used it like a scrying tool, like Brooke does sometimes."

"I'm glad to know we have a witch on our side," said Caris, and she saw that she'd surprised Morgan.

"I wasn't sure you'd feel that way," she said. "It's still not a popular occupation, and it makes some people uncomfortable."

Caris laughed then. "We have faeries and monsters all about us, and I should find myself concerned about a witch? Our preacher would be horrified of course, but people in my village were appalled by many things that have since proved to be without harm. As for myself, I'm thinking we need all the magical help we can get."

"Good answer," Morgan said, and smiled.

As Ranyon brought more books for his chair, Caris helped him stack them, then put a gentle hand on his spindly arm. "Are you certain Jay will be safe?" she asked.

"As sure as little fishes," he declared. "Anghenfilod are big, and deadly dangerous if you blunder too close to them, but most are shortsighted. It'll think our friend's just part of his horse. But since the good beast has plenty o' spots, there was never anything to be worrying yourselves over."

Caris waited in vain for an explanation and finally Morgan ventured: "Okay, I'll bite. How are Dodge's spots going to help the situation?"

The little ellyll looked surprised. "Why, a pied creature repels faery sight, dontcha know. 'Tis the mix of light and dark that does it, and even scrying will not reveal it. Few creatures outside the human realm can see such an animal unless they happen to touch it, because only touch can break the illusion.

"And as fer yer good Dodge, a horse as speckled as *that* one is a powerful shield against magic as well. Brooke told me that the peoples who once lived in these hills were wise about such things, and treasured their applesauces."

Morgan's mouth twitched. "Appaloosas," she corrected.

"Aye, those are the very ones," said Ranyon, heaving one last book on top of the pile on the chair.

"But . . . But you didn't have any trouble seeing Dodge, did you?" she asked.

Caris knew the answer to that question. "He's an elemental. His power is drawn from the earth, and it's not the same as fae magic at all." She looked at Ranyon, hoping he didn't mind.

"There are many in the Nine Realms who say that the magic of the Ellyllon is far stronger than that of the Tylwyth Teg."

Morgan goggled at him, but he only shrugged. "'Twas not strong enough to save my clan from betrayal and murder," he said quietly. "And the blow of it robbed me of much of my strength. Oh, I can still make a powerful charm, dontcha know. I have all the knowledge I ever did, and I'm forever learnin' more. But my talents are not what they once were."

"I'm truly sorry about your people, Ranyon." She put a comforting hand on his shoulder, and he reached up to clasp it with his twiggy fingers. "But I think you're the cleverest fellow I've ever met, and your charms and talents are truly amazing."

Morgan's words had the desired effect, and a small but genuine smile returned to the little man's face. "I do believe there was some mention made of a meal?" he asked.

"Well, we've been working on it, but the windows didn't just break, they *exploded*. There are glass slivers from hell on every surface in this room," Morgan explained. "I've cut my finger twice trying to wipe the counter, and frankly, I'm afraid to get any food out just yet."

"No food!" It was Ranyon's turn to goggle, as he clasped both hands over his stomach. "Well, we'd best be remedying *that*!"

"If I may, I think we need to remedy quite a few things," added Caris. "From what I can see, the rest of the house is the same as the kitchen or worse. We can't have Liam coming home to such a mess. With that lump on his head, he'll be having to rest—and not even a lazy man could relax in a house like this. I'm thinking I could start upstairs and . . ."

Ranyon winked at her. "Not to worry, good lady. The house is as anxious to be in order as you are to tidy it up." He scrambled up the tower he'd made on the chair, motioning to Caris to sit next to him. She did so just as he spoke a few words in a faery language so old she'd seldom heard it spoken (and her time as a grim had exposed her to countless languages both mortal and fae). A drawer in a massive oak buffet flew open, and Morgan jumped back out of the way as a variety of silver items flew to the table: teaspoons, saltshaker lids, pickle tongs, and tiny creamers. A kitchen drawer by the stove spit out several iron trivets and a cast-iron ladle.

"What did you mean about the house?" asked Caris. "You made it sound like it was alive."

"Well, most houses are, dontcha know. At least, they are after enough years go by. They gain a sense of themselves, so to speak, and they don't like to be disturbed overmuch."

Morgan sat down abruptly at that. "But I was planning to paint my kitchen!"

Ranyon chuckled. "Yer dear old farmhouse won't mind a bit of paint, good lady. She'll be like a woman with a new dress. Same if you move the furniture, or hang a fine picture. Nay, it's the bigger things that disturb a house's peace. Leo's neighbors, the ones that just moved in, barely introduced themselves to the building afore they were knocking out walls and windows, and building on a whole new wing. That poor old house has been grumbling for months over it now."

Caris looked around, wondering what Liam's house thought of the three strangers sitting around the table. *I hope it knows we mean well.*

While the little ellyll's skin appeared wooden, his movements were anything *but*. Ranyon was quick to select a number of things from the pile, then pulled out some treasures of his own, stones and gears and wire. His long fingers were adept at fine work, and Caris watched in fascination as he rapidly assembled a growing pile of copper-wrapped kitchenware. Each was bound to some little item with a flourish—a feather, a stone, a button, even a pencil—and the wire was knotted and woven into intricate designs. Ranyon's lips wove words over his creations, and in no time at all, he was finished.

"They're all quite pleasing to the eye," she said, and Morgan agreed.

He nodded in satisfaction. "Clean magic often is." Scooping up all his creations, he deposited them into a large bowl that Morgan had found. "Caris, with all the heaps o' glass everywhere, I'm thinking yer the one fer the job. Ya have the stoutest shoes of any one of us."

She tapped the boxy toes of her borrowed footwear together and chuckled. "I surely have the *biggest* shoes."

"Not for much longer," said Morgan. "My truck's out by the road. As soon as we're done, I'll go see if there's a pair of my runners in there that you can use instead of those work boots. They'll be much more comfortable for you. You know, I might have some other clothes too."

The ellyll cleared his throat. "When yer done with yer fashion planning," he said, handing the bowl to Caris, "Would you be so good as to take these and place one on the sill of each and every window or any other opening ya happen to notice. Don't miss a one, now, even if it's not broken." He patted her hand. "Top to bottom always works best, so make yer beginnings in the attic. It helps the magic."

As soon as Caris went upstairs, Morgan turned to the ellyll. "*It helps the magic?* Are you kidding?" she whispered fiercely. "You're not just fixing glass, you're charming all the entrances to the house."

"Aye, well, the glass will be put to rights too, so where's the harm? And top to bottom *does* help with some spells, dontcha know? Ask yer friend Brooke the next time we visit her fine shop." To Morgan's surprise, Ranyon deposited several of the strangely wrapped charms into her palm. She could have sworn he'd put them all into the bowl. "Yer a tall lass, so could you be placing one of these o'er the top of each door that leads to the outside? Set the rest along the kitchen sills, if you please. And best to be checking the cellar fer windows as well."

Morgan complied as quickly as she could. Hell, if the ellyll had asked her to run around the house three times naked, she'd probably do it—she trusted him that much, and his unusual brand of magic had saved many a situation. But she had a feeling he wasn't telling her all he knew. When she returned she laid a hand gently over Ranyon's twiggy fingers. "Are we still in danger?" she whispered. "I've never heard of an anghenfil. You said it wasn't mortal or fae, so what the hell is it?"

"Anghenfilod are shadow creatures, beasts of the Inbetween."

"The *what*?"

She must have looked as blank as she felt because Ranyon patted her hand as if she were a child and started over. "D'ya know how Lurien brings his Wild Hunt all the way from Wales to here, or how Gwenhidw comes to pay you a visit, or how any of the Tylwyth Teg travel over the Wide Waters to this place?"

Morgan nodded. "Sure, they use what they call a *way*. It's some kind of magical shortcut or a door between places, right? Sort of like being in Los Angeles, and on the other side of the door is New York. Jay and Brooke got into a big discussion one night, and they think the ways are really interdimensional gateways or space-time wormholes."

"Worse things than worms dwell in the Inbetween, good lady."

She was about to explain that there were no actual worms involved, but the solemn expression on his face stopped her. In fact, his uncharacteristic seriousness was more than a little scary. "Ranyon, are you saying that some kind of creatures actually live *inside* the ways?"

"Aye, and not just Anghenfilod," he continued. "There are as many kinds of monsters in the Inbetween as there are fae in the Nine Realms. Maybe more."

Of course there are. The more things Morgan learned about the faery realm, the more it sounded like a bad sci-fi movie that she couldn't walk out of. *I don't even get popcorn . . .*

"Most of the ways are very small." The ellyll held up a long, twiggy finger. "One person can come and go. Or one grim, but few will hold more than that. 'Tis how I made my own way here, dontcha know."

"*You* had to go through a way?"

"Aye, and a narrow one it was. If I had ta be doin' it again, I'd be choosin' an airplane. It must be a *brammer* of a way to travel— ya don't have to use a bit o' magic!"

There was no point explaining that modern air travel was anything but a wondrous experience. Instead she asked, "Can anyone go through a way?"

He shook his head. "Only if they have enough power to do so. Even a small way requires a great deal of magic in order to use it. Ya must open the way, and hold it open long enough to pass through, but ya must also repel the creatures that live there."

That doesn't sound good. "What happens if you don't?"

"Then you won't be returning, good lady. The creatures of the Inbetween feast upon magic, which is why they devour travelers like the Fair Ones whenever they can."

"But . . . But Queen Gwenhidw . . . and Lurien. They both travel here a *lot!*"

"And they command a great deal of power, dontcha know. Enough to use the Great Way that King Arthfael discovered, a way that leads directly from the Nine Realms to Tir Hardd. The Lord of the Wild Hunt alone has enough magic that all who follow him can travel it freely. 'Tis a fine highway I'm told, wide enough that five or six can ride abreast. A'course, there's a bit of a drawback," he said, and rearranged his Blue Jays cap on his head. "The monsters in it are bigger too."

Of course they are . . . Morgan rubbed her head as if trying to work Ranyon's words into her brain. Where the hell was Jay when she needed him? This interdimensional travel stuff was definitely his department.

"The Great Way is where the Anghenfilod live," continued the ellyll. "'Tis the only place big enough to hold them. An anghenfil is a great huge shapeless beast, like a soulless shadow, and blacker than anything in yer mortal world. They exist nowhere else—and thank all the stars fer that—and never have they been known to leave."

"Um, wasn't there one outside just now?"

Ranyon folded his arms. "Well, now, some fool's been stirrin' the pot, now hasn't he?"

"Maelgwn."

"Aye, it's his fault fer certain, that idiot prince and his private band of troublemakers, that an anghenfil came here. It's not likely Maelgwn would have enough magic of his own to open up the Way, mind ya, but all he'd need is a bwgan stone or two to magnify whate'er power he's got."

"I thought those stones were pretty darn rare." Her husband, Rhys, had one, a big one. He'd been forced to battle a monstrous bwgan that the Tylwyth Teg had sent to kill him, and had pried the dark glittering stone from the skull of the creature after slaying it. Morgan couldn't help but shiver as she thought of the horrible, toothy skeleton that was buried somewhere on their farm . . .

Archeologists in some distant future are going to have a field day with that *thing.*

"As a member of the royal family, Maelgwn likely was given a bwgan stone of his own. If not, he knows where to find a few of the cursed things. One way or t'other, he's opened the Way." Ranyon looked thoughtful for a moment. "If he was too stupid to close it properly, one of the monsters might have trailed him, hoping to make a meal of a grim or two. The prince had at least half a hundred of the great black dogs with him when he ran his hunt through Liam's farm."

"Grims? They like to eat *grims*? You didn't tell me *that* part!"

"I told ya, they'll eat anything fae, even warths and bwganod and the Fair Ones themselves."

"And ellylls like you?"

He slapped a twiggy hand over his heart as if it pained him. "I keep tellin' ya, 'tis one ellyll, and two *ellyllon*!"

"Sorry. I do try to remember, but the language still confuses me."

"*Hmpf.* But as fer yer question, no. 'Tis as Caris said: elementals have an older, deeper magic from the earth itself, dontcha know, and 'tis fair to say"—he held up a narrow fist—"it doesn't *agree* with the likes of Anghenfilod."

Just as Morgan was starting to relax a little, he added: "The creatures of the Inbetween do seem particular fond o' death dogs, though. I don't think one's been eaten in the past hundred years—they're far too quick to be caught as a rule—but the Anghenfilod aren't about to give up the notion."

"*But Caris was a grim!* Surely, she can't be safe here? And what about my husband? And Aidan?"

"Now that's a different story, dontcha know. Neither of *us* detected Caris, did we? If it weren't for the silver collar we found, we'd never have known what she used to be."

Morgan wasn't convinced. "What about smell? Or—or maybe the color of her aura? Is there anything to give her away, anything at all that you or I might not notice, but one of these monsters would?"

The little ellyll shook his head. "The only thing that could detect her now is another grim. Remember when Rhys and Aidan met? They knew each other's secret the moment they shook hands. But an anghenfil wouldn't be interested in them or in Caris, 'cause none of them are grims anymore. They're human." He shrugged. "No magic in 'em. And it's only magic the beasts are after."

Morgan wanted that in writing. The whole story just didn't fit in with any of the faery stories she'd read as a child—although she had to admit, *Monsters of the Inbetween* hadn't exactly been on her bookshelf. "Just for my own sanity, Ranyon, tell me again that they don't eat humans. Please?"

"Anghenfilod can't eat *anything* that belongs to the mortal plane," he said. "Now meself, on the other hand, I'm more than fond of the food here. And I'm fearful if that meal doesn't happen along soon, I'll be lying on the floor, too weak from hunger to move so much as a finger."

Ranyon proceeded to mug his most pathetic expression, complete with big sad eyes and quivering bottom lip, until Morgan couldn't help but roll her own eyes.

"I am *so* not letting you watch *Shrek* anymore," she said. "And we're definitely not done with this conversation. What I'm hearing is that we have a bunch of very large monsters running around that won't eat humans but might kill them anyway if they get too close. Am I right? Is that why you're charming the house?"

"No fae creature has come near yer own home uninvited lately," said the ellyll. "And yer the dearest of friends with the queen herself. Yet you and yer good man still take plenty o' precautions just the same."

It was true. If someone melted down all the iron horseshoes and nails that studded every roofline, every doorway, and every fencepost of the Celtic Renaissance Training Center, they could probably make a cauldron the size of a ten-person hot tub. Rhys added more iron charms all the time and regularly salted the fence lines and gateways for good measure. As much as she'd like to believe they were finished with the darker forces of the faery realm, she knew better. *There's never going to be an end to it. They're going to come back, sooner or later.* "We're just trying to be prepared."

"Aye. And I'm preparin' too." The ellyll sighed deeply. "Because it's worrying me greatly that the anghenfil might not be alone. Where there's one, there's usually many, dontcha know. And if they're still here, then maybe Maelgwn hasn't left at all. Otherwise, they would have followed him back into the Inbetween."

"Now wait just a minute! I thought the hunt had to return to the Nine Realms before dawn. It's a rule!"

"The *true* Hunt, the Wild Hunt led by Lurien himself, must return to the kingdom at the end of the night. Private hunts are expected to return as well. And if fer some reason they cannot make the trip in time, they must camp where'er they be until the night comes round again. That's only because it's written in the fae law, mind ya, not a'cause of any necessity. They're not like umpires that sparkle in the sun, dontcha know."

"*Vampires.* And in most books, they don't sparkle—they burn up."

"Aye, well, a hunt doesn't do either one of those things."

"Then why have a law?"

Ranyon looked aghast. "Good lady, the law was made to allow respite for the mortal realm during the sunlight hours. 'Tis not fair to humans for the fae to trouble them *all* the time."

She wasn't sure how *fair* it was to have the Fair Ones troubling them at all. Just the thought of the Wild Hunt roaming freely 24-7 made her feel ill. "Well, then, what about a *rogue* hunt, like Maelgwn's?"

The ellyll sighed again. "They'll do as they please, now won't they? Until someone from the realm stops them. But I imagine the prince has prepared for that."

Morgan studied Ranyon's face carefully, and what she saw there astonished her. "You think Maelgwn left the Great Way open at this end *on purpose*! But—but he's Tylwyth Teg, isn't he? You just told me that these creatures eat his kind."

"That they do. And he might be counting on that very thing. Caris did say that the prince wanted Tir Hardd for his very own. But he's far from strong enough to take it and keep it by himself."

It didn't take much to put it together, but it was nearly overwhelming to say out loud. Her voice came out as a whisper. "What if—what if he's formed an alliance with the residents of the Inbetween?"

Ranyon's expression said it all.

TWELVE

⌒⌒⌒

Despite her relief at being indoors, away from whatever might be skulking about and watching them, Caris felt like an intruder herself to be wandering through Liam's home without him. And that feeling was amplified by Ranyon's revelation about the house being alive in some strange way. Was it aware of only itself, or was it aware of her as well? Did it understand her intentions? Her curiosity was huge about other, more basic things, too—whatever did Liam do here in such an enormous space all by himself? It would take two of her father's stone farmhouses to fill it, and there'd be room left over. The attic alone, filled with dusty boxes and old furniture, would shelter a fair-sized family.

Caris had hoped to gain just a *little* insight into Liam from his home, but the house had definitely been decorated with a feminine hand. No doubt his aunt had lovingly chosen the pretty floral wallpapers, elaborate quilts, and lace curtains in the upstairs rooms. Of course, even if Liam *had* added any male touches to the house, it would be impossible to tell now. Glass was everywhere, pictures had fallen from walls, and countless things had toppled from shelves and shattered. The lush carpets were rain-soaked and dirty, shards of glass driven into them. Even the lovely hand-sewn bedding glistened not just with moisture but with millions of crystal-clear slivers. She entered a once-attractive bedroom that had been done up in delicate fern greens. The hues reminded her of Rhedyn, the faery who had attempted to help her.

Now the pleasing colors were just a backdrop for a thick scattering of dark, wet chestnut leaves . . . As Caris placed one of Ranyon's magical charms on each broad sill, she glanced out the gaping gabled windows. What had the yard looked like before the storm? There was only a mass of broken trees and a giant's dustbin of garbage as far as the eye could see. Added to the scoured fields and the great roofless barn, it was a sobering reminder of the immense destructive power that Maelgwn and his hunting party had unleashed.

Just for sport.

Anger surged through her. Anger about the yard and the house, about the farm and the livestock, and most of all, anger that Liam had been injured. *He could so easily have been killed*, she thought as she continued her task of placing charms as she'd been instructed, sometimes having to brush away a pile of glass to do so. *The Tylwyth Teg have neither care nor concern*, she thought. *And there's no one to stand up to them—or to Maelgwn—but Lurien and Queen Gwenhidw*. Did they know where the prince was? Did they have any notion of his grand plans to rule Tir Hardd? *And if I were to tell them, what could I say? He said he wants Tir Hardd, but he didn't say how he planned to get it*. Maybe Maelgwn had no plans at all. Maybe he was simply speaking out of temper, still furious that he didn't get to be in charge of the place. *Rather like a spoiled child who didn't get what he wanted*, she thought—except that this child was incredibly dangerous.

She finished her task on the second floor and went downstairs to the living room, depositing the little talismans along its tall windows. The bowl was empty when she entered the kitchen where Morgan and Ranyon waited at the table.

"I've set out the charms but—oh, I see you've done these ones already." She stopped and took a good look at her new friends' faces. "Whatever is wrong? Both of you are like to have seen a ghost. Is Liam okay?"

Morgan put her hands up. "He's fine. Honest."

"We're just not certain how fine he'll be after we tell him about the fae," said Ranyon.

"You're going to *tell* him?" Caris could hardly believe what she was hearing. "Then we must surely be in dire straits, for it's dangerous for mortals to know such things. The Fair Ones have been known to kill to protect their secrets."

"Aye, but we won't be asking their permission, now will we?" asked Ranyon. "And as fer killin', the Tylwyth Teg have never needed any particular excuse to shed blood, fae or human."

Or to imprison them forever, she thought, and shivered in spite of the heat. "You're both right, of course. It'll be a hard thing for him to hear, but a good thing. Liam deserves to know what he's facing and a chance to defend what's his." He would want that, she was sure of it. "But will he listen to us? Couldn't Ranyon just, well—just *appear* to him instead?"

"If he sees a strange and mysterious creature . . ." began Morgan.

"Who are ya calling strange?"

"Not like that, Ranyon, honest," she explained. "I mean, if Liam sees something he's *not familiar with*, he's sure to think he's hallucinating, and he'll probably blame it on his concussion. I think our best shot is to talk to him reasonably first."

Caris wasn't convinced. "Reasonable? There's not a reasonable thing about it. If we tell him a wild story about faeries, he's sure to think we're *all* touched in the head." It bothered her a great deal that Liam had questioned her sanity. She understood what it must have sounded like when she'd talked of the fae, but still . . . "I surely wish we didn't have to tell Liam at all."

Morgan rose and put a kind hand on her shoulder. "I under-stand. You don't know how much *I* wish we didn't have to tell him, but not because he'll think we're nuts. It's because once you know about the fae, you can't ever go back and *unknow*. It's like a loss of innocence for a human being," she explained. "And then you'll be watching your back forever."

"I hadn't looked at it that way," said Caris. She hadn't consid-ered that perhaps Liam—or anyone for that matter—might *prefer* to remain in the dark. For a moment, she remembered her own younger self, carefree and without fear, completely unaware that the faeries and monsters of the old stories were far from imagi-nary. It was indeed easier not to know—but it had also left her vulnerable.

"I see danger everywhere now," continued Morgan. "I'm learning to live with it, which is why I'm able to leave my home and go to work every day—I refuse to let the Fair Ones win by being afraid to live my life. But some days it's hard, and I can't help but wish I didn't know what I do."

The ellyll rolled his eyes. "Seems to me ya did everything ya could think of in order *not* to know the truth o' things!"

"Yeah, you're right about that. I really did fight it." She shook her head. "When Rhys first tried to tell me, it caused us a lot of problems and pain, long before we were ready to handle them. I hadn't learned to trust him yet, and I couldn't—*wouldn't*—accept the existence of the fae. Not until they nearly killed us."

"Here's hoping that Liam won't be as stubborn," said Ranyon.

Caris hoped so too. "Who's going to be telling him?"

"I say we wait for Jay, and then we tell him together as soon as the opportunity presents itself," said Morgan. "Normally, I'd wait and tell him on the weekend when Rhys can be here too—but with monsters running around, I don't think we should wait."

"And after we tell him, then what?"

"And then it'll be up to Liam to find the strength to believe," said Morgan.

He can do it, thought Caris, her instincts certain of it. *I know he can, if he puts his mind to it.* But she suspected Liam Cole was also a stubborn man, and she'd seen for herself a fearsome amount of anger and pain behind his vivid blue eyes.

"First things first, good ladies," said Ranyon, and motioned for them to sit on each side of him. "Both of ya hold tight to yer chairs. It's time to put things to rights."

Grinning, he clapped his narrow palms together *once* . . . And the entire house heaved beneath their feet like a live thing.

Liam stepped out of the cab in front of his roadside mailbox and paid the fare. His head was sore, his brain was sore—hell, even his goddamn *hair* was sore. At least he'd had his wallet in his jeans when he'd been taken to the hospital, and a kind nurse had come up with a tent-sized T-shirt so he didn't have to travel home barechested. He tried to ignore the fact that purple wasn't his color and, in fact, matched the bruising that was spreading out from his hairline over his forehead.

The driver eyed him with concern. "I'd be happy to walk you to the house, mister."

"I'll be fine," Liam replied automatically, although he wasn't so certain of that now that he was standing up. He knew the house was set back from the road, but it seemed like a frickin' mile away. Maybe two. "I'll go slow," he promised, wondering whether maybe he could just lie down on the grass and rest for a while first. Instead, he waved a hand at Morgan's truck that was parked across the driveway. "I've got friends here, so I'm not going to be by myself."

"I'll let them know you're here, then," said the driver, and cheerfully hammered out three skull-searing blasts of the horn on the steering wheel.

The noise echoed and pulsed inside Liam's injured head, and he fully expected to throw up or black out, or both. All was forgotten when a curvy woman with long black hair and a bright smile opened the seldom-used front door. Liam simply stared, not even noticing when the cab drove away.

Caris Ellen Dillwyn was even *more* appealing than he remembered.

She ran down the sidewalk and slipped a supportive arm around his waist before gravity could overpower him. Her body was solid and warm against his—and it felt more than simply good. It felt *right*. If only he had the strength, he wouldn't mind standing there until the proverbial cows came home just because she fit so damn nicely under his shoulder.

Smells good too. Of course, anything would after being inside a hospital, but Caris possessed a unique scent, subtle but heady, something like wild roses mixed with fresh-cut hay. How had he missed that earlier? As she looked up at him with dark, chocolate eyes, every question he'd so carefully planned to ask her about her canine claims evaporated. *Time enough for that later.* Right now, he couldn't care less if she told him she was a unicorn.

"Here, now, whatever are you doing back so soon?" she asked. "I thought you were going to let your physician watch over you tonight."

"I didn't like the food," he said. She didn't even crack a smile at the classic hospital complaint, but then he was pretty damn rusty at telling jokes.

"Well, then, I'll be glad to make you a bite to eat," she said. "Whene'er you're feeling steady, we'll head in and sit you down."

In spite of the fact that he was clutching her shoulder for balance, Liam didn't think he would ever feel steadier than he did in this moment. Somehow, it seemed that Caris hadn't righted his body but instead had gimballed the rest of the world into its proper place . . .

"I'd like to stay right here for a minute." *Or twenty.* He reached out with his free hand to lightly cup the side of her face. Her chocolate eyes widened, and her lips parted slightly in surprise, but she didn't pull back. Her skin was soft against his palm, and if he'd had the strength (and a mouth that tasted less like old carpet) he might have thought about coaxing a kiss from her. Instead, he held Caris's wondering gaze with his own as he withdrew his hand slowly, circling his fingers on her cheek in a soft caress as they left. He even managed a slight smile—at least he hoped it was a smile. His face didn't quite feel like his own yet.

"I'm as steady as I'm ever going to be, I think," he said. *Because of you*, he didn't say.

Caris seemed to come back to herself, as if she'd been far away. "Right, then, let's give it a go, shall we? We'll take it slow and easy."

Of course, his lower brain couldn't help but get ideas from a line like that, but there was also something simple, earthy, and oh-so-pleasant about it. It made him smile enough to aggravate his headache, which of course brought his attention back to where it was needed a hell of a lot more: trying to walk to the house.

Caris was a good deal stronger than Liam expected, but he was also a good deal weaker than usual. His balance was out of whack too. After a few awkward, halting steps, it was evident that she wasn't *quite* strong enough to keep him from listing further and further to the left. Thankfully, Jay appeared just as Liam was about to keel over entirely. With both sides bolstered, plus frequent stops to rest, Liam made it all the way into the house and onto the couch—but barely. *What was that, a whole hundred feet or so?* He felt drained and shaky, shocked that such a short distance had completely exhausted him, even when he'd had two people practically holding him up. Jay headed upstairs to get pillows and a blanket. Caris was more pragmatic. She eyed Liam's face appraisingly and passed him a wastebasket exactly two seconds before he threw up.

~

On her way to the evening milking, Caris was glad to find Ranyon sitting in the porch swing, his long, twiggy toes waggling contentedly in the summer breeze. She lifted the cloth from a plate.

"I brought you a little bit of something."

"Now that looks to be a *brammer* of a sandwich!" he said, quick to seize it in both hands. "My thanks to ya, good lady. Is our Liam still asleep?"

Caris chuckled. *Asleep* was too mild a word for it. "Morgan says he's 'down for the count'—I'm taking it to mean he won't wake again tonight. She said it was his own fault for not staying in the hospital, but that's a man for you. He's definitely overdone himself."

The sandwich—a wild creation of meats and cheeses that had been in danger of spoiling with the electricity not working—was nearly as big as Ranyon's head, but she'd already learned that the little ellyll could put away an astonishing amount of food. He'd proved that soon after he'd worked his charms on the house. She would gladly have cleaned the entire disaster, top to bottom, herself—the day hadn't come when she was afraid of hard work, no matter how tired she was. But with Liam insisting on coming home so early, there'd been no time for human effort alone to get the job done. "I should be thanking *you*, dear Ranyon. You worked wonders today, and you managed it all before Liam walked in the door."

"Seems to me, the man was half carried in the door," he said with his mouth full. "And no thanks needed. With a bump on the noggin like that, Liam Cole deserves a bit of calm and order in his house." He swallowed and grinned. "Besides, 'tis always a pleasure to undo the handiwork of the Fair Ones, dontcha know."

Undo it he had. When Caris had set the curious little charms on the windowsills, she'd thought Ranyon was only going to fix the window glass. Instead, everything in the house had suddenly begun flying back to its original place. "A spell o' restoration" was what he called it, as he sat watching his handiwork with satisfaction fairly glowing from his gnarled features. "And a fair bit o' protection thrown in fer good measure," he'd said.

It was the need for protection that still concerned her. Ranyon seemed certain that neither the lone anghenfil nor the rogue hunt were likely to return very soon. Morgan and Jay also seemed convinced that Steptoe Acres would be safe for at least a few days.

So why didn't *she* feel reassured? "Ranyon, I'm worried for us."

Almost half the giant sandwich was already gone, as the ellyll paused midbite and looked up. "Because of Maelgwn? That fool's already had his entertainment here," he said. "Look around ya, good lady. What havoc is left for him to loose? What trouble left to cause? Nay, he'll be on the move, at least for a time. He's got a big new territory to explore now, and he'll want to leave his mark on every bit of it like some great stray dog."

The broken trees and the roofless barn seemed to underscore the ellyll's point. And hopefully Maelgwn wouldn't be causing trouble anywhere for very much longer: Morgan had promised to try to get a message to the queen.

Yet the disquiet within Caris refused to settle.

Perhaps it was her time spent as a fae creature herself, perhaps it was the many occasions she'd had to witness Maelgwn's mercurial nature. Whatever it was, she felt right down to her now-mortal bones that the cruel prince and his rogue hunt would surely gallop this way again. Tonight? Tomorrow night? Next week, next month, next year? There was no way of knowing when. *But best to plan for it just the same.*

Jay knew of the existence of the Fair Ones, but he hadn't witnessed firsthand what they could do. Morgan had more experience in that area, and she agreed with Caris that Liam's farm needed to be fortified. She had promised to bring along as many iron horseshoes as she could on the weekend—and that was likely to be a considerable number, since her husband, Rhys, had built a forge at their own farm. The metal was a deadly poison to almost all faery beings, and most particularly to the Tylwyth Teg, and it was all the more potent as a ward on a building if the iron was first formed into the horseshoe shape. Just the presence of iron on the property would repel most fae—and Ranyon had promised to charm each and every piece as well. The iron would then be mounted on every building and fence post until the metal's influence formed a secure barrier around the farm, just as Morgan and Rhys had done with their own land.

But would Liam consent to the strange decorations? *Morgan and Jay are planning to tell Liam in the morning about the fae.* Would he believe what Caris had told him then? Or would he simply decide that all three of them were daft as brushes?

One thing she did know: if Liam Cole refused to believe in the existence of other realms and other beings, refused to be on his guard or take precautions against them, then he would be in terrible danger.

And there would be precious little she could do about it.

THIRTEEN

⌒୍ୠ୍ଽ

A trio of roosters crowed in the yard, each trying to outdo the other. Caris didn't know who was winning, but they'd succeeded in waking her. She glanced at the dark windows of the fern-green room she'd chosen for her own: daybreak was still a long way off, making it a very short night. Everyone but Liam had stayed up long past midnight, and her many fears had kept her awake for a time after that. She'd been afraid for Liam, certainly, and fearful of what the new day's revelations would bring. But at the bottom of it all, she'd been terrified that she would awaken as a great black dog once more.

Tired she might be, but she couldn't find it in herself to be anything but delighted. She was alive, awake, and a human being.

A tabletop clock displayed glowing green numbers, suggesting that the electricity had returned. Sure enough, she was able to turn on the pretty stained-glass lamp by the bed. Caris rose and pulled off the thin knit tunic—a man's T-shirt—that Morgan had suggested she use as nightwear. On the back of the door was a mirror larger than any Caris had seen in her previous life, never mind had the privilege of using. She leaned in close to examine the reflection of her face, then stood back to study her body. Still a woman, as mortal as could be—she pinched herself for the silly fun of it—and still looking much as she had the last time she'd gazed into the tiny mirror of her bedroom in the family farmhouse. The thought that entered her head was brand new, however: *does Liam like how I look?*

It still embarrassed her that he had seen her naked, but not as much as it would have in her earlier life. Though the Fair Ones had a weakness for fine and colorful clothing—the better to display status and power—nudity raised few eyebrows in the Nine Realms, and neither did uninhibited coupling. Caris had thought herself perfectly well acquainted with sex, thanks to being raised on a farm. As it turned out, what she knew was only the most basic mechanics of the act. And that was nothing compared to the artful intimacies of the Tylwyth Teg. Knowing their shallowness and their envy of human emotion, however, she wondered if perhaps they had no choice but to craft such elaborate lovemaking in order to feel anything at all.

And what would it be like to be in Liam's arms?

Caris left both the thought and the mirror abruptly. Her body felt just a little stiff as she crossed the room, but she welcomed every ache and pain from the previous day's labors, every evidence that she was mortal. And blessed whatever powers had given her a second chance at life.

That life included a wealth of new experiences too. Caris washed slowly, luxuriously, chuckling every now and then over the ridiculous opulence of having a bathroom just for her very own self. And indoors no less! The shower was indeed a "*brammer* of an invention," just as Ranyon had described it to her—she'd witnessed its development over the decades of course, was aware that it had adjustable hot and cold water, but she'd never actually experienced such a splendid thing. Great fluffy towels, fragrant soaps, lotions, and more—an embarrassment of riches surrounded her. Morgan had kindly explained which bottles were meant to be used for washing her hair—and in what order—and Caris was amazed by the exotic aromas and silky textures of the contents.

After such grand pleasures, she sat on the bed to indulge in a much simpler enjoyment: brushing out her long hair. "Black as a raven's glossy wing," according to her father, who had often said her mother's hair had been the same. It was also full of unruly waves—the exact opposite of most of the Tylwyth Teg. Thinking of the Fair Ones led to a whim: Caris decided to braid her hair around her head twice in a style that a few of the Gypsy women had worn. The Kale had always prided themselves on being a free people, and she was feeling gloriously free herself.

She opened the finely built door of the closet, where she had carefully hung the spare clothing Morgan had shared with her, and she was particularly grateful for the fine pair of shoes on the floor. They were white and blue, and even silver, in color—*imagine that!*—and strangely supple, yet strong. At first she hadn't wanted to wear such fashionable things in a farmyard, but then Morgan pointed out the scuffs and scrapes, and the dried dirt caked into the soles of the shoes. "They're definitely for work," she'd said.

Well, there was no lack of work to do on a farm. And Caris didn't mind one bit—it was grand, really, to have purpose again. She was about to close the closet door when something on the top shelf caught her eye. While the main part of the closet was empty, save for the handful of odd little plastic hangers that held her clothing on a rod, above it was a different story. She pulled the light cord to a single small bulb high overhead, illuminating old bundles of files, shoe boxes with the corners of photographs sticking out of them, stacks and stacks of books and albums too. But resting above it all was a narrow case of some sort—and if she stood back far enough, she could just barely see that the top of case was bowed outward by design.

In the end, she had to borrow the chair from the little writing desk by the still-dark window in order to reach the curiosity, but her hand trembled as soon as she touched the smooth ivory leather. Bound by dark-brown straps of heavy leather and fastened with bronze clasps, it looked like a tiny *cês dillad*, complete with a hinged handle. She used it to draw the diminutive suitcase to her. Even after she climbed down, Caris held it tightly with both hands. *It isn't. It can't be*, the sensible side of her scolded. *Goodness, you're getting excited over nothing. It doesn't even look like your old case.* "But it *is* the right size," she whispered. "You know it is." She was shaking all over now. Finally she laid the fine case on the bed, took a deep breath and unlatched it.

The *ffidil* was firmly nestled in soft white velvet like a shining chestnut still in its hull. Caris's heart pounded in her ears, she could feel a hot flush of color rise from her breasts to her throat, and she had to keep reminding herself to breathe—and breathe again. Flawless varnish gleamed golden yellow on the fine-grained wood of the instrument's top. *Spruce, most likely.* Her fingers automatically brushed along the strings, and she nodded as she felt the give in them. *They should be loose when a fiddle is stored*, she thought. Just as the strings of her grandfather's fiddle, *her* fiddle, had been loose when she first found it in the old trunk . . . The wooden pegs were cool and smooth between the pads of her fingers, and it was all she could do not to turn them.

Suddenly, without forming the intent in her mind, those fingers curved around the slender neck of the elegant instrument and lifted it from its bed. Turning it over, she gasped—the back was grandly striped, glowing like a gold-and-mahogany tiger. Her fiddle had been striped too, though more subtly, made of what a Gypsy had told her was flamed maple. She marveled at the vivid pattern, ran her hands over every inch of the fiddle, and then hugged it to her like a lost babe. Without warning, two centuries' worth of raw emotions exploded within her small frame—joy and grief, elation and bereavement, vindication and loss. Shaking from the force of it, she slid to the floor, helpless to fend off the storm of tears bearing down on her like raging floodwaters. She had the presence of mind to do one last thing, and that was to yank the quilt from the bed and bury her face in it to muffle her sobs.

~

Dawn finally brought an end to the catharsis. Thoroughly spent, Caris lay on the floor upon the rumpled quilt, still clutching the precious fiddle like a child holding a doll for comfort. *Crying is such a miserable business.* Her head throbbed, her eyes were swollen, and she still shuddered with each breath. The unexpected purge had wrung her out completely. Sleep was what her body needed now, but her spirit needed something more.

She needed to draw music from the exquisite instrument in her arms.

In the bathroom, she winced at her reflection in the mirror. She splashed cold water on her face, then held wet cloths to it until some of the swelling went down and the redness retreated. Some tendrils of hair had worked loose from her braided crown, but she wove them in as securely as she could. Finally she felt presentable. With luck she would be the only one awake, but if not, then at least there wouldn't be anything glaringly wrong with her. She glanced out the windows and realized it would be cool outside. She wrapped the quilt around her like a shawl, tucked the ivory leather case beneath its folds, and tiptoed into the hallway.

The door to Morgan's room was still closed. There was no sound from downstairs, so Jay must be still asleep in the back guest room. Liam had spent the night on the couch exactly where he'd collapsed—it just hadn't seemed like a good idea to move him. Carefully, Caris crept down the stairs, hoping against hope that they wouldn't squeak and wake him. At the bottom, she paused. Shouldn't she ask permission before she borrowed the fiddle? After all, it must belong to his aunt or uncle . . .

A light snore interrupted her thoughts, and Caris peered over the couch at the sleeping Liam. He was a strong man, but he'd certainly spent every bit of his strength yesterday. It would do him no good to disturb him. Instead, she pulled the blankets up around his shoulders, then gently leaned over and kissed his badly bruised forehead. "*Cysga'n dda,*" she whispered. *Sleep well.*

He didn't wake, but she could swear he smiled a little.

Meanwhile, the need to play was beating at her like the wings of the owl that had once gotten itself shut in her sheep barn. It needed to escape, it had to escape, it *would* escape. She hurried on. Her music was rapidly brimming to the surface—would it, too, explode from her as terribly as the tears had done?

Leaving by the back door, she saw the porch swing empty and wondered where Ranyon might be. Try as she might, she hadn't been able to coax him to come in the night before. She'd hated the notion of the little ellyll sleeping outside, especially after Jay had told her that Ranyon lived with his human friend Leo, where he had his very own room and his own bed. In the end, the little man had simply patted her shoulder and confided to her that he just didn't need to sleep as much or as often as a mortal: "'Tis more for the pure enjoyment of it, dontcha know. That grand feeling of lying down in cozy sheets and lettin' yerself sink into a soft mattress. Most nights, though, once Leo and Spike are both snoring up a storm, I go back downstairs and work a mite on my own little tasks."

She wondered what "little tasks" he'd undertaken while she slept. Wherever the ellyll was, that giant sandwich he'd eaten last night had surely worn off by now. Caris reminded herself to take him a bite of breakfast before she started the milking.

But before the milking, there would be music.

"Enlarging a *way* to such a size has never been attempted!" a kelpie gasped. The horselike creatures were often found gasping during the assembly. The air in and around the palace was pure, as unsullied as crystal, but Kelpies were designed for the fluid environment of their native rivers.

Still, Lurien knew it would be a mistake to assume they were any less deadly on land. He kept a watchful eye on the creatures, as he did all of the envoys in attendance. On the first day, only a well-timed snap of his light whip had prevented a pair of coblynau from being bitten in half by an ill-tempered basilisk. Since then, all the battles in the great garden courtyard had been waged with words alone—but that could change in an instant.

"The magic is ancient," said Gwenhidw. "But it exists. For the sake of our peoples, we must not be afraid to try what is new only to us." Though enormous in scope, her plan was simple enough in concept. The ways were the portals between dimensions. They linked places within the realms, connected the fae kingdom with the mortal plane, and even bridged the continents. If the Great Way leading to Tir Hardd were successfully made larger, the territory could be seeded with enormous *samplau*—bits and pieces of every environment from every corner of the Nine Realms. Infused with fresh energy from the new land, the samplau would flourish and expand until the kingdom was replicated, and every fae creature had what it needed to thrive in their new home.

The seventy-nine envoys had been deadlocked over this issue for days and nights on end. It rubbed Lurien's patience raw at times, but then, he was a hunter, not a diplomat. He would utilize any weapon to defend his queen, but he did not command words the way he controlled magic. Fortunately, no one was more masterful than Gwenhidw herself at tact and discretion. Her insightful negotiations were pointed and shrewd, yet their true effectiveness lay in the fact that she genuinely cared about each and every one of her subjects.

Including, apparently, the Draigddynion.

The Lord of the Wild Hunt still hadn't forgiven the queen for deceiving him. She'd known he'd never agree to let the dragon men into the castle, not after they'd slain the king and tried to kill her all those years ago. Not after the recurring participation of the Draigddynion in the many conspiracies that had plagued the Nine Realms ever since. Even as he seethed, however, he couldn't help but admire the clever trick Gwenhidw had played on him, and the sheer brilliance of her direct invitation to the new ruler of the dragon territories.

Even as he thought about her, Aurddolen's amber gaze fastened upon him for a moment. Then she strode boldly to stand in the midst of the bickering delegates. "Peoples of the Nine Realms, hear me now. The Great Way *can* be enlarged. Her Grace is correct—the spells required are old, older than the realms themselves, but they exist. As a member of the royal house of Draigddynion, I too have knowledge of these spells, and the ability to use them," she declared. "But as the queen has pointed out many times, such a massive undertaking will require every one of us to work together. I myself stand before you as a testament of our ability to put aside our differences for the greater good and to act as one."

He fully expected the room to erupt into argument as usual, to noisily end in yet another stalemate. But this time something was different. There was a thoughtful silence . . . and it was rapidly followed by a clapping and thrumming that swelled until it bounced off the walls of the courtyard. It would seem that at long last, they had reached an accord. The queen's bold plan would go forward.

The next time Aurddolen looked his way, Lurien inclined his head.

Caris already knew where she wanted, *needed*, to go. A stand of trees grew at the base of the ridge nearest the farm, and the high hillside at their back had sheltered them from the storm's violence. Even from the house she could see the high inward curve of gray rock above the treetops—and instinct told her that her music would flow through the space and fold back on itself, a tidy circling of sound. It was one of the reasons she'd chosen her favored spot on the mountainside above her father's farm, all those years ago.

Caught up in memories, she had crossed both the farmyard and the field east of the barn before she knew it. Stepping from the plowed earth and into the thick brush was a little scary. Ranyon had said the anghenfil was gone, and no one expected the outlaw hunt to return, not yet. Still, her heart beat faster with trepidation, as much as excitement. Alert for any sign of danger, she saw no peculiar shadows, heard no strange horns. There was only a thick grouping of trees gathered around rocks and fallen logs, leaning over a small stream like women visiting over the stalls of vegetables on market day. A few bursts of tiny yellow flowers dotted the area like sunshine dappling the ground. It felt good here, friendly, and *clean*, like the clean magic the ellyll had spoken of.

A tall mossy rock, long ago fallen from the hillside above, made a fine table. One-handed, she pulled the quilt from her shoulders and spread it over the stone before she relinquished the precious leather case from her grasp. She freed the bow from its clever little drawer, then unclasped the main compartment. Her breath caught as she viewed the exquisite fiddle in the early morning light. "Come here, *fy un hardd*, my beautiful one," she crooned.

The instrument was familiar and yet strange, as she worked patiently to bring it into tune. "We have to get acquainted, you and I," she said, and drew a long experimental note with the bow, then another—and another. The sound seemed to fill the forest around her, and just as she'd hoped, the hill sang it back to her, full and rich. That was the moment she stopped being afraid. Afraid she'd forgotten how to play, afraid that it wouldn't be the same, that somehow, her music—and with it, *who she truly was*—wouldn't come back.

All her fears fell away from her, time fell away, the world itself fell away, as she began to play . . .

FOURTEEN

⌒⌒⌒

The song . . . The song in the woods . . . The song pushed at him hard, rattled long-locked doors, pulled at latches, yanked open drawers and flung aside shutters . . . The song and the storm were one, and evil itself was coming, something dark and monstrous on feet that didn't touch the ground . . .

Liam's eyelids snapped open, but it took several seconds for him to realize he was lying on the living room couch. His own living room and his own couch, yet the familiar surroundings didn't reassure him at all. Nothing was comforting in the wake of such a nightmare—and even the beautiful part that had preceded it had shaken him to his very core. For a long moment, he remained motionless, alert and listening, but heard nothing. He relaxed a fraction, but part of him continued to be on guard.

It didn't help that the sun was in the wrong place. It should be late afternoon, maybe dusk at most. Yet there was a glowing pinkish orb just above the horizon, framed by the east-facing window. The good thing was that the light wasn't yet bright enough to stab Liam's eyeballs. The bad thing, that he didn't remember falling asleep, didn't remember anything before the dream-turned-nightmare in fact, except the upchucking part.

Great way to make an impression on a pretty woman.

Small wonder Caris Dillwyn was nowhere to be seen. But then, he couldn't see very much from his vantage point, and he wasn't about to make the mistake of sitting up just yet. Just the act of moving his eyes reminded him sharply of why he was sacked out like a drunk on the couch, although the throbbing headache was like no hangover he'd ever had in his entire life.

Maybe I'm not really awake. Obviously there hadn't been time to look around when he came home from the hospital. But the *last* time Liam had been in his living room, the better part of a chestnut tree had speared the wall right where Brewster the Mooster used to hang. The tree was gone now, and a sheet of plastic-wrapped plywood was fastened neatly over the area. He didn't know how his friends had managed to look after that so quickly, but he could accept that it was possible. As for the rest of the room? It was definitely causing him to question his state of consciousness.

Like many old houses with high ceilings, the windows were tall and narrow. The living room boasted six single-hung sashes, and every one had been destroyed. He'd heard them break during the storm, and he'd witnessed their remains the next morning. Yet now, the panes were not just intact but gleaming—which was a miracle all by itself, since he knew for a fact that they hadn't been cleaned once since Aunt Ruby lived here. He was no slob, but hey, *windows.*

Further study revealed no visible glass shards littering the floor. There were no leaves on the rug. The curtains weren't wet, dirty, or shredded. *What the hell?*

Slowly Liam turned his head to see more, and there was old Brewster, present and accounted for. The ancient moose head was propped up in a far corner and looked none the worse for wear—well, at least no more moth-eaten than usual. Someone had even glued his glass eye back in. *And nothing else was out of place.* Books and knickknacks were back on the shelves, pictures were back on the walls. If it weren't for the plywood patch, Liam might have concluded that either he was still asleep, dead, or had imagined everything he had seen during and after the storm.

Maybe he'd been out a lot longer than he thought. Christ, maybe even *days*. There was just no other way for his house to be back together—unless it had never been wrecked in the first place. Was that part of the damn nightmare? Maybe he'd simply dreamed that he'd awakened in the first place. *Maybe, maybe, maybe . . .*

No, dammit! I was in the hospital the first time I had that dream, I'm sure of it. And what about Brewster? The old moose didn't just jump off the wall by himself. And then there was Caris, of course. No matter what had happened to him, he sure as hell hadn't made up that gorgeous, dark-haired woman. His imagination definitely wasn't *that* good.

Liam put a hand to his aching head as if he could physically stop his chaotic thoughts. He couldn't feel more disoriented if he'd just stepped off a roller coaster. He never expected to have to question what was real and what wasn't, but in the middle of all the confusion, he was strangely certain of one thing—and his gut was certain of it too: his dreams were trying to get a message to him . . . Come to think of it, so was his damn bladder. Time to see if he could survive a trip to the bathroom. Slowly, gingerly, he eased himself up into a sitting position.

"Hey, welcome back!" The new voice belonged to Morgan. "Thank goodness we caught you before you face-planted on the carpet last night. Not trying to do it again, are you?"

"Morning to you, too," he said as she came into view and sat on the coffee table in front of him.

"Took three of us to get you back onto the couch, bud. You're totally *dead weight* when you're unconscious. Remind me never to go drinking with you—I'd hate to have to carry you home." She stood and put out both her hands. "Let me just steady you while you get vertical, okay?"

The natural fallback response of all males is "I don't need any help," but this time, common sense just laughed at that notion. "Sure, thanks," he managed.

A moment later he was standing on his own—and he was sweating by the time the dizziness cleared and his stomach climbed back down where it belonged. Whether Liam liked it or not, he had to admit that the damn concussion had kicked his ass and handed it to him.

"What do you think?" asked Morgan. "Stay up, or sit back down?"

"Up." He took an experimental step. "I'm okay." And he was, more or less. It was a long, slow trip to the bathroom even though it was close by, but he managed it. Morgan hovered as a precaution and waited outside the door in case he got dizzy again, but she needn't have bothered. He felt completely lousy, but he was elated to be mobile.

Liam surveyed his reflection—it was worse than at the hospital, the bruising more extensive and much more colorful this morning. His brow was swollen and his left eye was puffy, as if he'd been in a fight. *Hope I won.* He took the opportunity to lean on the counter, where he could brush his teeth, then drink a boatload of water.

Outside the door, he waved away Morgan's help—although the couch looked further away than he remembered it. "I can't believe you guys stayed the night," he said, striving to distract both himself and his friend. "That's some dedication."

She shrugged and followed him. "Veterinarians pull night shifts more often than you think. Like during calving season. So it's not that big a deal. Besides, nobody felt like driving home by the time we finished up."

Just a few more feet to go . . . Liam could feel his energy flagging fast. "Rhys is going to kick my ass for keeping you."

"Naw, he's still in California with the horses till Friday or Saturday. He wanted to get them settled into their new home before he left, make sure they were working well for the buyer."

He immediately thought of his own horses. "Did anyone find Chevy?" *Three more steps, two more steps.*

"We sure did." Morgan caught Liam's arm to slow his descent to the couch. "Your sensible mare came home on her own late last night. We found her standing by the backdoor steps, waiting for someone to come out."

"Thanks." He sank into the cushions with enormous relief. "She's all right?"

Morgan nodded. "'Right as rain,' as Caris says it. Maybe when you're up to it later today, you can come out and see her."

Liam closed his eyes and was just plain *thankful* for a long moment. It was an incredible piece of luck that both horses had come through the storm unscathed. He eyed the tall vet then. "The cattle?"

"Most of them made it. I'll let Jay tell you. Which reminds me, the power was on for a while this morning but it's off again. I'm afraid it's going to be like that for a few days, but Jay finally got your generator up and running late yesterday. Caris did the milking by hand last night, but we were able to put it in the cooler right away. Once the goats are milked this morning, Jay's going to run the whole batch through the pasteurizer for you. Oh, I found the number for your cheese maker too, and let him know what's going on . . ."

Although she kept talking, Liam had stopped listening the moment he heard Caris's name. *She did all the milking? By frickin' hand?* Forty does was no small feat for one person. Even Aunt Ruby in her younger days, before they could afford the luxury of milking machines, would have found it a challenge. He knew that his own hands, as accustomed to hard work as they were, would still be cramped and sore this morning if he'd milked the whole herd the old-fashioned way.

Morgan had mentioned on the phone that Caris was actually willing to stay and help Liam out on the farm for a few days. There was no denying that the timing was perfect. He'd heard plenty of storm stories at the hospital, and he knew his farm was just one of many places that had suffered damage. The demand for extra hands and equipment would be huge right now, and most would already be spoken for . . .

Yet Fate had somehow seen fit to deliver this unusual and remarkable woman to his very doorstep. Someone had once said, "There are no coincidences," and Liam turned that over in his mind. Any able-bodied person would have been welcome in his particular situation. But Caris, as capable as she was, was no mere hired hand. He wasn't stupid: maybe the help he really needed didn't have a damn thing to do with the farm. But he was so frickin' out of practice it wasn't funny. *When was the last time I actually talked to a woman I didn't already know?*

He interrupted whatever Morgan was saying. "Look, I'm not used to having a woman around, you know? I don't know how to make this situation work."

"Liam, you're not used to having *anybody* around anymore," she said. "But you don't have the luxury of being choosy. Jay and I both have to go home eventually. And you aren't in any shape to look after things alone, especially with the power being unreliable."

"I get that. I do. I'm not being choosy, honest, but I've still got a problem."

"Look, bud, right now all your problems are solved for a while. Besides, you've got a big house, so you'd hardly have to see her."

Liam knew it wouldn't help if he owned a fifty-room mansion. He'd done nothing but think about Caris Dillwyn every waking minute when he was nowhere near her. Dreamed about her when he slept, too. Even as he napped in the goddamn cab on the way home, she was in his mind.

Morgan was still talking. "I know you care about your animals, and Caris is downright gifted with them. I've even offered her a job at the clinic, that's how convinced I am of her competence. I'm vouching for her. Jay is vouching for her. Do you have any idea how hard it is to find someone like her?"

"Yes, the lovely Caris is intelligent, competent, great with animals, a hard worker, and probably sews clothes for orphans in her spare time. I agree with you, okay? But I'm trying to say that she's more than that. She's something incredible and—and *rare*—and I don't even know how I know, but I do," he said. His voice was louder than he wanted it to be, but he couldn't seem to help it. "I totally agree that I'm goddamn lucky to have her help. But I've done nothing but make a lousy impression on her so far. I don't know what to do or how to act, and now you're making that poor woman *live* with me?" He sounded angry, even to himself. "Shit, I'm sorry, Morgan. See? See what I mean?"

"It's probably just the concussion," she said gently.

"I'm not so sure of that. You know I'm used to being alone—in fact, I'm pretty sure you called me a 'Howard Hughes wannabe' the last time you were here."

"Hey, there's no tissue boxes on your feet yet, so there's still hope," she grinned.

"Thanks—I think . . . But do you get what I'm saying? You're not doing poor Caris any favors by leaving her here. I mean, I'll pay her well, no question, but—"

"But you *like* her. That's what this is really about, isn't it?"

After a long moment, he finally nodded. There was no point pretending differently—at least not with Morgan. One of the things he'd always liked about her was her directness.

"You," she said firmly, "are simply going to treat Caris with the utmost kindness and respect. And some honesty never hurts either. She's been through a lot that you don't know about, but she's not fragile. Give her a chance. Give *yourself* a chance."

"About that stuff she's been through—she's said some really weird things, you know."

"And all *I'm* going to say is that you don't need to worry about her. She's not a serial killer, or a con artist, or even a goat rustler. She's just Caris. In fact, if you really want to get along with her, you could try being yourself."

And wasn't that the real problem? "I'm not sure who that person is anymore."

"Maybe she'll help you figure it out."

Maybe. Trouble was, he wasn't sure that he wanted to know.

Morgan got to her feet and stretched. "Hour's up. I think that's enough couch time for now—for me, anyways. You get to stay there and rest up."

"Not going to add counseling to my bill, are you?"

"Depends. I'll waive my therapist fee if you promise to suck it up, smile, and make a reasonable attempt to get along with your new hired hand. Deal?"

"Deal. Except for the smiling part—I think that might be harmful or fatal right now with this headache."

"I'll accept that as a valid excuse. But only for a while."

Morgan brought him some coffee and a couple of pieces of buttered toast, then headed out to the barn, leaving him alone with his thoughts. And this time, he couldn't chase them away by moving hay bales.

One of Uncle Conall's oft-heard sayings immediately sprang to mind: "Receiving is harder than giving, son. But gifts are made to be accepted." Caris Ellen Dillwyn certainly qualified as a *gift*—and on so many different levels, that it made his head spin.

Something his Aunt Ruby said was finally starting to make sense too. Ever tactful and considerate, she'd kept her advice and her opinions to herself after his return to Steptoe Acres with his heart and soul in tatters—except for one puzzling thing. Just before the couple left for their new home in Arizona, she'd taken her nephew firmly by the shoulders: "Sometimes the universe conspires to give you what you really want, Liam. And it's your job to let it."

Could he let it? Could this exquisite gift really be for him? His head and his heart were divided on the issue, and any opinions from below the belt were automatically suspect. But his gut was saying, "Yes, yes, yes." At the hospital, the situation had seemed so clear-cut, so black-and-white. There was still no question in his mind—or his gut, where it counted—that he wanted Caris, but now he had a new consideration: Why the hell would Caris want *him*? What had he said or done so far to impress her, except argue with her, be an unsympathetic moron, and, as a finale, throw up in front of her? Christ, he couldn't have done a better job of turning her off if he'd been a teenager on a three-day bender.

Maybe there was still a chance to show her his *better side*. Mind you, he'd have to find the damn thing first. Kissing and foreplay and sex were simple compared to communication. Hell, even the most basic of conversation could be downright hard. *It's your own damn fault*, he told himself sternly. *You've been alone too long. You're gonna have to go slow and easy until you get your sea legs back.*

If he were really lucky, he wouldn't hurl in front of her a second time.

FIFTEEN

⌒⫯⌒

Exhausted but joyful, Caris lowered the fiddle at last—and jumped as she heard a sound like tree branches slapping together. Whirling, she saw Ranyon in the bushes at the edge of the woods, rapidly clapping his strange little hands for all he was worth.

"Dear heavens, you startled me!" She realized she had instinctively clasped the fiddle to her breast with both hands, as if to shield it. And that she was far from where she'd started too—her feet had danced her all the way to the head of the tiny stream, where spring water burbled out of the high stone wall of the ridge itself.

The ellyll grinned as she made her way back toward the quilt-covered rock. "And ya surprised me too, good lady. Yer gift fer music is a rare and wondrous treasure." He hopped onto a log and spread out a cloth of his own. On it was a lovely little feast of bread and cheese and apples, with twin bottles of ale, but though she was hungry, she barely saw it. Instead her gaze was arrested by something that gleamed on top of his bright blue shirt—and as she got closer, she recognized the wide silver collar she'd been forced to wear as a grim. The severed edges of the intricate chain creation were bound together with copper, and broken links hung from it on wires like beads. The entire thing was looped over one of Ranyon's skinny shoulders and draped across his narrow chest like a bright bandolier.

"Why are you wearing my collar?" she asked, and immediately felt distaste for having called the thing *hers*. It wasn't hers at all—she certainly hadn't wanted it. The collar was as clever and exquisite as only fae craftsmanship could make it, but it was nothing more than a tool to imprison her.

"Why, I'm hiding it, good lady."

Ranyon grinned at her as he slathered a thick slice of bread with butter, and she couldn't help but smile just a little.

"'Tis in plain sight, good sir."

"Ah, but it's not, dontcha know. As long as I'm wearing it, there isn't a creature in any realm that can see it or sense it unless I allow them to. 'Twill be safer that way."

Safer? All the disquiet that had been nagging at her yesterday returned. "Please tell me what's wrong, Ranyon. I feel that you're my friend, yet I can also feel there's a peril here that you haven't revealed."

He motioned to her to sit on the log with him. "Eat up. Ya brought me a *brammer* of a sandwich last night and 'tis my turn to offer a meal." He waited until she finally nibbled at a piece of cheese, then he nodded. "Aye, there's more to the truth than what I told ya. The real answer is that we're in deep troubles, good lady. I didn't want to cause more concern for Morgan and Jay until I'd thought it through a mite. And I didn't want to worry ya for something that's not yer doing."

"My doing? I don't understand."

"There was an anghenfil here yesterday."

She nodded. "You chased it away."

"Aye, it left in a hurry, but not all the danger left with it." His twiggy fingers held out an elaborately tooled sphere of silver, no more than an inch across. "I poked about the ruined shed last night and found *this* atop the rubble. 'Tis made of the same silver as this collar."

"What does it do?"

"It lures fae creatures—and it traps them. If ya were still a great black dog, this little charm would call to ya, lure ya to it like a fish to a hook. And then you'd be rooted to the spot until the monster came to collect ya."

Horror made her break out in goose bumps. "*Duw annwyl*, I could have been eaten!"

"If ya were still a grim, maybe—but I'm not thinkin' so," said Ranyon. "Anghenfilod feed on magic, but they have none o' their own. They can't use spells and they can't make these little things, or they'd have eaten their fill o' grims and every other kind of fae a long time ago. Only the Fair Ones can create these."

"*Maelgwn* gave it to the beast?"

"Aye, and then that fool prince sent the monster here. It wasn't looking fer any of us, dontcha know. It was searching fer a lost grim to take back to its master." He pointed a finger at her, and her goose bumps gave way to a chill that went right to the marrow. "Maelgwn is wantin' proof that yer dead, good lady—or he's wantin' ya back."

"Why?" She leapt to her feet. "Why isn't it enough that he kept me a prisoner all this time? How much more must I pay for my sins? I've lost everything and everyone to the fae. How much more punishment must I bear?" A burst of angry tears surprised her—surely she'd already used up a lifetime's worth of them that very morning.

Ranyon came over and patted her hand gently, handing her a cloth napkin. "What's all this about sins? You've too kind a heart to have many, and there's not an ounce of evil in ya that needs punishin'."

"I . . . I wouldn't give up my music. That's what started all of this. I couldn't do it." She explained her strict upbringing as best she could, and the little ellyll's eyes widened.

"'Twould be far more of a sin to stifle such a pure gift," said Ranyon. "And as fer the fae, 'twas never yer fault, dontcha know. Lurien alone is Lord of the Wild Hunt, and only he has the power to ride down the guilty. Was it he that came for ya?"

"No," she sniffed, blotting her eyes and wishing she could stop. Crying was giving her a headache again.

"A'course not. That idiot prince is the one who took ya, but it's kept me thinkin' half the night that he must have a reason behind it."

"I don't understand."

"Made no sense to me either, leastways not until yer songs filled my ears. Has Maelgwn heard yer music?"

Puzzled, she nodded. "I was playing in the forest above the farm when his hunt chased me down. He ordered me to play for them, and I didn't see as there was much choice. I . . . I thought if I just amused them, they'd let me go."

"Aye, they might have. Or they might not. 'Tis difficult to predict what the Fair Ones will do. But tell me now, d'ya remember what was said afore ya became a grim?"

She couldn't forget. It was the scene that changed her life, and she'd replayed it countless times in her mind, always wondering what she might have said or done differently. "Maelgwn was determined that I should go with him, and it angered him when I refused. I tried to explain that my father needed me—and I took care to be polite about it, truly. I even offered to go with him of my own free will in twenty years' time, but his temper just grew uglier." Caris thought carefully. "There was a faery in green—Rhedyn is her name—who begged him not to take me. Maelgwn shouted something about kings needing weapons, and that I was a 'sword upon the ground.' It didn't make a bit of sense to me, but I might not have heard it right."

"Or maybe ya did." The ellyll folded his skinny arms and rested his chin on them. "The Fair Ones have stolen away mortals since the very beginning. Not an eyebrow would raise if the prince showed up with a pretty human woman like yerself. So I'm thinkin' Maelgwn must have wanted to keep ya a secret from the rest o' the Tylwyth Teg."

"By making me a death dog?"

"Aye. No one in the Nine Realms would spare a grim a second glance, now would they? And under all that black fur, they'd never notice that ya were a tad different from the rest."

That was true enough. Grims weren't treated like dogs in the human world. Instead, they were little more than silent shadows, fae creatures and yet outsiders. She'd felt completely invisible most of the time—except from the bad-tempered prince. "But why would he hide me?"

"Yer music, good lady." The ellyll folded his arms in front of him with certainty. "As soon as I heard it on the morning air, I knew. He wanted ya fer yer music. 'Tis a weapon indeed, and a powerful one."

Her eyes widened. "Whatever are you talking about?"

"I'll tell ya a secret, Caris Ellen Dillwyn." The ellyll lowered his voice to a whisper, but it didn't diminish the impact of his words. "An old secret, one that few of the Tylwyth Teg themselves remember. Music has power, dontcha know. It enhances fae magic, and it makes magic of its own as well."

What? She could feel her face flush with indignation. "Well, then, why don't they be making their *own* music? What did they need me for? The old stories talk about the Fair Ones singing pretty songs to lure mortals away. And Rhedyn talked about the songs I could learn from them if I came to their Court. *Duw annwyl*, they sang the great crystals of the Glass Throne itself into being! So whatever was the point of stealing me away from my da?"

Ranyon reached across the little picnic and took Caris's hand firmly in his twiggy fingers. As before, she was surprised by his strength, although he didn't hurt her in the least. "Listen to me, good lady. 'Tis not a matter of singing the *right* song, 'tis a matter of singing a song *right*. The Tylwyth Teg can make all the music they wish, and 'tis true that it pleases the ear, and sometimes their songs can even bewitch a weak mortal mind. But I ask ya, are not the Fair Ones cold of heart? Do they have any deep feelings besides spite and senseless anger?"

She shook her head. "Not really, no. In truth, they envy the feelings of mortals."

"Aye, that's right. *Emotion has power.* And that's the key when yer making yer music. How those songs are born outta yer very heart and soul, how they're a part of you, is a complete mystery to the Tylwyth Teg, dontcha know. And that's why older stories than the ones you know tell of mortal musicians being spirited away to the faery kingdom. D'ya think the fae created the Glass Throne all by themselves? They may have written some of the words, but they had to have human help, dontcha know. Because only humans can give power to a song."

"But—but I don't have power like that."

"Look around ya, good lady."

Caris frowned but did as he said. What she saw made her catch her breath—the ground was carpeted so thickly with yellow flowers that the grass was nearly invisible as far as the eye could see. As she watched, more flowers grew up and blossomed before her eyes. "What's happening? Why are they doing that?"

"Ya did it yerself. Or rather, 'twas yer music that did it."

It couldn't. "That never happened before! Not ever!" she protested. "I'm not magic!"

"Yer music is."

"No, it's not!"

He patted her hand patiently. "Good lady, the last time ya tucked a fiddle 'neath yer pretty chin, had ya been to the Nine Realms?"

"I . . . No. No, I hadn't." A thought occurred to her that made her whisper: "Dear heavens, am I changed?"

"Aye, a little," said Ranyon. "Yer not fae, if that's what ya fear. But truly, think of what yer poor heart and soul have suffered. 'Twould change anyone, dontcha know. Yer feelings will be all the deeper for it—and so will yer music."

"I suppose they will," she murmured. "So what do I do now?"

"I'm not knowing that. But we'll figure it out, all of us together. And in the meantime, we'll keep ya safe as houses, good lady."

"It's not myself I'm worrying about. I can't bring more danger upon Liam. It's not fair to him. And Morgan and Jay should be warned as well."

"Aye, well, yer forgetting that Maelgwn and his cursed hunt have already set their sign on this farm, like a wolf marks his territory or a badger marks his trail. I know I said there was little left to interest the prince here, and that's true, but you and I both know he'll consider it part of his holdings forever on. So Liam has himself a problem with the fae already—he just doesn't know it."

She shook her head. "It'll be much worse if I'm here. I should leave, and quickly."

"Ya certainly should *not*! First, ya must know there's no runnin' from the Fair Ones. They'll find ya wherever ya hide. Best to make a stand, like Morgan and Rhys have done." He shook his twiggy finger at her. "But more'n that, d'ya think there's no rhyme or reason ta things? Out of all the places in the worlds above and below, you were brought *here*, and *here* is where ya were made human again. I'm thinkin' there's purpose fer it."

Caris couldn't imagine what that purpose might be. Her fears lessened somewhat, however, as she realized there truly might be more at work than she'd realized. Were there not two people in the house at this very moment who not only knew about the fae but were brave enough to live their lives in spite of them? And among their families and friends were Rhys and Aidan, who had once borne the grim curse as she had. Ranyon was right—what were the chances she'd end up here of all places?

"Feel better yet?"

She nodded as she wiped her eyes one last time. "Thank you, I believe I do."

"Here, then: I made this fer ya. Maybe it'll even put the smile back on yer pretty face." The ellyll placed something into her hand, and she gasped with pleasure. It was the nugget of blue stone he'd charmed when he first met her. Instead of being wrapped with grass stems, however, it was bound with exquisite copper leaves and vines, and suspended on a long copper chain with fine blue beads scattered throughout.

"Ranyon, your work is so grand," she breathed. "It's the loveliest thing I've ever seen."

"After hearing yer songs, I'm thinkin' that fiddle is the loveliest thing you've seen."

She smiled then. "We won't count that." Caris carefully slipped the ellyll's creation over her head as if it were made of spun glass, and tenderly cupped the pendent in her hands to admire it further. "How did you know I liked this stone?"

"Because it liked ya too."

Laughing, she threw her arms around the little ellyll. She was careful not to squeeze him too hard, but although he looked like he could blow away in the next good gust of wind, Ranyon was surprisingly solid. *Goodness, he is just like a tree!*

He chuckled and sat back. "A smart man would be givin' ya a gift every day, just fer a fine *cwtch* like that." His gnarled face sobered then. "But ya must know, the stone is much more than it looks. 'Tis as strong a charm as I've ever made. D'ya trust me, good lady?"

She didn't have to think about it, though she hadn't known the little ellyll for long. "Yes. Yes I do. Absolutely."

"Good." He held up a twiggy finger, and wagged it at her. "Now, fer the love of little fishes, *never take it off*. Not fer a single minute."

"But—"

"Not even if Maelgwn himself threatens to do harm to ya, or to someone ya care fer."

"Wait, I can't do that!"

"Ya can, good lady, and ya must. He can't see it around yer neck, dontcha know, but ya might think to bargain with it. *Don't.*" The ellyll waggled his finger at her. "I can't explain all the magical workings to ya, but 'tis fer good purpose. Some things ya have to have a bit o' faith in." He held out his skinny hand to her. "Will ya make a solemn pledge on it?"

Caris swallowed hard. It wouldn't be hard to keep a pledge when someone was trying to bully *her*. But if someone tried to harm Jay or Morgan or Ranyon—or worst of all, *Liam*—how would she ever keep her word?

"It really is that important?"

"Aye. Or I wouldn't ask it of ya."

She took his hand and shook it solemnly. "Then I promise."

"Right then!" He slapped his knobby knee. "Let me just be teaching ya a few little tunes that might come in handy some day . . ."

∽

"Liam, you've come back to us!" The voice startled him, and in the same moment, *eased* something within him. Everything in Liam's world was fine as long as the owner of that sensuous voice was nearby . . .

Caris walked around the end of the couch, and it seemed to him that the room became brighter. She wasn't in scrubs anymore, but wearing faded jeans and a simple blouse in tropical shades that loved her skin. Her long black hair was cleverly worked into a double braid that circled her head like a dark crown—and it was sexy as hell. But it was her broad smile that warmed him like good brandy. "Are you feeling better?" she asked.

"I wouldn't go that far." His voice came out hoarse, and his tongue was doing an imitation of a dried-out sponge again. With the pounding in his head, simply smiling could be harmful or fatal—but what a pleasant sensation to *want* to smile! He wished she hadn't caught him lying down, of course, but his body had insisted on more sleep right after Morgan left. "At least I've been up once, so that's an improvement."

"Morgan was saying so."

"Been checking up on me?"

"Well, now, someone needs to, don't they? Here, I brought some water in case you were awake." She produced a tall glass with a straw sticking out of it, holding it steady so that all he had to do was drink.

He took a couple of welcome sips, swishing it through his dry mouth before he swallowed. "Christ, that's better." It was only water, but it was sweet and cold, and he could swear he could feel his tissues expanding as he drank. Still, Caris pulled it away just as he passed the halfway mark.

"Your stomach's likely to be tender still," she cautioned. "Just let that settle a bit before you finish the glass while I make you a bit of lunch."

"Not going to boss me around, are you?"

She smiled again. "Are you going to be needing it?"

"Probably not today. Maybe when I have more energy."

"Let me know when that is," she laughed. Liam decided he was definitely in love with her laugh. His sensible side said that wasn't much of a basis for a relationship, but it made perfect sense to the rest of him.

He reached over and took one of Caris's hands in his larger one, holding it captive while he examined it gently. "A little bird told me you milked all the goats by hand last night."

She looked baffled. "Well, of course I did, and this morning too. I know you've got clever machines to do it, but they need electricity. Jay's already got your generator running some of your other equipment to cool down the milk. Your cheese maker's coming by today to collect it."

A small hand, yet strong. Her skin was soft, but there were also calluses here and there, badges of hard, honest work—and God help him, he'd do anything to feel those hands on his body. Liam looked boldly into her dark eyes as he brought her hand to his lips and tenderly kissed each fingertip. It was a delight to see the color rise in her cheeks, as a flurry of emotions passed over her beautiful face. Shocked, as he pressed his lips to the pad of her thumb. Apprehensive, as he kissed the first finger, and downright confused as he kissed the second. His lips lingered on the ring finger, long enough to shield the furtive flick of his tongue from view. Her eyes darkened with arousal, and crimson blushed at her throat. Caris tugged at her hand, but he didn't release it until he had kissed her pinky—and nipped it lightly. She stammered something about making lunch and left the room as if it were on fire.

But unless he was very mistaken, she was the one who'd been set alight . . .

SIXTEEN

⌒⫯⌒

"We have accomplished a very great deal this day," declared Gwenhidw. "And I think it well worth celebrating. I know that we had planned to do more, to attempt an even greater merging of our magics to send the first small seedings to Tir Hardd, but I believe we would do far better after a refreshment of the mind and spirit. Tomorrow will be soon enough to carry on our work. For now, let us rest and make ready, then repair to the great throne room when the moon reaches her height. It has been far too many years since we danced there. Let us remedy that together with a party, shall we?"

The envoys cheered her suggestion mightily and hastened to their quarters, laughing and talking as if they were the best of friends. Lurien didn't know which was more astonishing—that the diplomats were getting along so well, or that Gwenhidw had suggested an actual social event.

As for the vast throne room, it was seldom used at all, never mind for a celebration. In fact, outside of the queen's recent gathering to discuss her plans for Tir Hardd, there hadn't been a crowd in the throne room since . . .

Since the king died.

For some reason, the thought of the merriment to come filled the Lord of the Wild Hunt with a curious melancholy. Perhaps it was because the assassination of Arthfael was never very far from his mind. Though Lurien had arrived in time to save Gwenhidw from the murderous attackers, he would never be rid of the terrible sense of failure that trailed him like a hungry wolf. As for the queen, she had mourned her husband for nearly two millennia.

Did the announcement of a *party* mean that she might be healing at last? Or was she, as always, simply doing what she felt her people needed her to do? He didn't know.

Nor did he know what an actual *party* would be like. Lurien searched his memories, trying to recall past fêtes. He hoped to Hades it wouldn't be like the chaotic Court. The shallow and chattering assembly was perpetually seeking amusement and diversion, competing for the attention and admiration of their titled peers. Luckily, their lustful galas and raucous entertainments were restricted to the outermost ballrooms.

Lurien never attended the Court unless it was to escort and guard Gwenhidw—and thankfully, her appearance there was rare indeed. She hated the silly and small-minded assemblage as much as he did. In fact, battling the snapping beaks of *adar gwyn*, the white-headed gryphons, during a hunt was far less dangerous than an hour spent with the sharp-tongued wags of the Court.

No, he thought with relief, *Gwenhidw's party would be nothing like that*. She would host something tasteful and elegant. It would still be boring to *him*, of course—after all, his own ideas of entertainment involved untamed faery horses, ghostly hounds, and a fresh trail to follow over rough countryside. But while the envoys enjoyed the festivities, he would simply focus on guarding his queen and ensuring her safety. He would assign every one of his hunters to the occasion as well and . . .

"Lurien."

Startled, he bowed instantly at the queen's voice, but in the wrong direction entirely, causing her to laugh aloud. A thousand crystal bells were blended into that unique laugh, and the sound was all the more breathtaking for its rarity.

He turned to smile at her, an expression uncommon to his own face. "My apologies, Your Grace. Once again, you have surprised me. One might think you enjoy doing so."

"I believe you may be right." Her face was exquisite as always, her flawless gown capturing the delicate saffron hues of wild rockroses. The crimson-spotted flowers were plaited into her shining hair, where he knew they would remain fresh and living as long as they stayed within the energy of her aura. The queen of the Nine Realms gave life to everything and everyone around her. Only Lurien, with the perception of long acquaintance, could see the weariness in her eyes.

"Do you think it wise to have this party so soon?" he asked. "I would sooner see you rest, your Grace."

She groaned. "Do not 'Your Grace' me again," she said quietly but firmly. "We are quite alone in the courtyard now. You are my oldest and dearest friend, but you have become far too formal, even to the point of *stuffy*, since I called you to be my *llaw dde*."

"Stuffy? Now there is a word I haven't heard in this kingdom before. I believe your visits with Morgan Edwards are giving you a new vocabulary."

She favored him with a laugh again and motioned him to sit with her on a green malachite bench hedged with flame-colored foxgloves that grew nowhere else in the realms. "That may be so, but I miss your own irreverent tongue, Lurien. There is no one, past or present, who has ever spoken his mind in my presence with such piercing canniness. There was a time when a single word from you would shock many of our elders while silencing many fools. Yet throughout the labored proceedings of these past few days, you have been as silent as a shadow. Has nothing been said, no opinion voiced, that you have felt the urge to answer?"

"Gwenhidw," he said, and her name on his tongue was easy and familiar. "Most of my urges the past few days have been violent at best. I have not wished to speak so much as throttle most of the delegates at one time or another. When the coblynau proposed seceding from the kingdom? I very nearly volunteered to throw them all off the high face of the palace into the great chasm below." He sighed. "I do not have your patience, nor your gift for diplomacy. You are as perfect a monarch as there has ever been. The expansion into Tir Hardd is a mighty undertaking, and no one could bring about such a momentous thing, save *you*."

"I am very far from perfect, Lurien. And we are not in Tir Hardd yet." She placed her porcelain hand upon his black-gloved one, their contrast sharp and clear, yet balanced in their combination. "I truly fear for my people."

"I know it. But I fear for you far more. You work as if you never tire, and you take many, many risks." He clasped her hand as if holding a delicate bird in his palm. "I will do all within my power to keep you safe."

"You always have, my dear friend. But this time, promise me instead that you will keep our *people* safe. Promise me you will see them to Tir Hardd should I fail to do so."

Lurien's heart pitched within him. He had spent most of his entire life fighting to protect Gwenhidw, and the thought of anything happening to her was simply unbearable. As for the concept that his determined queen might not accomplish her goal? *Impossible.*

"You cannot fail," he said gently. "You love the realms and all that are in them. And while I'm more inclined to solve things with a sword and a spell, you've proved again and again that love is a far greater magic."

"I hope so," she said, sighing. "Promise me one more thing?"

He could not deny her. "Anything."

"You're so vigilant all the time. Always watchful, always on guard, forever hovering and seeing to my safety. Particularly with the envoys recently."

"I should not have told you that I wanted to kill some of them," he teased.

She smiled at that. "You did not ask me if *I* did. Tonight, at the party, I want you to delegate your responsibilities and just enjoy yourself."

What? "Have I grown tiresome to be around, dear Gwenhidw?"

"No," she chuckled. "Never that. Sometimes the weight of responsibility for everyone and everything seems too great, and it presses down on me. It would ease me greatly if just once, you attended as a guest and not a guardian."

"I will always watch over you," he said simply. "I cannot do otherwise."

"But you can still be a guest. You can still have fun, can you not? Just this once? I already know you'll put your very best hunters in the room with me. You could put two on each side of me—even three or four—if that would free you for a single night. Please?"

"'Tis a strange request, but I cannot say no to you."

She sighed and leaned against him with her head on his shoulder. Her satin hair spilled across the black of his riding leathers, like moonlight upon still, dark waters. "Since you cannot say no, will you also permit me to rest here a while, dear Lurien?"

His queen continued to surprise him. "Rest here for as long as you wish, Gwenhidw. For as long as the stars wheel in the heavens if that is your desire." He put his arm around her and drew her close, but whether he was comforting her or himself, he could not say.

⁓

Snatches of lively song came from the direction of the kitchen, and Liam realized he was hearing Caris's voice as she worked. No radio accompanied her, no music video on the TV, yet her voice was pitch-perfect. It was unearthly, idyllic even—and it shook him to his very core. The tune was lower, softer, as if it had been tamed down from its ancient wild origins, but he recognized it instantly nonetheless.

It was the very same cascading song he'd heard her play in his dream.

He didn't have a perfect voice himself, but he did have a faultless ear when it came to tunes. Liam knew without doubt that he'd never heard such music before his battered brain conjured it as he'd slept in the hospital. What the hell did it mean?

Aunt Ruby believed in psychic abilities. Uncle Conall believed in his gut and said it was the very same thing. Liam wasn't so sure, since his own gut had never showed a tendency toward precognition before. Yet it wasn't the prophetic aspect that bothered him. He could explain it away easily enough if he really tried. He'd simply heard Caris humming or singing sometime while he was asleep, and the tune worked itself into his dream. It was no mystery that she'd played a fiddle in his dream either. It was an instrument he himself played and loved. *Once.* If he'd been a tuba player, he'd probably have dreamed of Caris's bare skin pressed against the shining gold surface of the great brass horn . . . *Ah, hell. No question where the naked part came from,* he thought as he readjusted his jeans, and his focus, at the same time.

The issue was how the music made him feel—no, that wasn't quite right. *It was the fact that the music made him feel anything at all.* The song opened something inside him that he had hammered shut. And dammit, it was going to *stay* shut. It had to, it . . .

Caris was still humming as she came out of the kitchen and rounded the couch.

"Why are you singing?" The words were out of Liam's mouth before he could think and sharper than he would have chosen.

She froze in place, a plate and a cup of coffee in her hands. "I beg your pardon?"

"Why are you singing?"

"Ah. I'm very sorry to be making noise," she said gently. "I should have thought it might bother your poor head."

"No, I just—it's not *noise*. Don't ever call it that. It's beautiful, really beautiful, but I just can't have it around me. I can't have you singing near me." His voice rose a little in spite of himself, as if instead of explaining, he were underscoring the words that were pouring out of his mouth unbidden. "I know it makes no sense, but I have to ask you not to make music while you're here. Please don't sing anymore—don't hum, don't whistle, don't do anything. At least not here, not around me, not anywhere that I can hear it."

She stared at him as if he had struck her. Setting the food on the coffee table in front of him, she turned and left the room without another word. He heard the back door open and close— quietly.

So much for showing Caris his *better side* . . .

"Fuck!" he yelled, and threw his pillow across the room, where Brewster appeared to regard it with an accusing expression. "I know it," he muttered at the silent moose head. "I'm being a total moron. Again." When the hell had that become his default setting?

Liam muttered every curse he knew, sitting up carefully as he massaged the explosive pounding pain that was his head. He survived the change of position without passing out or throwing up, but he was unable to avoid the rush of purest guilt as he regarded the colorful plate with its tidy sandwich, trimmed and nestled next to a fan of sliced radish and pickle. Dammit, hadn't he just been thinking about what an incredible gift the woman was, that just maybe he'd like to take a chance on opening his heart again?

"Nice way to treat a gift, asshole," he told himself. When he was young and his mom was ill, and he was angry at the whole damn world most of the time, he'd come home with a note from the teacher about his latest outburst or scuffle. Aunt Ruby would sit him down privately and hold what she called "a social autopsy." Kind of like *CSI* investigating a social error—*Here's the corpse of the situation, what do you think killed it?*—with the hope of preventing further fatalities. Often as not, it boiled down to missed cues.

Hell, he'd done more than miss a signal this time. Caris hadn't gotten a chance to give him a cue of any kind, not in time at least. He'd bolted from a musical dream that turned into a nightmare, and the very first time he heard her singing, he practically jumped down her throat.

Liam had seen something in her face *then*, all right, something that didn't add up.

Okay, moron, think. He'd probably been too loud, but he hadn't yelled, not exactly, and he hadn't been particularly rude. He'd even said *please*. Puzzlement in her eyes at his strange request would have been understandable. Concern for the crazy guy with the head injury, certainly. Rolling her eyes at him for being "cranky as a wet cat"—as she'd once put it—would also be an appropriate reaction. So would some solid indignation, if she thought he was criticizing her talent or insulting her in some way, although he'd *said* her singing was beautiful. *Yeah, so lovely that you asked her not to do it! Who wouldn't believe that?*

Instead, Liam had seen a raw, deep hurt and an even deeper disappointment, laced with grief and anger. *I hit a nerve of some kind*, he thought. But he couldn't begin to guess what it was connected to.

On top of it all, what the hell had struck his own nerves? Liam was as baffled by his outburst as he was by Caris's reaction to it. Maybe he should have told her the real story. That he'd turned his back on his own music—and then it had turned its back on him. He could neither play nor write, and worse, he didn't want to. And dreaming of Caris's song, that primal, enlivening tune, had set off a terrible struggle within him. He was torn between following it and running away from it.

Her music had not only made him feel; it made him feel much too deeply, tearing him wide open and laying bare much more than his heart: it had uncovered his goddamn *soul*.

And while his gut might persuade his heart to consider a relationship, his soul was not on board with anything of the kind. His soul was where his music lived—or *had* lived—and it was definitely closed for business, windows and doors nailed shut. If Caris could cross that barricade with only a casual tune, how on earth could he bear to have her around?

Boundaries. He'd have to set boundaries, that's all—and in the moment he thought it, he realized how crazy that was. *You can come this close to me, but no further. You can make me feel this much, but no more. Yeah, right, that'll work. Not!*

Obviously, it just wouldn't work out. She'd have to go, that was all there was to it. He could still send her away, back to wherever she came from, couldn't he? It wasn't too late to ask Morgan and Jay to give her a ride, not too late to pull back from where his heart was headed. Not too late to put the brakes on and . . .

Hell yeah, it was too late.

Liam slumped back on the couch. He'd had the very same dream twice, heard Caris's strange wild song in that dream and again in waking life. It wouldn't matter if he sent the flesh-and-blood woman to the other side of the damn world. He had no control over the dream woman that lived in his head or the tune that was stuck in there with her. *And when you have that nightmare again, or think about Caris for the hundredth time in a day, what are you going to do* then, *smart guy?*

He had no idea. But for now, he'd better be thinking up a damn good apology. It might be too late to fix things—Christ, he hoped it wasn't—but she deserved to hear him say that he was sorry. Of course, that meant he had to fight his way off this frickin' couch and follow her . . .

The back door slammed behind her, but Caris didn't even notice. She walked briskly into the living room to find Liam standing unsteadily, with his hand braced on the bookcase for support. The surprise of seeing her nearly took him down again, but he grabbed a shelf with his other hand and tried to adopt a casual pose. Normally she'd offer to help, ask if he was okay, but at this particular moment, she didn't care.

"How dare you," she said. It was not a question, and the fury that was in her made her voice thick. She'd barely gotten halfway across the yard before raw anger erupted from somewhere deep inside her and turned her right around. "How *dare* you tell me not to sing!"

"Caris, I was wrong. I'm sorry. I just got myself up to see if I could follow you—as you can see, I wasn't nearly fast enough. I want to apologize, explain—"

"Let me explain something to *you*, good sir. I grew up with everyone and their dog telling me it's a wicked, wicked sin to sing, to make up songs, to play music, *to be who I am*. And I've spent an even longer time without the ability to sing or play or do any of those things that make me *myself*."

Her feet took her across the room until she was within what her da would have called "spittin' distance" of Liam Cole. She had to look up into those vivid blue eyes, but she wouldn't let them mesmerize her this time. She needed music like she needed air. Hadn't she always told herself that it would better to be alone than to be with someone who couldn't understand that? It was yet true—though she hadn't expected it to hurt so much. Still, the words had to be said. "There's no denying there's something between us, Liam. We've done nothing but make eyes at each other since we met. But you need to be understanding that if you cannot abide music, then you cannot abide me. I'll not be separated from it again."

Fully expecting that she'd burned her bridge, Caris turned to leave, but a big hand on her shoulder tugged her back.

"My turn," said Liam. "You've said your piece, and you're right. You're right about all of it, except for one thing. *I don't want you to be without your music.* I wouldn't wish that on anyone, because that's what happened to me."

When she looked up into his eyes this time, she saw the shadows in them too, all the anguish and the anger she'd glimpsed at their very first meeting. His words registered slowly in her brain, perhaps because she was afraid she hadn't heard them right. *Dear heavens, does he feel the same way about music as I do?*

"Will you tell me?" she managed at last.

He closed his eyes and nodded once.

SEVENTEEN

~⫘~

The moon was at its apex. Lurien might not be enthused about the party, but he would not draw attention to himself by being late. He entered casually through a side door of the massive throne room and stopped still . . . If this was indeed the majestic hall in which the queen had so recently called a great gathering of her people, then every whit of its formality had been very well hidden. The towering agate pillars glittered with the many-colored reflections of thousands upon thousands of floating lanterns. The glowing lamps hid almost the entirety of the vast vaulted ceiling, save the high clear center of the dome itself, which was reserved for the moon to shine through. Lurien was almost embarrassed for the orb—it was at its fullest and most perfect, and it had garbed itself in warm yellow gold for the occasion, yet its light was all but swallowed up in the splendor below.

Cleverly tooled shapes cut away from the gently rotating lanterns cast countless, ever-changing shadows on the polished walls: creatures of every kind, from every realm and every world. Lions danced with unicorns. Deer pranced with warths. Songbirds circled bwganod. Lurien frowned however at the numerous dragons among the shadow figures—dragons with great horned wings, dragons that breathed fire, dragons with sharp teeth and long tails . . .

As if that didn't make Lurien uncomfortable enough, Gwenhidw had neglected to mention that she had planned a *costume party*. Frustrated and furious, his powerful fists clenched hard enough that they would have driven his nails deep into his palms if it hadn't been for his black leather gloves. For reasons he could not fathom, his queen's main mission in life seemed less to expand the kingdom and more to imagine new and awkward surprises for her *llaw dde. Surely no right hand in the history of the Nine Realms has had to contend with such a security nightmare.*

The seventy-nine envoys had been joined by all their advisers and assistants, and every one of them was masked. *Masked!* And from the crush of guests in attendance, it was obvious that countless invitations had gone out beyond the palace walls. Like the myriad shadows on the lofty walls, the costumes drew from both fae and human realms. The effect was nothing short of fantastical. Lurien was looking out over a sea of wildly imaginative guises and headdresses that bobbed and bounced as the wearers danced, pranced, minced, conversed, and even sang—some quite badly.

For the most part, Lurien could not distinguish who was an envoy and who was not—except for a few of the larger and more obvious creatures such as the kelpies and the glittering fire drakes. It took every ounce of his self-control not to stare, however, as a huge basilisk slithered by him wearing a kitten mask . . . Meanwhile, an entire contingent of knee-high coblynau, dressed as human football players replete with shoulder pads and helmets, were sampling more or less continuously from the groaning boards of exotic foods that lined one wall. Elaborate silver fountains had been strategically placed around the vast dance floor, dispensing jewel-colored streams of exquisite wines and rare ales. A pair of eerily beautiful *undines* with large, luminous eyes lounged in one of the bigger fountains. Their notion of costuming appeared to have been to paint their naked bodies with crushed gems. As each enticing curve caught the light of the multicolored lanterns overhead, it was hard to argue with their choice.

Still Lurien's dark eyes didn't linger. He was studying the crowd, seeking the person behind the party—though whether to throttle her or protect her he didn't yet know. Perhaps both. At one end of the cavernous room, the great Glass Throne sat empty upon the green jasper dais, save for a shining drape of silver fabric carelessly tossed over one clear arm. *Of course she wouldn't be there. She'd be in the very midst of the chaos.* He changed his focus then, looking instead for the hunters he had assigned to watch her. Lurien alone wore black, and only black. It was as much his signature as his waist-length dark hair, and it was eminently practical when trying to blend with shadows while hunting or while carrying out his duties to the queen. What his men would be wearing, however, was anyone's guess. They were not soldiers, per se, but simply trusted followers and friends, loyal to him and, more important, to their queen.

"She's all right, you know," a silky voice whispered in his ear.

Lurien whirled to find himself face-to-face with a lioness. The mask was exceptionally realistic, right down to a muzzle wrinkled back to expose long bared fangs. Ever the hunter, he admired the big cats that still roamed the human world and wished that such felines lived in the Nine Realms. Automatically he scanned the rest of the costume—and discovered that the leonine fur was not a garment at all. Rather it was a whisper-thin pelt that blushed over a completely naked female body. Golden nipples peeked shamelessly from the fine, soft fur that defined rather than covered rounded breasts. The only marking on her tawny pelt was a long narrow stripe of palest gold that ran all the way from her delicate throat to the enticing female cleft between her long, shapely legs.

He wrested his gaze back to the lioness's face, and one of her amber eyes winked at him wickedly. "Aurddolen," he acknowledged, finding that his voice betrayed him. His attempt at disapproval came out mixed with amusement—and interest.

"Come, I'll show you the one you seek." Aurddolen linked her arm with his and guided him through the jostling throng of revelers to the tightly packed dance floor. Here, the dragon-woman-turned-lioness stopped. "See?" she half shouted to him.

He didn't see, not at all. Where the dancing was at its most feverish, the Lord of the Wild Hunt studied the crowd—and finally focused in on a tall fae dressed as a terrifying warth. As the unlikely creature stepped lively to the tune, the tip of a diagonal scar across its throat became visible for a mere eyeblink. It was enough to identify Trahern, one of the men he'd assigned to the queen's side. And only Lurien knew that the scar was from a long ago battle with a *real* warth.

Quickly, he discerned Iago, Wren, and Nodin—and even as he continued to search for Gwenhidw, Lurien made a mental note to commend Nodin later (with much jesting) for his unlikely mermaid costume. Finally a monstrous black horse cleared some of the dancers in front of Lurien with a burst of flame from its nostrils. The nightmare creature with glowing yellow eyes was a pwca, and several of them had accompanied their envoy to the palace. It seemed to be having a fine time. Festive flowers, copper bells, and silver ribbons had been braided into its long mane, and sparks flew from its sharp silver hooves as it danced nimbly . . .

Gwenhidw!

Thankfully, a lifetime spent stalking prey made him shout her name only in his mind. As if she'd heard him just the same, however, she wheeled and insolently flicked him in the head with her long tail. Before he could protest, Aurddolen seized his arm and dragged him into the crowd.

"I told you she was fine," she shouted into his ear. "You'll only draw attention to her if you stay." She grinned then and raised her mask so that her lovely and unconventional features were revealed in the shadow of the lioness's teeth. As a wild tune began, she grasped his hands and playfully whirled him away.

Lurien didn't dance as a rule, but that didn't mean he didn't know how. He knew this tune and its implications. It was part music, part sexual enchantment, and lovers often used it to excite each other. The charmed song was a long one, building slowly from something light and merry to a final frenzied culmination— and at that point there would be many uninhibited couplings in the midst of the dance floor. No one would think twice of that, of course, particularly if they had visited the ever-salacious Court.

So Aurddolen thinks to play with the Lord of the Wild Hunt?

Lurien closed his gloved hands over hers, and their gazes locked. It was satisfying to see her sudden understanding that she had just lost control of this encounter, and before she could think, he spun her swiftly across the floor. With grace and power, he ably threaded them both through the pulsing crowd, and as the music demanded more, he made bracelets of his strong hands and slid them over her wrists and all the way up her slender arms. Manacled thus, she could neither escape nor strike him should she wish. Aurddolen didn't appear to want to do either one, so far at least, but he found himself with an urgent craving. He pulled her close and bent his head to her ear. "Unfasten my tunic," he said, in a low resonant tone he knew a draigddynion could hear despite the background noise. "I would have us skin to skin."

Her eyes widened, and her pupils swelled from narrow cat-like slits to round black moons. Only the barest glimmer of amber iris was visible, as if eclipsed by desire. As the throbbing beat and anxious keening music intensified, she brought her hands up with difficulty—he wasn't foolish enough to let her go—and slowly undid the rich black leather that covered his chest.

She spread his open tunic wide, splaying her hands across his muscles as she did so, and he wanted more. As the music pounded faster, the dance brought their bodies close, closer. Her golden nipples, her soft breasts, the fine velvety fur she had cloaked herself in—all brushed over his skin and electrified it. He leaned into her so that his own nipples could be lightly caressed by hers, and his cock immediately reared within in its leather confines, fighting to be free like a stallion fought its bridle.

Enough, thought Lurien. He flexed his magic like a well-toned muscle, willing both he and Aurddolen far from the sights and sounds of the writhing crowd.

The palace had many gardens, but unlike most, this one was private. It was one of the few that was neither manicured nor maintained but instead permitted to grow as wild as it wished. Lurien had claimed it long ago as a personal sanctuary, a place to come and think, or simply to compose himself when life at the palace irritated him beyond all bounds. He was coming here a lot lately . . .

The exquisite statuary was nearly overgrown by prowling vines. Riots of night-blooming flowers were attended by tiny white *ystlumod*, batlike creatures unseen during the day. Their trilling song was usually soothing, but Lurien didn't even notice it this night. Instead, the enchanted tune from the party was still pulsing hard in his veins. He stripped off his gloves and shrugged out of his tunic, grateful to be rid of them. The cool night air was soothing to his feverish skin, but he did not wish to be free of the fire inside. Not yet.

"I like it here," whispered Aurddolen, drawing her mask from her head. Her long tawny hair fell in a wild cascade of braids down her back, and she smiled broadly at him. "Shall I resume my usual skin, my Lord Lurien, or do you like the fur?" She chuckled: "I'm able to do feathers as well. A lesser known feature of the Draigddynion royal family."

Feathers? That certainly presented some intriguing prospects . . . His mouth quirked as he reached out and stroked the side of her lovely face, running his fingers down her throat and around a velvety breast. Circling his hand over her hip and down her thigh, he imagined *all that softness* rubbing full-length against him. "Your pelt is alluring to the senses in every way, but I believe I find your true form most appealing." His answer obviously pleased her, and he watched, fascinated, as the fur seemed to withdraw from sight. Once again she was covered in minute pearlescent scales of palest gold. The full moon gleamed from each and every one, and Lurien sucked in a breath at the exquisite beauty of her. But he planned to do far more than look.

And so did she. Aurddolen approached him with a subtle swagger that undulated the curves of her hips. She kept her eyes on his as she boldly unfastened his knife belt and threw it over her shoulder. She refused to free his shaft all at once, though. Instead she teased at it, brushing it with her fingertips, revealing it a fraction at a time. It swelled and strained toward her, and a quiver ran up and down Lurien's spine. He very nearly moaned aloud as she breathed on its tip. It was too much and not enough all at once. Impatiently, he willed his leathers away completely. He stood naked, and the fiery heat of his proud cock was eased not at all by the cool air. Instead, his magic crackled within him and around him, and a sudden wind picked up and sent the ystlumod fleeing in fear.

A storm was coming, one that heeded only the Lord of the Wild Hunt. Lightning would strike the garden repeatedly this night—and still the dragon woman was unafraid. With claws that were only partially retracted, her hand slid around his erection, gripping him hard as she worked his nipples first with her soft full lips and tongue, and then with her teeth. Lurien growled out her name and pressed her down to his cock. She laughed at him, then set her lovely mouth to work as he tangled his hands in her hair.

Thunder rumbled nearby as he fought to stop his hips from rocking. He rode the fine sharp edge of pleasure, and his breath hissed between his own teeth as hers scraped him. Merely watching the exotically featured woman made his pulse pound in his veins, and he was captivated by the utter perfection of her comely backside . . . He knew what he wanted then, what he wanted *now*. In a flash, he had pulled Aurddolen to her feet and turned her in his arms so that delicious ass was grinding into him. He held her tight with one powerful arm, then parted her legs with his knee, making it easy to slide a hand between them. His cock rubbed insistently against her hip, yet Lurien took his time exploring her wet heat. Pressing his fingers into her again and again, he began to splay them inside her, erotically stroking the soft walls of her core. The honeyed scent of her pheromones wafted upward, dizzying him and eroding his control.

She arched her back and thrust against his hand, wanting, seeking, aching for release. Aurddolen was no Tylwyth Teg, however. Her desires were as feral as the lioness she'd pretended to be—but he knew his timing had to be perfect. Nuzzling aside her heavy spill of braids, Lurien licked and kissed her nape until she shivered uncontrollably and he could feel her minute scales pebble against his skin. In the same moment that he thrust his cock deep, he sank his teeth into the back of her neck. Lightning strobed around them as she bucked in his arms, pumping her hips in a violent paroxysm of pleasure that set its own hard rhythm, until the whiplash of ecstasy ensnared him as well.

With a satisfied moan, Aurddolen sank to the ground, and he

followed her. They lay side by side gazing up at the golden moon without really seeing it.

Finally, she leaned up on one elbow to grin at him. "Again!" she laughed.

"Definitely again." His mouth quirked, and an abrupt downpour of rain soaked them both.

Startled, the dragon woman's skin flared with strident patterns of green and blue. "Where did that come from?" she demanded of him. The clear night sky was still aglow with a lustrous full moon—but she could not look upward for the heavy pelting drops. He pointed at a small cloud, hidden from view by the overhanging trees.

"At least it's warm," she said grudgingly.

"And so are you," he said, and reached for her, but she eluded him, leaping to sit astride his lap.

"You may control the storm, but I have powers of my own," she said playfully, and drew a circle around one of his nipples with a single sharp claw. "I think I will begin with—"

The explosion heaved the ground beneath them, buffeted the air around them. It shook the foundations of the entire palace and the mountain upon which it stood the way a fierce terrier shakes its prey.

The vibrations hadn't died away before Lurien was in a defensive crouch over Aurddolen, his long black hair spilling across his bare skin in thick wet ropes. He'd already called his silver hunting knife to his hand and held it at the ready while magic gathered in his other fist.

A glance at Aurddolen showed her wide-eyed but unhurt. "Get the traitors," she hissed. "I will see to the queen."

In answer, he shook his head—and a binding spell instantly shackled her with invisible chains. She would not be able to move from the spot.

"You cannot think I had anything to do with this? Lurien, you need my help!" she shouted in fury and frustration, but he barely heard as he raced in the direction of the blast. His leathers materialized on his body as he ran. The explosion hadn't been the throne room . . . that much he knew. Lurien raced down a hallway at full speed, intending to cut across the central courtyard. Only well-honed instinct allowed him to stop in time.

Barely. The central courtyard, where the envoys had succeeded in putting aside their differences and learned to work together, no longer existed. A blackened crater surrounded by fallen or failing stone walls was all that was left, save for the nine arched doorways that led into the palace. All of the smaller samplau, the seedings from the Nine Realms that had been painstakingly readied to be sent, had been destroyed.

Lurien stood at the still-smoking edge of the pit. Looking across, he could see many of the guests gather at the doorways to peer at the disaster, some curious, most nervous. Was a traitor among them? He felt the presence of Gwenhidw at his elbow, no longer in the guise of a fearsome pwca, and sensed all four of his men close behind her. He was thankful for their diligence—he knew from experience just how difficult it could be to keep track of the woman. "Someone seeks to undo your work, Your Grace."

"Someone always wants to undo that which is good. They will not succeed," she said simply. "They have cost us *time*, perhaps, but fortunately time is quite flexible in this dimension." Gwenhidw leaned over to view the depths of the hole. "Thank all the stars that we were not working here this night."

"Obviously you should have more parties." Lurien won a weak smile from her, and then she called out across the chasm to her guests for a return to the throne room—and the celebrations. The faces in the doorways slowly disappeared until only Lurien remained. The queen had also returned to the party, and he knew she would not resume her pwca disguise again. Instead, she would make a point of being seen by her people in hopes of allaying their fears. And also, Lurien knew, to thumb her nose at whoever dared to try to disrupt the peace and progress of the kingdom.

He drew a symbol in the air and waited for two of his hunters to come to his side.

"Go to the westernmost garden, the one grown wild. Arrest Aurddolen o'r Draigddynion at once. She is not to be released, even by order of the queen herself. Put my seal on the door." He was glad he had that one little bit of power under fae law. As *llaw dde*, he could act directly to protect the monarch—even against her wishes.

Was Aurddolen deliberately distracting me? he wondered. *Ensuring that I was not at Gwenhidw's side when the plot was carried out?* If so, the dragon woman must have been frustrated by the change of venue, with all the envoys at the throne room this night rather than in the courtyard. Lurien had detected no such feeling from her . . . and if he was wrong, she was going to hate him forever. Yet even she could not deny that most of the conspiracies over the centuries had involved the dragon people in one way or another.

As for himself, he would not trust Aurddolen again. He could not take the chance with Gwenhidw's life at stake.

EIGHTEEN

⌒⌒⌒

I'll have to be thanking Ranyon for fixing this. Caris loved the porch swing, even if they'd decided not to rock it in case Liam's bruised head didn't like the movement. She loved the entire sprawling porch with its sturdy roof. It was like a room without walls, where you could enjoy being out of doors while still feeling sheltered.

It was a sheltering place in which to speak of difficult things too. It had been hard for Liam, of course. What man was good at talking about disappointment and lost love? But he had managed to tell the tale through as honestly as he could. And he'd held her hand the entire time—for her sake or to steady himself? Perhaps both.

"What do you think went wrong?" she ventured at last.

"Hell, I've lost count of how many times I've asked myself that. Maybe it was too easy," he said. "We got together in high school, when we were just kids, and just kept on going. Maybe we got too comfortable."

Caris frowned. "Why is being comfortable a bad thing? I should think a couple would cherish being at ease with one another."

"I just meant that sometimes people stay together because it's easier than being alone. Jade and I never had to worry about who we were going to sit with at lunch, or finding a date for the dance, or who we were going to hang out with on the weekend. We didn't have to put any effort into it, you see?"

"That's almost more like being friends or school chums, isn't it? I mean, my cousin, Enid, lived two farms over and we played together whenever we could, but we weren't really close. We didn't even like each other all that much. It was simply convenient."

"Convenient." He said the word like it tasted bad. "That's a helluva lot worse than *comfortable*, but maybe that's what it boiled down to in the end. Although it didn't start off that way. I was in love with her, I know that, and yet I also know that I didn't put her first. Not ever. And what kind of love is that?"

"Maybe just an inexperienced love," she said simply. "You're so hard on yourself. You were young but you had good intentions. You didn't use her and discard her. Instead you made plans to spend your whole life with her." And just for a moment, Caris felt a twinge of envy and even a little jealousy toward a girl she didn't even know.

He sighed. "What I really wanted was a marriage like Aunt Ruby and Uncle Conall have. You were talking about *cherishing* a minute ago? After all the years they've been together, they're still crazy about each other. When I was growing up, I had no idea how much work love really was, didn't realize how much work the two of them put into their relationship—I guess I thought it all just happened by magic."

Curious, she asked, "What do you mean by *work*?"

"They put each other first, always. And I couldn't begin to list all the little stuff they're always doing for each other."

"Ah. I didn't think of that as work. Surely that's just what comes naturally?"

He snorted. "To a woman, maybe. To men, not so much. I know that's one place I screwed up for sure. I put my music career first, above everything else, thinking I was doing it for Jade too.

I wish I'd gotten smarter sooner, paid a little more attention to *how* my aunt and uncle stay close. They don't take each other for granted. Me? I definitely took it for granted that Jade would always be there."

"*Gwr dieithr yw yfory*," said Caris. "It means, 'Tomorrow is a stranger.' 'Tis human nature to be thinking that tomorrow will be just like today." She certainly hadn't expected her own life to change so dramatically. *What would I have said to Da if I'd known I wouldn't see him again? What might I have done?* The thought pricked her heart and tears stung her eyes again. She quickly changed the subject. "Did her family want her to marry you?"

Her question surprised him. "Yeah, actually, they seemed pretty enthused about me. I think they even pressured her a little, asking when I was going to propose. Friends and family on both sides did that, figuring marriage was a foregone conclusion, you know? I thought it was too, actually, although we didn't really discuss it."

"Truly, she wouldn't be the first girl that didn't know how she really felt until it seemed like it was too late to stop the wedding."

"Wait a minute. I thought you'd be on my side," he grumbled.

"Well, of course I am." She used her free hand to cup his cheek for a moment. "I'm just trying to understand."

Liam looked out over the devastated farm, but she didn't think he was seeing it. "I'd like to think I'd have found a way to *understand* too, if she'd just told me she'd had second thoughts, had changed her mind. I wouldn't have liked it of course—I know damn well I would have tried to talk her out of it. But I hope I would have seen sense eventually," he said. "If only she hadn't gone through with it . . ."

Liam rose and paced the porch slowly. She knew by his pallor that the exertion was making him dizzy, but she also knew she wouldn't be able to talk him into sitting down. Not yet. His hurt and his anger were too close to the surface now, and Caris thought of the lurking pike with their needle teeth in the cold mountain lakes of her homeland. He wouldn't bite *her*, but it was plain he was biting at himself, over and over.

"If she just hadn't gone through with it," he continued. "Hadn't stood in front of me and spoke vows she'd already broken and wasn't ever going to keep. But she did." His voice rose. "She did, dammit. And it nuked everything, me included."

His story reminded Caris of the yard. She could imagine how pretty it must have been before the storm, all fruiting trees and blossoming flowers, peace and tranquility. And now there was nothing left but a tragic and terrible mess. No hint remained of what was once picturesque, and all of the calm had been upended by chaos.

There was no peace within Liam, that much was certain. The heartbreak and betrayal had been as cataclysmic as the storm, leading to the collapse of the bridge between his music and his soul. True, Caris herself had been discouraged from expressing the music that lived within her during her human life. And she had been physically prevented from doing so as a grim. *But what kind of pain does it take to dam up the songs inside when there's no one and nothing to stop you?* She'd learned that Liam Cole had once had a burning need to create music, just as she had. But while hers still blazed, his own fire had died out as surely as if a river's worth of water had washed it away.

"You said you haven't played since. Not even once?"

Liam sat down heavily beside her then, plainly exhausted. Caris guessed he'd been wrung out far more by rehearsing the past than by pacing.

"Not a damn note," he said. "It's like all the music that was in me just packed a bag and left town. And the thing of it is, I don't even know if I want it to come back. Music just—I don't know, it kind of opens you up to the bone. Takes you over. It's not something that exists in you, it *is* you. It's why I couldn't bear to hear you sing, as talented as you are."

She nodded. "Perhaps you're just not ready to feel that much again."

"Maybe."

"Then I'm needing to say something. Your pain and your anger are like a festering wound. If you don't find a way to let go of what happened to you, it'll poison you." That much she knew. The Fair Ones had stolen her life once. Instinct told her that if she allowed herself to dwell on her own anger, if she spent her energy on hating the fae, or simply permitted herself to wade too deeply into grief, then her new life would be lost as well, swallowed up in the pain of a past she couldn't change.

"How would you know a thing like that?"

"What do you mean?"

"You *know* what you're talking about. I can hear it in your voice."

"It's because of my da," she said quietly. "My mother passed on when I was but two. He loved her desperately, and he grieved for her his whole life. He never let go of it, don't you see? Instead of remembering the good, he hung on to his pain, and that's why he drank so much. It wasn't so bad when I was small—he'd only drink at night after the farm was looked after, and after I was in bed. But once I was grown, he started his drinking early in the day, and he drank more all the time. And then . . ." Her voice trailed away, and she bit her lip.

He brushed a finger over her cheek. "Shit, I'm sorry. I have no business acting like I'm the only person who's ever had it rough."

"There's no need for you to be sorry. Not for me." Caris forced herself to meet his blue gaze. "Be sorry that you're well on your way to an empty life yourself, Liam Cole. Don't you see that I can't be in it if you can't lay the past to rest? How can you divide your heart from your soul? Your life from your music? It would be like a wall between us." She took a deep breath. "I'll abide by your rules for singing and music making because I care about you and don't want to cause you pain—but I'll not do it forever."

"You don't pull any punches, do you?"

She didn't know what that meant, but she couldn't say anything more over the lump in her throat. Instead, she simply squeezed Liam's hand. Caris herself had never borne the heartbreak of losing a lover—although as new as her relationship with this man was, she already felt something of that raw, deep ache at the very thought of walking away from him. *But walk I will if I have to.*

She had already endured the loss of her father, her entire life as she knew it, all that was dear to her, her own human body, and her music. It had been crushing and cruel—yet she had refused to relinquish her sense of *self.* Was that what the soul really was? She didn't know, only that she would not give it up to the fae or to anyone else. She had waited more than a lifetime to be able to play her music again. The memory of sobbing over the instrument she'd found only this morning was still a dull ache in her heart, as two centuries of grief had finally broken loose. But when the floodwaters had ceased, pure exultation had burst from her like a star as she played that fiddle. It had been liberating beyond all bounds.

Of course, through the course of their conversation, Caris realized that it must be Liam's own fiddle she'd found and borrowed. And she had no right to it. *Best to be setting that straight.* At least she'd gotten a chance to play the marvelous instrument once, and while it would be hard to relinquish it, she would return to her original plan and work until she could buy one of her own—though she would be unlikely to afford something of such amazing quality. "'Tis my turn to tell *you* something now," she managed.

Her voice must have sounded far too grave because Liam looked almost alarmed. "You're not married, are you?"

"Dear heavens, no!"

"Why the hell not?" he shot back.

"What sort of a question is that?"

"Because you're too damn pretty to be running around single. Are all the men in your country blind?"

"What a perfectly silly thing to say," she said, giving him an exasperated look—though she was privately delighted that he thought her *pretty*. Had anyone ever said such a thing to her in her life? "'Twas my da that raised me, remember? There was just the two of us, and he was a straightforward man. I learned to act the same, and even more so when I was running the farm on my own. I think perhaps I was too bold, too outspoken, because no boys brought flowers to me when my friends or my cousins were being courted. I likely scared them all off because I knew my own mind."

"But you must have met someone, some time?"

"Are you hearing yourself? And how many strange women are there dropping by your farm to visit?"

"You're the first. And I'm busy anyway."

"Aye, and I was a bit busy too, you know. There was none but my da and me to run the sheep. No hired man, no herder, no cook. Only us. Not only that, but we lived halfway up the side of the mountain. If I went down to the village at all, it was to church with my da or to buy and sell at the market." She didn't mention all the hours she'd spent with her music. "Or do you suppose I must have simply forgotten to find myself a man?"

"Well, I just thought for sure you'd at least have a boyfriend."

"Ah, well—when I was ten, perhaps," she chuckled. "Collen Edwards and I agreed to try kissing, behind a tent at the market. His big sister had a sweetheart, and he wanted to see what all the fuss was about, and I was curious too. We kept bumping noses until I couldn't stop laughing, and that was the end of that."

Liam grinned. "A little hard on his tender ego."

"I guess it was, since he didn't ask again. And when I was twelve, I was fair to swoon o'er Bran Tommer each Sunday when I was supposed to be listening to the sermon. His family had their own pew, third from the front. I didn't get to see much but the back of his *cochyn* head—he had the most splendid red hair! But I never said a word to him, and then he took up with Mary Shippey after that."

"So no husband, no boyfriends, no one at all, then?"

"Not a one," she said, amused at the now hopeful note in his voice.

"Don't take this the wrong way, but good. I'm damn glad for my own selfish reasons." He picked up her hand with both of his and held it to his lips like it was a holy relic. "You were right that there's something between us. It's new but it's real, and I want to build on it. Look, I know I'm no prize—I've been festering in my own frickin' juices for way too long." Scrambling for words to explain himself, he stumbled on new revelations: "The breakup made me question everything I thought I knew. Like I thought I knew Jade, thought that she loved me. And I was dead wrong. I guess I just stopped trusting myself to be right about anything anymore."

Caris nodded. "Perhaps she thought she loved you too. How could either of you know for certain if you hadn't felt it before?" She put a gentle hand on his chest and leaned in until their faces were close. "Tell me how would I know, Liam Cole? Because I've not been in love before."

"You listen to your gut," he said without hesitation.

She wrinkled her nose and pulled back. "What does *that* mean?"

"It's not something I understood back then, but I've had three years to think on it." He summed up Uncle Conall's famous rule of thumb for her. "Your gut is your instinct, it's what tells you the things you can't see or feel. It's a lot more reliable than your heart or your head. That's why people say, 'trust your gut.'"

They did? After all her years as a grim, and all the languages she'd learned, the phrase was altogether new to her. "Trust your *gut*." She tried out the words. "It's not very pretty, but it makes sense."

"I didn't know how to listen to it before—I probably didn't want to listen because I was young and headstrong and determined to have what I thought I wanted. But I know enough to listen now. And my gut's telling me that I want a chance with you more than I've ever wanted anything. It's not—well, it's not flowers and candy, but like I said, it's real."

She was quiet for a long moment, long enough for him to berate himself. *Nice going, Cole. Could you possibly have been any more romantic? What woman in her right mind wants to hear about your damn gut?* He realized then that he was still holding her hand with both of his, and that she hadn't tried to take it back. The seconds dragged on in an agony of hope . . .

Finally she nodded, and relief washed over him like a cool waterfall.

"I like to speak plainly, but 'tis difficult when it comes to feelings," she said. "Never have I laid eyes on a man whom I wanted more than I want you. But I'm thinking it's not going to be easy for us because you've been sore wounded, heart and soul. You've some healing to do yet, Liam Cole."

"I know it," he said. "Can you wait?"

She laughed then. "I seem to have a bit of time on my hands as they say, since I have a whole new life ahead of me. So I think I can spare you a little patience."

"That's all I can ask," he said. It would have been a great time, a perfect time, to seal that agreement with a kiss, but before he could act on that notion, Caris jumped up and straightened her clothes.

"I'd best be getting back to the barn."

Hard to be disappointed when this appealing woman had just agreed to give him a chance—but he managed to feel let down anyway. He'd wanted that kiss. As if she knew, she turned and cupped his face with her small hands, then kissed his bruised forehead so tenderly that he could swear it really did make it feel better.

"I nearly forgot," she said as she pulled back. "I meant to tell you that I found a fiddle in the closet of the room I stayed in. It was too early to wake you, and I was far too excited to wait—I must confess to you that I borrowed it."

A fiddle? He was damn glad to be sitting down. "*You* play the fiddle? *You* do?" His voice was incredulous as his dreams came back to him in a rush, the wild woman creating primeval music in the forest . . .

"Are you all right?" she asked. "You've gone pale."

Small wonder, he thought. "Yeah. Fine."

"Anyway, it's not so odd that I play the fiddle, surely. The Kale—the Gypsies—taught me. They camped on the mountainside above our farm each year when they came to shear sheep in our village. I had to keep it a secret though—I could only play in the woods, far away from the farm."

"Why a secret?" he asked.

"Because when I was growing up, any music outside the church was frowned upon, you see. Between the preacher and my da, I was certain to lose my fiddle if anyone found me—" Her voice abruptly failed her then, and her eyes filled. She wouldn't let the tears fall, however.

Somebody did *find you out, didn't they?* "That must have been pretty rough," he said, grasping her hand and tugging her down beside him again. It wasn't enough to simply put an arm around her. He wanted to draw her in close and shelter her from her hurts with his body. He didn't expect the exquisite sensation of wholeness it brought to him. She fit exactly in the hollow beneath his shoulder, as if it was meant just for her . . .

Had Caris noticed that too, or was she too busy trying to recover her composure? She cleared her throat, yet remained pressed to his side. "Anyway, I'm truly sorry that I took the fiddle. It's in my room—I'll put it back in the closet where it was, or I can give it to you now so you can put it in a better place."

"Like hell you will. I want you to have it."

Big brown eyes looked up at him in shock. "I . . . I can't take it from you! It may not mean much to you now, but it did once."

"It did," he agreed. "Maybe someday it will again. But it's just plain wrong for a fiddle, for *any* musical instrument, to be locked up in a case and never used. And it's not good for it, either." He saw that she wasn't convinced. "Look, if you feel uncomfortable accepting it, would you just keep it for me? Tune it up and play it until I need it again. It would be good for the instrument, and it would make *me* feel better that it's being used. Can you do that?"

In answer, she threw her arms around his neck. "Thank you, Liam. It means more to me than I can begin to tell you. And I'll take very good care of your fiddle for you."

Liam pulled her the rest of the way into his lap so he could wrap his arms around her too. She felt so good there, so right. His bruised head didn't spoil the moment by complaining, either. Holding her, Liam heartily wished he had a dozen fiddles to bestow upon her. The downer was that he had to request one condition. Just one, but damn, he did *not* want to do it.

Yet if he didn't, he wasn't sure if his heart, head, or gut would be able to handle the situation.

NINETEEN

Liam wished he didn't have to spoil the moment. "Caris, honey, I have to ask you a favor."

"Of course." She pulled back so she could look at him, and those big brown eyes just made it harder for him to spit out the words.

"It's about the fiddle," he said. "I feel like a jerk asking this, especially when you told me how you always had to hide when you wanted to play your music. But—I need you to take it where I can't hear it, okay? Just for a little while. I'm just not ready to hear it, not yet." She frowned, and he braced himself, certain he'd blown away whatever ground he'd gained with this beautiful woman.

Instead she nodded slowly. "I think I understand it, now that we've talked for a time. The music hurts something inside you when you hear it, doesn't it?"

Only like his insides were being scooped out with a melon baller. "Yeah," he managed. "I don't understand why, but for now, it does."

"Then, *for now*, I'll practice somewhere else. I've found a lovely place out by the ridge, so I won't mind playing out there a bit. And I can sing around the farm when you're in the house." Caris placed her finger on his chin. "*For a while.*"

He got her meaning, loud and clear. "Thanks. For understanding and for being patient while I try to work this out."

Her finger slid around his jawline and upward, until her small palm was cool on his cheek. She delighted him by placing a tender, lingering kiss on his other cheek—and then apparently thought better of doing more. Liam could see that she was flustered again, and he found it completely endearing. That rosy blush bloomed along her throat once more, and he wondered just where it originated . . .

"I have work to do," she said, pulling back.

As she wriggled to get off his lap, *endearing* was replaced by, well, something completely inarticulate. His lower brain must have sent out a message to keep her gorgeous butt exactly where it was, because instinct had Liam catching her around the waist before his upper brain even got the memo. *There, yes, right there . . .*

"Don't go just yet—I think I need a little more TLC," he murmured and cradled the back of her head in his hand.

"What's that mean?" she asked. "It's not about guts again, is it?"

"Not at all. TLC stands for 'tender Liam care.' I really think a little more kissing could do me a whole lot of good."

"You think so, do you?" She didn't sound convinced, but she was smiling as he brought her face close to his. That pretty mouth was made to be kissed, he decided, but he wanted to take his time—like saving dessert for last. Meanwhile, it was oh so pleasant to brush his lips lightly along her hairline, where that intriguing crown of dark braids made her look like a sexy Princess Leia on Endor. He lightly nibbled at the tops of her ears and noted that they were hot—and an answering heat echoed deep within him. Liam nuzzled into the ear closest to him until a shiver rippled through her and her heart beat loudly enough that he could feel it in his own chest.

His hands wanted nothing more than to explore every tantalizing inch of her. Instead, he restricted them to slowly kneading the fine, smooth arc of her back from neck to tailbone—and no further. His body wanted everything *right now*, of course, but this time, this one time, Liam wanted something else, something slow and intimate, *something less that was so much more*. Instinct told him that Caris Dillwyn was a woman to be savored. And savor her he would . . .

He teased at the corners of her lips with his tongue, but moved on. Kissed the end of her nose and made her laugh. The pleasing contours of her face were mapped and committed to memory with only his mouth. Finally, he sensed the flutter of her eyelids beneath his lips. It evoked an image of her small figure quivering like a bird's wings beneath him as he pleasured her . . . and as he claimed her.

It nearly undid him then and there.

It was definitely *go forward or fall back* time, and Liam would cut his own throat rather than spoil this moment by taking things too far, too fast. But there would be a time, and damn soon, he promised himself as he fought to calm the powerful craving that raged within. His cock was straining beneath his jeans, and with their bodies molded together as they were, he knew she could feel it pressing against her, seeking her. *Down, boy.* He needed to get out of this face-to-face position, and fast.

Regrettably, enjoying Caris's soft, full lips would have to wait for another time. *This is what you get for not having dessert first,* he chided himself. To her, he said, "I think we might want to take a break now." And he kissed her forehead with all the tenderness he could muster.

"Right. Of course," she said, and her voice was as unsteady as if she'd had too much to drink. Before she could make a move to leave, Liam placed his hands firmly on her waist and lifted her clear of his lap. It was pure self-defense—one more wriggle of that gorgeous butt and he was going to embarrass himself. He was already sweating, and he could swear the air had turned to syrup as he tried to drag it into his lungs.

Once her feet were back on the porch, Caris barely took a moment to compose herself. She said something that sounded like "good-bye" and was set to take off, until he seized her hand in his. Whether he was trying to steady her or just couldn't bear to let her go, he wasn't sure. Probably both. Worse, he couldn't think of a damn thing to say. He settled for planting a soft, lingering kiss on her palm and releasing her with as much of a smile as his bruised head would allow.

She smiled back, a little shyly he thought, then hurried off toward the barn. That's when what she'd said about no boyfriends in her life struck him like a lightning bolt. *You frickin' idiot, she hasn't been with anybody before.*

Liam waited until Caris was out of sight before he got up and shuffled into the house to stretch out on the couch. He couldn't help but moan a little as his body sank gratefully into the cushions. How could he be so damned tired already? He hadn't done much of anything with Caris, except get extremely aroused. Apparently that was enough to wear him out—but it had been worth it. *I guess I'll just be glad this stupid concussion didn't interrupt anything.*

His concussion was likely to get aggravated all to hell, however, just by trying to sort out all the thoughts that were presently trampling like wild elephants through his head. The discovery that Caris had no sexual experience meant that he needed to be damned careful. It was more than just taking it slow and easy—he needed to take his cues from her, and let her tell him what she was and wasn't ready for. *Great, like reading cues is a real talent of mine. Not!*

However, Uncle Conall had once said, "There's nothing you can't figure out together if you give it enough time." His uncle had actually been talking about disagreements, not sex—but it seemed to Liam that the advice applied. Since he'd already made up his mind that Caris Dillwyn was a woman to be savored, then surely she was a woman worth waiting for, too. Somehow it would work out. *It has to . . .*

What was giving him even more of a headache was the discovery that she was a fiddler like himself! So much for his theories on his weird dreams. All his rational and reasonable explanations had been completely blown out of the water. Liam had always been respectful of Aunt Ruby's interest in psychic matters, but privately, he'd taken it with a very big grain of salt. *I'm going to have to apologize to my aunt, big time.* He could no longer deny what his dreams had revealed to him. Somehow, for reasons he couldn't fathom, he'd been given knowledge *in advance* about Caris's incredible music. And just in case he needed any further verification, his gut concurred.

He stilled suddenly. There had been *two* parts to the dream. If one was true, then the other must also be true. Something dark and dangerous was coming—and it was coming for her.

Liam shook his head, not with denial but with determination. "No," he said aloud, and his resolve tempered into steel. No matter what happened, he would damn well stand between Caris Dillwyn and whatever the hell was trying to threaten her.

If only he knew what it was.

The rest of the afternoon passed in a satisfying rhythm of work. There was no lack of things needing to be done before the milking, and gradually Caris found herself singing over every task big and small. After all those years of being a voiceless grim, she finally had both a reason and the ability to express the music that lived within her. When she came to the end of a song, she laughed with sheer delight and started another. The work became a joy. It was a joy, too, to know that when the work was done, the exquisite fiddle would be waiting for her.

It was exhilarating to be so free, much like being a small child again—before her da's lectures and the preacher's sermons tried to repress and contain what was second nature to her. She remembered the silly little songs she'd made up as she played with her doll. When she was big enough to have chores, she sang over them as well. Caris recalled how she'd chanted to the oxen when they plowed, crooned to the chickens to call them to feed, sang to the sheep as she and the dogs took them up to the higher pastures.

Entering the barn, she greeted the goats with a nonsensical rhyme. Looking over their heads to the back of the building, Caris expected to see Chevy watching her too—but no vividly spotted head or broad speckled back was visible. Quickly, she pushed past the goats and ran to the makeshift enclosure. *The mare was down.*

"On the weekend, Jay and I will come back with Rhys and some of our friends and see if we can finish cleaning things up around here," Morgan was saying, as she helped Liam slowly down the steps to where his ATV was waiting. It was a fairly new side-by-side quad with a small cargo box, and it had been a welcome sight on several levels. The handy little vehicle had been buried in the machine shop wreckage the last he'd known, and he'd assumed it was a goner. Steadying himself with the overhead bar, he settled into the passenger seat (and hoped he didn't look too pathetically grateful to be sitting down). His stomach lurched only once, then the nausea subsided as if it had never been. The dizziness? That seemed to come and go more or less continuously.

As the quad moved forward—and thankfully, Morgan had a light touch on the gas—Liam was surprised at the progress all around him. *Somebody's been awfully damn busy.* His battered skull protested as his head kept swiveling—but he'd already learned it was better to turn his whole head rather than move his eyes.

A broad driving path had been cleared through the debris. There'd be no more picking his way through an obstacle course to get from the house to the barn. There were still a lot of fallen branches littering the rest of the yard, but an assortment of fallen trees and large limbs had already been piled at the head of the driveway, and topping the heap was the chestnut tree that had pierced the living room wall. *I'm going to have a lot of frickin' firewood this winter.*

"I've been meaning to ask, how the hell did you get all the windows fixed before I got home?" Liam had witnessed the flawless glass on the first floor but had yet to tackle going upstairs. From the outside, it was now apparent that the panes on the second floor were perfect as well. "And it isn't just clean inside, it's *immaculate.* Aunt Ruby would totally faint. I can't believe you got a company to come out here that fast."

Morgan chuckled. "Let's just say that I have *connections,* and leave it at that." Steering the quad toward the farmyard, she parked by the corral, where the yearling goats were pulling alfalfa from their feeder with adept lips. She pointed out the injuries that had been treated, and Liam felt relieved. He didn't like to think of his animals suffering, and it was pure luck that nothing seemed to be too serious. At the milk house, the generator was still running nicely—no small feat considering its many idiosyncrasies.

As a result, all the milk from the previous night and the morning had already gone through the pasteurizer.

"When's the cheese company coming?" he asked.

Morgan laughed. "Been and gone already. You slept through it, bud."

Jay hitched a ride on the back of the quad as they headed for the paddock. Morgan pulled in close to the fence so Liam could rub Dodge's questing nose without having to get out of the vehicle. The Appaloosa nickered low, glad to see him too—and blew grassy slime all over the front of his borrowed purple shirt. "Nice one, dude," chuckled Liam. "I think you improved it." Maybe he could consign it to the rag bucket in the machine shop without too much guilt.

"Dodge is a great cow horse," said Jay. "Zeroed in on the cattle right away and knew just what to do to get them together and moving toward home. Although after a night like that, I don't think they needed much persuasion. I'm sorry to tell you that I counted six dead by lightning strike a couple miles south of the ridge. The good news is that the rest are fine: no injuries at all that I can find. I put them in the small pasture on the other side of the creek. The fences are still solid there, there's a fair amount of decent grass, and they have access to water."

"I can't thank you enough for finding them and bringing them back. I'm damn lucky to have any livestock left after that storm." Dodge abruptly angled his big head under Liam's hand, nearly shoving him into Morgan. "Hey, go easy on me, will you?" The horse had a huge fondness for having his closed eyes rubbed just *so*—and as Liam delivered what the big spotted goof was asking for, he realized something was wrong.

"I thought you said Chevy came home. Why isn't she here with Dodge?"

"She's in the barn with the milk goats," said Morgan. "Caris is with her."

"Chevy's all right, isn't she? She didn't lose her foal?"

"She's just fine. Come see for yourself."

Liam stood in the small side door of the barn and waited for his eyes to adjust. It didn't take long—with the roof missing, there was a hell of a big skylight overhead. The late afternoon sun was waning, and there was a soft yellow glow to everything in the barn. The Saanen and LaMancha does seemed calm and content. Some sported blue spots from antiseptic spray, a few had vibrant-colored elastic bandaging on their legs, but otherwise, the herd looked good. Beyond them, he caught sight of a familiar speckled hide in the back section of the barn where he usually kept the yearlings at night. He was out of the quad and heading for the mare, heedless of any need to take it easy, not even noticing Morgan and Jay rush to flank him.

Halfway there, he stopped. Time stopped. There was Caris, kneeling in the straw at Chevy's feet, supporting a tiny foal and encouraging it to stand on gangly legs and drink from its mother. A *second* tiny foal lay sprawled beside her, taking in its brand new world with big curious eyes. The golden light lent something reverential, almost otherworldly to the scene, gilding it like a Renaissance painting. The big mare's coat might have been speckled with glittering coins. Caris's upturned face glowed, and rich amber highlights shimmered in her dark hair. Even the simple straw might have been spun from purest gold, as dust motes glinted diamondlike in the air over all.

Caris turned to see him and laughed in delight, shattering

the spell into a million shining pieces, but not before he was utterly, completely dazzled by her. He'd thought he had feelings for her already, but he could actually *feel* his heart take a long, slow, glorious tumble . . .

"Look, Liam! Your good mare has given you a fine gift."

He nodded dumbly, and half sat, half collapsed on a hay bale. The sun slid just a fraction of an inch lower and the light in the barn lost its golden tones. The feeling within Liam lingered, however. It was part of him now. *She* was part of him now, whether Caris knew it or not.

"Chevy's given you *two* gifts," added Morgan. "We had no idea she was carrying twins."

"Wait a minute, that's pretty rare for a horse, isn't it?" Liam managed. As his brain finally kicked in, he already knew the answer. It was not only rare; it was dangerous. Horses weren't really designed to carry more than one foal.

"Live twins only happen once in about ten thousand pregnancies," affirmed Jay. "I've never even seen any, never mind delivered them."

"Now you know why we're still here," said Morgan. "We noticed that Chevy was acting strange early this morning. Her water broke about midafternoon, and we had a healthy foal shortly afterward. He's got contracted tendons, which is why Caris is helping him stand, but it's a pretty minor case: he should recover on his own pretty quickly. But he was awfully small, and that made me suspicious. Sure enough, along came a second foal."

They don't even look real, he thought. *More like toys.* "I've gotta see them." Gripping the wooden boards of the barn partition, Liam made his way slowly over to Caris's side and sank into the thick straw. Chevy swung her head around to greet him, nosing his shoulder gently and blowing in his face—and thankfully, unlike Dodge, it was just air. He caught at her bridle to support himself as he scratched under her jaw in her favorite spot. "Good job, girl," he said soothingly. "Those are real nice babies you have there." Inside, however, his heart wrenched as he wondered whether they'd make it. *They're so damn little . . .*

"How much do they weigh?" he asked. As if in answer, the foal that had been nursing staggered over to Liam, where it collapsed in a flurry of long legs onto his lap. It was like having a sack of grain fall onto his legs, but fortunately his head wasn't involved and didn't complain overmuch at the jolt. He was even more thankful that the creature hadn't landed on his crotch.

"Isn't he a handsome fellow?" asked Caris. "Here, feel his coat!" She seized Liam's hand and drew it over the foal's fuzzy pelt. He didn't know which felt better, her touch or the soft baby fur. He grinned at Caris (whether his bruised head liked it or not), and they leaned in toward each other as he stroked the little creature.

"We figure the twins are about a week or so early, so they're a lot smaller than average," said Morgan, kneeling beside him and checking over the gangly creature in his lap. "I'm guessing this little guy's weight is maybe fifty or sixty pounds. The girl is smaller—forty pounds, tops. But she's got plenty of zip. She was up on her feet long before her brother, and he was born first. No obvious defects, nothing wrong with her tendons, and she doesn't seem to need any help to nurse."

Morgan looked at Liam squarely. "I think they have a chance, but you'll have to watch them like a hawk for the next two or three weeks. Dammit, I hate saying it, but you have to understand that the survival rate for twins is pretty low for horses, even if they make it through the birth, even if they look just fine. You have to be prepared for that possibility."

"I know it," he said, and glanced over just in time to catch Caris's expression. She didn't look scared or worried in the least.

Instead, she looked downright *fierce*. What the hell was that about? "We'll give it our best, both of us," he said, and put an arm around her shoulders. "Right, Caris?"

"They'll grow up just fine, the both of 'em," she said, and it wasn't like a wish or a hope or some kind of positive thinking. Instead, it sounded to him like a statement of *fact*. "When I was young, the Gypsies would camp each summer on the mountainside above our farm. They told me that twin horses are a good omen, a male and a female, just like these." She cradled the little female close to her. "These foals are here to tell us that things will turn out right."

His gut told him he was missing something here. *What things?* "Of course things will be all right. Steptoe Acres will recover from the storm, and we'll be back in business in no time."

The veterinarians looked at each other. "It's as good a time as any," said Morgan. Jay shrugged, and they both sat down in the straw across from Caris and Liam.

Okay, this is just plain weird, Liam thought. "If there's going to be a campfire sing-along, I want out now," he said.

"We have something we need to tell you," said Jay. "And it's going to be difficult to hear. That thing that wrecked your farm wasn't a natural storm."

TWENTY

~~~

"More gifts from the Nine Realms. How kind of them to furnish our new home," said Maelgwn, and wheeled his horse with his spurs for a better look. All of the horses were restless and fitful, chewing their silver bits, anxious to be galloping over the hills below. Instead, the prince and his followers had spent the early morning hours atop this odd little mountain, watching the Great Way gleaming like a dark, wet mouth in the blue sky. From its depths floated enormous shining spheres as delicate in appearance as soap bubbles.

The appearance was deceiving of course. Each transparent orb was as formidable as faery-forged silver. It was only that strength that allowed them to pass safely through the glittering passage at all. The living magic they were infused with attracted the ever-hungry Anghenfilod and other unsavory residents of the Way.

Many anghenfilod sat clustered together on the hillside, only a stone's throw away from the Way's entrance. They had been nervous at first to be outside of their strange realm. Now the shadow figures fairly vibrated with excitement. *Like hounds awaiting scraps from the master's table*, Maelgwn thought. Unlike dogs, however, every anghenfil towered over the prince and his followers—and absorbed all the light that touched them. Theirs was a darkness that *lived*. The prince's own followers kept a wary distance, and every black grim hung back from the scene, clearly uncomfortable with the presence of the Inbetween creatures. Or perhaps they were simply frightened by the fact that Maelgwn had just thrown one of the fae dogs to the biggest anghenfil, the one that had dared to venture farther from the Great Way than any anghenfil before it at the prince's command. That the monster was unsuccessful in finding what Maelgwn was searching for was unimportant, at least for the moment. It was like training a hawk to *seek*—they had to be rewarded when they returned to the glove.

Meanwhile, the creature's efforts hadn't been entirely fruitless. If anything, it had given the prince a ray of hope. The fact that a hungry anghenfil was unable to home in on the missing grim's magical collar meant that *perhaps she still lived*. And if she did, he could still employ the power of her music to aid him in his plans. Maelgwn signaled one of his riders to approach. He would send the other grims out hunting . . .

The order given, Maelgwn ceased to concern himself with anything but the contents of the spheres emerging from the Way. Within each orb was suspended a samplau, a living portion of one of the kingdom's countless *amgylcheddau*, the unique environments and habitats of its fae flora and fauna. Unimpeded, each sheer container was designed to pass through the solid quartzite hilltop as easily as a fish glides through water. There, it would descend from the human plane to the fae realm, following the core of the ancient rock to Tir Hardd—and assume its assigned spot. The magic-infused sphere would dissolve, nourishing the samplau so it would expand and grow with great speed. Thus the new territory would be seeded.

My territory.

The fae portion of it, that is. Maelgwn had already decided to claim the human realm above it as well, something that no fae ruler had ever attempted. Endless rolling hills and deep-gorged rivers stretched out for hundreds of human miles before his keen sight—and he was going to own them all. One of the first things he would do is rename this odd pinnacle of rock where he now stood. Blissfully unaware of the magical energies centered here, the mortals had named the mount after an unsuccessful general—Steptoe Butte. It was not much more than a hill really, at least not here in the mortal realm, but it was an upthrust of purest quartzite from the very heart of Tir Hardd. It was the selfsame rock that formed the foundation of the great mountain Mynedfa in the Nine Realms, which towered high into the human plane to become a lowly hill on a Welsh island. *Interesting that the Great Way links one mount to the other.*

But it wouldn't link them for long.

Maelgwn kept an eye on the mouth of the Way as it hovered above them. He also watched the broad scrying pool he'd called into existence in the center of the hilltop. With his breastplate of bwgan stones, he had not only the power to view the Inbetween but also the ability to see beyond it to the other side. He knew who was working to send the orbs—and exactly where they were.

Just then, a new orb bobbed out of the Way. As with the others, its contents could be seen plainly. This one held a samplau of the forested marsh in which Bwganod typically lived.

"I no longer care to hunt Bwganod," declared Maelgwn. Although he affected a bored and careless tone, his blue blood was pulsing hard with near-sexual excitement as a bright ball of energy formed in his palm. "In fact, I don't believe we need any swamps at all in Tir Hardd, do you?"

His followers agreed with him wholeheartedly. He lobbed his spell skyward, and the glittering sphere blew apart in a loud, fiery shower of silver sparks and debris. The riders cheered and clapped in a rare display as their horses stamped and snorted. The noise, coupled with the snarling anticipation of the anghenfilod, hid Maelgwn's startled gasp as his cock convulsed. It had happened with every sphere he'd destroyed this day—and there had been many. Still, thanks to his breastplate of bwgan stones, there seemed no end to either his magic or his prowess. In fact, he eyed Rhedyn. The highborn daughter of a *dryad*, she dressed in green perpetually as a sign of her status, but he would surely bend her naked over her horse's back before the day was out.

First things first.

He motioned to the Inbetween creatures, and they erupted into action, pouncing on the remains of the *samplau* from the faery realm and the magic-infused shards of its container, devouring all until nothing remained. It was a simple arrangement, really, and it surprised him that the mighty Lord Lurien hadn't thought of it rather than having to bludgeon his way through the Way's residents each and every time he traveled it.

The Anghenfilod would obey whoever fed them.

And right now, he had a task for them. It was true that they had no magic of their own, but only in the sense that they did not work spells. Instead, they devoured magic and utilized the raw energy—and they could link together to increase that energy.

Maelgwn wanted to find out if they could direct it . . .

Liam was baffled by Jay's words: *not a natural storm . . .* "Look, I was here. I saw it. I was *in* it, for chrissakes. It was a first-class thunderstorm." He pointed straight up at the blue sky where a roof had once been. "And you can see by the damage all around us that Mother Nature threw in a frickin' tornado just for laughs."

"Yes and no," said Morgan, as gently and carefully as if she were delivering bad news to a pet owner. "Yes, you had a monstrous storm here, Liam. And no, *nature* didn't have a thing to do with it."

What the hell? His mind was racing like a hamster in a wheel, trying to think of something else—anything else—that could have caused what had happened. All he could come up with were the shaky plots for a dozen or so late-night movies: *Military experiment gone wrong. Alien invasion. Nanobots. Battle between superheroes. Arrival of travelers from the future.* "Okay, I got nothing," he said at last. "Somebody better start telling me what's going on."

"The best way to do that is to start small," said Jay. "We see in three dimensions, right? But Einstein suggested that time was actually a fourth dimension."

Liam shrugged—and the jolt in his head made him wish he hadn't. Caris gripped his hand tightly as pain sharpened his voice. "So what?" he asked.

"Well, I'm just trying to establish a base here. We have theories now that indicate there are a lot more than the dimensions we're familiar with. Follow?"

"Yeah, I read something about that. String theory, or some damn thing. Still not seeing where this is going."

"Those extra dimensions aren't far away, they're not on some distant planet, they're *right here*—we just can't perceive them."

"Sure, why not." Liam barely stopped himself in time from shrugging again. "Now explain what that has to do with the damn storm."

Jay glanced at the others and took a deep breath. "Here it is then: Humans live in this dimension, the one we can see. Other beings live in the dimensions we can't."

"And they visit our little slice of space and time whenever they please," added Morgan.

Liam was stunned into silence for several moments. Then his temper kicked in. "Jesus H. Christ, if you're trying to say that frickin' *aliens* wrecked my farm, it's a piss-poor joke."

"No, not aliens. *Not* aliens," said Morgan quickly, her hands making calming gestures.

"Well, what the hell else is it then?"

"The fae are here," said Caris.

Liam nearly saw stars as his head whipped around to stare at her. He yanked his hand away from her so he could use both to cradle his head, half wondering if his brain had just popped like a cheap balloon. But he was far too angry to give in to his body's desire to pass out just yet. He was damn well going to see this conversation through to the end, once and for all. "Faeries again? You're *still* on that damn faery kick? I was hoping I just didn't remember that right."

Caris didn't flinch in the slightest. "Some call them faeries, but they have many names because there are many kinds," she continued, her face as solemn as a funeral. "The fae can be found in the old stories of many countries, and they're there for a reason, Liam Cole. *Maent yn bodoli.* They exist."

How could this be the same woman he'd fallen for? And what about the two veterinarians? When did they change from his caring and sensible friends into card-carrying members of the fringe?

"You really, truly want me to believe that *Tinkerbell* tore the goddamn roof off my barn?"

"Not Tinkerbell," said Morgan. "The Tylwyth Teg. They're the ruling class among the fae, and they aren't little and cute, and they sure as hell aren't friendly. We're talking about extremely powerful beings here, creatures that don't particularly care about right and wrong."

"Right. And I suppose they use magic too?" Liam took his hands from his head in order to sign quotation marks around *magic*.

Morgan was incensed. "How do you think we got your house back together in such a short time if there's no such thing as magic?"

"I . . . Well, I admit it was pretty damn impressive, but it wasn't magic," he persisted, though his gut was telling him his friend had a hell of a point. "You called someone. You said you had connections."

"Okay, bud, you're welcome to phone around. Go ahead and check with every company you can find in a hundred-mile radius," she dared him. "See for yourself if anyone was here. I have connections, all right, but not to any human company that can houseclean like that, or believe me, I'd be paying them to tidy up my own place regularly."

Liam looked to Jay for support but didn't find it. "Magic, dude," he said and shrugged. "Could be technology we don't understand yet, but it's magic to us. Starr and I have both seen it in action."

Holy-o-shit, he thought. *They're not backing down on this.* What the hell was going on? Vaguely he wondered whether it was a strange and elaborate joke—and a hugely unfunny one at that. *Why would these guys mess with my head when I've just had a concussion? These are my friends!* "Look, this is just too far-fetched for me," said Liam. "I don't know what happened to you all, but this magic crap is stupid."

"*Magic* transformed me into a grim, just as I told you when you found me." Caris's voice had a curious dignity to it, like a victim reciting the unsavory facts of the crime against them to an unsympathetic cop. "'Twas Maelgwn, a fae prince, who did it. He used magic to change me, and magic to steal me away with him. I was forced to leave my father and our farm behind, and everything I ever knew and loved, never to see them again, all thanks to that *magic* you so easily mock."

Her words stung him, as if he was an insensitive creep, and not someone being asked to accept the impossible. *I wish I could believe you. I really do.* That's what Liam wanted to say, but the words wouldn't come out. The most he could do was put his hand over hers, and he was supremely relieved when she laced her fingers through his. *She wasn't kidding when she said it wasn't going to be easy for us.* He had no idea how they'd survive something like this. It wasn't like they had different religions—it was more like they had different realities.

"My husband, Rhys, and my friend Aidan became death dogs as well," added Morgan. "They were lucky to escape the spell that bound them. And luckier still that they weren't killed outright by the Fair Ones."

Not just faeries, but *homicidal* faeries? This was just getting better and better. "Oh now, come on. Since when do they kill people? I don't remember reading any books like that when I was a kid." He'd actually read superhero comics more than anything else, but that was beside the point.

"You weren't reading the ancient stories, the *real* stories like the ones my Welsh grandmother told me," said Morgan. "The faeries you see in books and movies now are sanitized and diminished versions of the real thing. Frankly, the real thing is usually big and terrifying."

"Most of the Tylwyth Teg are amoral. Many, like this Maelgwn guy, exhibit sociopathic behavior," Jay explained. "It's very apparent that they don't think like we do. In fact, it's safest to treat them all as extremely dangerous . . ."

"*Enough with the damn faeries, you guys!* I'm still not hearing how any of this connects to the storm."

Morgan jumped up and started to pace. "Look, if you've ever picked up a mythology book, you've heard of the Wild Hunt, right? It's a classic theme."

Why did that sound familiar? Liam frowned and was rewarded with a fresh burst of pain, but he soldiered on. "I dunno, I think it's some story the Norse used to tell. The god of the dead led a hunt of dark horses and hounds through the sky or some damn thing."

"Close enough. Well, Maelgwn and his gang of Tylwyth Teg ran a rogue hunt right through your farm. About forty or fifty riders came through this region and damaged every farm in their path between Pullman and Cheney. It was a helluva big storm, yes, but the thunderstorm is just a side effect of the light whips the riders use."

Riders . . .

Stunned, Liam fell silent. How could he have forgotten? He thought he'd seen a dark band of riders along Finger Ridge. In fact, they were the very last thing he saw before that damn crystal vase knocked him senseless. *No, wait—I saw something else. There were streamers of lightning snaking upward.* But that was a natural thing, right? Just a charge reaching up from the ground to connect with the lightning coming down from the clouds . . . except the phenomenon was very short-lived and rarely seen. And there had been not one but *many* streamers. They'd all been in the very midst of the riders, lingering long enough to illuminate the horsemen to Liam's incredulous gaze.

There was that feeling in his gut again, the sensation of truth. *What the hell is going on?*

"Okay, I think I've heard enough for one day," he said finally, with one hand cradling his head. "I'm tired and I have one helluva headache. If someone will give me a hand up, I definitely have a date with the couch."

Jay sprang into action as Morgan tried again to explain. "Look, I know how all this sounds, I really do. I used to think the fae were just make-believe too," she said, as Liam was helped to his feet. "But that's before they tried to kill Rhys and me one night. They're as real as we are, and their realm is right beneath our feet. Where geologists perceive nothing but rock and earth, where our damned *instruments* detect only rock and earth, the fae have enormous ancient kingdoms that dwarf everything we've ever built above ground."

"It's true. I've seen them. I've been there." Caris looked up at him, her face grave. "The Fair Ones existed long before mortals walked the earth, Liam Cole. And some of them still remember that time."

The woman he cared for—*ah hell*, he loved her and knew it—was telling the truth. His friends were telling the truth. Liam could see it in their faces, and worse, his gut confirmed it. *But that only means they believe what they're saying, right?* He'd heard that members of cults could pass lie-detector tests. But how did three intelligent people—two of them medical professionals, for chrissakes—get caught up in such a wild tale?

The sun had dipped behind the hills, leaving only a glow in the sky. Jay stayed quiet as he drove the quad slowly along the cleared path leading back to the house. Liam was thankful for that—he didn't think he could take in one more word about faeries, or anything else for that matter. But that didn't keep him from thinking about the strange things he'd been told. His head and heart and gut were arguing over the details of course—but the conclusion he kept coming to was: "Morgan and Jay are my friends." They'd come all the way out here to help him, and help him they had. *Caris too, when she barely knew me.* In fact, if you really wanted to talk about magic, the trio had pulled off nothing short of a frickin' miracle with his house alone, never mind taken excellent care of his animals. All three had gone above and beyond for *him*.

No matter where the truth lay, Liam felt he owed his friends more than a dismissal of their words. Somehow he had to try to understand. He owed that and more to Caris especially, and the future he'd like to have with her—but how? Where the hell did he begin?

The vehicle slowed to a complete stop about forty yards short of the house, startling Liam out of his thoughts. "Hey, J-man, can you please pull up to the steps? I don't think I'm steady enough to walk this far."

Jay, however, was staring straight ahead. "Um . . . there seems to be a party in the way."

"A what?"

Liam stared too. Between the quad and the house were dozens of canvas canopies in every bright color imaginable. Beneath their shade sat low round tables, not even a foot high, formed of smooth cross slices of tree trunks that had been polished to a high shine. Thick squat candles burned brightly in the twilight. And every setting boasted a rough-carved mug and a copper trencher laden with breads, meats, and cheeses of every kind, not to mention a cavalcade of pickles.

But the guests were the most startling of all. Seated all around the groaning tables appeared to be every last one of Aunt Ruby's beloved gnomes . . .

That's not possible.

Not pausing to consider his throbbing head or his flagging energy level, Liam slid from the quad and shuffled slowly through the bright panoply, bending a little to fit under the canvases. His last straw of hope—that somehow the local Ladies' Garden Society had arrived with emergency replacement gnomes for their beloved sister Ruby—dissolved almost before the desperate thought could form. He *recognized* most of these gnomes, having had to move many of them countless times so he could mow and trim and weed around them as a teenager. Large and small, fat and thin, cheerful or frowning—every last one had been painstakingly glued back together!

The cracks were tiny but apparent, giving some of them a faint Frankensteinian air. And definitely creeping him out. *This is crazy.* No one could ever have found and gathered up all the fragments from all over the property. No one could have sorted them all out, glued them back together, and then arranged a goddamn party in—he checked his watch—*barely a couple of hours!*

Feeling his strength slipping, and possibly his mind, Liam ducked under a vivid blue canopy with some of the bigger gnomes, where a tree stump afforded him a seat. These gnomes definitely had a sports theme going, with a large TV screen showing a baseball game in progress. There was a new gnome in the bunch, most likely one of his aunt's more recent acquisitions. Maybe even an antique, since it looked more like some kind of weird forest spirit than what his aunt usually collected. Even more peculiar, it sported an authentic Blue Jays cap.

"Not the Jays," Liam muttered aloud. "Anything but the damn Jays. Aunt Ruby is strictly a Mariners fan, for chrissakes." During one game, he and Uncle Conall had actually feared she'd have a stroke when it looked like Toronto might beat her favorite team.

The "gnome" suddenly turned to look at Liam with fire in its bright blue eyes. Indignation quivered in every word as the bizarre little creature demanded: "And just what, pray tell, d'ya think is wrong with the Blue Jays?"

TWENTY-ONE

⌒〜⌒

"C an you hear me? Come on, buddy, you gotta wake up."

It was dark, and Jay Browning's voice sounded a long way away. Couldn't be talking to him, surely. He just wanted to sleep . . .

"Liam! Liam Cole, you gotta wake up now."

Okay, maybe he *was* being addressed. "G'way," he muttered without opening his eyes.

"Here," said another voice. "Let me wave this under Mr. Mariner's nose."

The pungent scent of vinegar and garlic assaulted his senses, penetrating his sinuses with acrid fumes and kicking his brain wide, wide awake. Liam's eyes flew open, and he gasped for air but got only more of the powerful aroma. At first, all he could see was green, as an enormous dill seemingly the size of a fence post was being brandished in his face.

By a gnome wearing a Blue Jays hat, sitting on his chest.

"What the hell?" Liam tried to bat it away and scramble backward at the same time, which not only didn't work but also set off Klaxons of pain in his beleaguered head. "Ow, dammit! Get away, get off me!"

The strange woody creature sniffed and got up with great dignity to stand beside Liam, one hand on his hip and the other pointing the pickle at him like a weapon. "I'm not a bug fer ya to be shooing away, dontcha know."

Jesus H. Christ, I'm in a coma. What else could it be? Liam had heard of people not only dreaming but hallucinating while deeply unconscious. Maybe he was still in the hospital . . . Hell, maybe he was still lying in the guest room, with Aunt Ruby's vase next to his bruised skull. Or maybe he'd never been hit with the vase at all; maybe it was lightning, maybe the house was destroyed by the tornado, and maybe, just maybe, he was frickin' *dead.*

Jay leaned into his field of view, using his thumb and forefinger to move Liam's eyelids around to stare into his pupils. "Had me worried there, dude. Morgan and Caris would both have my ass in a sling if I let anything happen to you." Glancing at his watch, Jay checked the pulse in Liam's wrist. "Solid and steady," he announced. "A little rapid, but that's to be expected."

"I . . . I passed out, right? I mean—shit, I don't know what I mean."

"Lemme guess." Jay helped him to sit up against a tree. "You're a little worried about your sanity?"

Liam could see the gnome creature behind Jay. He was taking great smacking bites out of the pickle. And all around him was the scene Liam remembered last, the giant crazy gnome party beneath the colorful canvas canopies. Bright cheerful candles illuminated everything. "Christ, I'm not sure what to worry about *first.*"

"Let's try some introductions. Liam, this is my friend Ranyon." The young vet turned to the strange being and gently bumped fists with him. "Ranyon, this is my friend Liam."

Ranyon didn't seem terribly impressed. "So, Mr. Mariner, you've never seen an ellyll before?"

"Why are you calling me that?" asked Liam, genuinely perplexed. He turned to Jay. "And what's he saying about an eel?"

"First question: *baseball*," explained Jay. "You cast aspersions on his beloved Toronto team."

Okay, he could wrap his head around that much. "I'm sorry about that, er, *Ranyon*. My aunt's totally crazy for the Mariners. I just assumed someone had played a joke on her by dressing up one of her gnomes as the opposing team."

"Ya watch baseball yerself?"

"Not often enough to have a favorite team. I like a good game no matter who's playing, but I'm mostly a football kinda guy. Seahawks fan."

"*Hmpf.* Well, at least yer honest." The little man finished the pickle, licked the tips of his fingers, then folded his spindly arms in front of him. They resembled knobby tree branches more than anything, and so did his skinny legs. Maybe they *were* branches, since there were leaves sticking out of them here and there. Ranyon's face certainly looked like weathered wood, and his hair was filled with leaves as well. Despite the bright T-shirt and ball cap, he could easily be mistaken for an ancient shrub. Only his lively blue eyes said differently.

Jay continued. "Second question: he didn't say *eels*. He said he was an *ellyll*. That's a type of fae, an elemental, from the Nine Realms."

"Lately of Spokane Valley," Ranyon added proudly.

"Okay. Sure. Well, good to meet you." Not knowing what else to do, Liam offered his hand to the little tree man. After a moment, Ranyon took it, and Liam's eyes widened. Those long, twiggy fingers were damn strong.

And very, very *real*.

Holy-o-shit. He was seeing, hearing, and *touching* an honest-to-God faery. He nodded at Jay. "I guess I oughta apologize for not believing you."

The man just shrugged and grinned. "Hey, we all knew how far-fetched it sounded. When I first met Ranyon, it might have been a little easier for me because I already half believed in this kind of stuff anyway. I *wanted* to believe, you know? But your reaction was totally understandable. Most people aren't very receptive to having their reality shifted."

Liam nodded at the description. His reality had definitely been shifted—*like a damn earthquake shifts tectonic plates.* And like all seismic events, he knew the change was permanent.

The Great Way yawned open, a shimmering gateway suspended in the air between Lurien and the queen. Her proximity to the phenomenon had him poised on the knife-edge of alertness—they were scarcely a handsbreadth away from its reach—but Gwenhidw was never one to avoid risk. *Safer that she should pet a fanged warth*, he thought grimly. Crystalline motes of pure power floated out of its maw, wafting to the rocky ground beneath his feet and vanishing like snowflakes, but Lurien knew the mountain had simply absorbed the energy.

Within the Way, a vast tunnel of spun starlight stretched away as far as even his sharp eyes could see. It was undeniably breathtaking in its beauty—and like all things associated with the Inbetween, it was also dangerous beyond imagining.

As Lord of the Wild Hunt, he had now braved the bright and winding course a score of times, with the full force of his magic before him and the strength of his battle-hardened followers at his back. And still, creatures seen and unseen had attacked them from every side. He and his band were compelled to fight their way through each time—only to discover the return journey just as difficult. He'd lost two good hunters, a horse, and three white hounds on the last sortie alone. It still left a bad taste in his mouth: he wasn't accustomed to losing, not with the skills and powers he'd worked so hard and so long to master.

Lurien commanded a considerable wealth of magic, far more than most of the Fair Ones could imagine. And unlike many of them, he didn't rely on stones and relics and other amplifiers—he considered the practice to be both lazy and foolish. As a hunter and a fighter, he knew too well that weapons could be lost or taken. Instead, he had painstakingly honed his powers over the eons until he *was* a weapon.

He still believed in caution, however. The distant sound of fae horses stamping and blowing attested to the presence of the Wild Hunt on the shoreline below. As *llaw dde*, Lurien was bound to protect the queen from any and all dangers. He would use every tool at his disposal, including his own heart's blood, to keep her safe.

As well as her own ability.

After the assassination of King Arthfael, Lurien had insisted that Gwenhidw no longer rely solely on any protector, including himself. She had already been proficient in magics and spells, but with his guidance and encouragement, she'd developed her powers to the point that they now surpassed his own. He was proud of her for that. Though her royal lineage entitled her to every artifact of power housed in the vast treasure rooms of the palace, and although she commanded the loyalty of numberless beings, *she was dependent on none of them.*

Except tonight.

They would all be depending on each other tonight, as Lurien and Gwenhidw combined their magics with the varying powers possessed by the assembly of envoys. But would the combined result be sufficient to tame the Great Way?

Lurien surveyed the envoys, all committed to the plan to claim Tir Hardd. Only Gwenhidw could bring together such diverse beings with such long-held misconceptions about each other and so many genuine grievances against each other and persuade them to work as one. They had practiced together in the courtyard innumerable times. They had succeeded in gathering samplau and preparing them for the journey through the Way—and after the explosion at the palace, they had replaced all the ones that had been destroyed.

Their biggest accomplishment, however, had been the enlargement of first one, then several, of the small ways. Yet the tiny conduits could be stretched only so far, and not one had grown big enough for anything larger than a coblyn to walk through. Only the Great Way could provide what was needed—but were they ready for it?

They stood atop the faery kingdom's highest mountain, Mynedfa, the only peak that actually burst through the fae skies into the human realm. Mortals called it Holyhead Mountain, though in their world it was little more than a seaside hill whose sheer rock walls flanked Anglesey Island, where the druids had once made their home. Since that time, humans had forgotten how much magic resided in the mount. And not even the druids had known about the massive Way that Arthfael himself had discovered there.

Night had fallen in the mortal realm, its sky clear and filled with stars. The moon was full and round, echoing the shape of the glittering portal, but unable to compete with its glory. At the queen's direction, a circle had also been formed by the delegates of the Nine Realms. Large and small, they stood on the broad flat mountaintop in utter silence. Seventy-nine envoys, plus Gwenhidw and Lurien, made nine times nine. A goodly number for magical workings, he knew, even though he had fought hard to make certain that the envoys numbered seventy-eight.

Lurien had spent hours arguing with an infuriated Gwenhidw, advocating far greater precautions. No evidence had yet been found of who or what was responsible for the terrible explosion, and therefore *everyone* was suspect. With innumerable examples of Draigddynion crimes against the monarchy in the past, surely it was best that Aurddolen remain imprisoned for the time being. And perhaps the enlarging of the Way, the seeding of Tir Hardd, should be postponed until the current conspiracy was uncovered. Gwenhidw argued that there were those within the realms, even among the Tylwyth Teg themselves, who would not be above such a horrific deed, and he had to concede the point.

In the end, he was compelled to concede to her wishes regarding Aurddolen as well. Citing diplomatic necessity, the queen had insisted that the Draigddynion envoy not only be freed but also rejoin the envoys. Lurien had been ordered to apologize as well, but *that* he would not do. He would never be sorry for trying to protect Gwenhidw. And since the queen was doubly determined to go forward with her plans as quickly as possible, Lurien not only tripled the guards around her; he also set six guards on Aurddolen day and night.

As furious as she was certain to be, the dragon woman had neither looked at Lurien nor spoken to him. Not once. A pity, but he had made his choices, and he would live with them.

So far, they had been successful in sending several dozen samplau through the glittering Way, all of the ones that would fit its present dimensions. There remained, however, massive spheres like great ships, containing precious portions of the mighty Silver Maples forest, the Rainbow Chasm, and many more amgylcheddau, one-of-a-kind environments that provided shelter to numberless creatures unknown in any other world.

This is what we practiced for. The time had come to enlarge the Way.

Many of the delegates seemed mesmerized by the splendor of the bright tunnel. *Those with any sense*, thought Lurien, *should be awed by their queen.* Clad in a white gown that seemed created from moonlight itself, she wore the silver baldric of her royal office over one shapely shoulder. From it hung the sword of her ancestors, Deiliad Golau. The sword's name meant "Bearer of Light," and it seemed to Lurien that the queen embodied that name far more than the ancient weapon did. In the pommel of the faery-forged sword, however, rested the largest-known bwgan stone in the Nine Realms. By the glittering light of the Great Way, green fire leapt to life within the smooth black stone. Perhaps the assembly thought that the queen was using its magical properties to hold the Way open, but Lurien knew that she was unaided by anything but her own honed ability. He had agreed with her reasoning that she should demonstrate her power, so that the envoys would have full confidence in her—and therefore have confidence in her plan. But he also understood how much energy it took from her. *Hurry,* he thought silently. *We must do this now, while you yet have all your strength.*

Gwenhidw called to the delegates: "Come to me now, all of you! Join your powers to mine as we have practiced!" Keeping a watchful eye on the Way, she extended one of her hands to the closest envoys. No one moved for a long moment, then another . . .

Aurddolen leapt out of her place in the circle and ran to seize the proffered hand. "Quickly, everyone! There must be no hesitation. We must move *now!*" she shouted at the others, extending her hand in turn. The delegates shook off their qualms then and rushed to join hand to hand to wing to paw to hoof. As the chain of beings grew longer, the air became electric. Power surged through the group and came at last to Lurien. It was his task to complete the circle and combine the powers of all. He extended his hand to the queen.

And just as their fingertips touched, power surged around the circle like a chain of lightning. It shook them all, and some of the delegates—even the fierce kelpies and the *kobolds*—fell to their knees at the unaccustomed burden of energy. For a moment it seemed too much to bear. Then the enormous tear in the sky that was the Great Way seemed to draw in their collective power as it was a live thing drawing breath. This was what they had hoped for, this was what they had practiced for, trained for. The Way would feed on their power and *grow*.

"Do not break the circle!" commanded the queen, as more of the envoys collapsed where they stood.

"*Gwenhidw.*" Lurien didn't like the way this was going. Power was being sucked away from him at an alarming rate. The Way was draining them all. "We have to—"

Without warning, a shaft of blinding white light erupted from within the tunnel. The energy struck Gwenhidw full on, not only knocking her out of Lurien's reach but hurling her over the cliff's edge like a falling star. Instinct was made for moments like these, when shock robbed the brain of all thought. Without hesitation, Lurien threw himself headlong after her, and they both tumbled to the restless ocean below.

"So begins the rule of Maelgwn, King of Tir Hardd!" The prince rode his stallion into the midst of the scrying pool, trampling the vision of the falling queen and causing it to disappear from view entirely. His hand-chosen followers, three-score strong and every one of them a blooded noble of the Tylwyth Teg, cheered him heartily.

"A cheer as well for our good friends, the keepers of the Way," said Maelgwn, and forced his unwilling mount toward the towering creatures that seemed to draw all the surrounding light into them. The anghenfilod were pitiless and insatiable—and now absolutely essential to his plans. "Well done! Today, we have kicked the *cacwn* nest, angering the bees within. And hundreds upon hundreds of vengeful fae will come pouring through the Great Way, just as I promised you. If you lie in wait within, I will close the Way behind you as I promised, and they will be unable to escape you."

And all of Tir Hardd will truly be mine, he thought. Above and below, and no one to oppose him, human or fae. As for the loathsome Anghenfilod? They would be the old kingdom's problem. Thanks to the ancient Draigddynion spell in his possession, written on leather parchment stained with the former owner's dark blood, Maelgwn had the means to permanently seal the Great Way from this side. As for the power to enact the complex spell, he was already energized by the glowing stones in his breastplate. He'd need to draw on his followers' magic as well, but it might not be enough. Once the little mortal fiddler was back in his hands, however, his success would be ensured. And when the spell was complete, Tir Hardd would be unassailable by anyone from the Nine Realms.

The first wave of fae beings seeking revenge for their queen would find themselves trapped against a dead end and devoured by anghenfilod—and Maelgwn knew that would include the entire Wild Hunt and their twice-damned leader. After that, knowing that the Way was blocked at this end, no one would attempt to use it again, but they still wouldn't be safe. *The spell ensured the Way remained open to the great mountain, Mynedfa.*

As soon as the Anghenfilod were hungry again, they would spill out the opposite end of the Way, and begin hunting in the Nine Realms.

It was simply *perfect.*

Power surged through Maelgwn as he basked in his ultimate triumph, and accompanying waves of pleasure radiated from his shaft. Despite the intense gratification, however, the stones in the breastplate felt as if they were intent on burning through his upper body. Still, he dared not take off the cuirass for even a moment's respite. He *must* have as much magic at his command as possible at all times. And he could not risk anyone guessing the source of his power.

Rhedyn knew about it of course—the breastplate was too bothersome to hide when he took her, which was more and more frequently each day. And by necessity, she had become his personal servant as well. But what did that matter? He certainly wasn't concerned about *her* telling anyone anything. He kept her well under control.

Some of the smugness left his face when he glanced at her, however. Rhedyn's face was drawn into something like horror. "You do not share my triumph, my dear lady?"

"You didn't say you were going to hurt the queen," she whispered, fisting her hands in the folds of her green riding dress, as if to keep them still.

Spurred into a blinding burst of speed, Maelgwn's stallion slammed its shoulder into Rhedyn's mount, causing it to rear and stagger backwards until it threw her to the ground. The prince then seized her horse by the reins beneath its chin and yanked it down on all fours once more.

"There can be only one ruler in Tir Hardd—*one*, do you understand?—and I intend it to be me. I have planned and worked for this for centuries. You have questioned my decisions for the last time." He spun around in his saddle to look at all of his followers. *My subjects.* "You have all witnessed this woman interfere with the enjoyment of what is rightfully mine."

Rhedyn rose shakily from where she had fallen, clutching her shoulder. Not one member of the assembly made the slightest move to assist her. Instead, they only watched with mild interest as

Maelgwn uncoiled his light whip from his side. The dark anghenfilod watched too, with greedy anticipation in their soulless eyes.

A frantic baying suddenly filled the air, and a huge canine shape materialized nearby.

News at last. Rhedyn could be—would be—punished later. At Maelgwn's signal, the great black dog lowered itself until its belly scraped the ground and crawled toward him. "Tell me you have discovered my little lost grim," he commanded.

The animal dipped its head once, then twice for good measure, no doubt anxious that its message be clear.

Found! The hidden stones in the breastplate beneath his tunic seemed to heat of their own accord, as if they too were pleased. "Show me at once," he ordered, and the dog bounded away. Maelgwn's silver spurs drew blood from his horse's flanks as he rode hard in pursuit. The entire hunt wheeled and followed him, with all the grims howling like hellhounds at their heels.

Rhedyn alone was left behind. Maelgwn hadn't specifically given her to the anghenfilod, but they might think differently—if they thought at all. She had no idea where she was in the mortal realm, but she dared not stay here. Her fae mount, steady beast that it was, stood shaking but had not fled. Nor did it appear to be lame. Quickly she seized a fistful of its mane in her good hand and leapt to its back.

The horse didn't need to be told to run for its life.

TWENTY-TWO

M organ had left the barn on the pretext of checking on the goats again, but Caris knew the tall veterinarian was discouraged over her failure to persuade Liam to accept their story. *It's not your fault*, thought Caris. *You can't* make *someone believe in something.* Knowing that didn't make it any better for any of them, though, and she felt wholly at a loss. Should they try again? Would Liam even *allow* them to try again? He'd been so angry . . . but that was water off a duck's back to her. Her own da had been a gruff man more often than not, cussing at every frustration, and he was all the more so after a long night at the pub. Yet she'd known that her father meant nothing by it. She'd certainly never worried that he would send her away.

But what would Liam Cole do?

The man might rail at them all, order them off his farm, perhaps even banish them from his circle of friends. But Jay and Morgan had mates to go home to. Family. Other friends. Work to do and lives to lead. Caris knew she would be welcome to accompany them—and Morgan had already offered her gainful employment—but her heart could hardly bear the thought. Yet what choice would she have if Liam couldn't find it within himself to accept their story? Even if he wanted to continue their relationship, she couldn't do it. She simply couldn't.

Because you needed the person you loved to believe you. And there it was. She'd admitted it. She'd tried to be sensible and careful, conceded that she had *feelings*, agreed to give him a chance and all that. *Duw annwyl, I love him.*

Now, simply by telling the truth, she had surely lost the man's trust, and with it, all hope of love was dashed. Nor would she settle for less. It seemed foolish, even outrageous, to dare to want something as incredibly wonderful as love, when she'd already received the gift of being human again. *But humans have hearts!* As a rule, the Tylwyth Teg looked down their noses at mortals, usually with distaste and loathing for such inferior creatures. After spending time in the Nine Realms, however, Caris knew better. Most of the Fair Ones envied men and women their emotions, but particularly love in all its forms.

He touched my cheek . . . He kissed my fingers . . . He kissed my face. Most of all, he'd uncovered his secrets, revealed his past disappointments and pains to her.

Realistically, their relationship was barely more than the light of a firefly, blinking fitfully in the darkness. But she knew, as much as she had ever known anything, that their feelings could grow into a great blaze, bigger than the biggest midsummer bonfires she'd witnessed as a child.

Big enough, perhaps, to consume her.

The foals were well fed and dozing. Might as well walk back to the house and make up some semblance of a meal. Jay and Morgan hadn't bothered to eat yet, she knew, and she'd had very little herself—though she'd never felt less like eating in her life. As for Liam? If she was lucky, he'd already be sound asleep on the couch again, and if fortune was truly kind, he might even be stretched out in the back guest room.

Out of sight . . . but he'll never be out of mind. Caris sighed.

As she crossed the farmyard in the dusk and headed for the house, she caught sight of many glowing colors through the shadows of the broken trees. She couldn't see clearly at first and quickened her pace to get closer. Were those tents? Whatever was going on? No Gypsy encampment had ever been so dazzling. Drawing closer, she saw the many—what? Dolls? *No, they're garden statues, silly.* The whimsical figures were called *gnomes*, and they surely represented how humans viewed the faery world. As precious and sweet as children's toys, and purely imaginary . . .

Small wonder that Liam didn't believe us.

She regarded the red-capped one closest to her. Out of all the fae creatures she knew, Caris supposed the bearded gnomes best resembled the Coblynau. Most of them did, from the ones that were barely a hand high to some that stood as tall as her waist. But why had Ranyon—because it could only have been the ellyll—gone to the trouble to do all this? It was one thing to restore the gnomes, but the festive setting looked like a giant tea party. In fact, she remembered playing much the same way with her cloth-peg dolls and a pair of uncooperative kittens when she was small. She'd never seen such an abundance of food in her entire life, however, and the savory aromas made her stomach growl. *Whatever is Ranyon up to?*

The ellyll's excited voice burst from one of the tents closest to the house. As she made her way there through the bright gathering, Jay could be heard as well. It sounded like they were arguing . . .

And then a third voice made her heart jump.

Caris hurried as fast as was possible, dodging tables and figures and tent poles, until she reached a great blue canopy—and stopped completely still, unprepared for the sight of Ranyon, Jay, and Liam, lounging on an enormous leather couch. Great mugs of ale were in their hands, heaping plates of food in their laps, and they were far too busy exclaiming over something on the television to notice her presence behind them.

"Did ya see that?" Ranyon was sloshing ale as he pointed at the screen with his mug. "That batter's havin' a real power surge today. 'Bout time too!"

"Naw, it's the prevailing winds," said Liam, and took a hearty bite from a cold meat sandwich that was as thick as a brick. "Come on, just look at the direction the flags are flying. That ball got a ride."

"Are ya daft?" The ellyll punched Liam's arm. "My man's a solid contact hitter. That ball didn't need a bit o' help to clean off the bases."

"I haven't heard any commentary yet," added Jay. "You'd think the announcers would say something about the wind if it were a possible factor."

"You just watch the next batter," said Liam, with his mouth full of sandwich.

"Aye, well it's yer team up next," said Ranyon. "They won't be batting near as far as mine."

Liam shook his head. "I don't have a team. I told you: I'm a neutral observer."

"If ya don't have a team, then why can't ya be rootin' fer Toronto?"

Dear heavens, he's made a believer out of Liam! Relief sagged Caris's knees, and she sat down hard on a vacant stump between two enormous smiling gnomes made of concrete. She truly didn't know whether to laugh or cry. Ranyon had managed to work another miracle—only this was far greater than anything he'd done with the house, or even with the strange party around her.

The ellyll turned around and winked at her, as though he'd heard every word in her head. "There ya be, good lady."

Jay waved without looking, intent on something happening on the television, but she was shocked when Liam practically jumped off the couch and came to stand in front of her.

Instinctively she put out her hands to steady him—but it wasn't necessary. Not only did he not keel over; he looked as steady as a rock. His color was good, and she peered at his forehead in utter disbelief: the vivid purple bruising that had marred nearly half of it was completely gone!

Shocked, Caris looked around at Ranyon. He had a knowing expression on his face and waggled the mug he had in his spindly hand so that some of the foam sloshed over the side . . . and it glittered strangely as if shot through with pure gold.

"You gave him coblyn ale?" she mouthed at him, but the ellyll just smiled and shrugged as if he were perfectly innocent of any such thing. Liam still had his tankard in his hand, and she snatched it from him.

"Hey! That's my first one!" he protested, but she ignored him and eyed the contents. He'd polished off two-thirds of it, but there at the bottom was one of Ranyon's signature charms. Caris guessed it had healing properties, and she was glad for that. But the coblyn ale itself was a concern. When her da had a few too many pints at the pub, he'd eventually become drowsy and collapse to sleep it off (hopefully making it home first). Coblyn ale had a like effect on the fae. Fermented by the Coblynau deep in their mountain home, the powerful brew quickly produced drunkenness, and eventually stupor, even in the Tylwyth Teg. *But a human?* Their minds remained clear, their thoughts unmuddled, while their bodies were infused with energy. Liam Cole was probably feeling better than he'd had in years.

Like all things fae, however, there was a downside. The more ale, the more energy. Too much and it was possible for a mortal body to wear itself out in frenetic activity. She'd witnessed captive humans literally dancing themselves to death in the midst of the glittering Court, and the memory made her heartsick. Caris fished out the talisman and dumped the ale on the ground.

"You've had enough for today," she said to Liam, tucking the little charm into his shirt pocket.

He looked like he was about to protest further when Ranyon interrupted. "Aye, she's probably right about that," said the ellyll. "Don't want to overdo with that head o' yers. At best you'll be fair snobbled or, worse, you'll be tossin' yer cookies again." He winked at Caris and turned his attention to Jay, who was still focused on the screen. "I'll just be having a quick look 'round for Morgan. I'm sure she could do with a bite to eat," he announced much more loudly than he needed to, and seized his friend by the arm. "And I'm going to need a bit o' *help* finding the poor, famished dear."

"What? Oh, oh right. Sure." Jay jumped up and the two disappeared in record time, leaving Caris alone with Liam. He had both her hands in his before she realized it.

"Hell, it seems like all I do is apologize to you," he murmured. "This is twice in one day I have to say I'm sorry for being such a moron."

Moron? She looked at him oddly, then laughed. "Sorry. Once upon a time in Wales, I'd have thought you were talking about *carrots*. But I think it means something quite a bit different now."

"Lemme spell it out for you. It means *idiot*. Dork. Complete and total ass. Oh, and probably that word you came up with too: *dihiryn*. Did I say that right? Anyway, take your pick, I'm guilty as charged."

"I don't think you deserve any of those names, and especially not *dihiryn*." She stood on her tiptoes and whispered in his ear. "That's a brutal cad, you know. A bounder. A truly nasty and despicable villain, like Maelgwn."

"Okay, okay, maybe I'm not quite that bad." He touched his forehead gently to hers, and she was mesmerized by the intensity of his gaze. "But I didn't believe you when you told me the truth, and I did that to you more than once too. I'm guessing it probably hurt like hell. I'd do anything rather than bring you pain, you know, but somehow I seem to keep doing it—that whole misunderstanding about music for instance. I could have lost you forever before I'd even gotten a chance to know you.

"Before I got the chance to tell you I love you."

She couldn't think of a single thing to say, but her arms slid around his neck of their own volition. Caris had never had a lover in her life. She knew nothing about kissing save for that quick and awkward sampling when she was ten, and if she'd stopped to think about her lack of experience, she might have let this moment slip by. But she didn't stop, and she didn't think . . . Her lips tingled as they met Liam's—and they didn't even bump noses. His response, gentle but certain, left her breathless.

And wanting more.

The sunset had given way to full dark, and the many vividly colored canopies glowed like giant lanterns with hundreds of bright candles. The innumerable gnomes stood motionless beneath them, surrounded by all the trappings of a terrific party—although Liam cast them a suspicious glance from time to time in case any of them moved. Soon, however, he forgot all about them, and about everything else in the world.

There was only Caris.

The flavor of her soft full mouth was everything Liam remembered from their very first encounter, when he'd been convinced she was a dream for the taking. This time, however, it was all the sweeter for its willingness, and he drank from it for a long time.

"Stay with me. Be with me," he said at last. "I don't understand where you came from or why it was me that found you. I'm just grateful that you're here." His words were interspersed with the gentlest of kisses, giving and asking at the same time. "I'm sure you've noticed that I can be an insensitive jerk at times, but I hope you also know that I need you and I care about you. Just give me a chance to show you."

Caris looked up at him then. Her eyes were wide, yet dark with answering passion. She nodded solemnly, saying nothing.

But it was everything.

His arms encompassed her, and her warm body fit neatly against his as if she was made for him. Things long forgotten stirred within him, mingling with some things he'd never known. Desire was there, certainly. That first sight of Caris naked had already proved to him that he was very far from dead. It surprised him that there was so much *more*, things beyond even feelings or sensations. The notes of his heart were being strummed as surely as if she'd slipped her fingers inside his chest. Something about *this* woman, and only this woman, seemed to draw a quivering bow across the very moorings of his soul . . .

His lips didn't want to be parted from hers for a second, yet the need to memorize her shape had suddenly become essential. Liam's breath shuddered as his palms slid over the delicate angle of her shoulders and circled lazily down her spine. His strong fingers were feather-light as they outlined the curvature of her elegant hips, and—finally—his hands gently cupped the enticing roundness of her firm bottom.

Pull up! Pull up! his inner voice hollered at him, as though he were a pilot in a tailspin. Perhaps he was. Liam drew back from the kiss and used one hand to tuck her head beneath his chin. The other might as well have been glued to her glorious ass, but while his body was well aware of it, his brain wasn't paying full attention. He was too busy trying to pull oxygen out of air that had become too thick to breathe while attempting to gauge Caris's reaction. He might have gone too far already, for all he knew. So now, even if it killed him (and of course, his idiot lower brain was certain it would), he wasn't going to make another move without her explicit direction. Sighing, he rested his cheek on her hair and waited.

She was aware of her own heart, pounding like a small fist against the drum of his chest. Somehow it had picked up the rhythm of Liam's heart, and together they created a primal harmony. Caris's fingers tingled, automatically anxious to pick up her fiddle and pluck out a tune to that perfect drumbeat. The rest of her wanted other things—wonderfully physical things, elemental things, sensuous things.

And she wanted them all from Liam Cole.

His breath was ragged, as if he'd run all the way to the barn and back, but she knew it had nothing to do with his concussion. Thanks to Ranyon and his healing charm—not to mention a magical boost from the faery ale—Liam was right as rain. And if she doubted that, she had only to pay attention to the arousal bulging in the front of his jeans. She was pressed against it tightly enough that she could feel it throb against her belly in time to his heartbeat, a heartbeat she shared. It was intoxicating to think that she had somehow caused it, exhilarating to know that this strong man wanted her. More than that, he *loved* her.

His powerful arms held her firmly, yet she sensed how they sheltered rather than imprisoned her: she wasn't caged in the least. Caris knew that she only had to speak a word, and he would release her. That wasn't surprising. Despite the disappointments life had dealt him, despite his lingering anger and hurt, her instinct—or her *gut* as Liam so colorfully called it—told her that he was a good man. Not a perfect man, but one she could depend on, a man she could trust.

A man she could love with everything she had.

What *was* surprising to her was just how powerful, how overwhelming, her own desires were. They were not the barely formed feelings of the young woman she'd once been, nor were they the careless and lascivious appetites of the Fair Ones. And her desires were not sinful, she decided. There had been a time when she had worried deeply about her list of transgressions—but surely she'd been punished enough to pay for more than she could ever think to commit.

No, her desires were simply *hers*. And she could choose what she would do with them.

Far below him, *too damned far away*, Gwenhidw's pearl-colored hair and moon-white robes billowed around her like wings. A wounded swan falling from the sky . . . and by all the stars, Lurien *had* to catch up to her. His powers, usually so formidable, had been almost completely drained from him. Even at his best, he didn't have the capability of flight, but he tucked in his arms and legs and made himself a streamlined bolt, willing himself to go faster, *faster*.

If I can just touch her . . . He had so little energy left. Normally he could spell them both to safety but that wasn't an option now. Desperate, he ripped the light whip from his belt and snapped it downward against the uprush of resisting air with all of his physical strength and the last of the natural powers at his command. The end of the whip grazed her precious ankle, then, incredibly, half wrapped around it. *It was enough*, and although his magical energy was gone, his knowledge wasn't. Lurien didn't hesitate. He shouted the word, pouring his own life essence into the spell to give it power, and the queen vanished from his sight.

A half second later the impact of the blue-green water drove the breath from his body. The waves were strong this close to the sheer rock face of the mountain. Ruthlessly, they dragged him under, buffeting him, and yanking him back and forth between them like warths fighting over prey. Lurien drifted in and out of consciousness as he spiraled downward to where the full moon's light was only a faint glitter high overhead.

There was no pleasant sandy bottom below him, that much he knew. No shell-strewn seafloor. Only dark, jagged rocks waiting to receive him. Lurien searched within, seeking an overlooked spark of energy, a modicum of power, anything at all. He'd even be grateful to conjure a common kitchen spell—but he was well and truly drained. *At least if he was dying, he'd done so for just cause. He had saved his queen . . .*

A shadow blotted out the last of the light above him, and he supposed he must be dying—until the ferocious face of a monstrous, horselike kelpie appeared before his eyes. Its blue hide glowed slightly, enough to reveal its powerful shape. The water around it churned with the powerful downstroke of its broad hooves as it swam. No horse ever had such a mane—thick and green, it floated upward like an impenetrable wall of seaweed.

You're too late to drown me, he thought as the water creature seized his leather tunic in its sharp teeth. Like something out of a dream, a pale gold figure parted the seaweed mane as if it were a curtain. She grasped Lurien by the arm, pulling him through to the kelpie's broad back.

Aurddolen? It was his last thought before blackness engulfed him.

TWENTY-THREE

⌒⁊⁊⁊⌒

Just as Liam figured that Caris must have had enough, and that maybe he ought to back off for a while, she surprised him. With painstaking deliberateness, she lowered her arms and slipped her hands beneath his shirt. For a moment he simply stared, disbelieving, as she slid the material upward—then he hastened to shrug free of it.

She began planting slow, small kisses across his chest, even as she explored it with her hands. He hissed in a breath as she fondled his nipples—and he nearly imploded when she took his hands and placed them squarely on her breasts. Soft and rounded, they were heavy in his palms. Ever so gently, he squeezed them and thumbed her own nipples erect through the thin material that covered them.

Her low, throaty moan was electrifying.

Too bad he was in nine kinds of pain. Blue-jeans zippers were all too good at restraining expanding cocks—and his was nearly bent in half at the moment. "Honey," he managed. "I need to know how far you feel you'd like to go. Because I need to either stop now or get naked." *Before there's permanent damage.*

Her eyes were huge and dark with passion as she regarded him. "I think my gut is saying I'd like to lie with you."

"Now?" It was all he could do to get the word out.

She nodded—and laughed out loud as he scooped her up and whirled her around.

They were heading for the house, hand in hand, pausing to kiss every few steps, when the night sky was suddenly split asunder by a strange white light that blazed upward from the northeastern horizon like a large shooting star. Cometlike, the object grew brighter by the second and trailed a long, frost-colored tail as it hurtled in a high arc and then began a downward trajectory. Alarm bells went off in Liam's head: *It's headed for the goddamn farm!* He grabbed Caris's hand and ran.

The storm hadn't left much standing by way of shelter, except the house itself. Quickly, he flung open the cellar doors—and for the first time ever, it was a good thing the entrance *was* on the outside. He yanked Caris down the concrete steps into the darkness and around the corner, sheltering her against the cement wall with his body when . . .

There was no explosion, no sound at all. A brilliant flare of white light abruptly illuminated everything in the cellar as bright as day—it must have lit up the entire farm like a baseball stadium. He could see Caris's anxious face looking up at him. And then all was dark again, seemingly darker than before. He knew that was simply an illusion, but it wasn't comforting.

"What was it?" she asked, her voice revealing how shaken she was.

He wasn't feeling too steady himself. "I don't know. Probably just a meteorite." Liam had seen online videos of such occurrences—*funny how you always wish you could witness cool stuff like this until it happens to you*—but he found it far more disturbing that the area had become some sort of epicenter for strange events. *First a tornado, then faeries, and then a meteor . . . That's gotta be some kind of frickin' record, but I don't think Guinness has a category for this kind of shit.*

Outside in his corral, Dodge could be heard kicking up a fuss—and making a strange sort of sound between a neigh and a bellow. A cautious glance outside revealed a fiery glow behind the barn—and then Liam was running full out with Caris close at his heels. Morgan, Jay, and Ranyon were in there!

His fears that what was left of his barn was burning down were put to rest almost immediately. As he got closer, Liam realized the glow was about a hundred yards beyond the building, out on a rise in the alfalfa field. Even as he looked, the glow seemed to be fading—but it still gave enough light to see that all three of his friends were out there. Forced to slow down to a jog purely by the distance, Liam was thankful that his head was still in good shape. Ranyon had worked wonders, practically erasing the concussion, and that alone was enough to make him believe in magic. Otherwise he was certain he not only would have face-planted at the bottom of the cellar steps but would have probably still been there, trying hard not to upchuck.

"Dodge is really upset," said Caris, as they neared his corral. "Though I'm not thinking he's taken a fright."

The big Appaloosa stallion didn't looked frightened to Liam, either. The horse was pacing, switching his tail and shaking out his mane, and even occasionally planting his front hooves on the rails. Liam frowned. If he had to guess, he'd say there was a mare nearby that Dodge wanted to impress . . . *Probably Chevy.* Mares sometimes came into heat early after foaling. "Cool your jets, bro," he called out to the horse. "She's too damn busy being a mom right now." He'd be certain to check on the big goof later—then stopped dead as he saw the horse canter to the middle of the corral and drive hard for the fence. Liam waved his arms. "No! *Don't you dare, dammit!*"

Too late. Dodge cleared the top rail easily and charged past Liam and Caris. Instead of heading to the barn where Chevy was, however, the stallion galloped hell-bent-for-leather toward Finger Ridge and was quickly lost from sight.

"What's up with that?" shouted Liam. He had just gotten his damn horses back. "I swear, ever since the storm, *nothing's* been normal around here."

"No doubt he'll be coming back on his own, just as he did yesterday." Caris caught Liam's arm and tugged him along, until they finally caught up to their friends.

No one greeted them. Liam had been prepared to see a smoking crater in the ground, a glowing fireball—hell, even an engine off a jetliner wouldn't have raised his eyebrows at this point in time.

He was not prepared to see Morgan kneeling next to an impossibly beautiful woman. In fact, *beautiful* was far too ordinary a word. This *being*—instinct told him she was not human—was more than exotic in appearance, she was sublime beyond description. It put him in mind of the delicate heirloom angel that Aunt Ruby brought out every Christmas. A candle inside gave a warm glow to the white porcelain—and this woman's fine features somehow glowed as well.

Her thick, lustrous hair had fanned out in a silken cape around her. It was as long as she was tall—and luminous white. *Who has hair like that?* Her long white robes were as iridescent as the inside of a seashell, finely embroidered with animals Liam recognized and many he did not, and the wide hem of her garb, as well as the ends of her sleeves, were couched with pearls. A silver harness looped behind one shoulder—and the gleaming hilt of a sword was clearly visible.

Morgan was holding the woman's hand and speaking to her—and she smiled back weakly. *At least she's alive.* How badly hurt she might be, Liam couldn't begin to imagine. He looked around, a little desperately, for some sort of craft, some method of flight, *anything.* How could this woman possibly have gotten here? And why was he the only one who seemed to be wondering?

All too aware that something was going on that he didn't understand, Liam broke the silence with what he hoped was a nice, safe topic: "Does anyone need me to call 911?"

Only Ranyon seemed able to shake himself free of the thrall cast by this woman's presence. The little ellyll looked up at Liam, with his beloved Blue Jays hat clutched in his long, thin fingers. "'Tis the queen herself," he said. "'Tis Gwenhidw, and mortal medicine is of no help to her."

Lurien did not expect to awaken in his chambers in the palace. He did not expect to wake at all, in fact. And just to add to his surprise, his hazy vision picked up a pale-gold goddess who looked an awful lot like Aurddolen.

"You're an idiot, oh mighty Lord of the Hunt," she said.

It was definitely her. "Are you here for your revenge?" he managed, and discovered he was parched.

She moved in close, lifting his head and putting a goblet to his lips, and the contents made his eyes widen. There was no refusing it, not at the rate she was pouring it down his throat. "I just finished rescuing you and staying up all night to make sure you lived. If it was vengeance I wanted, I had only to leave you at the bottom of the ocean."

"You may already have wrought your revenge with that cup," he gasped. "What in the name of the Seven Sisters was that? It tasted like warth piss."

"Nothing poisonous, if that's what you mean. My mother was accomplished in herbs, and she passed her knowledge to me. You've taken in a great deal of seawater and spent all of your magic, but worse, you've been as close to a ghost as I've ever seen. You used your own life to send Gwenhidw somewhere, didn't you?"

"I had to. I had nothing else with which to save her. Is she all right?"

"I wish I knew. She's still missing."

He tried to sit up then but his body wasn't the slightest bit interested in obeying him. "I have to go after her, I have to find her. More, I have to find whoever attacked her."

"You really think someone was behind that? Lurien, we poured a lot of power into the Great Way—surely it was simply a backlash, some sort of surge from the Way itself."

"No." He was certain of it. Every hunter's instinct he possessed told him that there had been intelligence behind the energy blast that struck Gwenhidw. And as for where she was—he tried to recall what he'd said, what spell he'd cast, in those final desperate moments . . .

Somewhere safe. He'd tried to send her somewhere she couldn't be found by her enemies yet would also be among friends. For a long moment his brain would produce no plausible answer. Then a new idea illuminated his mind: *I must have sent her to Morgan Edwards.* Morgan's family had guarded the powerful pendant Gwenhidw wore—the Sigil, emblem of the royal house—for twenty generations. Had the frantic spell chosen the mortal woman to guard something far more valuable?

Dozens of thoughts vied for his attention: Was Gwenhidw all right? Had Morgan indeed found her? Could he fight his way through the Great Way to get to his queen? He tried again to move but realized that he would be fortunate indeed to fight his way out of bed.

"You aren't going very far, at least not for a while," said Aurddolen, as if reading his mind. "Even if you were hale and hearty, we've got plenty of trouble right here. The envoys are in a state of panic. I've tried to allay their fears, calm them and get them back on task, but they seem to lack confidence in me. Apparently, my credibility is in question after being arrested by your hunters."

She paused, as though waiting for him to apologize. It would be a cold day in Hades before that happened. "You would have done the same," he said curtly. "The palace was under attack, and I had no choice but to act quickly to secure the queen's safety. I will never take chances when it comes to Gwenhidw."

Aurddolen's voice was soft. "So I've noticed."

"I am her *llaw dde*. How else would I behave?"

"I think you misapprehend your own motives, dear Lurien." She walked around the bed as if to change the subject and looked out the window. "So, as soon as you're up to it, I'd say your first task should be to talk to the envoys before they leave—and mind you, several delegates are already packing as we speak."

She turned to look at him then. "Do you understand? We may never be able to get them together in one place again. That alone was something that no one but Gwenhidw could have accomplished, and it would be a shame to see it fall apart. You are, as you say, the queen's *llaw dde*. More than that, you are the Lord of the Wild Hunt. They will trust you, as they will trust no one else at this time."

Something Gwenhidw had said tugged at Lurien's memory: "This time, promise me instead that you will keep our people safe. Promise me you will see them to Tir Hardd should I fail to do so . . ."

He cursed himself soundly for agreeing to such a promise. It was all too plain that Aurddolen was right. As *llaw dde*, he had to establish order here, restore confidence in the envoys, and keep the queen's bold plans for her people alive and moving forward. Gwenhidw would expect no less of him.

But as Lord of the Wild Hunt, someone was going to pay with their life for what happened on Holyhead Mount.

~

Liam was appalled. "You told me she was a *queen*, for chrissakes—you *can't* put her in the damn barn!"

"She's too weak to move far," said Ranyon, as they carried her in a strange gossamer sling he'd produced from one of his charms. "And the barn will hide her from her enemies. Better a safe hut than a dangerous castle, dontcha know."

"Okay, I'll give you that. But let me bring out a mattress from the house at least," said Liam.

The ellyll shook his head. "Already got a charm fer that."

Liam stepped inside the barn just in time to see something bizarre growing between the goat pen and the horse enclosure. Four pure-white saplings had burst straight up through the dirt floor.

"How . . . ?" he began, his eyes wide.

"I had a few seeds with me," said Ranyon. "They just needed planting."

Of course they did, thought Liam, as the trees rapidly twisted themselves into a great braided platform, replete with a bower of coin-shaped leaves. Neither Chevy and her foals nor any of the goats appeared concerned in the least that a living bed had just sprung up in their midst.

"Now this here is a simple spell of multiplication." The ellyll laid a single downy feather from his favorite spotted hen upon the center framework, which instantly proliferated into thousands until there was a feather mattress a foot thick, though what held them together, Liam couldn't begin to guess.

Gwenhidw, queen of the Nine Realms and the faery kingdom, was gently laid with the utmost care upon the soft and splendid bed, her silver sword placed beside her.

In my barn . . . Just as Liam thought his brain would explode from the overdose of strangeness, Caris grabbed his arm and pulled him outside where sunrise had pinkened the sky over the eastern hills.

"Liam?" She cupped his face with her small hands and made him look at her. "I know it seems terribly rude to put Gwenhidw in such a place, but no one will be looking among the goats for a queen, don't you see?"

"Hey, I'd sleep in there myself if I had a bed like that. And I *have* slept in there once in a while in the straw while the goats were kidding. It's comfortable enough, I guess, and it's not cold. But she looks like she's in bad shape—and I'm even more concerned about who's going to come looking for her. Hey, is that Dodge?"

He stared dumbly as his Appaloosa stallion trotted proudly over the hill into view. With him was a smaller horse, undoubtedly a mare, and Christ only knew whose farm the amorous Dodge had visited this time. *I swear, you're going to end up gelded yet, you butthead.* Of course, Dodge wouldn't make things simple by coming straight to his owner or anything like that. Instead, the stallion veered to the left with his famous look-at-me canter. The mare wheeled to follow . . .

And revealed a rider lying low over her back.

They took off at a sprint to catch the horses, but Caris already knew the identity of the rider. She would have recognized that exquisite green gown anywhere. Getting close enough to help Rhedyn was something else again. Dodge was maddeningly certain that Caris and Liam wanted to play. Horses being herd animals, the mare followed the stallion's every move, her finely shaped head pressed close to her new friend's flank. It was a fortunate thing indeed that the unconscious woman did not fall off.

Finally Liam made a fast feint to the right, then dove like a quarterback to the left, grabbing Dodge's halter at last. Caris quickly grasped the mare's silver reins and found that Rhedyn had knotted them tightly around her gloved hands. Thankfully, a pulse still fluttered at her slender neck. "She's alive," Caris called out, breathless.

"Good," Liam managed. "I'm not." He leaned over to suck in more air but kept a solid grip on the halter. "Remind me to kill you too, you big dope," he whispered fiercely to the horse. In a more charitable voice, he asked Caris, "So who is she? And why are so many women showing up on my farm all of a sudden?"

He almost said *beautiful* women, but thought better of it. He'd been out of the dating game a hell of a long time, but Liam figured Caris would probably want to be the only woman he thought attractive. And in truth, she was. When he looked at her, he felt warmth and want and a wealth of human emotions. Pleasant, welcoming emotions.

As lovely as they were, both the queen and this newcomer possessed an ethereal quality, an *otherness* that made him want to keep his distance. *They don't belong to this world.* If he'd never even heard of faeries, he instinctively knew that much.

Liam had to yank on Dodge's halter more than once as they made their way across the field to the farmyard, and he was glad Caris was leading the mare. The stallion continued his role as a complete pain in the ass, still trying to show off for his new conquest. The mare was a pretty thing, red in color and as fine-boned and built for speed as any Arab. She'd been running hard too—she was exhausted, and lathered from her bit to her flanks. Had she spooked and bolted? Or had the woman been trying to escape something?

As they approached the barn, Liam hollered for the others. Jay and Ranyon ran to meet them. Morgan poked her head out of the doorway. "What's going on?" she asked.

"If you figure it out, let me know," said Liam. "Someone attend to the rider. I've got to put Dodge away, then I'll come and get the mare."

Dodge didn't like the idea, of course, but Liam had had enough of the stallion's antics for one day. Thankful beyond all measure that the horse stalls were still standing, he locked him in and bolted the top door for good measure. When he returned, he was surprised to find the group by the back porch of the house. They were gathered around the woman in green—and she was awake.

"I cannot stop," she whispered hoarsely, and Ranyon handed her a drink. Her delicate fae features were pale and anxious, and her gaze flicked back and forth over the rim of the mug as she downed the contents quickly.

Liam noticed that the stranger wasn't looking at the ellyll or even at the humans that surrounded her, but beyond. *Hunted*, he thought. *Or haunted. Maybe both.* He glanced around the farm himself, just in case, but saw nothing amiss.

"I cannot stay. I have to find a way back," she said. Her voice was a little stronger now, but still thick with fear. She was sitting on the bottom step, and Liam didn't think she looked strong enough to stand, never mind go anywhere. Caris appeared with a blanket from the house and draped it around the woman's narrow shoulders, then sat down beside her.

"You're safe here, Rhedyn," she said.

The cup tumbled from the faery's fingers, and she stared at Caris. "By the Seven Sisters, you live!" She seized her hand with both of hers. "I am so glad. I thought surely you had been slain."

"I'm happy to see you too. Did you escape as well?"

"No." Rhedyn glanced around again. "No, I've only been forgotten for the moment. I have to go."

"Go where?" asked Morgan.

"I have to find a way back to the Nine Realms. It's of the utmost importance that I get a message to the queen. I have information for her."

"Well now," said Ranyon, looking at his human friends. "We just might be able to help ya with that."

TWENTY-FOUR

~~~

"Okay, lemme see if I have it straight. The green faery is Rhedyn, and she's hiding out from her boyfriend," said Liam. "He, of course, just happens to be Maelgwn, who is trying to kill the queen so he can rule over everything in his world *and* ours. Right so far?"

Caris nodded. Rhedyn had made a full confession to Gwenhidw in the queen's makeshift chambers—closely watched by Ranyon, Jay, and Morgan. They'd then escorted the faery to the house and locked her in a bedroom, with custom-made charms on the doors and windows for good measure. Caris couldn't blame her friends for their abundance of caution: the queen's safety was paramount. As much as Caris herself pitied Rhedyn and appreciated that the faery woman had once tried to defend her, she dared not trust her. Rhedyn had been under Maelgwn's control for a very long time and, for all anyone knew, he could be controlling her even now.

With the green-clad faery confined to the house, and Gwenhidw residing in the barn, the most privacy Caris and Liam could find was under a canopy at the colorful gnome party. They chose the leather couch where he'd recently watched a baseball game with Ranyon, and just held each other for a while. The TV screen was blank, and while the numberless garden gnomes were still present, they were blessedly quiet. Jay had volunteered to milk the goats, so she had the luxury of lying down in Liam's arms for a while. For a long, sweet moment she could pretend they were like any other couple in love . . .

If only Liam would stop asking questions.

"And Maelgwn is also the asshole prince who turned you into a dog, and then tried to kill you?"

"One and the same," she said. "But don't you see? I'm the lucky one in that he thinks me dead already." She decided not to mention what the ellyll had said, that the prince would likely be wanting proof of her demise. She would have to cross her fingers against evil and hope that Maelgwn would be too busy trying to implement his plans—which Rhedyn had revealed were far more grandiose than anything Caris had imagined.

"Rhedyn will never be safe anywhere," she continued. "But as he's a fearful bully, he's more likely to torment her than kill her. The queen is the one in the truest danger. Having dared to make an attempt on her life, Maelgwn will not be satisfied until he's finished her. And that is why we're hiding her in the most unlikely place we can think of. Besides, Ranyon says the spotted horses have charms that will help conceal her."

"Wait just a minute—you're saying my own damn horses are magic too?"

"Everything is, *cariad*," she said gently, and slipped her arms around him. "Small or large, everything is." She'd meant the kiss to comfort him, but it quickly became something more. Liam needed her, but she needed him just as much. And ached with the desire to finish what they had begun in the night.

"Sorry I have to interrupt you guys." Jay ducked under the canopy, and Liam groaned so loudly that Caris giggled like a girl.

"Okay, *really* sorry." He put his hands up in a gesture of peace. "Please don't kill the messenger."

"Depends on the damn message," growled Liam.

"Actually it's for Caris. Ranyon wants you to play for the queen. I didn't know you were musical—I thought he must mean Liam, but he definitely asked for you."

"Me?" She felt stunned. In an instant she was reliving a moment in time, when she was surrounded by a faery hunt and their prince commanded her to play . . . *Who am I to play for such a being? What songs could a mortal possibly offer?* "Whatever for?"

"The little guy seems to think it would help, and I agree," said Jay. "My wife, Starr, could tell you all about energies and resonance and such. But the bottom line is that music has healing properties."

It was daunting enough to be asked to entertain the queen. But to help heal her? Ranyon's words came back to Caris then: "Music has power, dontcha know. It enhances fae magic, and it makes magic of its own as well."

"What kind of music should I play? What if I play the wrong tune?" She hoped Ranyon would give her some instructions because she felt completely overwhelmed.

"Hey." Liam squeezed her hand, bringing her back to the present. "You can do this," he said aloud, then whispered in her ear, "And I'm proud of you that you can."

She eyed him strangely. "But you've never heard me play a note."

"Oh yes, I have," he said quietly, and stroked her hair. "More than once. I'll tell you about it later." He kissed the little frown on her forehead.

Jay looked uncomfortable. "Um, the sooner you can come, the better."

"I cannot say no," she said. "Give me a few more minutes, and I'll come."

Jay gave a mock salute and gratefully disappeared.

Caris looked up at the blue-eyed man who'd become so vital to her in only a couple of days and held his hands in both of hers. "I don't know what you were meaning. Just don't be thinking that I care not for your pain, Liam Cole. This will be hard for you, I know. I need to ask—will you be all right if I do this?"

"*Right as rain.* And if I'm not, then you'll just have to nurse me back to health." He winked, and she couldn't help but smile. "Look—if it can help the queen in any way, then it's important. You go ahead and find out what kind of songs they're looking for. I'll get the fiddle from the house and bring it out to you." Liam kissed her lightly on the forehead, then seemed to think better of it, kissing her on the lips with a soul-deep tenderness that went on and on until she felt buoyant enough to fly. "Remember where we left off," he said as he got up and headed for the house.

Caris clung to the sensation of that kiss and all the emotion behind it as she walked slowly toward the farmyard. She paused in a clearing between the barn and the house that had been filled with tall trees before the storm. As she looked, one sad and broken trunk had already sprouted a brand new twig with a tiny tender leaflet. It filled her heart with encouragement that beauty could yet overcome destruction.

And then she saw something else.

High on the ridge that flanked the farm, an animal moved against the gray stone and straw-colored grasses. It wasn't a wolf—it was bigger and blacker than any wolf had a right to be. And a wolf would have shown concern that a human had spotted it. Instead, the creature watched Caris with an intensity that made her shiver despite the warmth of the morning sun. It didn't even try to hide.

A grim didn't have to.

The great black dog lingered a few moments more, no doubt until it was confident she had seen it and knew it for what it was. Then it vanished, leaving behind a mocking howl that echoed off the ridge and chilled her to the bone.

She'd been found.

Caris stood there for a long moment, considering. *Run or hide?* If she asked them, she knew that her friends would immediately jump in their truck and take her far away from here, and maybe—*maybe*—Maelgwn wouldn't find her again for a long time.

But the queen would be left behind. The prince would come to the farm looking for Caris, and he would find Gwenhidw instead. *He'll kill her.*

Caris had no love for the fae. In fact, she had every reason to hate them for what had been done to her. Their petty quarrels and power struggles among themselves were none of her concern. *And yet . . .* Minding her own business hadn't been enough to shield herself from disaster. The fae's problems spilled over into the human world regularly, whether humans knew it or not. And there were too many like Maelgwn who interfered with mortal lives regularly and inflicted cruelty for the sheer sport of it.

Ranyon wasn't like that at all. His heart was bigger than he was. Even on short acquaintance, Caris couldn't help but love the little ellyll. During her time in the fae realm, she'd observed that Lord Lurien valued honor; he was as different from Maelgwn as night was from day. And the dear queen herself? Somehow Caris understood that Gwenhidw's breathtaking beauty came from within. She radiated what she was, and she represented all that was good and worth fighting for in any domain. *She can't die!* If the queen perished, then the power-hungry and the heartless—like Maelgwn and his followers—would take her place.

They would rule the Nine Realms beneath Caris's home country and they would rule Tir Hardd beneath this new land too. And things would be worse for both the fae and the human worlds. Caris looked around her again at what a rogue hunt had done to this once-charming farm in a single night.

Dear heavens, what would happen if those fae were free to wreak such havoc every night?

There was no other choice she could make that she could live with. She had to play for the queen, had to try to help her, strengthen her. The grim would surely tell Maelgwn where Caris was, but perhaps—just perhaps—Gwenhidw could be saved.

But what about Liam? *If I tell him, he'll be wanting to take me away. If I don't tell him, he'll be wanting to fight the prince when he comes to take me.* She hoped Ranyon had an idea as she ran for the barn as fast as she was able.

But the first thing she had to do was warn them all.

The ivory leather case was sitting on Caris's bed. Liam didn't expect the mere sight of it to punch him in the gut, didn't expect something inside to twist hard enough to hurt when he picked it up. Part of him wanted to *open it, open it, open it,* to see and touch the fiddle within, to heft it and stroke music from it—and another part of him wanted nothing more than to throw it from the window as if it were on fire.

He did neither. A wild grief coupled with a fearful yearning blew like a cold wind through the empty rooms of his soul. He clutched the case to his chest, although it seemed to grow heavier with every step. But he'd already determined that he was going to get the fiddle to the barn for Caris's sake, no matter what effect it had on him.

The sun had cleared the hill when Liam entered the barn. The air smelled fresh and clean. Pretty impressive for a barn, really, but probably because it had no roof. He looked up to see candy-pink and pale yellow clouds in a robin's-egg sky and wondered what his royal guest thought of the extra-large skylight.

Someone would explain to him eventually how a faery queen came to be here on his farm. At the moment, Liam decided he wasn't ready to ask those questions. He just hoped that Caris's music would help the injured woman heal. On the other side of the barn, he could see Morgan and Jay sitting on a bale to one side of the bowered bed, Caris and Ranyon on the other. He pushed his way through the goats and looked up just in time to see Chevy's appallingly enormous nose nuzzling Gwenhidw's elegant face—but rather than be shooed away, the gentle mare won a broad smile from the queen that could have melted a glacier. Liam slipped into the enclosure—and got his second surprise. The foals, both of them, were up and playing together like a pair of fawns, capering around the bed with their short little tails wagging.

He was still staring at them in wonder as Caris came up and gently took the fiddle case from him. "*Diolch i chi*," she said, and kissed his cheek. "Thank you, *cariad*. I'll wait until you're gone from the barn before I start."

"No, you won't. I'll leave when I have to, but I'll stay here 'til then."

She paled. "Truly, I would feel better if you were in the house."

He didn't know what to make of that. He could understand if she was nervous about playing for a queen. *She's probably just as worried about me. After everything I said about music, she probably thinks I'm going to have a damn breakdown or something.* Again, he shook his head. "Don't even think about me, just do what you need to do—play our fiddle for the both of us, okay? Remember what you said about the twin foals? They're here to tell us that things will turn out right—and just look at them." He kissed her full on the lips. "It'll all be fine. You'll see." A fleeting smile crossed her face, and it satisfied him.

Liam found a bale by the stable door and sat down to watch. He had every confidence in Caris. But in himself? *Big fat zero.* From his dreams, he could guess what he was in for—and after everything that had happened in the past day or so, why wouldn't he believe in dreams too? He seriously doubted he could handle the wild music at all. But damned if he would leave while Caris was under such enormous pressure to perform. He would be here to provide moral support if it killed him . . .

"Aye, and it might unless you be listening to me now, Liam Cole."

Liam stared as Ranyon sat beside him. "Did you just . . ."

The ellyll seized his ear and whispered fiercely. "No time fer that now. Maelgwn is comin' to take Caris—*no*, don't ya be gettin' up."

Liam's instincts would have had him lunging to his feet. Instead, he suddenly discovered he could do little more than give the ellyll a dirty look as the little tree man continued.

"We cannot fight him here, Liam. Understand? You will die. Morgan and Jay will die, and the queen will die—and that fool prince will *still* be taking Caris with him. He'll not hurt your good lady, dontcha know. *He dares not hurt her.* It's her music he needs to give power to a spell."

"The hell with that. He hurt her already. He hit her with one of those power whips you and Jay have been talking about. I saw her when she was still a dog, remember? Broken leg, busted ribs, burn marks . . . I'm not letting him have another chance at her."

Although Ranyon had hold of Liam's ear like some sort of fierce little grandmother, the ellyll also patted his arm with his other twiggy hand. "Maelgwn has a foul temper, true, but he won't be letting it get the better of him again. Not with so much at stake. His entire plan to take over Tir Hardd is resting upon your lady's music."

"She's got to be warned." Liam stopped dead at the ellyll's expression. "She knows, doesn't she? She already knows that bastard's coming to get her." *Truly, I would feel better if you were in the house* . . . Dammit, they were going to have some words about this—if they got out of it alive. He shoved that thought aside. "You're saying I'm supposed to just sit here and watch it happen? That I can't do anything about it?"

Ranyon shook his head. "I'm saying ya can't do anything about it *now*. But fer certain, we'll be doing plenty about it after." His bright blue eyes widened in his woodlike face. "D'ya truly think I'd leave the good lady in that idiot prince's hands?"

Liam glanced up, but no one, not even Caris, seemed to be hearing their conversation or even looking in their direction. *What did he do, put up a cloaking device like in the damn movies?* Not for the first time he wondered about the true extent of Ranyon's powers. "Okay, okay, let's say I go along with this, this frickin' *stupid* idea." It ran counter to every instinct he had just to say the words out loud. "But you'd damn well better have a spell or a rocket launcher or something else up your skinny little sleeve that's going to help us get her back."

"Oh, aye." Ranyon grinned then, a wickedly feral smile with a wealth of satisfaction behind it. He released Liam's ear and rubbed his twiggy hands together. "I've *plenty* of charms fer that."

Liam leaned forward and whispered in the ellyll's ear. "Good. Because if a single hair on her beautiful head goes missing, I'll swear I'll find a way to make birdhouse out of you."

Ranyon only laughed. "Yer a good man, Liam Cole. 'Tis hard ta have trust and faith in things you've never laid eyes on afore." He laid one of his strange spindly hands on top of Liam's, and his voice softened. "Have ya heard of a faery oath?"

Liam raised his eyebrows.

"'Tis rarely given, but 'tis unbreakable," continued Ranyon. "There's not a creature in the Nine Realms that can go against his own word. So here's mine fer ya: we'll get yer lady back, or I'll die in the trying."

They shook hands solemnly—and then the ellyll actually bumped fists with him.

Maybe he was just trying to distract himself or release the terrible tension, or hell, even lighten up, but he simply had to ask: "Where the heck does a faery learn to do *that*?"

"Why, baseball, a'course!" said Ranyon. "Like Jose Bautista and Dan Johnson right after the Jays beat Tampa Bay." He adjusted his hat proudly, then wriggled back and made himself comfortable on the bale. "I'll tell ya all about the game, but first we'll let Caris work a little o' her magic fer the queen." They watched as Caris gently laid the leather-bound satchel on the end of the leafy tree bed, and drew the bow from its hidden drawer in the bottom of the case. Next, she unlatched the main compartment and Liam could swear he *felt* each fastener open. She reached in her small, strong hands and there it was—the fiddle. *His* fiddle. The morning sun seemed to brighten and set fire to the tiger maple of its back, dance over the golden-yellow spruce of the top. Caris plucked the strings, but Liam's infallible ear told him it was in perfect tune. He didn't notice, however, that his fingers had wrapped themselves into the twine that bound the bale he sat on, as if to brace himself.

Time seemed to stop as she drew the opening stanzas of a tune. The notes built softly and slowly, like a gentle rain, then came faster and stronger like a downpour in a desert. Caris's long dark hair flew about her with each expressive sweep of the bow, and she danced as she played until her entire body was an instrument of joy.

In Liam's dreams, she had been naked. Another time he might have joked that it was simply wishful thinking on his part, but now, in this moment, he thought it might have been symbolic. As she played, she hid nothing—he could see all that she was. Even her very soul seemed visible. With pitch and timbre, she created the primeval music of forests and fields, of rivers and earth. Liam had never heard such things in his conscious life, and he wasn't so certain that he perceived them with his ears alone. Every cell in his body resonated with the notes that were both exquisitely assuaging and agonizingly painful. And once again, the long-dormant songs hidden deep in the recesses of his own soul called out to her.

The strange, wild music reached inside him with questing fingers, both merciless and merciful, lancing wounds he'd assumed were healed, tearing away the scar tissue that had grown over pain, and releasing the anger that poisoned him. Through it all, he could not have found the strength or the will to leave even if he'd wanted.

It was riveting. It was exhausting. It was a revelation. It was a benediction. When Caris stopped at last, she stood perfectly still, her head bowed and her long dark hair curtaining the bow and fiddle tucked against her.

All was hushed and silent—until the sound of a single pair of gloved hands clapping made Caris's head snap up. The expression on her face, fearful yet fierce, told Liam all he needed to know.

Maelgwn was standing in the doorway of the barn behind him.

TWENTY-FIVE

~⌒⌒~

Such a rough and rustic place for such superbly crafted music," said the prince, as he strode confidently toward her. The goats could hardly move fast enough to get out of his way, parting for him like the Red Sea. Maybe they were repelled by his fake charm. Liam certainly was—and worse, he could see the loathing on Caris's face. If it hadn't been for Ranyon's hand on his arm (and whatever binding spell the ellyll had thrown over him like a goddamn net), Liam would have inserted himself between her and the prince in a heartbeat.

"I'm liking the company here," she said, with her chin high.

"It must be all that time spent as a dog that's made you so comfortable with ill-smelling animals." Maelgwn smiled at his own witticism as he passed by Liam, though there was no warmth in his voice.

He can't see us! The realization shot through Liam's brain. In some incredible feat of camouflage, Ranyon had hidden both the humans and the fae in the barn. Caris stood squarely in front of the strangely crafted bed that sheltered Gwenhidw herself—but the prince perceived only the woman he'd come for!

"No matter," Maelgwn continued. He seemed almost amiable . . . or was it smug?

You think you've already won, you bastard.

"You can sleep among the grims if it pleases you, just as soon as you play a few songs for me," continued the prince, as though he were speaking to a recalcitrant child. "Come along now, I have much to do, and you've already kept me waiting long enough."

"And if I do not?"

The witty charm and amiability disappeared. "Then you'll come anyway, and I'll burn this entire farm down to naked bedrock, including every living thing that has ever set foot on it. Surely you must have friends around here somewhere, four-legged and two-legged, whose lives you value?"

"You are truly all-powerful, good prince." She bowed her head, but she was far from finished. Although she was in jeans, Caris curtsied prettily and very low. "As you are soon to rule Tir Hardd, it has ever been a human custom among royalty to celebrate their coming coronation by granting gifts to the poorest of the poor." She dropped to her knees then. "I beg for your kingly word that the farm and all in it will be safe. And it will be my greatest pleasure to play for you *every* song that I have learned."

"Always the little bargainer, aren't you? I'm sure you recall how well that went the last time you tried it," he taunted, yet it was plain that he was pleased by her subservient display. "Fortunately for you, however, I'm feeling somewhat benevolent. I already rule Tir Hardd, and my position will be unassailable by mortal dawn on the morrow. As my first *celebratory* gesture, then, I will extend my royal word that what's left of this paltry farm will be unharmed by me or my followers. As for those you care for, they will be unharmed *as long as they do not leave this place.*" There was menace in those last words, although he gave her a mocking bow. "That is as far as my generosity and my patience will extend. Enough games."

In a single blur of movement, the prince crossed the floor and seized Caris's arm. The two of them vanished from sight.

Ranyon's spell abruptly ceased to hold Liam back, and he nearly stumbled as he ran to the spot. Strangely, the fiddle and its bow had been left behind. He scooped them up from the straw, holding them tenderly as if he were somehow holding part of Caris. He looked toward the queen then, who was being helped to sit up by Morgan.

"She did this for you, didn't she?" demanded Liam. "She knew that bastard was coming for her, and instead of trying to escape, she played her music to help *you*. She sacrificed herself, do you understand that?"

"I understand far more than you know," said Gwenhidw. "Caris Ellen Dillwyn showed rare courage and great love, but it wasn't for me. She had to protect both the human and faery worlds, in order to save all of you. That is what she gave herself for—and I have the feeling that she is far from beaten yet."

It was the first time Liam had heard the queen speak, but that was not the amazing part. Even though her voice was weak, his perfect ear detected something within her voice very like a cascade of crystalline bells. The unique sound reached deep within that part of his soul that created music and resonated there . . .

"We have no time to waste if we are to stop Maelgwn," the queen continued. "Morgan, you must help me get a message to the Lord of the Wild Hunt immediately. Maelgwn himself has verified Rhedyn's words: he plans a full-out rebellion, and Lurien will need that information. There are plans and preparations for us to make, and quickly."

Liam shook himself free of the strange effect that her voice had on him and stared instead at the fiddle and bow that were still in his hands.

"Why are these still here?" he asked suspiciously. "If all he wanted was her music, why didn't he take her instrument?"

"Most likely, the prince has procured a faery fiddle as a way of controlling her," said Morgan, but her face was pained. "Fae instruments are often spelled so that mortals can't let go of them. In the old stories, human musicians would play until they collapsed or until the faery party was over, whichever came first."

"Ha!" Ranyon snorted and folded his spindly arms. "I made sure she has a charm fer that, one that he can neither see nor remove. A faery fiddle—or any other spell Maelgwn tries on our Caris—won't be having the effect he's hopin' fer. 'Tis in the blue stone I gave her, ya see."

"Starr says that most blue stones enhance truth and inspiration," said Jay. "She uses them in her therapies to calm people and help clear their minds."

"Aye, but this particular stone is good fer protection as well."

Liam leaned over to speak into the ellyll's ear. "Please tell me you used your *multiplication* spell on it, like you did with the feather bed. She's going to need all the protection she can get from that dickhead."

"Our Caris is as safe as she can be fer now, and she has the freedom to play what she pleases." Ranyon grinned up at them all then. "And, well, ya see, I may have taught her a tune or two meself. Just in case, ya know."

Morgan simply dropped to her knees and hugged him, and Liam almost felt like hugging the ellyll as well. *At least she didn't go unarmed*—though what kind of tunes Ranyon might have taught her, he was afraid to ask.

"Glad to hear it. Now where do I have to go to get her back?" demanded Liam.

"To the entrance of the Great Way," said Gwenhidw. "According to Rhedyn, Maelgwn needs Caris's music to power a spell that can seal up the Way forever."

"That's at the top of Steptoe Butte, believe it or not," offered Jay. "The same place your farm is named for."

"The butte? Why up there?"

"The story goes that Native Americans used to call it the Power Mountain. If you climbed to the top and you were worthy, you would receive a gift of power from Bull Elk, a guardian spirit said to live there."

"I've heard that legend since I was a kid, but it doesn't help unless this Bull Elk tosses Maelgwn off the butte for me."

"Well, I just meant that people have known for a long time that there's something different about the place. Turns out that Steptoe Butte is far older than the surrounding hills. They're made of fifteen-million-year-old basalt, but the butte is like an amazing island of pure quartzite about four *hundred* million years old. We think the electromagnetic properties in the quartzite help to create a wormhole effect."

"Jay!" hollered Morgan and Ranyon together.

"Right. Too much information. Okay, here's the skinny: the Way will look like a tear in the sky, kind of a rip in reality, if it's open. It's a door that leads directly to the old faery kingdom beneath Wales. Oh, and it's full of monsters that feed on magic, especially on anything fae."

And you don't want a thing like that sealed up? Liam decided against asking any more questions. Better to keep things simple. "Okay, well, see you later."

"Wait," said Morgan. "You can't just go charging off. We haven't got a plan."

"You do whatever you have to do. I already have my plan," said Liam. "It's called 'I'm going after Caris.'" He left the barn without looking back.

"'Tis a good plan," said a voice at his knee. "But ya won't be going alone."

Thanks to Aurddolen's gut-churning herbs, Lurien was on his feet. He had no energy to speak of, but he threw everything he had into acting as if he did, as if he were yet a force to be reckoned with. And mentally, he was. He called a meeting of the seventy-nine envoys in the throne room, including those who had already left the palace. Some had made it all the way back to their territories, but no matter where they were in their journey, they were politely *retrieved* by his hunters in one way or another.

Lurien stood tall on the green jasper dais, a few steps away from the clear crystal throne. He wanted the association with it—he was the *llaw dde*, after all—but didn't want anyone to think he had designs on it. Aurddolen had suggested wearing something less formidable than his black riding leathers, but he refused. *Formidable* was exactly what the delegates needed to see right now. Drained of their magic on that hilltop by their attempt to enlarge the Great Way, they were frightened and confused and missing their queen. They needed to see *strength*, even if he had to fake it.

"Esteemed delegates. Lawfully chosen envoys of your peoples. We have grown together in friendship and understanding as we have worked together this past while." Actually there were still several of them that he'd like to use his light whip on—or even just his fists. Curses ran in a constant stream through his head, as he fought for the right words, words that Gwenhidw might use in such a formal setting. Finally, he gave up and sat down on the edge of the stage. He motioned to all of the delegates to sit as well.

"Let us deal in truth. We have not always gotten along. Many of us disagree on issues. Some of us have little or no liking for others in the group. But when we were atop Mynedfa, what mortals have named Holyhead, we accomplished something. We managed to set aside our differences and work together. We fed our collective power to the Great Way, and I believe we would have succeeded in our goal had not our queen been attacked."

There were many gasps around the room. Aurddolen had been right. Most thought that the blast that hit the queen had been a natural recoil of power from the Way. "It was indeed another attempt on her life."

A coblyn jumped to his stubby feet. "Is she all right, then?"

"Where is she?" hissed a fire drake. Others took up the questions, clamoring for details.

Lurien put his hand up for silence. "Her Grace, Queen Gwenhidw, is unharmed." He hoped like Hades that was a true statement. It had to be. As for the other question, he'd thought long and hard as to whether to reveal her location. Finally, he'd come to the conclusion that to win the cooperation of this unruly group, he'd have to take the risk. And embellishing the truth *ever so slightly* might help all the more.

"Our beloved queen has been taken to Tir Hardd against her will." True, in a matter of speaking—she certainly hadn't asked him to send her there. Although she wasn't actually *in* the faery territory—if she was with Morgan, she was in the human world. "She is alone and undefended." Mostly true. Her mortal friends would do their best, but they had no magic with which to protect her. "And I need every one of you to work with me to open the Great Way again, so that the Wild Hunt may ride to her aid and bring her back to us." That was completely true, regrettably enough. For the first time in his long, long life, he *did* need their help. He, Lurien, Lord of the Wild Hunt—who could not only open the Great Way by his powers alone but could hold it open for the passage of his entire entourage—didn't have enough magic left in him to so much as light a candle.

He'd expected some hesitation, at least some discussion, but where Gwenhidw was concerned, her people were united. They stood and yelled, cheered, growled, roared their assent. They would return to Holyhead and tear the Way open with their bare hands, claws, and teeth if need be.

That was where the clamor died down and the gathering suddenly looked rather lost. "How will we do such a thing?" gasped a kelpie—the same one who had helped Aurddolen save him. "Our magic is drained, and we have not enough between us to open the Way."

"We need time to recover," said a tree nymph.

An undine hissed at her. "The queen has no time for you to rest!"

Lurien raised his hand as arguments broke out. "It seems that a solution has already been found." It hadn't been his idea, but he knew a good one when he heard it, and he'd acted on it with all the haste at his command. Better that the author of the idea presented it, however, and he motioned to Aurddolen to speak.

The dragon woman declined to climb the dais but stood in front of it.

"Each of us owns *cyfareddau*—relics, artifacts, stones, items that hold energy and power, that amplify the magic of living beings. We value and collect such things. Most of us are reliant on at least one *cyfaredd*, although some of us who are learned in magic eschew these objects as if they were mere props." She shot a meaningful look at Lurien before continuing. "But they are not props, they are *tools*. And at such a time as this, when our resources and our magics are low, and our queen and our kingdom are in danger, we need all the tools we can get our hands on. Every monarch has known this from the beginning, and a collection of such objects has been preserved in the treasuries of the palace. Under the direction of Lord Lurien, we've brought these things here."

He wished it had been that simple. No records had been kept over the endless centuries, no tally made of such things, as royalty tended to be somewhat casual about numbers. It was enough that the treasures were secure—somewhere. In the end, many trusted hands had been conscripted to hunt through the very roots of the palace, and many doors were forced open whose hinges had not moved in millennia. As the queen's *llaw dde*, he had indeed directed the search though it seemed more like ransacking. Still, he would have torn down the entire palace, stone by stone, with his bare hands if it would have helped save Gwenhidw.

Lurien drew a symbol in the air, and his hunters entered the room bearing ornate golden boxes, elaborate silver urns, containers and chests embellished with gemstones and jewels. The rich trappings on the outsides were valued highly in the human world. Here, in the Nine Realms, the contents were the real treasure.

Bwgan stones. Thousands of them. From the size of a fingernail to the size of an apple, they had been accumulated over eons and stored in the very foundations of the palace, saved for a day of need.

And Aurddolen had been right: that day had come. Lurien watched as some of the envoys rubbed the stones on their skins and hides as though bathing with them. Others pressed them to their foreheads, and a few, like the basilisks, curled up on little nested piles of the stones with strange blissful looks on their faces.

The dragon woman grabbed Lurien's hand and plunked a large bwgan stone into his palm. He was about to protest that he didn't want to look weak, but the sensation was simply too good. The dark chatoyant stone, laced with hidden fires, filled the void in him with clean, enlivening energy. He was a desert wanderer drinking deep at the shaded spring of an oasis . . .

"Tools," she said wryly. "Once in a while, you need them."

Once in a while, indeed.

"My Lord!" One of his hunters, Trahern, raced through the vast room and handed Lurien a palm-sized leather pouch sewn shut with rough individual stitches, as though someone had been in a hurry. "This just came through one of the small ways."

He held it in his gloved hand. "Odd. Who brought it?" he asked.

"It was tied to the back of a fat speckled bird. Actually, I could not see the fowl at first, only the pouch moving in the air by itself. When I touched it, the bird was revealed to my eyes—but I have never seen one like it here."

Lurien frowned. If the bird had spots, it was no surprise that it had remained hidden. It was a curious fact that few fae beings could discern a creature both dark and light by sight alone. But Trahern had been a hunter all his life—what bird could he not identify?

"Nodin says it's called a *chicken*."

It must be from Gwenhidw! Lurien opened the packet and read the letter within. He read it a second time, then stood before the assembly. This time it wasn't long before they quieted and turned their full attention to him.

"Friends," he said. "It seems we need to alter our plans. There has been treachery, and a trap has been set for us. We will have to combine our talents to find another way to send the Wild Hunt to Tir Hardd. And we will have to do all within our power to keep the Great Way sealed at this end."

He read aloud every word of the queen's letter.

Mounted on Dodge, Liam followed the top of Finger Ridge. The basalt formation curved away from his farm and melded into the Palouse Hills. His brow was even more furrowed than usual, trying in vain to anticipate how to free Caris while reflecting on the incredible events of the past few days. The existence of faeries didn't amaze him as much as how he'd come to love a woman in such a short time. Such things happened only in the movies—or maybe they just happened when you met the right person. He'd never known anyone like her, and he needed her like he needed air—but right now she needed him. *Hold on, Caris. Just hold on.* He still had no idea what he was going to do once he got to the butte, but get there he would.

At least nobody had to look for the place. Steptoe Butte was easy to see. It was a wide conical hill, thirty-six hundred feet or so above sea level. That might have been impressive somewhere else. Here, it was merely the tallest bump in a sea of rolling hills. In fact, it didn't even look like a proper butte, at least, not like the kind you saw in cowboy movies. The tourist pamphlets often described it as "thimble-shaped," but the truth was, the small flattened top remained hidden until you were practically standing on it. At twelve years old, Liam certainly hadn't been impressed when he'd gone there on a school field trip. That is, until he got out of the bus at the summit and got his first look at a view that stretched two hundred miles in all directions. It had taken his breath away.

Now, that same view could get him killed before he ever got a chance to help Caris. If that asshole prince and his followers were up there, surely they'd see anyone approaching. "Ranyon—tell me again how this spotted thing works?"

The little ellyll urged his mount alongside Dodge. Ranyon had insisted on riding a goat, and he'd chosen one of Liam's herd sires, a big solid buck with a fine sweep of horns and a coat nearly as spotted as Liam's horses. The animal had certainly never been used as anyone's mount before, yet it behaved with all the dignity of a noble knight's destrier. *Perhaps it is one*, thought Liam. After all, the little tree man certainly had a noble heart.

Noble or not, damned if Liam didn't have to rub a hand over his mouth to keep from smiling. Ranyon wore an ornately fashioned silver bandolier over one shoulder. Despite the ellyll's explanation that it had been Caris's magical collar at one time, Liam automatically thought of a Wookiee every time he saw the thing. Even harder to ignore was the fact that the ellyll didn't use reins, but simply guided the big goat by steering it with its big sweeping horns. They looked for all the world like ape-hanger handlebars on a motorcycle . . .

And it didn't help a bit that the buck's name was Harley.

"Ya needn't be worryin'," said Ranyon. "That fool prince won't even see us coming, not when we're mounted on such fine pied creatures. As I was tellin' Morgan, the mix of dark and light repels faery sight. Only touch can overcome it—and he won't be layin' a finger on what he can't see! Your good Dodge there will protect ya without ya havin' to do a thing."

"The fae don't have to see us—they'll hear us coming a frickin' mile away." Liam was referring to the strange creations of copper wire, gears, stones, keys, bells, and feathers that had been loosely fastened around all four of Dodge's legs between the fetlocks and the hooves like bizarre ankle bracelets. They jangled as the stallion walked, and Liam could swear Dodge liked them. Harley was similarly festooned. "I don't understand why we have to have these."

"You'll be understandin' soon enough if we find ourselves with a pickle," snorted Ranyon.

"*In* a pickle."

"'Tis sour either way. Fae horses are faster than any mortal creature, dontcha know, and every one o' Maelgwn's followers has one. Plus that traitor's got fifty grims that can keep up with faery horses. If we have to make a run fer it, you'll be glad fer the extra speed those charms will give yer mount."

Liam was impressed. The Appaloosa stallion was already fast. It could be fun to see how much speed Dodge could muster with the charms—but not if riders and hounds were at their heels. "You're absolutely certain they can't hear us? Because *I* can sure hear us."

"Ah, but *yer* ears don't matter, now do they? I promise ya that *fae* ears won't be hearin' a thing," said Ranyon. "Did ya not see the thistledown woven into each and every one o' the charms? That's fer silence, dontcha know. We're going to be as quiet as gorillas."

"You mean *guerrillas*, right?"

"A' course—them things that swing through yer trees."

Liam gave up then and simply trusted that Ranyon knew far more about magic than about some of the details of the human world. He couldn't argue with the fact, strange as it was, that they'd covered more miles in a couple of hours than they should have been able to. Still, it bothered him that the afternoon sun was on the wane. Instinct told him he'd rather not encounter the fae after dark.

Instinct *still* wasn't giving him any great strategic plans as to how to save Caris, however. A lot was going to depend on what the situation was when he got there. He didn't have much for weapons, just the fiddle in his backpack, and his uncle's .30-30 Winchester carbine shoved into the scabbard on his saddle. Ranyon said the fiddle was the most useful of the two, but Liam felt better with a rifle along. Whether it was any good against a faery prince remained to be seen.

He studied the looming shape of Steptoe Butte and felt like a hobbit heading into Mordor.

TWENTY-SIX

The sound of dripping water echoed in the sea cave. Lurien held the lantern aloft and peered further into its depths. It was one of many dark and uninviting places he and his hunters had investigated today, and this one didn't look any more promising than the last six. "You're certain there's a way through here?" he asked the undine with the long blue hair. Her name was Morien, and she was the only one who would speak to him, although several others stood huddled together at a distance to watch. Perhaps they were intimidated by the dark image he presented.

"We found it when we were playing in the tidal pools. Sometimes we find pretty treasures in caves." Morien twirled the gold chains that spilled over her naked breasts. "So my sisters and I like to go exploring."

The undines liked lounging naked in fountains at parties too, but that didn't matter. The important thing was that they were among the few creatures that could simply *sense* the existence of a way. He had the kobolds and coblynau combing the area, as well as a pair of basilisks. And word had gone out to everyone in the realm to report any way they knew. The kingdom was honeycombed with them, so much so that no one spared them much thought. Of course, that was because most were disappointingly small and therefore useless. The one that the chicken had obediently followed under Gwenhidw's direction, for example, would hold nothing larger.

"Did you go in it?"

"Teleri did. She has more power than I do, and she's not afraid of anything."

Except me, apparently.

"She thinks it comes out somewhere near Tir Hardd, but she wasn't sure. None of us has ever been there before. The way is big enough to walk through, but only one at a time."

"Horses?"

"I don't know if they'll fit. I don't think so."

Worth a try just the same, Lurien thought, as he thanked the undines for their help. He couldn't afford to rule out any possibility—even one that would leave his riders without mounts. "Iago, take three of your men. Find out where it goes and if we can use it."

Lurien rode back to the palace and returned to the throne room, which had become the unofficial headquarters for the envoys and their retinues. Those who didn't have natural talent like the undines were helping with the search using more pedestrian methods. It was a testament to how they all felt about Gwenhidw that no one fought, no one griped, and no one gave up. A huge hairy bwbach, with his ever-present cask of beer, was helping several kelpies pore over ancient maps—in some cases literally pour, as the waterhorses tended to drip a lot and the bwbach's mug sloshed freely. Lurien didn't care, as long as someone, somewhere, found a way to get to Gwenhidw.

He felt naked without his magic, and even if he rolled his body in a *barrelful* of bwgan stones (he'd spotted a fire drake doing just that), he knew of only one spell that could transport someone halfway across the world without using a way. He'd used it to save

Gwenhidw's life. But moving a company of horses and riders? Not a chance in Hades. One person would be the extent of it, and one was far from enough. In fact, since Maelgwn had essentially initiated a rebellion, it would likely take the entire Wild Hunt to put it down—and Lurien wasn't sure even that would be enough. The prince was young by fae norms, arrogant, cruel, vain, and ambitious, as were those who followed him. But Maelgwn had proved he was far from powerless. Lurien knew all too well what it took to open the Great Way. The prince was also far more cunning than anyone had suspected, according to Gwenhidw's letter. Somehow, the upstart had persuaded the Anghenfilod to help him.

A head like that needs to be removed from its shoulders . . .

Aurddolen came in with Trahern and Nodin. They looked as tired as he felt, but there was a spring in their step. "We found one," said the dragon woman. "And you won't believe where it is."

Lurien was on his feet at once. "It goes to Tir Hardd? You tested it?" Too many ways had looked promising at first only to end up back in the Nine Realms. Others led to strange, unknown places in the mortal world. Sending the Hunt to the frozen land the humans called Antarctica would help no one.

"It comes out on the mortal plane, amid the sea of hills surrounding the mouth of the Great Way," said Trahern. "There's no room to spare—the horses cannot fit. But it'll work. I left Emrys and Heulog there to keep an eye on things."

"We cannot ask for better. Sound the horn," Lurien commanded, even as he hated the idea of leaving their mounts behind. "Tell our men to arm themselves well. Summon the hounds. We will leave at once." He grabbed Aurddolen's arm as she made to follow Nodin and Trahern. "Someone must lead the envoys, someone with sense and the nerve to push them to their limits. *The Great Way must not open.*"

"They're still drained. We all are. Even at full strength, it would take all of us together to come close to the magic of the queen or the Lord of the Hunt."

He nodded. "And you are both a queen of the dragon territories, and a hunter in your own right, are you not? Besides, you will not be without resource. Save for the ones the envoys are carrying in their pockets, I've had all the bwgan stones gathered and moved to the top of Mynedfa, where its summit becomes Holyhead Mount in the human realm."

"Not giving me directions are you? I've been there."

"And I need you there again. There is no one else I can trust with this task. The envoys must not fail. *The Way must remain closed at all costs.*" He pulled her close and leaned his forehead to hers. They stood like that for a long moment in silent communion.

When she looked up at him at last, she grinned. "The Anghenfilod will find no entrance here—even if I have to tie rocks to each and every envoy and toss them into the Great Way to fill it up." She knotted her hands in his hair then and kissed him hard on the lips. "*Hela da,*" she said, and spun away.

"Good hunting to you as well," he murmured.

For his queen, Lurien would endure anything. If it had been anyone else who required aid, he might have wished he'd traded places with Aurddolen. For one thing, with her smaller frame, she'd feel far less cramped in this infernal way that they'd found. The location, as she promised, was a surprise. It was in the kitchen of a very large and very busy tavern—for coblynau. The little fae were gracious enough, wanting to help their beloved queen in any way possible. They cheered and lifted their glasses as Lurien's tall men trooped through the hazy atmosphere of the pub and into the bakery end of the squat-ceilinged kitchen.

The way itself wasn't much larger. In the end, the entire Wild Hunt had to walk single file, and slightly stooped as well. Although the tunnel was formed of bright blue energy rather than rock, the walls were just as solid. Every man held a dagger at the ready, the rest of their weapons on their belts or on their backs. There were frequent stops to readjust a sword or a bow or a pack in order to fit through the cramped passage. Lurien set a brisk pace, but it was still slow going on foot, and he cursed at his inability to get to Gwenhidw any faster.

At least the way was relatively short, considering it was taking them to another continent completely. And it was far too small for fearsome creatures like the Anghenfilod to inhabit. But glowing leechlike creatures did live here, and they were starved for the taste of magic. It wasn't long before every man had been bitten several times, and their weapons were slimy from killing the pests. Lurien sighed and yanked another one from his sleeve—the *gelau* had worked its needlelike teeth right through the charmed leather.

The only good thing about this ordeal was that Maelgwn would never suspect their approach. As far as anyone knew, the Wild Hunt could travel only through the Great Way—and the traitorous prince was counting on that.

Lurien was looking forward to disappointing him.

～

"We will have but one chance, Rhedyn," said Gwenhidw. "Are you certain your magic is up to this? More important, is your resolve? Maelgwn has had much power over you."

The fae woman bowed her head. "I am strong enough. I will take any chance to redeem myself, Your Grace. And to be free of him."

Morgan watched from the doorway of the barn. She hadn't been convinced when the queen first proposed the idea. Now she looked from one woman to the other, then turned to Jay. "You know, I think this could actually work."

He nodded. "As long as their horses cooperate. Kirk Leland brought over a pair of his best Quarter Horse mares, just like you asked. Both of them are real splashy Paints, so they should be spotted enough to do the job."

"They're here already?" Kirk lived in the area, but still . . . Morgan looked at her friend suspiciously. "How the hell did you get him to move so fast?"

Jay looked positively embarrassed. "Well, he thinks the world of you since you saved his daughter's champion barrel racer last spring. So I said the only thing I could think of. I told him you wanted to buy the horses as a surprise gift for Rhys, and he was coming home tomorrow."

There goes the livestock budget, thought Morgan. *Hard to worry about that when you're trying to save two worlds.* "Most people look over an animal before they make a purchase. He didn't question that I wasn't there?"

"Of course he did—and I lied accordingly. You had a *veterinary emergency* and so I examined them and wrote him a check. Said you'd seen both horses at the state team roping finals—but actually, I'm the one that saw them there. It got a little convoluted after that, so I'll have to write it all down for you so you have the story straight the next time you talk to him."

Good grief. "Kirk left the trailer he brought them in?"

"Are you kidding? He was so happy to be paid up front that he would have left his truck, his wife, and his dog if I'd asked. We're good to go. I've got the trailer hitched to the clinic truck, I found enough tack in the shed, and the horses are saddled and loaded."

"Well, then, let's see how close we can get the queen to Steptoe Butte." Morgan thought of phoning Rhys again. He'd been adamant that she wait until he could fly back to help—and frankly, his warrior skills might be damned handy—but she'd already checked the schedules of the flights from California. *He's going to be absolutely furious, but we can't wait for him.* "Your Grace, if you're certain you're up to this, it's time to go. We'll get you and Rhedyn as close as we can before you'll have to ride."

"The Nine Realms are in grave danger," Gwenhidw said, sliding the baldric and its sword over her shoulder. "I *must* be up to this. Sometimes action cannot be delayed for a more opportune time."

Yeah, tell me about it, thought Morgan.

The sun was a flame-colored ball just a finger's width from the horizon, and they'd traveled only partway along the road that wrapped two and a half times around the broad butte. That's when Liam heard a fiddle. Ribbons of music carried through the air from the hilltop, winding through the air currents like streamers. He felt that if he just squinted hard enough he'd be able to actually *see* the perfect notes floating by. Only Caris's incredible talent could have produced them—but they didn't have the passion he remembered.

In fact, none of the tunes he was hearing had the stamp of emotional power—probably because they weren't from her heart and soul but were being commanded and coerced.

Hope that slows down Prince Asshole's plans.

Rounding a corner revealed two mounted fae guarding the halfway point, right in the center of the narrow road. Liam reined in Dodge and put a hand on the stock of the rifle—but the guards didn't react at all. In fact, they looked bored. *What the hell?* While it wasn't quite broad daylight anymore, Ranyon and Liam were right out in the open, and all the charms jangling like Santa's sleigh bells. *Nothing.* It was like being a ghost. He hadn't really believed in that whole spotted-animal magic stuff, but it was tough to argue with the evidence. *I owe the little guy an apology.*

Liam looked around only to find that the *little guy* had left the road and was urging Harley straight up the side of the god-damn hill! Ranyon glanced back once, and beckoned him to follow, though it was impossibly steep and treacherous terrain for a horse. *He really* is *trying to be a gorilla.* "Whaddya think, Dodge?" he murmured. "He's been right about everything else." The stallion answered by simply following the goat and its rider without any hesitation. Liam quickly laid flat—well, as flat as the saddle pommel would allow—and wrapped his arms tight around Dodge's muscular neck as the horse climbed at a gut-wrenching angle. Liam didn't bother looking down. He already knew that what they were doing was absolutely physically impossible, and that if they fell, there'd be no hope for either of them. Instead, he made himself concentrate wholly on the music and on the woman he loved who was creating it.

And the need he had to save her. As long as there was breath in his body, he would *not* leave her in the hands of the fae. She'd suffered that cruel nightmare once already. Not again. Never again.

They came up on the paved road just below the summit. Above them was an ugly assortment of telecommunications equipment, microwave relay and transmission towers clustered on one side of the flat-topped butte. Liam dragged himself off Dodge, grateful to be on level ground. Ranyon dismounted as well, and together they climbed the rock behind the towers, made their way around the fence, and lay flat to look out over the top of the butte.

As a hilltop, it was unimpressive, a small plateau fringed with bushes and rocky outcroppings but otherwise barren. Directly in front of Liam, a paved parking lot stood ready to receive about twenty cars and buses. Thankfully there were no vehicles at the moment—no doubt due to the faery guards stationed at various points along the road. Instead, Liam counted about sixty horses clustered together, as close to the edge of the butte as they could possibly get. At their feet huddled a monstrous pack of the biggest, blackest dogs he had ever imagined. They could only be grims, the death dogs his friends had spoken of. *That Caris had been cursed to be one of . . .*

But she hadn't been this big. Some of the grims looked like oversize wolves, others like immense mastiffs. Immediately he thought of the war dogs spoken of in ancient Roman history—and yet these mighty canine specimens seemed not just subdued but fearful. Stranger still, both horses and dogs were motionless, as if cemented in place. Every one of them faced northeast, their eyes fixed on something at the other end of the—

Liam recoiled, staring in both wonder and horror. He would have sat up without thinking if Ranyon hadn't yanked him back down into the dirt.

Suspended in the air was a gaping maw with glowing blue edges. Jay had described the Great Way as a rip in the fabric of reality, some kind of wormhole like in a science-fiction movie, but nothing prepared Liam for what such a thing would actually look like. The surreal phenomenon was round like the eclipse of a moon—or Alice's rabbit hole. Within, however, was darkness so complete that even the dogs looked pale gray by comparison. Liam could swear he felt a punch to the stomach when he realized that the darkness was not the tunnel. Instead, a monstrous shadow appeared to move aside to reveal a shimmering passage of light beyond—and more nebulous shapes moving within it.

What the hell are those things in there?

As if he'd heard him, Ranyon whispered. "Those are the Anghenfilod—monsters of the Inbetween."

Liam clamped his teeth together rather than reply, because only curses would come out. He'd expected scary dogs and armed fae hunters and a big dick named Maelgwn in charge of it all. *No one mentioned honest-to-God monsters.* Maybe he should have stuck around for the queen's planning meeting instead of charging off. *But I had to get to Caris.*

He forced his gaze away from the gaping tear in the landscape to study the figures on the far side of the entrance of the tunnel—and noted with relief that the woman he loved was indeed there. As far as he could tell from a distance, she was okay, but it scared the hell out of him that she was standing so close to that hulking anomaly with goddamn monsters living in it.

Caris was still playing, swaying slightly in time to the music, but not dancing as she usually did. Maybe she was tired? *More likely she's just holding back.* She wasn't the type to cooperate one bit more than she absolutely had to, and she definitely wouldn't put her heart and soul into this forced performance.

The prince's followers, close to sixty strong, were as strangely motionless as their animals. Seated in a great half circle, they formed an impromptu stage for Maelgwn—and he was definitely putting on a show. Hands upraised, he chanted strange words in a loud voice. His wine-colored leathers had been covered with a golden robe, and his white hair hung in a long, thick braid behind him. Wisps of scented smoke curled up from some sort of squat bronze kettle at his feet.

"That idiot prince is trying to close the Great Way," said Ranyon. "And he's draining the magic from every fae creature on this hilltop to do it. Ya see how strange they are?"

No kidding. Liam watched as a pair of ravens landed near one of the fae and plucked silver beads from her clothing. She continued to stare straight ahead, even when one of the birds yanked a shiny pendant from her throat. "Christ, that's creepy," he whispered. "They're not dead, are they?"

"They're alive fer now. But there's not a one of the Tylwyth

Teg that would volunteer to part with their powers, not even if Maelgwn promised them the earth itself. He's tricked them fer certain, and he'll kill them all if he's not careful."

Liam couldn't help but flinch as Ranyon continued to speak in his normal tone of voice. Yet a quick glance at the grims, who should have been the first to hear, revealed no reaction at all. Only the occasional quivering of their flanks revealed them to be anything more than statues. *Definitely spooky.*

"So if he's sucking in power, will *you* be okay?"

The ellyll snorted. "I have a charm fer that, a'course! Besides, I'm thinkin' the fool may have overreached himself—leaned too much on that fancy breastplate o' bwgan stones that Rhedyn told us about. And counted on Caris's music to make up the difference."

"Let's tip the scales a little further then."

"Aye, it's time," said Ranyon. "The Way is beginning to close."

The new king of Tir Hardd sucked in great lungfuls of air, yet it felt as if he wasn't getting enough. The atmosphere of the mortal world wasn't of the same purity as the fae realms, but it should have been adequate. It was the spell—the spell was exhausting him. So was the pain. The thirty-three bwgan stones were searing his skin to the point that he could smell it, and the silver breastplate that held them had heated accordingly. He wanted to claw the metal from him, peel it off before his skin became fused to it. But he wanted Tir Hardd more, and he fisted his hands until his nails made his palms bleed. He let the blue drops fall into the brazier at his feet as he continued the chant. All he had to do was seal the Great Way, and he would have all the power he'd ever dreamed of, including the power to heal himself of terrible burns if need be.

The spell should be working by now. It has *to be working.*

He was close to completing the first recitation of the spell when the perfect roundness of the portal distorted, one side indenting the way a full moon wanes to a lesser one. *Finally!*

Maelgwn redoubled his efforts even as he strained against the excruciating pain. He'd taken such care to create perfect conditions for the spell, particularly since it had never been tried on such a large way. The brazier at his feet contained great nuggets of pure amber from long-ago forests and the ground bones of dead bwganod, to facilitate and enhance magic. He'd ensured that he had more than his own powers to draw on too. His ambitious followers all thought they'd chosen him, but he'd been grooming each one of them for years, cultivating only the allegiance of those who possessed large natural wellsprings of magic—magic he was now using.

He *knew* he was performing the incantation correctly. He'd studied the bloodstained parchment every day since he'd first snatched it from the aged sorcerer's broken fingers. Maelgwn had practiced the archaic language it was written in, and memorized not only every word but every nuance. The lengthy spell had to be recited perfectly three times—once to initiate the process, once to close the Way entirely, and once more to seal it for *all* time.

The music was wrong. That had to be it. Music should have eased the entire process. In fact, the mortal-spun melody should have caused things to happen far more quickly, should have delivered more power than everything Maelgwn was drawing from his followers and his breastplate combined. He finished the first recitation to the last syllable, then whirled to regard the small human woman playing the *ffidil.*

TWENTY-SEVEN

⌒⌒⌒

Caris swore she could feel her very bones chill as the prince suddenly turned his attention to her. His gaze seemed almost mad, his perfect features drawn tight as if in pain, and his breathing ragged and gasping. Still she made certain her bow never hesitated, that tunes were drawn from the strings of the instrument without ceasing—he must not suspect that the faery fiddle could not compel her. Silently she thanked Ranyon for the blue-stoned charm she wore around her neck, and she was doubly grateful that fae eyes could not perceive the pendant. She still had no idea how she was going to escape, however.

Meanwhile, the prince snarled at her like a feral animal. "You," he hissed. "You're playing like an ungifted student, when I know you have far superior talents. *I will have your passion, your heart!* Play like your life depends on it, like the lives of those you care about depend on it—because surely they do."

"You generously gave me your royal word, good sir," she said quietly, not wishing to incite him further, although the title of *good sir* tasted foul on her tongue. Truly, there was nothing good about him. Even Rhedyn, who knew the prince better than any-one, had admitted he was both ruthless and cruel, and ever had been. Like most of his followers, she had been foolishly drawn to his rapidly growing power, willing to endure his foul treatment of her in exchange for the elevated position it provided, and the chance to rise even further with him.

Maelgwn laughed at Caris. "Ah yes, that little *gift* to celebrate my coronation. You forget that your friends are protected only if they do not leave their dirty little farm—and you know they will not stay there forever. My men will be waiting to seize them and then I will have a gift for myself—their skins taken while they yet live. *All* of your friends, four-legged and two-legged"—he pointed at her—"and you will watch."

Caris's stomach lurched, but she dared not show any reaction. Nor did she dare interrupt the vibration of the strings beneath the press of her fingers and the glide of her bow.

"Animal skins are useful, of course," he continued. "Human skin is another matter. It's far too flimsy to be made into saddles or boots. Shall I have soft cushions covered with them? Perhaps make them into fine clothing?" His eyes narrowed. "You hold their fates in your hands. Play from your mortal heart, *now*."

She couldn't stall him any longer, could buy no more time. Caris slid skillfully from the song she'd been playing into "*Dacw 'Nghariad.*" It was an old Welsh folk song, a sweet lover's tune, but she made it a bold anthem as she faced Maelgwn. He grunted in satisfaction as she poured her heart into the notes without further bidding. In her mind, she sang the words:

Away is my sweetheart, down in the orchard
Oh how I wish I could be there myself . . .
Here is my harp and here are my strings
Who am I without him to play my songs to?

She watched the prince take up his position before the brazier and begin chanting once again. *What am I going to do?* She knew her music was strengthening him and energizing his spell, the very thing she'd sought to avoid. When should she play the songs that Ranyon had so carefully taught her? He'd told her to wait until help reached her—but as yet, she saw no sign.

She allowed herself to dance a little as she played the song over again, thinking of Liam the entire time. *I'll wait in the shade until my love comes . . .* Caris twirled near the stony lip of the plateau and bent low . . .

She was so astonished by what she saw, she nearly stopped playing. There was Liam himself, perched on a small rocky ledge on the steep hillside just below her—*with a fiddle in his hand.*

He grinned as Caris's eyes widened in surprise. She brilliantly managed to render her tune without missing a beat, even as she risked a glance over her shoulder to where Maelgwn was shouting words at the Way in a language Liam didn't recognize.

She looked back at Liam. "'Tis time for Ranyon's songs. Can you follow me?" she whispered.

He nodded and tucked the fiddle beneath his jaw—and he could swear both heart and soul jerked as if electrified into life. There was no time to practice, no time to find out if he could still play. Everything he cared about was on the line. Knowing Caris had been the last one to touch the bow, he kissed it quick for luck. And hoped like hell that the ellyll knew what he was doing.

Liam's own plan had been simple: bring his rifle to bear, take out Maelgwn, and whisk Caris off the summit with Dodge. The ellyll had had to explain twice over exactly why that would *not* work. Apparently fae princes weren't that easy to get rid of with human weapons. In fact, even an Apache helicopter with laser-guided missiles might not do the job. So Liam had agreed to Ranyon's scheme even though he didn't understand it in the least. But the little guy hadn't been wrong yet.

His back against the rocky hillside, Liam held the bow poised and waiting, ready to jump into whatever song Caris played next. He glanced down only once. It wasn't a cliff, but it was the next thing to it—the steepest side of the entire hill. The good part was if he fell, he wouldn't roll all the way to the bottom. The bad part? It would be a toss-up as to whether the jutting rocks would break his fall or the narrow strip of road even further below. Either way, it would definitely leave a mark . . .

There! Caris had launched into something Celtic, and he listened intently for a moment, then drew the bow long over the strings, the sound strong and true. He followed her lead, every sense he possessed straining to hear, to anticipate. Caris fed him the notes, and he picked them up, scarcely a heartbeat behind her, his tune an underlying counterpoint to her song. By the second verse he was improvising, and by the third they took turns leading.

He could still hear Maelgwn's voice, and it seemed to him there was a note of desperation in it. Was he already feeling the shift in the music, or was it the strain of the task he'd undertaken? *Just keep on chanting, asshole,* Liam thought. Ranyon had said that the words to a spell could not be interrupted. When it was done, however, all hell would surely break loose.

Lurien, his hunters, and every last Cŵn Annwn from his kennels, emerged onto a grassy slope. Like all the hills at this time of year, it was dried and golden, the color of a lion's pelt. He scanned the tawny landscape until he spotted Steptoe Butte looming higher than the surrounding hills—and he cursed when he saw the glittering black tear hovering at the edge of its summit. How in Hades was he going to get there in time without a mount?

"Lord Lurien?" It was Trahern. "The hunters I left here, Emrys and Heulog—they've got something you'll want to see."

What else is wrong? he wondered, but followed Trahern around the curve of the hillside. The men in question stood in a swale between the hills. And with them was a large herd of tall, heavily muscled creatures with great sweeping antlers. The humans called them elk.

For the first time since the attack on Gwenhidw, Lurien smiled. "It would seem that Arthfael himself is watching over us." The king had always preferred his great gray stag, Hydd, to any fae horse.

"Collect the hounds and keep them silent," he ordered. "Every man mount up and follow me. Don't sound the horn until my signal."

The twilight had faded to full dark, and the glowing rim of the Great Way was vivid against the night sky. The portal's shape now resembled a half-moon—and remained so, despite all of Maelgwn's efforts. He faltered slightly, struggling to continue the spell. He was weak and dizzy, and for the first time he wondered if he'd miscalculated just how much power was needed to seal the Great Way. He could see more and more anghenfilod gathering near the entrance he was trying so hard to close—and they seemed agitated. Undoubtedly it was the immense volume of magic he was wielding that was attracting them. Shouldn't the Wild Hunt have galloped into the shining passage by now? Where were all the indignant fae seeking vengeance for their dead queen? They should have been racing by the hundreds down the throat of the Great Way. He'd promised the Anghenfilod a fine feast, and then they would be free to spill out into the Nine Realms to hunt at will.

Instead, several more of the featureless creatures appeared—and some were poking dark appendages through the glittering aperture.

If only he could get the twice-cursed way *shut*.

At least there was no more pain from the stones or the breast-plate. A small voice in the back of his mind suggested it was because the flesh beneath it had been burned away, and he hushed it immediately. Dizzy or not, weak or not, burned or not, he would continue the spell. Another thought occurred: *the little mortal . . .*

He'd obviously been successful in frightening her, as her music had burst from her with unfettered power ever since. Who knew but that it was the real reason his pain had stopped? Yet . . . Surely it sounded as if there was a *pair* of fiddles, not one. No doubt a trick of his hearing, considering the state he was in, or the sound was being affected by the magic it contained. He shook his head and doggedly continued to recite the ancient words, though the Great Way gave no appearance of closing any further.

That's when it occurred to him that there was an unusual tone to the woman's now-passionate songs, a resonance, a repeating cadence that . . . *The little witch is stealing my power!* The realization shot through him like lightning. His increasing weakness was not because of the difficulty of his task but because her music was draining his magic away!

Blinded by temper, he abandoned the spell and took a step in the human's direction, freeing the light whip at his side with a single smooth movement. Tiny blue-tinged fingerlets of energy crackled along its length, a far cry from the streamers of raw lightning he had once called down. Knowing he had so little power left planted a cold thread of fear within him, and his rage immediately swelled to cover it. *I require no magic to wield this weapon!* The snap and bite of leather could still remove tender flesh from mortal bone.

"Stop playing," he hissed, and took another step.

The woman was afraid, but she refused to heed. She jutted her chin and drew her bow ever more fiercely. He could feel his energies ebbing, like water leaving a cracked bowl—and for the first time he clearly heard a countering tune, an undercurrent of supporting notes, from somewhere nearby.

Another ffidil! He had not been mistaken after all. Maelgwn had already lifted his hand to strike her, but now a different tactic was called for. He lowered his arm as if he'd changed his mind—then snaked the whip out sideways. It caught her full around the waist and the prince yanked her to him. His free hand gripped her by the throat and shook her until both instrument and bow dropped to the ground. All he had to do now was wait . . .

Pressed tightly against him, Caris's fingers clawed at the prince's gloved hand around her neck, and she kicked back at him with her feet. Through her thin clothing, she could feel the unyielding breastplate beneath his garb—and the fiery heat from it shocked her. It was like being held against a hot stove, and she fought harder to free herself. The prince stood perfectly still, however, unmindful of her struggles as if focused elsewhere. *He's waiting for something.* That's when Caris realized that all was quiet save the prince's harsh breathing. She seized Maelgwn's thumb with both hands and bent it away.

"Liam!" she screamed. "Don't stop play—"

The prince's hand closed like an iron trap. As she thrashed and choked, she turned one wild eye toward the edge of the hillside, terrified that Liam would climb up where Maelgwn waited with his whip ready. But even as her vision began to darken, there was no sign.

A flurry of notes sounded from far behind them, and the prince whirled to face it. The movement and the distraction loosened his fingers just enough to let Caris draw a shallow, desperate breath. The bluish glow from the Great Way suddenly illuminated Liam as he emerged from the darkness, drawing one of Ranyon's songs from his gleaming fiddle.

"Let her go!" he commanded, his bow arm never slowing. The tune was sprouting new branches here and there, new leaves and buds in the form of flourishes and grace notes that lingered as if suspended in the night air. Rather than diminishing the song's effects, they seemed to strengthen them.

Caris felt Maelgwn shudder, and without warning, his fingers released her as if he couldn't hold her up any longer—or because he was desperate to conserve his strength. She dropped to her knees gasping as the fae prince stalked toward Liam. The whip was no longer alive with energy, yet it was coiled and dangerous just the same. She wanted to shout a warning but could coax no sound from her throat.

His magic might be gone, but Maelgwn no longer cared. He was running on white-hot rage now, and he was still physically stronger than any foolish mortal. He would enjoy killing this one—right after he destroyed the cursed *ffidil*. In a blur of motion, the leather struck out like a viper, but his aim was off and he missed the instrument. The results were still rewarding however, as the whip laid open the man's face from temple to jaw. Blood—that strange bright scarlet that separated human from fae—rushed from the wound, but though he reeled from the blow, *the mortal would not stop playing*! His intense blue gaze was locked on Maelgwn like a warth who had singled out his prey, and every pull of his relentless bow was like a punch. The blood ran freely over the fiddle—and Maelgwn realized with horror that it was fueling the already-powerful magic of the song.

He had just added oil to flame.

Desperation collided with madness. A wildness overcame the prince, and he tore his robe away from his body, revealing the shining silver cuirass set with glowing stones. Advancing on the mortal, who stubbornly held his ground, Maelgwn raised the whip again.

The blow didn't fall. Instead, an enormous *goat* materialized out of nowhere and knocked the prince to the ground. Before he could recover, the beast rammed him again, kicked him in the face twice, then bounded away as its diminutive rider made an insolent sign with long twiggy fingers. Both vanished as abruptly as they'd appeared.

Wheezing and winded, Maelgwn nearly choked on his own anger even as he fought his way to his feet. He would *not* be beaten by such inferior beings! Yet the unrelenting song was still beating at his brain, still dealing blow after invisible blow . . . And the prince realized for the first time that if he didn't stop this musician, he would lose more than his magic. His very life essence would follow it.

"Maelgwn of the House of Ash!"

The voice from behind him caused him to freeze in place. He knew it—every fae creature knew it—but it wasn't possible. Slowly he turned and found himself face to face with a ghost: Queen Gwenhidw of the Nine Realms, *Brenhines* of the Faery Kingdom *dan Cymru.* Her long hair fanned out behind her like a cape, her shining robes fluttered as if by phantom wind, her iridescent eyes were as flames as her gaze locked on his, and she held the sword of her ancestors before her.

"I killed you," he spat out.

"I live," she said. "And so will my kingdom."

With an incoherent roar, he slashed at her with the whip. The sword caught the blow and a withering blast of magic traveled up the leather and staggered Maelgwn, buckling his knees until he dropped the weapon and fell to the ground. The image of Gwenhidw, however, abruptly wavered and faded to reveal Rhedyn standing defiantly before him.

"How dare you betray me!" he shouted. Still on his knees, he sought the light whip, spotting it just out of arm's reach.

A slender and delicate foot, fair of skin and perfect of form, placed itself firmly upon the fallen whip before his fingers could seize it. "It is you who are the betrayer."

The prince looked up at the white-robed figure, his face contorted by hatred. He would feed this woman to the Anghenfilod a piece at a time . . . "Think you to deceive me a second time?"

"Think you to rob my people of their future?"

Maelgwn had only a heartbeat in which to glance back and see that Rhedyn had not moved in the least. He looked up just in time to recognize the true queen—and the shining silver sword that was already descending from its high arc.

The blade passed through his body from neck to hip, sundering it and the silver breastplate like paper.

TWENTY-EIGHT

G wenhidw wanted nothing more than to put some distance between her and what she had been constrained to do, but she hadn't gone many steps before her knees wobbled and she sank to the ground, physically and emotionally spent.

Rhedyn dove at once to catch her. "Your Grace, are you all right?" she asked, cradling her in her arms. "Tell me what to do for you!"

It was on the tip of her tongue to say that she was just tired and *not to worry* . . . but as the queen looked up at the fae woman's anxious face, she saw the glint of steel against the night sky above them.

Before she could react, the clash of swords rang directly overhead. And then there was silence, save for a single heartfelt curse from a familiar voice. Gwenhidw quickly put her palms together for a moment and opened them like a book. The small sphere of light that rested in her hands revealed the Lord of the Wild Hunt, his sword blocking the downstroke of another fae's weapon. Lurien also held a dagger that was currently buried to the hilt in the heart of the queen's would-be attacker. Lurien shoved the heavy body away from him and knelt at her side.

"Are you saving me yet again, Lurien?"

"I cannot seem to help myself, my queen. Are you hurt?" He glared at Rhedyn suspiciously. "There is blood all over your gown."

"It is the prince's, not mine," said Gwenhidw. "I am simply resting before I undertake my next task."

He digested that for a long moment. "I truly fear to ask what you have planned."

"Why, I must negotiate with the Anghenfilod, of course. The Great Way cannot be left open here, and we have not the power ourselves to close it. I believe the creatures of the Inbetween can do so. Besides, it is long past time we made peace with them."

She could see his jaw clench as she smiled up at him—and was that a slight twitch at the corner of his eye? Truly, she never tired of surprising her *llaw dde*.

"We will speak of it after you rest, Your Grace," he said with great effort.

She didn't doubt that there would be a great deal of speaking, mostly on his part as he attempted to dissuade her. She looked forward to it. "I assume the rest of Maelgwn's followers have fled the hill?" she asked.

Lurien nodded. "I have set six men to watch over you here. I must return to the Hunt."

A great antlered creature emerged from the shadows. As Lurien mounted the great stag, Gwenhidw's heart leapt and broke between one beat and the next.

For an instant, he was the very image of her Arthfael . . .

Caris savored the haven of Liam's arms as long as she dared. Then she made him sit on the ground so she could take a better look at his face. The glow of the Great Way revealed that his left eye was swollen shut, and the long gash across that side of his face had covered the front of his shirt with gore. "*Duw annwyl*, you're a proper mess," she said, pulling off her outer shirt and tearing a sleeve from it. Wadding it up, she pressed the cloth gently against the wound, and he obligingly placed his palm on it to hold it in place. "Now, whatever has happened to your leg?"

His right leg was a dark crimson mass of shredded blue jeans and deep, ugly bite marks. "One of those damn grims got me," he said. "Everybody woke up when the queen finished off Maelgwn—his followers, the horses, the dogs—and they were in a helluva panic to get off this hill. I was headed in your direction when a couple of the fae ran right into me and knocked me down. And then a grim chewed the frickin' daylights out of me until a goddamn *elk* charged by and scared him off."

"I was scared for *you*. I thought Maelgwn might kill you."

He shook his head. "You were brave as any lioness, the way you faced him down. I was more worried he'd try to kill *you*. And I wasn't going to let that happen, no matter what. Besides, now you get to nurse me back to health, just like I told you."

"Gladly." She leaned in and pressed her lips to his as tenderly as she could. He wasn't satisfied with that, however, and hooked his free arm around her neck, pulling her off balance and kissing her soundly until they were both lying on the ground in a heap.

Liam laid his head back and laughed as he clumsily repositioned the cloth against his face. "I want about a week of that, at least. It's got to be the best medicine for me."

"I'll be pleased to oblige you too," Caris smiled. "But I need to be binding up your leg first." She squeezed his hand and was surprised when he winced. Looking down, she saw that the ends of most of his fingers were bleeding, the skin not only blistered but rubbed raw. Liam hadn't played his fiddle in years—but tonight he'd played for hours with everything he had. For her. He bore far worse wounds, and she ought to be tending to them, but for some reason, it was his dear fingers that brought the tears to her eyes.

"Shh, don't worry about them," he said. "They hurt like hell but I swear, they've never felt so good. *I've* never felt so good. Well, okay, maybe a little better on the outside, but inside? My music's back where it belongs, and it's because of you."

Caris kissed him again, softly and slowly, then sat up and began tearing the rest of the shirt into strips. "We both had help this night," she pointed out.

"True. The faery queen was really something else. I thought the sword was just ornamental or something—I never suspected she could wield it like that. Maelgwn got his just desserts."

"*Diwedd y gân yw'r geiniog*," Caris said solemnly. "At the end of the song comes payment."

"Like paying the piper, huh? I like that. It fits. And Ranyon had my back for sure—what a stunt! It did my heart good to see that asshole prince get kicked in the head."

A loud whisper startled them both. "Don't be tellin' it about, but I almost didn't have a charm fer that one!" A big goat pranced out of the shadows, with Dodge ambling along behind. "Spotted creatures can't be seen by the fae as a rule," Ranyon explained as he slid off his mount. "But I was wantin' Maelgwn to get an eyeful o' Harley here as a detraction."

"*Distraction*," corrected Liam. "And it was a helluva good one, buddy."

Ranyon beamed as Caris hugged him, then peered more closely at his friend on the ground. "Yer a mess, dontcha know."

"So I've been told."

The clarion call of a hunting horn rang out from the sea of hills below. It was deep and bell-like, a rallying cry in battle, and the sound of swift judgment to the guilty. Caris's heart beat faster, remembering another time and another horn. Liam, not knowing what the sound meant, sat up and put his arm around her, gathering her into his shoulder. The horn sounded again, and the wild baying of spectral hounds took up the cry from the dark valleys all around them.

"'Tis Lurien's horn," said Ranyon. "The Wild Hunt is giving chase."

"Sure, after we've done all the hard work," chuckled Liam. "*Now* the cavalry shows up."

TWENTY-NINE

⟨≻⟩

The sun was up, and Caris lingered in the shower. She'd never get used to the sheer luxury of the thing.

And its many uses. She laughed out loud as a large masculine form slid in behind her and big hands began soaping her breasts in sensuous circles that made her nipples stand out immediately. In all her imaginings of what it might feel like to be with a man, she had not expected laughter to be such a sweet and tender part of it.

"Good morning, Mrs. Cole." Liam's voice rumbled in her ear above the water spray—then cursed as he bumped his head on the handheld shower. She always adjusted it to her own height, and he almost always forgot.

"And a good morning to you, Mr. Cole. The goats are waiting to be milked."

"The goats will wait just a little longer."

Caris laughed again and turned in his arms for a watery kiss. The goats often waited *just a little longer* in the mornings . . . and she found it to be a wondrous fine way to begin the day. And only yesterday, kissing Liam in the kitchen had turned into *clearing the table*—and not for breakfast. It hadn't been the most comfortable of surfaces, but the heated urgency of their need for each other made it perfect in the moment.

That was the most amazing thing of all, the craving for each other, the drawing together, that intense pull like iron to a magnet. Caris rubbed her slick, soapy breasts back and forth on Liam's chest. She locked her hands around his neck and stood on her tiptoes to greet his nipples with hers, sharing again that sweet, knowing laughter like a secret joke between them. His hands were busy all the while—his hands always were!—tracing intricate patterns with a silky sudsy brush all the way down her spine. She'd never thought of her back as a sensuous area before, but everything Liam did to it made her want to arch like a cat and purr.

Caris lathered her hands and reached for him, and his moan of pleasure was echoed by a subtle quiver between her legs. She loved to touch him, loved the heft and feel of his shaft in her hands as she slid her slick fingers up and down it and marveled at the growing impatience of her own body.

He touched her then and the sensation was electric. She lost her grip on him as he encircled her waist with his strong arm and bent her back so his hot mouth could reach her breast . . . Then Liam slyly slid the slender showerhead between her eagerly parted legs. Caris gripped his shoulders as he worked the clever nozzle back and forth until her breath was ragged and gasping, yet her body was greedy for more.

He carried her dripping and laughing from the shower and tossed her on the bed. The sheets would get soaking wet, but it didn't matter to either of them. Nothing mattered, only the need to be skin to skin, hands to skin, mouth to skin.

And nose to skin. She adored the smell of him. That clean male scent that was so uniquely *his* enticed her whenever they hugged and kissed throughout the day—and even when Liam was sweaty with exertion, she couldn't help but be aware of an underlying primal lure that tantalized her. Whenever they were naked together, she indulged herself, inhaling his scent deeply as she nuzzled, kissed, tasted.

She tasted him now, boldly taking as much pleasure from it as she was giving, relishing the feel of Liam's hard shaft in her palm, the fascinating contrast of its velvety skin against her lips, and the immense satisfaction of coaxing growls of pleasure from a strong man. Her body fairly vibrated with anticipation too, knowing that her subtle sense of power would be delightfully brief.

Caris laughed when Liam's hands suddenly pulled her upward, when he rolled atop of her to blanket her with his muscled body. She held him tightly to her—her man, *hers*—as he kissed her, as the weight of him pressed her into the softness of the mattress. Her fingers teased his nipples when he reared back—then gripped his arms as he parted her, filled her, slow and deep, again and again. Her body took up the rhythm as she would take up a tune. It was a dance, it was a song, and then it was *glory.*

They lay wrapped around each other for as many minutes as they dared. Definitely longer than they should when there was milking to be done, but Liam made a mental note to buy the goats off with an extra ration of grain.

"I know we're traveling to visit your aunt and uncle next week, but Morgan phoned yesterday to ask if she and Rhys could come by this weekend," said Caris, as she rearranged herself next to him. "They're wanting to bring Leo and Ranyon along too—Ranyon's anxious to visit Harley." The ellyll had been reluctant to leave his mount behind but had finally understood that a goat, particularly a fully intact and frequently *smelly* buck goat, would not be welcome in a residential neighborhood. And he had had to concede that Harley lived a very good life at Steptoe Acres, considering that there was no shortage of does to keep him company.

Fortunately, the queen had arranged for the fat spotted hen to be returned to the farm, and Liam had promptly gifted Ranyon with it. Delighted, he'd named it Fiona, and the hen went nearly everywhere with him. *The damn chicken is even in our wedding photos*—and so was Ranyon, of course. Caris and Liam simply couldn't imagine their big day without the little ellyll being part of it. In the end, they'd decided to hold a small and intimate ceremony at the farm—utilizing the entire collection of flower-festooned gnomes as decorations. Ranyon had been willing to trade his beloved Blue Jays cap and shirt—"Fer one day only, mind ya!"—for a gnome costume, lovingly sewn by Caris, complete with red stocking cap.

Cousin Tina, Uncle Conall, and Aunt Ruby had all commented on the charm of the whimsical décor—right after they fell in love with Caris. But Tina and Liam's uncle were too caught up in getting to know the bride to notice anything unusual. Aunt Ruby's sixth sense could not be turned off, however. She'd taken a long hard look at the strange spindly "gnome" with the treelike features—then walked right up and introduced herself to him. They'd become instant friends, although Liam wasn't certain how that would stand up the next time Toronto played the Mariners.

This weekend, the ellyll would no doubt rearrange the gnomes again. He'd finally admitted that they appealed him because of their size—"I feel like I'm with my own clan again," he'd said. It had become a tradition almost, that every time Ranyon visited, the gnomes ended up in a different activity. At present, just to please Liam, they were arranged in a football scrimmage in the front yard, complete with two opposing bleachers of gnome fans. One team was Seattle of course . . .

"It'll be great to have them all come over," Liam said to Caris. "Rhys and Morgan will get to see the foals again before we deliver them to their new home." Gwenhidw had fallen in love with the twin Appaloosas she'd shared a stall with and had purchased them. *With pure gold.* Liam had nearly choked when he'd come in from the barn one day to find a heavy oak chest of the yellow stuff sitting in the middle of the living room floor. It proved useless trying to tell the queen that she'd paid too much. Faery custom dictated that the buyer determined the price in such matters, as long as the value was met.

Maybe she still feels guilty about the farm being wrecked, Liam thought. Although Gwenhidw had, as Caris said, put things to rights as soon as she regained her strength. The roof was back on the barn. The trees were restored to their former glory. Everything that had been damaged by Maelgwn's rogue hunt had been repaired—and long before the wedding took place. That seemed fair enough to Liam. The chest of gold? That was just plain crazy. Apparently, though, Morgan and Rhys were experiencing a similar excess—the queen had insisted on purchasing the Paint Horses procured on her behalf. The strange effect of their light-and-dark coloring had enabled Gwenhidw and Rhedyn not only to reach the summit of Steptoe Butte unseen but to get as close to the prince as possible. That success had inspired the queen to breed the mares, crossing them with her best fae stallions. *Stealth horses*, Liam thought. *Who'd have guessed?*

Now that the twin foals were weaned, he and Caris would be taking them through the Great Way. And Gwenhidw had requested a concert from them while they were there. In all the dreams he'd once had of a successful music career, a command performance for a faery queen certainly hadn't been among them. Come to think of it, he hadn't imagined sharing the stage with someone either—but it had since become a source of joy.

Something new sprang to life every time he and Caris performed, as if their love for each other informed their music.

One of their best songs so far was titled "The Wild Hunt." Liam had turned down several music companies' offers, no longer wanting the demands of that business—he liked his life with Caris on the farm too much. Instead, he hired his former agent, Mel, to handle the private production and marketing of their recordings, and to book small and intimate venues in which to play now and then. And at every concert they gave, Liam spotted small groups of fae in the audience, disguised as humans. He chuckled. *Who would have thought we'd become popular in two worlds?*

"What's funny?" asked Caris.

Liam rested his chin on her hair. "It's been a few months now, and it still seems like I fell down a rabbit hole. I'm friends with faeries, I'm on a first-name basis with a queen, I travel through an interdimensional tunnel . . . and that mare that Rhedyn left here has grown honest-to-God horns. Tough for a guy to get his bearings some days, that's all. Do you know there's a kelpie in the irrigation pond?"

"I did have a chat with him about it. He was just passing through."

"I just feel like I've wandered into a completely different world."

"It's not different, not really—just a bit bigger, is all."

Bigger . . . he hadn't quite looked at it that way. But was bigger necessarily better? *Hell, yeah*—if Caris was in it. Liam grabbed her and rolled her on top of him, where he kissed her soundly. "You know what? Any world that includes *you* is the one I want to live in."

EPILOGUE

L urien made his way to the enormous circular courtyard at the heart of the palace and found it unrecognizable. The stone walls were gone. Towering monoliths of tourmaline crystals rose high on all sides: resplendent in cool reds and purples at their bases, graduating through blues and glacial teals until they topped out with brilliant emerald greens that could rival any rainforest canopy. Within that perfect arena, the ground was inlaid with complicated spirals and continuous knots in a fascinating combination of polished stone and short succulent plants designed to be walked upon. Blossoming trees shaded many carved crystal benches, all in multicolored tourmaline like the walls. Despite the vast scale, the entire place beckoned and soothed.

Hard to believe it had been nothing but a blackened crater the last time he'd been here.

In the center of it all, like the sun in a galaxy, the queen directed a team of artists and gardeners as they put the finishing touches on the creation of a new mosaic map of the Nine Realms. Set with bright agates and other gemstones, it was pleasing to the senses, particularly when it caught the sunlight. It was much larger than the first had been—and there was something else different.

"You've included Tir Hardd," said Lurien, pleased.

"How could I not?" she smiled at him and extended her hand. "The new territory is a vital part of our kingdom. Perhaps we will have to start referring to our lands as the Ten Realms."

He shook his head. "A little uneven, when the tenth is larger than the other nine combined."

"Well, then we will simply have to think of something more clever to call it." The queen warmly thanked her workers and dismissed them so that she might converse with her *llaw dde* in private. "You escorted the colonists without incident?"

He thought about that. This group, the twentieth so far, had been composed mostly of coblynau, and that meant there had been plenty of *incidents*—mostly squabbles, fistfights, and the occasional refusal to go any further. Nothing unexpected, however. And they'd been happy enough once they'd arrived in the new territory and witnessed its vast potential for themselves.

"The truce with the Anghenfilod holds," he said. "Once again, we delivered the offerings as you promised them, 'paid the toll' if you will, and they both opened and closed the Great Way. I still don't know quite how they do it without magic of their own, but then, it *is* their natural environment, and they understand it as we do not. All was peaceful, both coming and going." In fact, although those strange featureless faces and soulless eyes revealed nothing, Lurien's instincts told him that the tall, dark creatures of the Inbetween were quite *pleased* with the new arrangement. As for himself, he was still in awe that Gwenhidw had so ably managed to negotiate a pact with them. She had defended their right to live and recognized their sovereignty over the Great Way—and then she had given their leader the giant bwgan stone from the very pommel of her ancestral sword to demonstrate good faith. *There is no one like her . . . and will never be again.*

"The land thrives?"

"The samplau are flourishing throughout the new land. I believe that one day soon, Tir Hardd will outstrip the old kingdom for sheer wonders. The new grove of Silver Maples alone will soon exceed the height of their parent forest here." He shook his head in wonder. "The land is vibrant, vital, energizing. It would do you much good to spend time there. The people look forward to your presence."

"Soon," she said. "And what of Aurddolen—how does she find Tir Hardd?"

What could he say? He and Aurddolen had worked together, and well, for the good of the kingdom, joining forces to save both the queen and the new land. The dragon ruler had indeed managed to rally the envoys and inspire them—threatening them only a little—into holding the Way closed at their end. She'd even forgiven Lurien for arresting her. *Mostly.* But when he'd suggested a pairing, she'd refused. There had been perfectly understandable reasons, of course, not the least of which was that Aurddolen had a challenging territory to rule and her people would not approve of one of the hated Tylwyth Teg as her consort. But it was the last thing she'd said that stuck with him: "I much prefer to be the only female in my mate's life." It was almost embarrassing to admit that he hadn't understood right away . . .

He decided to keep the explanation simple. "She did not wish to see Tir Hardd at this time. She cited pressing responsibilities and returned home to govern her people soon after your safe return."

"She left?" Gwenhidw looked surprised. "And you did not go with her?"

"I found that I did not wish to."

The queen sighed and sat down on a carved agate bench by the pond. Glowing blue fish with enormous eyes hastened to the surface, hoping for crumbs. "I had so hoped you would find more between you. That is why I encouraged her to seek you out. Why I insisted you enjoy the party as a guest and not a guardian."

"You would send me from you?" Lurien was incredulous.

"I would see you happy."

"Perhaps you would see yourself without temptation."

She frowned. "Have a care, Lurien. You overstep your bounds."

"Really?" Instead of apologizing, he sat beside her on the bench. "What bounds have I, Gwenhidw? We have been in each other's shadow for time immemorial, you and I. And grown ever closer. Never did I allow myself to think I was worthy of you, and I am no blooded prince. But lately I have dared to hope that perhaps you might open your heart again, if not to a husband, then at least to a lover."

"I will have neither," she said, with a sad smile. "Many have said that when Arthfael died, much of me went to the dark lands with him. I do not think it is true, though I walked in shadow for a very long time. It is simply that I am wed to the Nine Realms, and my people are my children. My heart rests with them—and none else."

"Noble sentiments and lofty ideals," he said. "Your words have great power, Gwenhidw, enough to move an entire kingdom from its very foundations. You speak to your people of growth and change, and the need to entertain new ideas in order to live— and yet you will not hear your own words. You talk of the future, yet you do not release the past."

"Is that not the way of our peoples? Is it not written on our banner? 'We relinquish not that which is ours.'"

"Not even a dead king," he said, and saw her eyes flash as the barb hit home. *Good. You can still feel something.*

She rose to her full height, then, and power radiated from her as if from the heart of a star. A lesser being would have quailed or fled before the queen's outraged countenance. Lurien did not even stand but simply folded his arms and waited. When she finally spoke, her voice was thick with shock and anger. "He is mine, and you will not speak of him to me again."

"I *will* speak of him. I loved him too, Gwenhidw. Arthfael was my lord, but he was also the closest thing to a brother I have ever known. I will always miss him, but he has been gone for *millennia*. I will not be a prisoner to his memory as you have become."

"No? I have watched you suffer ever since that terrible night. I have never blamed you for his death, Lurien. Never. But you still do. What else are you but a prisoner?"

What indeed? He softened his voice as he stood. "We all have our regrets to bear, dear one. But to shut yourself away from love is to deny who you are. Mortals say that the Fair Ones have no hearts. You and I know that is not true."

"I love my people. It is enough."

"Is it? Truly, they return that love. But tell me this"—he encircled her with his powerful arms and pulled her close, though she held herself stiff and unyielding. "You need no arms to hold you in the night when you are weary from the burdens you carry? No shoulder upon which to rest your head? It seems to me you asked for that very thing not long ago."

She shook her head and pushed herself away. "I will have no husband, Lurien. And no lover. Not even you, though you are my dearest and truest friend, and the nearest to my heart."

Near it. But not in it, he thought, and let his arms drop to his sides. "You may not need a love that is flesh and blood, Gwenhidw. But I do. And I find I have other needs as well. I hereby cede the title of *llaw dde*, Your Grace, and resign as your right hand."

"What? You cannot!"

"I just did. I have guarded you well all these centuries and served you with all of my heart and soul. These palace walls have been as a cage to me, but I bore it gladly for your sake. Now, however, I see it is time for me to leave this place and return to my true self."

"And who is that?"

"I am the Lord of the Wild Hunt, Your Grace. And that is not a title that even you can bestow or take away. It is simply who I am." He turned and left the shadowed garden.

No voice called him back.

ACKNOWLEDGMENTS

Nobody writes alone. I'm more than grateful to the usual suspects for their encouragement and unflagging support in this endeavor.

First and foremost, my deep appreciation to those who helped refine the creation of *Storm Warned*: Sharon Stogner, Melody Guy, and Ron Silvester. Thanks for reading—and rereading—and re-rereading countless pages! Your suggestions were invaluable.

Thanks to my editor, Maria Gomez, for your enthusiasm and patience. Also, I feel very fortunate to have a fabulous author team at Montlake to whom I can turn with any question, and who do so much of the behind-the-scenes hard work of producing and marketing a book. You guys rock!

A shout out to my agent, Stephany Evans, for helping me get to this point in my writing career. Thanks for believing in me.

Love and hugs to Samantha Craig, who provided a veritable hotline of emotional support during the tough times, and to Jordan Craig, who gave me some great survival ideas that changed my perspective. Much love to Abby Craig for sharing suggestions and creative fun, and to Jaime Craig for cheering me on no matter what. I adore you all.

Meanwhile, there just aren't enough words to express my thanks to my Alaskan mountain-man husband, Ronald Joe Silvester, who has endured several months of privation in the form of not only cooking for himself but voluntarily learning to process an explosion of garden produce. I'm certain he would far rather have wrestled a fifty-pound salmon with his bare hands and hauled home a bull moose by the nostrils, than peel a bumper crop of apples and slice up an unrelenting supply of tomatoes. Not only are you are my hero; you have the greatest heart of anyone I have ever known.

ABOUT THE AUTHOR

⟨⟨⟩⟩

Photo © 2011 Ron Silvester

Dani Harper is a former newspaper editor whose passion for all things supernatural led her to a second career writing fiction. There isn't anything she likes better than exploring myths and legends from many cultures, which serve to inspire her sizzling and suspenseful stories.

A longtime resident of the Canadian north and southeastern Alaska, Dani now lives in rural Washington with her retired mountain-man husband, Ron. Together they do battle with runaway gardens, rampant fruit trees, and a roving herd of chickens, with the assistance of three dogs and several grandchildren.

Dani Harper is the author of *Storm Bound* and *Storm Warrior* (the Grim Series), as well as *First Bite* (Dark Wolf), for Montlake Romance. She is also the author of a shapeshifter series, which includes *Changeling Moon*, *Changeling Dream*, and *Changeling Dawn*. For full details, visit her website at www.daniharper.com.